We Pretty
Pieces
of
Flesh

We Pretty Pieces
Pieces
of
Flesh

A NOVEL

COLWILL BROWN

HOLT
NEW YORK

Henry Holt and Company
Publishers since 1866
120 Broadway
New York, New York 10271
www.henryholt.com

Library of Congress Cataloging-in-Publication Data is available.

ISBN: 9781250342881

Our books may be purchased in bulk for promotional, educational, or business
use. Please contact your local bookseller or the Macmillan Corporate and
Premium Sales Department at (800) 221-7945, extension 5442, or by e-mail at
MacmillanSpecialMarkets@macmillan.com.

First Edition 2025

Designed by Omar Chapa

All emojis designed by OpenMoji—the open-source emoji and icon project.
License: CC BY-SA 4.0

Printed in the United States of America

1   2   3   4   5   6   7   8   9   10

To my bezzies, past and present

We Pretty Pieces
of
Flesh

Victory

Remember when we thought Donny wut whole world? Before we knew we wa Northern, when we seemed to be central, when we carved countries out ut farmers' fields, biking through neck-high rapeseed, cutting tracks. Stalks flattened beneath us wheels, releasing sweet smell of honey and rot, pollen dusting us skin wasp yellow. Bike chain clacking, thighs burning, daring each other to go non-handed. It warra state of mind, non-handed—you had to just let go and believe. When Coops' chocolate concrete warra delicacy. When sex facts wa currency, dead-eyes warra language, when kicking littler kids off back seat ut bus warra career. When romance wa gerrin mashed on Smirnoff Ice on summer nights by t'canal's stretch of still brown water, lazing ont grass int late-evening light. So late we stopped believing int creeping dusk. When it wa cheeky tinnies guzzled beneath hay-bale tower that loomed like a ship's mast behind house rows, that wa shaped like a sad man staring at his outstretched feet. Time we tried climbing tut top, stalks sticking in us bras and socks, and accidentally set whole fucking thing ablaze wit flick of a half-smoked cig.

Ask anyone non-Northern, they'll only know Donny as punch line of a joke or place they changed trains once ont way to London.

1

They'll recall afternoon they wa relegated tut station platform for fifteen freezing minutes, warming their hands round a paper-cup cappuccino, waiting fut LNER express route to tek em off somewhere else, suspecting that if they stepped beyond station doors forra second they'd be asked by five blokes—and at least one bloke'd ask twice— Alreyt, love, you got 20p fut phone? No point venturing intut town centre, exploring place affectionately described by natives as "Dirty Donny," and spitefully described by posher towns as "chav central," "a scowl of scumbags," "a collection of small former mining villages who won't stop complaining about Thatcher," or "home ut country's worst football team." Some folk reckon Doncaster boasts kingdom's highest boozer-to-human ratio, but that's an honour also claimed by residents of every lost borough in England. Any commuter foolish enough to breech station's threshold would backstep sharpish intut concourse's promise of elsewhere and thank fuck they dint get themsens stuck here. If trains dint have to pass through it, they'd tell themsens, Doncaster wouldn't need to be a place at all.

They wouldn't know about sleeping in cornfields under t'stars, nested in makeshift stalk beds, chatting till dawn. They wouldn't know about keeping a campfire burning all night int ancient woods, or tiptoeing back int morning, dodging clumps of bluebells we couldn't bear to trample. Or spending a weekend building thrones from smooth boulders we found ont riverbank, beside waterfall's roar and rush. Or us three perched on us thrones—sweaty, knackered, happy—pinkie-swearing we'd always have each other's backs.

They wouldn't know about us parents, time they sang and hugged and cried, dancing ont sofa till four int morning, night Tony Blair's Labour Party got elected. About hope us parents held forra fairer future: things can only get better. About all of us, how loud we laugh, how sharp we feel, how hard we love, how soft.

And they wouldn't know about Donny's still visible chunk of Roman fort, but to be fair, neither did we. We dint recognise eighteen-foot stretch of weathered stone for warrit wa, mossed and grassy, thicker than a body is long. We dint feel centuries beneath us chilly bum cheeks when we bought two litres of cider, spent afternoon sat on that wall gerrin pissed in us Adidas Poppers. We dint imagine soldiers in leather sandals fighting battles wi their iron-tipped javelins. We wa too busy fighting us own battles.

Remember when we wa so young, we dint even have run ut whole town yet, when big school warrus universe, when slightest victory med us feel invincible, like as long as we stuck together, we could tek on any fight and win—like time us PE teacher said we had to play football wit lads, even though there wa only three of us and sleet screamed across school field like a fleet of angry bees. Sight of it from window med chills run through us, even int warmth ut changing rooms. Lads'd had their growth spurt by then; they all wore shin pads and spiky football boots. We just had us Reeboks, shorts, unpadded shins, naked knees. They jeered when they heard us begging Sir to lerrus off: S'up wi yas? they said. Are you ont rag, like? But Sir wouldn't gi us special treatment just because we wa lasses. We dint see why Sir got to decide whether we gorrus teeth kicked in. We dint understand why we weren't allowed to say no.

We decided we'd play in goal together, three of us in a row. But when we gorrup top field, wind pelting ice pellets at us cheeks, goal hanging ovver us like a giant staple, we realised we'd volunteered oursens fut bullseye. We linked arms, connected at elbows.

Ont pitch, nineteen lads threw meaty thighs intut muck. From nowhere, a ball coming at us, white missile flying through sleet. We scattered like pigeons. Ball smacked one of us square int tit, knocked down, winded. Circle of mud on white T-shirt like a target, like a brand.

Lad who scored pulled *his* T-shirt ovver his face, streaked across field wi his arms outstretched like Fabrizio Ravanelli.

"DICKHEAD," we said. Wind caught us syllables, chucked them back.

Knees grazed, stung. Elbows siren red and flayed. Pain flaring up int wind's icy gusts. We checked us limbs for blood, searched for gashes that'd heal into scars, but lads dint gi us owt that day except knocks that'd blotch into bruises then fade. We pulled oursens together, shook off shock, locked arms. We took shallow breaths, lungs seizing int cold.

Sir blew his whistle; lads ran back down field, re-formed. At second whistle, lads weaved slowly back towards us. Their hard bodies, blank shapes int mist. We clenched, afraid of gerrin broken up again.

Lads cem close enough that we could mek out their T-shirts, streaked brown, clung wet to torsos. Wind hammered us eardrums. Their voices reached us in snatches, echoes, protesting violent tackles, bad ref calls: As if! Since when? Us silent, watching lads come. Close enough to mek out breath clouds shrouding heads.

Ball shot back and forth across pitch. Nearer it cem, more it seemed like soon we'd have to let go of each other, fend for oursens. Us goosebumped skin, cringing, waiting fut ball's thud, fut bone-bruise ache that'd follow.

Then we could mek out calves, muscles carved tight. Int heat of their coming our arms unwound, elbows freed.

Then we could mek out faces, contorted wi fury as they heaved down last twenty yards, gorrin formation like her majesty's fighter jets. Int thunder of their feet, drumming of their spiked soles ont frozen pitch, we turned to each other.

We said, "Fuck this!"

We fiddled wit hems of us PE shirts. Then we could mek out eyes, trained on us, squinting through swarming sleet. We curled us fingers ovvert fabric's rim. They angled a foot, took aim. We pulled up T-shirts, pulled up us bras beneath.

Our tits gleamed int sleet.

Sir's whistle blew, long screech like an outraged bird. Ball veered, scuttered off. Lads threw up their arms: *Fuck are you doing?*

Sir ran towards us. "Oi, you lot, gerrinside!"

We let down us tops and walked off, arm in arm, feeling like we'd be this strong forever, like nowt could tear us apart. Before us: changing rooms, steamy warm. Behind us: whistle went, lads re-formed.

Legend of Arms-Out Simon

Arms-Out Simon died same weekend me, Kel, and Shaz took train to Sheff forra night out, tried to dodge fare and got caught. Shaz reckoned she knew bouncer at Gatecrasher, Sheffield's megaclub, reckoned he'd lerrus in wi'out ID. We wa fifteen, but we could already gerrin most places in Donny wi us boobs hoicked and us slap on, so we decided to gi it a go, see if we could blag us way in. Arms-Out Simon, whose real name wa Dave, warrout in Donny that night—we warra city away, so all I've got to go on is what folk said who wa there.

Ont train in, Shaz taught us how to blag fare: find an empty seat int last carriage, pretend to be asleep. Conductor will think you've been on since Scunthorpe, and if you stop your eyelids fluttering, if you keep smirk from your lips while he paces aisle, voice going up and down like a bingo caller's—Tickets from Doncaster? Your Doncaster tickets, please—if you keep yoursen still till you hear swoosh-suck ut carriage door behind him, you'll feel blush of excitement down every inch of you, rush of being naughty bubbling up, and you're alive knowing your purse still holds that £4.80 you didn't surrender.

"Told ya, knobheads," Shaz said when I opened mi eyes ontut empty carriage, found misen a first-time criminal. She wa pissed off because I hadn't believed it'd work and she reckoned that meant I didn't trust her. I didn't trust her, but I wont about to say so. Shaz reckoned she'd done it loads, reckoned her brother taught her— her Kyle did it every Satdi night to gerrin to Rotherham from Goldthorpe, him and his mates spending their giros in Club Envy, 80p entry, proper buzzin lads, lads, lads.

We giggled from giddiness. We stoked feeling wi a voddy-spiked bottle of Coke. I wa extra giddy because I'd just started seeing this lanky lad int year above. We'd only been going out a fortnight and he'd already gi me a pet name. "Monkey," he called me, all his texts ending in a semicolon, hyphen, close bracket. *Miss you so much, monkey ;-)* This wa mi first proper boyfriend—I hadn't been near a lad since that psycho from Barnsley, who definitely didn't count— and I hadn't told Kel and Shaz about him yet. I wanted it to be special; I'd been waiting fut right moment. I wa busting to tell them right there ont train, but before I could open mi gob, Kel declared it a "girly night," which meant strictly no talking about lads.

Better to wait till we warrint club, anyway, when Kel'd be too drunk to remember her rule, and we could have a proper celebration.

We sipped voddy, let looseness fill us, raised us voices over t'clatter ut tracks, shrieked and laughed. We talked nonstop about whether or not we wa gunna gerrint club. Thought of sneaking past door intut heat and noise of a rave burned me wit thrill of it. But no matter how much Shaz insisted it'd be reyt, because Keith, this bouncer mate of hers, had promised, mi nerves still raced themsens around thinking about moment we'd step up tut door, about t'now or never of it. Crasher nights wa legendary, even for us Donny lot, who warra million miles from Sheffield most weeks. We had us own clubs, but they were nowt like Gatecrasher. If Gatecrasher wa South Yorkshire's Ibiza rave, Donny warrits wedding disco.

I didn't know or care back then, but building Gatecrasher wa housed in used to belong to a manufacturer called Roper and Wreaks. Int War, Roper and Wreaks made cartridges and howitzer shells int two-storey brick warehouse, which stayed industrial till 1989, which makes sense if you think about when Thatcher fucked us, and how. I'm not sure what I mean by "us," if I'm honest. Mi proper "us" is Donny, but fair do's, Tories fucked Sheffield same as they fucked us—they're no more Steel City than we are a mining town—and sometimes, when I'm stewing over posh cunts down south and what they've done to this country, it's comforting to think of a bigger "us," though I know we're still a small wound int history of a dying body.

Kel and Shaz unzipped their purses, fingered crinkly notes they'd earned working Satdi shift at Home Bargains. We'd agreed we wa bringing thirty quid fut night, or "neet," as Shaz would say, and as Kel started saying day we met Shaz. They counted out loud: fifteen fut door, tenner for booze, fiver for scran.

"What about you, Rach?" Shaz asked, since mi purse wa still buried in mi handbag. "You got thirty?"

I had forty quid pocket money saved and I'd brought whole lot. I'd meant to leave extra tenner at home but panicked last minute and nabbed it, thinking about mi mum saying you're always meant to carry more than you need.

I didn't wanna lie to Kel and Shaz. But having more than them made me feel guilty, or ashamed, or left out, or summat. Me and Kel had always been same, born ont same street, went tut same primary school, wore same school uniforms, same tracky bottoms ont weekends, same neon-orange Kappa jackets. Went nursery together, childminder's together, played out together every day ut six-week holidays, climbing over stone walls and breaking into building sites and gerrin lost int woods by canal. It wa me and Kel who first stole down Sprotty Road to make calls int piss-reeking phone box, ringing operator and speaking clock fut thrill. Us who strapped platform heels to us feet when we were ten, tottered tut corner shop to buy twenty Regal Superkings from nicotine-yellow bloke behind counter, who did think it over, lighting hope in us guts, but turned us away when I bodged mi fake birthdi ont second ask. Us who thieved two of Kel's mum's More cigarettes—long, slim, brown, not stumpy white like normal ciggies—and four Cook's matches. We snuck down t'Dip, an old train line wi its track removed, haunted, so we wa told, by pot dealers and pedos. We tried sparking up by striking match heads across a concrete post, spent us matches before we got ciggy lit and had to creep back intut house and nick more. It wa me who watched Kel take her first inhale, one hand on her cocked hip, cig caught between two taut fingers, quick breath in then blowing up at sky, lashes down, as if now, suddenly, she wa grown.

In 1998, same year me and Kel moved up to comp, met Shaz, and became a three, mi parents moved us up tut posh end—tut "Village"—to a bigger house wi a double garage, conservatory, and water feature int garden. Village wa called "*the* Village" even though it wa one among many villages. It warront other side ut A1 motorway bridge to Kel's, and houses were twice size. People from t'Village called where Kel lived "t'Shit End." People from t'Shit End called people from t'Village "tossers."

Then Kel and Shaz wut same, same single mums they called "mam," same state-sponsored quid-a-day dinner money, same missing dads. Shaz called hers "mi fatha," wi two short *a* sounds like "apple," and by us first half-term so did Kel. Shaz's fatha wa dead—black lung—Kel's had only run off. My dad played fut local cricket club, tea and quartered sarnies int pavilion between innings every Satdi, mums carrying plates of orange slices ontut pitch fut fielders to suck, juice dribbling from their mouths, staining whites their wives'd hand-wash all Sundi. I wanted to say "mi fatha" an' all, but I knew it wouldn't sound right between mi teeth, knew somehow wi'out asking that I weren't allowed.

Shaz wa from Goldthorpe, same as Arms-Out Simon. Even before I first went Shaz's for tea, I knew Goldthorpe warra different kind of village to mine. Goldthorpe wa anciently a small medieval farming village. It wa recorded int Domesday Book. Its pit closed in 1994. If you ask someone who lives there now, they'll tell you it's teenagers staggering up streets fucked out their eyeballs on Co-op beer; it's dole queue out post office door every Mundi, Thursdi, and Fridi. It's bagheads sleeping in cardboard boxes, bloody scraps int Rusty Dudley every Satdi neet. They'll say it's difficult to get to, impossible to leave.

Us train would've tore past Goldthorpe ont way to Sheff that night, council estate blip beyond fields we dashed through. We didn't notice owt beyond windows, though, which sundown had shellacked into shiny black sheets, making me feel already hemmed in by nightclub walls.

I gorrout mi purse, showed Shaz three tenners waiting inside. "I've got thirty, don't worry." I'd folded extra note thin, hid it in mi bra. It dug intut flesh of mi left boob.

This war-works-cum-warehouse-cum-megaclub morphed intut home of Gatecrasher in 1997, five years before us three stomped to its doors in stripper heels. Mine wut classiest because they weren't clear, they wa iridescent magenta. Bought from New Look specially. I only wore them that once, though, because they made me too tall, straps cut into mi feet, and they never were same after that night. We arrived shoulders back, tits out, ready fut rave of us lives.

We stood int queue for years. Shaz had a little baggie of Es, reckoned her mam gave it her, and she doled them out. Pills slipped down us throats. We waited fut come-up while we waited fut queue to do its slow agonising shrink, feeling sting of missing out on what-ever wonder wa palpitating ont other side ut wall.

Building had become a metallic palace, wi a new front soaring above old warehouse roof. We stared up, necks crooked, at Gate-crasher's British-lion logo, a gargantuan steel cutout ont fascia. According to Google, building had a "fragmented style of Gehry-esque fractured geometry." According to Rachael Gifford, BA, PGCE, Who Wa There at the Time in Classy Platform Heels, it warra dystopian manor house of steel slabs and wonky mirrors. Building survived till 2007, dying five years after we rocked up there looking forra rave. Fire started int DJ booth, tore through building's core, made it permanently unsound. Locals reckoned you could taste smoke in every Sheffield postcode. No-one expired int fire, but someone left a bouquet ont steps. Card pinned tut plastic wrap: "The music, the lights, the spirit of the people, we will always remember you."

No-one can remember if flowers were left for Arms-Out Simon, at least no-one I've asked. If you forced me, I'd say there weren't any, no, because you couldn't pinpoint spot he went like you can forra car wreck—wreathes and teddy bears bunched against letter-boxes and telegraph poles, marking place tarmac broke flesh. We couldn't have found place he lost consciousness, so we couldn't have bundled tributes, left them int rain to get soggy and rot. Shaz said 150 turned up tut funeral, and for once I didn't think she wa chatting shit. Arms-Out wa Donny-famous as a happy skaghead, part-time pillhead, preeminent bus stop philosopher, best known for pulling his signature moves at every Donny rave: head-banging tut bass, arms windmilling in every direction, legs scissoring back and forth. He always wore sweatbands and a plastic whistle. Nobody knew where he slept.

When we finally gorrup tut door, we got told it wa IDs, ladies, please, or off you pop. We barely had time to look longingly through entrance before we wa shooed away, forced to turn us backs on Gatecrasher's gleam. Exact moment bouncer turned us down—or thereabouts, so I could glean from various accounts, high as those witnesses were—Arms-Out Simon passed through entrance ut Ware-house, legendary venue ont Donny rave scene since 1989. Warehouse warranother postindustrial ruin turned iniquity den, same story as Sheffield's, except we didn't have imagination to call it anything other than warrit wa—and ours never got a £1.5 million revamp to look "Gehry-esque" or esque of any other kind.

I never made it inside either club. Mum had warned me off going Warehouse since I warra kid, every time we drove past it ont North Bridge ont way into town. She said it wa where people went to do naughty things and heroin. It's where people go to shoot up, love, where people die of overdoses and nobody helps them because it's lawless, underground. From Mum's car it always looked desperate, a lonely towering stack, windows smashed, char lines trailing down brick walls as though place had been torched and burned out. I imagined ravers gathered between crumbling concrete pillars on a dance floor of broken glass. I never saw slick new entrance, which must've been round back, a stout shipping-container-looking thing painted in black-and-grey chevron. Round back must be where famous double-decker bus still sits, though I can't imagine where there'd be space. Through car window, all I could see warra tall spectre of a building squeezed between train tracks, river, and bridge.

We walked away from Gatecrasher, down a cobbled alley, cold in us skimpy dresses, all of us clasping us middles against wind.

I said to Shaz, "Fuck do we do now?" Last train to Donny had already left. Since Gatecrasher wa open till six, plan had been to stay out till 05:24 to Scunthorpe, first train ut day.

Kel said, "Chill out, Rach, this int Shaz's fault."

I wanted to say, Then whose fucking fault *is* it.

"Keith must've been on his brek," said Shaz.

Usually, I tried to keep quiet when Shaz wa talking bollocks, but mi shoes were nipping and mi toes were numb, and it'd been forty-three minutes since mi fella's last winky-faced text. I said, "Oh aye, yeah, *on his brek*."

"Fuck's that menna mean?" Shaz swivelled to face me, heels going scrape-clack, halting all of us. We stopped beside a pub kicking out "Down with the Sickness" to an empty dance floor, three dizzy disco lights whirling primary colours through t'windows.

I wa always wary of Shaz's version of events, suspicious of her stories—all t'break-ins, all t'funerals, all t'babbies, all t'scrapping int streets, all t'glassing. It wa too much to be real, too much for one person to have lived through.

And Shaz always "knew" everyone worth knowing. She knew all t'bouncers and barmen, all t'cokeheads and weed dealers, all t'criminals, both violent and petty. She knew every Donny lass or lad who'd died tragically young. She knew Arms-Out Simon, reckoned Arms-Out wa mates wi her brother Kyle, a not-so-happy skaghead who'd recently lost a knuckle in a prison fight. After Arms-Out's funeral, Shaz went on and on about how mint he wa, sweetest lad she'd ever known, but she'd said that about a few lads from her end who didn't make it, who'd been in and out of Doncatraz for assault, battery, GBH. Who'd had babies before they turned sixteen. Arms-Out never thieved, though, said Shaz—even withdrawing, shivering and sweating, hurt tut core, he'd rather lay clammy and sick in a festering squat than tek a knife to some poor cunt's throat.

"She's joking," Kel said to Shaz, but gave me eyes that meant, *Don't start*. A sulk brewed in me: Kel taking Shaz's side as per.

Shaz pulled a fag from packet in her bra and sparked it, turning away from me, body shielding flame from wind. She inhaled, picked at a scab on her wrist.

I said, "Don't, you'll make it bleed."

She kept picking, her frosted-pink fingernail prising scab's edge from her skin.

"His name's Keith Pickering and ah gorr'is number cuz ah fucked him other week, if you *must* know."

I could've pushed for more Keithy details, made her gi me fabrications that would eventually unpick themsens, but mi phone went, mi fella saying, *I love you more than 12,000 Fender Jazzmasters, monkey ;-)* I wanted to show Shaz and Kel mi fella's text. This wont how I'd imagined telling them about him, though, on a random street corner shivering us arses off. We wa meant to be raving, buzzin, euphoric.

I started walking. Shaz got moving an' all, quick-marching to make sure she warrout in front. We stopped again—we didn't know where we wa going. E wa kicking in; we wa coming up ont street wi no club to rave in.

"We'll have to get taxi home," I said.

"It'll be about fifty fuckin quid," said Shaz. "Ah'm not spending half mi wages on a fuckin taxi." Kel and Shaz agreed that they didn't stack shelves cash-in-hand every Satdi to go all t'way to Sheffield and not have a dance. I thought about whipping out mi secret tenner, offering to pay taxi fare. But then they'd know I lied, pretended I wa skinter than I wa.

While we lurked beneath illuminated yellow sign of a pizza takeaway on West Street, toeing pavement and feeling homeless, Arms-Out Simon, according to reports, ordered his usual bottle of Evian at Warehouse's bar, said Y'alreyt, mayte? to a dozen other regulars, before heading tut slashers, where he locked himsen int sole cubicle, did a line of Charlie off cistern, dropped a couple of Es. Then he claimed his fave spot ont dance floor, right up against guardrail below DJ booth, lifted his arms into a wide rigid V, and got down to what he did best.

We tried Fez Club, Leadmill, and Casbah before ending up in Kingdom because Shaz gorroff wit doorwoman who lerrus through, intut main room, wi its diamond-shaped neon lights, its vast dance floor overlooked by a balcony where lads supped pints and scouted for conquests. Speakers rattled wi air horns, distorted keyboards, bass notes kicking so low they wa more feeling than sound, thumping in mi solar plexus. Shaz and doorwoman disappeared tut loos together. I never could ask her if she really fancied lass or if she did it just to gerrus past door. There warra lot I felt like I couldn't ask Shaz. I always thought she warrall tooth beneath skin. I wish I'd known then she warrall bones.

I wanted to ask about every time it'd happened that way, ever since Shaz took us for us first night out round town when we were fourteen, steering us towards Spider's Web because she reckoned she wa seeing bouncer, who wa twenty-one wi a shaved head and "Rovers" tattooed on his neck. He said Ey up to her when we got there, and they went off tut car park together later, but we never heard about him after. I wanted to know how much of all that wa "lust." I wanted to know if lust existed, outside ut smutty novels Kel thought I didn't know she still read. If inside Shaz lived a core of lust fuelling all this public, open-air shagging—or if it wa just a tactic, just one of Shaz's schemes.

Me and Kel made us way intut smaller side room where DJ wa playing cheesy pop and bar area smelled like sick. We had to hold us breath to order us VK Blues. After half a bottle, Kel's tongue wa purple and her breath smelled like sick too, which meant mine did an' all. I leaned into her ear, tried to shout over t'music wi'out breathing on her.

"Where's Shaz *now*?"

Kel shrugged.

Shaz'd come back from snogging doorwoman int loos but absconded again almost instantly. We'd only been there five minutes and we'd already lost her twice. Whenever us lot went out, me and Kel wa forever having to hunt for Shaz, forever finding her pushed up against a wall in a shady corner, legs crooked round a torso, dress riding her thighs, mouth sucking on a mouth, till I didn't know if I wanted to slap sense into her or snog her misen, just to stop her wandering off. But this wa too much disappearing even for Shaz. At this rate, I wa never gunna get to make mi announcement about mi fella.

"What's up wi her tonight? It's like she's *trying* to get raped."

"Oi!" Kel slapped mi arm. I always knew I'd said summat out of order when Kel gave me that *oi*. Pins and needles prickled beneath mi skin, feeling I always get when I'm int wrong but don't know why.

"Aren't you sick of rescuing her?"

DJ switched from an Abba medley to House of Pain's "Jump

Around," and horn intro wailed over Kel's reply. I tapped mi ear, and she leaned in, shouted over a quiet bit: "You say that like she never rescues us."

We found her on a sofa in a nook under a staircase, sandwiched between two blokes. Bloke One's arm draped across sofa back, behind her neck; Bloke Two's fingers rubbed her thigh. Kel kept blokes chatting while I took Shaz by her arm, pulled her standing. She grinned silly, her face blissed till I wished I wa that high. I didn't think I wa high at all except that mi big hand looked funny and lovable against her tiny wrist.

She threw an elbow round mi neck and hung there, gi'in me a side hug. I put mi arm round her shoulders, side-hugged her back. Bloke Two's aftershave lingered on her skin; she smelled of lemon trees and a boxing gym, macho, unpredictable, aloof. She said we should go back tut blokes' flat because they'd gorra pool table and a fridge full of beer. I stroked top of her arm, patch of skin so soft I thought it wa melting away beneath mi finger.

I said, "Not tonight, babes." She laid her head on mi shoulder.

"Love you, Rach." She closed her eyes. We might've stayed that way all night, Shaz's chin digging at mi clavicle, if mi phone hadn't gone, mi fella texting. I couldn't help breaking us hug, pulling phone out, couldn't resist reading—*wish I wa huggin u right now, monkey ;-)*—couldn't stop spreading mi silly loved-up smile.

"What you grinning like that fo'?" said Shaz.

"I'm not grinning like owt!" I said, grinning like owt.

Shaz made a grab for mi phone.

"Oi!" I held it up out her reach. She tickled mi armpit, making me writhe, till mi arm clamped down and she could swipe phone off me. She read text, handed phone back.

"Is he your boyfriend or summat?" She said "boyfriend" like idea of me having one wa ridiculous.

"So what if he is?"

She went quiet, staring over mi shoulder gone out, gurning, mouth spasming down at corners, as if she wa so drugged up she'd forgotten what we warron about. This wont how it wa meant to go. Where wut giggles and shrieks. Where wut oh-my-gods. Where wut Honestly, Rach, I'm dead happy for ya. I nudged her arm.

She said, "Ya too good forr'im, ya know."

"Shurrup." I smiled, blushed hot, pulled her back into us side hug.

"Ah mean it." She put her hands on mi hips, forehead inches from mine. "You could do way better." Us foreheads touched, night-club a forgotten fuddle around us.

"What do you know that I don't?"

Shaz seemed to come back to hersen, then, out of a daze. She shook her head. Nowt.

"Shaz, what do you know?"

"Nowt, ah just—" She stepped back, fumbled in her bra till she found plastic baggie, fingers scissoring inside it trying to grasp a pill. I closed mi hand over t'bag, stilling her fingers. She looked away. "Ah just heard he's a cheater."

"From who?"

"Can't say."

"Yes you *can*, Shaz." I took her cheeks in mi hands, held her head so she had to look up at me. "You're meant to be mi best mate."

"Promised ah wunt."

I studied her face. A too-sincere roundness of her eyes informed me that she didn't really have owt to divulge. A too-innocent slackness of mouth. I should've guessed—she barely knew mi fella, and she wut type of lass who'd come out wi any old bollocks to conjure a scandal, plonk hersen at centre. Years, I'd played Friend #2, a supporting role in every one of Kel and Shaz's relationship dramas. Now I wa finally t'one wit boyfriend and she couldn't just be happy for me. Couldn't let me be centre of attention. This wut first time I'd been out wi a lad since I wa thirteen, first time one had said he liked mi chunky thighs, liked cupping his hands round their thickness. Mi anger fizzed beneath blanket of calm E had thrown over mi nerves.

"Did *you* fuck him, like?"

It wa meant to come out jokey but I knew it sounded wrong. Shaz's mouth wa half open, as if she'd been about to say summat before I cut her off. She closed it, her face blanking, emotionless, an expression I'd never seen her wear, laugh-lit eyes gone flat. She looked like someone I'd never met, like she'd donned a mask, or finally taken one off. I let go of her cheeks, stood back, braced forra sock tut nose.

"Ya look dead pretty tonight, Rachael."

Heat scattered over mi cheeks and neck. Shaz had consulted her arsenal of spite, selected weapon she knew would pierce flesh. Whenever she wanted me to feel small, she'd make a weird comment about how much prettier I wa than her. She wa always everything a lass would want to be: short slight frame, long glossy hair, dinky chin pinched and perfect. She never spent her school dinner money on food; she saved it up, and every few months she took it into town, bought a denim jacket, pair of gold hoops, so she wa always thinnest and best dressed lass int school. I wa always a foot too tall, curvy too early, mi hair too thick, mi eyes too small. I didn't understand why she had to be that cruel, why she had to hurt me that much.

Kel burst intut little space we'd made for oursens, shoulders pushing ours apart, to report that Bloke One had just grabbed her arse so it wa time to move on. She linked arms wi us both, making us one chain. I think me and Shaz wa always trying to make Kel love us more than she loved the other. Maybe that's why I didn't say owt about Shaz telling lies, and she didn't say owt about me accusing her of being a slag—Kel would've got pissed off at both of us for grassing each other up. We left staircase nook, one of Shaz's pills below each of us tongues.

I don't know how much E we took, but it wa enough not to

notice Kingdom's grimy floor, and lads in Fred Perry polos and Ben Sherman shirts prowling dance floor's perimeter, short sleeves choking their biceps, purple beams bouncing off their rock-hard quiffs, their scowls, and lasses int loos chugging voddy they'd snuck in like us, and Shaz untwining hersen from somebugger else, bouncing off sinks where she'd sat straddling them, seat of her dress wet, and handing Kel a baggie of coke she'd seduced someone into gi'in her. It wa enough not to notice black marks scuffing length of mi new heels, or Kel's nail polish glitter as she passed baggie below partition between her cubicle and mine, told me to tap powder onto mi thumbnail, hold one nostril closed, sniff. It wa enough not to notice happy hardcore tunes int first room, mass sing-along to "Angels" by Robbie Williams int other, and dank hands groping mi thighs while I stood int bar queue, hemmed between bodies. It wa enough to keep us dancing till two a.m. kick-out, and it wa too much: it made us buy mucky kebabs, shovel them from Styrofoam boxes to mouths, us drugs hungrier than us bellies, us bellies we filled till they were tight and pressing at us dresses. It made us trip over us shoes and strain us ankles, blundering downhill towards station, where we huddled on a metal platform bench, closing eyes against fluorescent lights but too wired to sleep, shivering int blue air before dawn.

Arms-Out raved all night too, fixed in his spot by t'guard-rail, whirling his arms, jacking his legs. He'd have stayed there till dawn, say those that saw, sweat bleeding through T-shirt, plastic whistle dangling from mouth, if it weren't fut lass who came up to him. If you ask regulars who'd known Arms-Out for years—"our Arms-Out," they call him—they'll tell you he never looked more alive than he did that night: summat about way this lass chose him, walked right up to him and copied his moves, spinning her arms and chopping her feet. It wa hypnotic, way their wasted bodies found each other, made silhouettes like sculptures of lovers int strobe light. You wanted to step out of your body and dissolve into them. Love looks that way sometimes, they'll say, but not often, not round here.

Some folk told it different, said two of them just spied each other's track marks and knew they'd found a running mate, someone to shoot up wi round back later, who'd feed needle between their knuckles and push drugs in. One person swore down there wa no lass at all, that Arms-Out spent his last night alone.

By five o'clock, we were chilled tut spine and coming down. Paranoia kicked in worse than I've ever felt, and I wa sure station staff knew—sure they could see drugs written in mi retinas, sure they'd call police and get me done. I tried not to look them int eye, tried not to look anywhere but at rails, where rats darted, then paused, then turned their little faces at me till I gorrup and paced between loos and station clock. I stared at egg-shaped stain on mi left shoe that could've been a lad's lager splash and could've been kebab grease, trying not to listen tut echoey splatter of Shaz throwing up int disabled loo, or Kel saying we should go in and hold her hair back. I wa so paranoid I started thinking Shaz wa telling truth about mi fella, sent him a dozen texts that began wi, *What the fuck is this I hear*, and were so jammed wi typos and fury that he nearly finished wi me moment he woke up that day—didn't have a clue what I warron about, he'd barely spoke to Shaz in his life. I haven't done coke since that night. It makes mad thoughts creep in.

Shaz wa sure we could sleep our way home for free again and I wa sure we couldn't. Ont way in, it wouldn't have mattered if conductor woke us; we had enough money to pay. I didn't wanna get Shaz riled, so I didn't say what I wa thinking: 05:24 to Scunthorpe departed from Sheffield; there wa no earlier station to pretend we came from. And 05:24 wut first train ut day, so there wunt be as many bodies on board. Only fools and scrubbers up at that hour, and by that stage we were both: Kel's burgundy lipstick wa swatched across her chin, and Shaz's scab had bled like I told her it would, left rust-brown spatters all down her dress. I didn't say owt about how fucked I wa sure we were because Shaz said faking sleep would work and Kel backed her up, and we didn't have a choice anyway because they were bare skint and I couldn't tell them about tenner I'd still got hidden, softened, now, wi body heat.

When 05:24 pulled in, we settled oursens int last carriage, chose seats alone. Train rattled off and we posed, heads juddering against windows, arms limp and lolling. Mi fingers and toes burned wit train's sudden warmth. Exhaustion scorched mi insides, roasted mi veins. Int dark of mi eyelids, mi head pulsed wit memory of Kingdom's dance floor, as if I'd stuffed a pounding bass line beneath mi skull. Mi brain wa too big. Mi thoughts zipped around like flies. Coarse bristles ut seat fabric itched mi bare thighs, making mi legs twitch. I couldn't sit still, waiting fut conductor to find us.

I hissed, "Need a slash," headed intut vestibule.

Louder there, train's walls thinner, line of sunlight bleeding along edge ut exit door. I passed loo, peeped through window ut next carriage. Conductor at far end, making his way down. Three rows in, he leaned over a bloke laid out across two seats. "Tickets, please." Bloke didn't stir. Conductor shook bloke's shoulder. "TICKETS, PLEASE."

I ran back to our carriage. Shaz and Kel were still pretending to be dreamers bobbing against glass. "He's waking us," I said, making Kel's eyes flick open. "He's shaking us awake."

Shaz's lids pulled back into slits that she dead-eyed me through. "Get fucked as if he is."

"Swear down."

Bleak terrace rows thrashed past. I fought to quiet mi heart. I'd never got in trouble before, not proper, not wit *law*. Never skived school like Kel did when she wa shagging Ando behind chippy every Mundi morning, never lifted a lipstick from Bargain Beauty like Shaz reckoned she did ont reg. Mi tenner wouldn't pay for us all. If I only bought mi own ticket, other two would never speak to me again.

"Fucksake." Shaz wobbled onto her heels. "We'll just hide int bog till Donny."

"He's int next carriage, he'll see us." Everything around me hummed, swayed.

Kel rose, stretched her arms over her head. "Be reyt," she said. "Come on."

Back int vestibule, blast of noise and cold air, wheels beneath us going yatatatack, floor shifting left and right. We weaved through fields, ferns and heather fringing tracks, nodding their heads at us, reaching their fingers up. Wind rattled exit door, but circular red light by t'latch promised me that it wa locked.

Int next carriage, conductor's hat bobbed towards us. Shaz opened boggy door and backed in, beckoned us wi a bossy hand. Kel sidled in wi her. Just me, then, int vestibule. I'd been awake so long I wa dreamy, like I might float, like I might slide into a different life altogether. Orange ut carriage seats throbbed like a heart. Had I ever seen orange before?

"Hang on," I said. "I forgot, I always keep a tenner in mi bra."

It wa warm when I pulled it out and held it up, curved tut shape of mi boob. I wont ready fut way it'd change air around us, carry its own weather. I wont ready fut way it'd make them look at me.

Kel said, "As if you do, since when?"

"You forgot?" Shaz's expression wa hard to read, as if her face had suddenly plunged into shadow.

"Yeah, I always keep it in there so I forgot."

"Fare is £4.80 each," said Shaz. "You're fuckin top set maths boff."

"It's enough for two."

"Oh aye." Shaz's voice turned savage. "So ya can mek sure you and Kel are alreyt and leave me in here to get fucked on mi own?"

Conductor: nearer, sun bouncing off his specs.

"Who said it'd be me and Kel?"

"Well, I'm stopping in here wi Shaz," Kel said.

"Go on, then, Rach." Shaz bared her teeth. "Get thisen fucked off and sat down."

Cut of Shaz's *g* when she said "go"—I thought it'd slice open mi cheek. But her *o* wa long, just like everyone's *o* from her end: "*G*oo on, then." Another of hers: she'd always say "Gi oo'er" when she heard summat she didn't believe. Gi oo'er, like a donkey's bray.

I saw a programme once, young lass from down south gerrin interviewed. Talking about her fella, she'd say "this is me" and "this is him" instead of "I said" and "he said." Like, "This is me: 'I don't know what I'm doing wrong.' This is him: 'You're clueless, that's the problem.'" I liked way it sounded, as if every time you speak you're saying who you are. I wished I could use it, fold it into speech like it wa mine, but I couldn't, not in Donny. Here we're not allowed to sound like we're trying to be from somewhere else. Here we say, "Then I goes, then he goes, then I went"—actually, we say, "Then ah guz, then he guz, then ah went"—as if saying is the same thing as leaving.

Then ah went intut boggy and closed door.

If I'd stayed int vestibule, there'd be a forever of just Kel and Shaz, bezzy bitches, me frozen out. I'd get accused of not being loyal. It'd happened loads over t'years: sometimes Kel wut outcast, me and Shaz linking arms, striding across school field. Sometimes it wa just me and Kel again, Shaz swallowed back into her Goldthorpe lot. Always, we angled forra villain.

I slid bolt, quiet as I could, intut latch behind me. We pressed against each other between sink and loo, rocking wit train in lockstep like a dance troupe.

Carriage door swooshed open. Conductor's boots tapped across vestibule. We didn't breathe. We made violent eyes at each other.

Mi left arm snaked Kel's waist; mi right pit housed Shaz's nose. Fermenting-fruit odour of old booze rose from all of us, gathered like heat beneath ceiling, mingled wit faintly stale smell of a thousand ill-judged aims. We swayed, me towering over them, a shot-putter sheltering two elves. We listened tut boots tap tap.

I'd gone so long wi'out dipping mi mind into sleep, I found misen outside time. I found misen drenched in eternity. And in that breathless silence I thought, mebs we'll just hold onto each other, forget every fight we've ever had.

We heard swoosh ut next carriage door and exhaled, unhooked us bodies, looked for places to arrange oursens alone. Kel inched her hips ontut metal sink frame and perched, one leg extended, toes anchoring her tut floor, neck bent to keep her head from banging ont mirror. Shaz lowered hersen ontut loo seat. I scooched down as far as I could—not enough floor for mi arse—and crouched, back against door, mi cauliflower knees taking up space int middle. Door buzzed wit train's motion, tickling mi ears. Comedown wa starting to hollow me out. Thirst crawled into mi mouth.

"Ya knees are in mi way," said Shaz, pushing against them wi her knees, forcing me to lean intut sink, into Kel's outstretched leg, which buckled and pitched her sideways. She crashed intut sheet of white opaque plastic ont wall that wa masquerading as a window.

"Fucksake, Rach," said Kel.

"It wa Shaz's fault."

"Int my fault your legs are too fuckin long."

"What's up wi yous two?" Kel said far too loud.

"Quiet," I said. Conductor had stepped into an empty final carriage. He'd be back any second. I pulled misen up again ont disabled rail.

"*Sozzard*," said Kel, at same risky volume.

Shaz said, "If we're too loud for ya, why don't you fuck off out?"

As her mouth formed "off," carriage door swept open. We froze. Boots tapped past us. We listened till t'noise got lost again int roar ut train.

"Why are yous so pissed off wi each other?" asked Kel.

Shaz crossed her arms, scowled at her knees.

"I told Shaz I've gorra boyfriend, but she can't be happy for me because it means she's not centre of attention."

Kel looked at Shaz, who wouldn't look at anyone. "To be fair," said Kel, "it *wa* menna be a girly night. We wont menna be talking about lads."

"Oh aye, there wunt even *be* a girly night if Ando hadn't dumped you—you'd be spending every last second wi him."

"Ando dint fuckin dump me, you dick." Kel turned her head from me, glowered at white plastic sheet.

I knew I wa saying unfair things now, but I couldn't stop misen. All I'd wanted wa five minutes of fuss, them two giddy and pleased, demanding to know warr'e a good kisser, and what did he say when he asked me out. I wont even sure if Ando did dump Kel. A few months back, Kel came to school covered in a weird rash. She wouldn't say what happened, but there wa no more Ando after that.

"Why are you in here, Rach?" said Kel. "You could just go out and pay, so I don't even know what you're proving by staying."

"We all know she'd've paid fo' thee, so wharra you doing in here an' all?" Shaz said to her knees. I knew what Kel wa doing in there. Proving her loyalty, proving she wa just as brave as Shaz.

"Look, I shunt've said owt about Ando. I'm just upset because this is mi first ever boyfriend—"

"What about that psycho from Barnsley?" said Shaz.

"That psycho from Barnsley dunt count! This is mi first *proper* boyfriend, and I just thought you'd be happy for me. Especially you, Shaz. You were t'one who told me to get wi him int first place."

Shaz's head snapped up, eyes trained on me. "Did ah fuck tell ya to get wi him."

"You bloody did. Other week, at Squiff's all-nighter." Either she wa lying or she wa too fucked that night to remember. "I wa saying how come nobody ever fancies me, and you said it wa only because I hadn't been near a lad since that psycho fro—"

"Ah said you've gorrer *flirt* if you want a lad to tek interest. Ah dint say flirt wi any old munter."

I had to dig mi nails into mi palm to stop misen from crying. I'd never say owt that nasty about a lad Shaz wa seeing.

"So now you're lying about that just like you wa making shit up about mi boyfriend earlier."

"Ah wont mekkin shit up." Shaz sighed. "Ah shunta bothered. Ah just thought you'd wanna know."

"Why do you always do this? Why do you always say owt you can think of to make sure everything's about you?"

Shaz returned to staring at her knees, fierce and fixed. "Go get thisen sat down, princess. Conductor'll be back in a minute."

We fell into a silence humming wi summat none of us could name. Mi feet burned to be out of mi shoes. If those two didn't want me in there, I may as well go. I groped fut lock behind mi back, fingered bolt. I closed mi eyes so I could listen for boots. But I didn't quite dare slide bolt back. Instead, I counted down stations in mi head: Rotherham, Swinton, Mexborough. Conisbrough next, then Donny Beaut.

At some point, say most ut people who were there, Arms-Out's lass took his hand, led him off dance floor intut chill room, where music throbbed soft and ambient, fairy light clusters twinkled pink, chairs stretched low and wide and squidgy—kind you sunk into, beanbag chairs, snug as wombs. They laid out and gazed at lights and strung their fingers together, talked happy babbling druggie nonsense till they leaned towards each other and their lips met and they forgot everything and their borders fell away and they dropped into an endless yes.

Person who claimed there wa no lass at all said Arms-Out warrin there alone, talking to hissen, staring up into nowt, probably thinking nowt but fuzz and coming up. Maybe he went back tut slashers and did too much skag, or maybe he stayed ont dance floor, throwing too many windmills till he passed out from heat.

Only event everyone can agree on is that sometime before dawn
he hoisted hissen from a beanbag and staggered off alone.

As minutes passed between Mexborough and Conisbrough, train
hissing and thunking around us, making me feel like I wa trapped
in an enormous mechanical serpent, I realised that we hadn't talked
about what would happen when train pulled into Donny Station.
How would we get out, off, and down platform stairs wi'out conductor spotting us?

I wanted to ask what'd happen if we got caught, but they'd only
keep on at me to leave. I wont sure, then, if I wa even off to uni—
whenever asked what I wanted to be, I said teacher, but I hadn't
thought about what that involved, or if it wa really what I wanted.
Most days I didn't think about leaving Donny, didn't think about
much except going out and gerrin pissed: I warrin love wit freedom
of it, of not belonging to yoursen, of losing memory and muscle
control and speech.

Mum had threatened to disown me, though, if I didn't go uni.
She warra hairdresser, but she wished she'd been summat else.
And thought of gerrin caught hiding in a bog ont Northern train
to Scunthorpe, being dragged out by coppers, dragged into court,
gerrin charged wi summat that would brand me wi Donny forever.
I couldn't get enough air. Mi lungs felt sawn in two.

Train tilted us into Conisbrough. I pictured town's medieval
keep, laid on its hill like a ragged animal, torn open limbs of its walls
and turrets, exposed stones like dragon scales rippling. Cowering
below it, maze of terrace rows, green lick of a cricket pitch, and
down by t'tracks, set of Stella-swigging chavettes, rounding off a
late sesh like us.

Train's exterior doors slid open, then footsteps, coughs and
sniffs, a crisp draft around boggy door as Conisbrough's finest
thrumbled in. It wa safer to talk now train wa filling wit shuffle and

thud of many feet, the dat dat ut boggy door lifting out and back into its frame each time a body pushed past.

"What are we gunna do when we get there?" I asked.

Shaz shrugged.

"I thought you'd done this before."

"I thought your tits wa sneezing cash."

I closed mi fingers back around bolt. I could nip out now, blend wi everyone else, pretend I got on at Conisbrough.

"What's fare from here? I bet I could pay for all three of us now."

Shaz laughed as though I'd asked what's a blow job. "Not tekkin owt from thee."

"Kel, do you want me to pay for you? If we go now, it'll look like we just got on."

"No, ta." Kel wouldn't meet mi eyes. "I stick by mi mates, me."

Maybe I'd already lost Kel. Maybe they'd both hate me no matter what.

"Fuck it," I said, and turned round to leave. As I faced door, someone knocked ont other side, loud dap dap dap ont plastic.

"Unlock this door and come out of there, please."

I raised mi hand tut lock, but Shaz lunged over and gripped mi wrist, sunk her nails in. She purra finger to her lips, shook her head. I tried to throw her off. She pinched harder.

I hissed, "Why not?"

Shaz pulled hersen up by mi arm, clapped her other hand round mi mouth. "Trust me," she said in mi ear. "Just shurrup and stay still." Her fingers pressed against mi teeth.

Conductor banged again. "Today, please, or I'll be forced to knock down this door."

"Do it," Shaz shouted. "Ah'll sue ya for sexual assault." She relaxed her grip on mi face, but I wa too sick to move. All I could hear wa mi heartbeat. We were proper fucked now.

"Are you threatening me, love?"

"Ah'll tek ya to court, ya pedo. Tryna watch me tek a shit, ya dirty fuckin cunt."

"Shaz what the *fuck*?" I whisper-screeched.

Shaz raised her finger to her lips again.

Train chu-chunked, gathering speed. I tried to push back panic that wa swallowing mi senses, leaving me bright and hot behind eyes, like sky at midday, bleached of contour.

Conductor said, "Look, just get yoursen out here and pay your fare."

"Shaz, please just let me pay. *Please* just let me. You wunt have to pay me back."

Shaz cocked her head to one side, weighing offer up. "Do you trust me?"

"Yes, just please let's open door and pay him."

"Giz your tenner, then."

I pulled it from mi bra, handed it to her.

"Ta."

"I'm opening door, then." I looked at Kel for support. Kel wa watching Shaz, who'd whipped coke baggie from her fag packet and wa tapping white powder ontut side ut sink. She rolled mi tenner into a cylinder.

"Go forrit," Shaz said, bending her head to her coke line, mi tenner threaded up her nostril. She snorted loud.

Sick, doom feeling in mi belly. I couldn't open door now wi'out exposing her—me, us—to a drug charge. This wa Shaz's way of taking back control. She'd rather us all go down on her terms than be saved on mine.

"Right, enough faffing about," conductor said. "If you don't open the door and exit the lavatory within the next thirty seconds, you will find yourself in breach of railway bylaws that mek it an offence to travel without a ticket." He spoke int proud, rehearsed rhythms of a kid who'd just learned his times tables. I could hear him breathe. Each breath gave me shape of him, as if I could gauge his heft just by sound ut air streaming in. "Such a breach is punishable by law, and if found guilty, you would be subject, at present, to a fine of up to £1,000."

Shaz tapped out more coke. "Fine me all ya like, ya nonce, I ant gorra grand."

"An operator can also prosecute for intent to avoid a rail fare under the Regulation of Railways Act of 1889, in which case you may be sentenced to imprisonment for up to three months."

Fucking *prison?* Mi pulse warra frog clucking in mi mouth. I could open t'door, play dumb about t'coke. Unless they took me in and drug tested me, for fucksake. I closed mi eyes, wished for owt that could rescue us—owt that could stop me tumbling down this forever pit. I wa meant to mess and dabble but come out of all this alright, gerra job and a mortgage, kids and a time-share fortnight in Tenerife.

"I'll count to three," he said.

Owt, I thought, over and over. I'll tek *owt* you've got if you'd just gerrus out of this. I suppose I wa saying a prayer. It wa mi very first prayer, and mi last.

Shaz bent her face over t'white powder. Train slowed, throwing her forwards. Her head knocked against mirror. Her coke line scattered into snow dust. We'd be pulling into Donny Station. Transport police would be lined up ont platform, waiting to book us.

Train slowed, and stopped, and gasped.

Silence.

I put mi ear tut door. No boots, no rustling bags, no squawking sinuses, no squeaky trainers. Nowt. Too much nowt.

"He's fucked off," said Shaz.

"No he ant!" I mouthed like a desperate mime.

Shaz yelled, "Are ya there, ya fat fuckin perv?"

We waited.

Nowt.

Shaz reached round me, unlatched door. We both half fell intut vestibule.

Green, all around us. I couldn't make sense ut view—fields and woods filled windows instead of Donny Station's brick and bustle. Train must've stopped early. By t'exit door, circular light shone green for unlocked.

Shaz hit release button. Door beeped, slid open. Brisk morning air rushed in. Shaz flung hersen out, vanished over t'embankment. Me and Kel looked at each other, feeling same fears: broken leg, electric shock, decapitation.

We jumped after Shaz, leapt over tracks, intut long wild grasses. We fell hard and bruising on knees and palms, rolled down, down, till we stopped at slope's bottom, wind knocked from us lungs. We laid on us backs, panting. Waited to hear an *Oi!* To hear boots scuffling above us, someone chasing us down. Door beeped shut. Train sat, quiet and unbothered, as if it'd never contained us.

We laughed and laughed and laughed. We held us aching bellies and laughed.

When giggles finally subsided, we crept away from t'embankment, unbuckled us stripper heels and slung them from us fingers, picked us way barefoot through woods. Smell ut dewy undergrowth, ut summer pollen, lemony morning sun flashing through gaps int trees—and whip ut wind making branches and leaves applaud like us own enthralled audience—it all made me feel a different kind of free than you get from booze. Free like clear, like scrubbed clean.

We hobbled, stumbled, danced, grit between us toes. Somewhere between miracle and hysteria of it, hatred melted off us, got lost int knee-high brambles. When Kel's feet hurt, I hefted her into a piggyback, ran till she squealed. Usually, Shaz'd beg forra turn. This time, she strode behind us, as if determined never to need me again.

I knelt in front of her, said, "Go on, let me."

She held tight round mi neck, breathed into mi hair, weighing almost nowt at all. But she didn't squeal, didn't laugh. She just clung, let her silence tell me that I'd said summat she wont gunna let me take back. Summat had shifted for me an' all. I never did feel same about Shaz after that night.

At edge ut woods we found River Don, which gi us our bearings. We crossed footbridge, followed river till we met curve of a familiar cul-de-sac.

When we hit main road, Kel and Shaz meandered towards Kel's house and I pushed on tut posh end, feet fiery wit tarmac's friction, shoes banging against mi thigh, plastic stiletto tip already worn to a sharp wedge. Dull worry that walk had delayed me too long and I couldn't sneak back in before everyone woke up.

But mi mum and dad'd been out wit cricket lot that night, end-of-season barby. They were still sock on when I climbed back through downstairs loo window and pulled it shut.

I slept all day, didn't wake till after dark, mi phone blipping in mi handbag ont floor. Seven missed calls from Shaz, twelve unread texts from mi fella. I wont ready to face mi fella, so I called Shaz back. I listened tut rings, mi body moaning in all its sore spots: scuffed elbows, grazed knees, shredded soles.

"Arms-Out Simon is dead," she said. "Died this morning." She wa crying, and that's when I knew she really did know him. "He got hit by a train, Rach. Our train."

For years, Arms-Out had teetered between shelter and streets. His mam didn't have cash forra funeral, so council wa gunna purr'im in a pauper's grave, his ashy parts mixed wit ashy parts of folk he'd never met. Warehouse threw a charity rave. Everyone ont Donny scene pitched in, bought him a plot at St. John and St. Mary Magdalene, a piss-up int working men's club.

At time, I didn't ask questions, I just took Shaz's word. I didn't read write-up int *Free Press*, didn't get involved int fun run following year in his name. I didn't know what South Yorkshire police chief said, or how Arms-Out's tox screen came back, and I didn't find out for sure if it wa our train. I think I wa ashamed of mi own safety, mi own clean record. Mi ten GCSEs, mi first car mi mum and dad bought me soon as I turned seventeen.

Recently, I tried Googling everything I'd never asked. Google wouldn't tell me time of death, or extent of his injuries, or if there warra lass he'd loved. Google wouldn't tell me if it wa our train.

Then, other week, me and Shaz passed each other on Clock Corner in town centre, both of us arms folded, bristling against wind. Years since I'd seen her, friendship dwindling from weekly drinks to monthly to nearly never. She'd shown up at mi wedding, too skinny again, pained look on her face all night as if it warra chore, seeing me happy. We hadn't talked since night she got arrested. Mi husband warrout round town that night, said she wa blind drunk, proper lost her mind, assaulted his best mate unprovoked. He'd said to me, Stay away from that batty cow, she's unhinged. He'd said, You hold onto relationships too long—time to let that one go.

She looked birdish and sad and weathered like sand. Her coat looked too thin as we stood saying, Y'alreyt, duck, it's been ages, so I steered us into Costa and we sat either side of us mochas, warming us hands on us mugs. We talked forra minute about Kel, who's long gone, America, left us both behind. Alright for some, innit, we said. Living it up in Yankeeland. We talked forra second about Brexit, but only to moan about how tired we were of hearing t'word. We knew better than to ask how we'd voted. I tried not to talk too much about mi teaching career or mi uni mates or mi marriage, or ask what she wa doing for work. Us chat kept guttering, snuffing itsen out. He'd been on mi mind, so I asked her about Arms-Out. How did she know it wa our train?

"Ah never said it wa our train."

"You bloody *did*."

It came out like an attack—like an uppercut, her head jerking back in shock or disbelief. I wanted to ram mi words back in mi gob, suck them down wit dregs of mi mocha. She took a long sip of hers, large eyes assessing me over t'mug rim.

"Ah can't remember, me." She shrugged. "If you say ah did, ah did."

That wont like our Shaz. Our Shaz never backed down, never doubted her own story. She wa full of fight no matter what. Mi insides seesawed, seeing her this depleted, this ready to give in. I missed her like fuck, then—missed Shaz I knew, wanted to span gap between us, rub out us lost years, find us way back to how we wa before, when Shaz warra gale-force wind, when she loved you as fiercely as she fought you. I didn't have mates like that anymore.

I didn't know how to rescue things, so I started telling her how much I'd been wondering about Arms-Out, how guilty it made me feel to think—

Her raised palm stopped me mid-flow. Her mug went clatter ont saucer. "It's not about you, though, Rach," she said. "You dint even know him."

There she wa, Shaz of old, glaring at me across table, eyes lit wi an ire so concentrated I wondered how I could've gorrit so wrong. Said summat so unforgivable. She wa right, I didn't know him. But I'd wanted to. I'd wanted to know any ut ones she'd lost. I wanted to tell her that—say, mebs she'd weathered more chaos than I'd gi her credit for. Say, mebs I used to get cross wi her because I'd wanted to be as interesting as she wa, claim some of her stories for misen. Touch tragedy wi mi own hands. I wanted to say, what if we just started again? Put past int past. But she wa already draining her mug, slipping into her coat, saying she had to gerroff home.

Nobody would admit to being wi Arms-Out when he died. Nobody but train driver—who, rumour wa, tried to hang hissen three months later—caught moment Arms-Out's body met tracks, or how his bones snapped, or shape his limbs made int air. Nobody could talk about how far he flew or how wide he scattered, or what pieces of him were saved for his mam.

I picture him walking out intut misty dawn. Laid ont grassy bank, admiring clouds rimmed in orange glimmer. Probably, he wa just looking forra quiet place to slash. Probably, he wa too smacked up to make ground from sky. Probably he choked on his own sick and convulsed, organs failing before he hit tracks.

You Cannot Thread a Moving Needle

Next day, they come round your house to mek sure you'll never tell.

But that's not what they say when you open door, find them ont step, two dense bodies int daylight. They say, Ey up, and you greet them back, Alreyt. They're int year above, little un wi dyed-black hair all t'goth lasses fancy, and lanky lad, who you're not sure, but you think might be seeing Rach. Lanky Lad's alreyt like, but you reckon Rach only fancies him cuz he plays bass in Little Un's band. You can't get past his mouth, two fat pink slugs sleeping one below other. His lips, always wet, saliva slick. You don't know how Rach can snog that mouth, if she is. Little Un, though, proper beaut, barely ever spoke to you till yesterday: mid-afternoon int backyard while your mam wa asleep, you and Kel and Rach, splayed ovver too-long thirsty grass in nowt but string bikinis you all went Primark together to get. Bacardi Breezer Watermelons from offy round corner that'll serve anyone, long as you've gorra backpack to hide it in. Giggle, bottle, clink. Pink liquid tang, swill down quick. Then Lanky Lad and Little Un appeared ovvert fence, surprised your boozy tanning sesh.

Now, Little Un grins. You go warm, arse to tit.

36

Little Un sez, "Fancy a walk?"

It's summer, so days are borderless, their edges shimmering int heat. Today feels like it's still part of yesterday, especially since you can't remember going to bed last neet. You leave your house and stroll between t'lads forever, or half hour, or five minutes, chatting shit, bouncing on toes while plastic flip-flops go flap flap, thinking, *lucky cow*, and legs shaky, and Little Un's grinning at you again. They flank you in a winding too-wide trio dance down slender snicket behind neighbours' sheds. Nettles and snapdragons poke between fence planks; damp and dog shite sings in your nose. They natter about Sheff Wednesday's shocking turnout and Donny Rovers' keggy midfielder, NOFX's punk purity and reasons Green Day are sellouts, their lips stretched across cheeks into smiles like rubber bands across fingers.

You wonder if your tits stick out far enough beyond your belly, if your nipples' silhouettes are bleeding through your Hello Kitty tank top, if Little Un will get top's irony, if hot sweat between your thighs is really your period starting, if it's pooling int seat of your short-shorts, if it's trickling down a leg. You wish there wa somewier private you could drop your kegs and check. You wonder if your short-shorts are showing too much arsecheek. If they're not showing any arsecheek at all. You wish you'd brushed last neet's booze off your breath, and you wish you'd put your Wonderbra on when you crawled out of bed, head banging, to answer t'door, and you can't think about owt apart from how flat your tits must look wi'out that bra till you notice crumbling corner of a brick, loose and hanging out somecunt's garage wall.

Reminds you of younger days, of graze, of flay, of scramble ovver under through broken-off battered fence gate wall. Pegging it ovver knackered train tracks, building sites, rubble piles. Lung-rasping cackle, stop dead when brick cement stone gravel bites, snatches flakes off your top layer, leaves runs in your skin down arms, legs, laddered like tights.

You look down now and there's a new rip across your wrist,

dried-blood trail of torn-away skin. These days, grazes come from neets ont lash, bottles of voddy downed ont hay bales and bench by t'canal. Limbs fall heavy int midnight grass. These days, you wake wi'out memory of cuts and bumps left on fingers, shins. What did you do last neet to get thissun? Warrit brick, or cement, or?

Glass: your trio reaches snicket's end, emerges intut road, straightens, expands sideways intut new space, like a concertina between two palms pulling away, squeeze box that appears in your mam's hands when t'gin flows, plays "Gypsy Maiden" and "Stone Outside Dan Murphy's Door." Old red phone box stands before you, one pane shattered into craggy diamonds spat across tarmac. Sun bounces off glass, off old stone wall, off cornfield's dabbing heads.

Yous three sit ont wall. Your arsecheeks flare, remembering this sharp pattern, places where flesh is bruised from this constellation of hard rock points.

"Good night last night," Little Un sez. You nod. He strokes your knee and your fanny guz mad, tingling between your legs. He touches you like he knows you, and you half realise, half remember: summat must've happened last neet.

You can't believe it—you and Little Un! You can't wait to brag to Kel and Rach. Everyone fancies Little Un.

"You're a reyt lass, you," he sez. "You're amazing. A goddess. And nobody sees it."

Lanky Lad nods. You nod too.

"Seriously, Shaz." Little Un holds your shoulders, turns your torso towards him. Soft eyes staring into yours, face slack and grave. "I could write a hundred songs about shape of your arse, about them two freckles on your right cheek." He swabs a thumb ovver them two freckles, shuts his eyes, teks a long breath through his nose, inhaling your aura. He exhales, recovers himsen from how much you over-whelm. "I know you. I see who you really are, beneath shit you do to disguise yoursen for them." He gestures at phone box wi its broken pane, but you know he means Kel and Rach. Mebs he means your Goldthorpe crew an' all. Mebs he means whole world. You look down at wall, shift your weight. "And if you tell them about last night, they'll call you a slag, won't they, Shaz? They'll call you a whore."

You stare at rounded pebble, greyish, caught between rough red stones, trying to catch up wi what's been done. You remember now—you and t'lads went off alone, cem down here, but you can't remember why. Most ut neet's still black.

"You waint have any mates if you say owt," Little Un sez.

Lanky Lad adds, "Rach will hate you—proper hate you," so you reckon he's def seeing Rach. Who must Little Un be seeing? Which lass'll bray you if word ever slips? You dint mean to do owt wi someone else's fella. You're not that lass. And you're always gerrin pegged as that lass, who backstabs and shit-stirs and slags it up. Mebs cuz you've gorra reyt loud laugh, or cuz you're cocky like a lad, or cuz you waint back down from a fight, or cuz you like a flirt, or just cuz.

You swallow, throat still coated wi Bacardi Breezer's pink acidy swill taste, wit burn of it coming back up. Did you vom in front of Little Un? Did you gerrit on his trainers?

"Ah waint say owt," you say.

Lanky Lad's lips pucker into soggy disbelief.

"What's face fo'?" you ask.

Lanky Lad's eyes say, *You know*, and you realise Rach must've told him you can't be trusted, mebs even gi'en him her version of that time a few months ago when bolshy cunt int Ivanhoe called you a clown cuz you wa wearing pink eyeshadow and thick liquid liner. You wont even talking to him—you wa just at bar wi Rach, waiting to get served—but he kept on, asking what did you come as, Ronald McDonald? He warra regular, so everyone knew him, and soon all his mates wa laughing at you an' all. Shame glistened in your mouth so sharp you couldn't stop your tongue telling whole pub he'd cheated on his fiancée wi Rach. Everyone went dead quiet. Then, "You fuckin *what*?" from a lass who Rach told you later wut fiancée's best mate. Rach grabbed your hand and yous legged it. She couldn't be mad at you, though, cuz it wont true—she'd never gone near that bloke; she'd fibbed about him cuz she wa sick of being single, sick of never having her own juicy goss. So she said sorry for lying and you said sorry for grassing, and she reckoned she forgave you, but maybe she dint.

"What we did is beautiful," Little Un sez, sweeping his arm across field as if it wut site of a miracle. "It's divine—it's what life's about. You're *living*, Shaz. You're really living. But twats round here wouldn't know living if it thieved their fucking giros."

Lads' lips press shut, one set dry, one set wet.

"Ah won't say owt to anycunt, ah swear down."

And you don't. You don't say owt to anycunt ont solo trip home, back down snicket, picking at scab on your wrist till fresh blood trickles, and your mobile jangling: *Fuck did you end up last neet?* You don't say owt when neet comes back to you in flashes, like looking at memory through strobe light ont Karisma dance floor. You try not to look at all, cuz it's whorish behaviour, innit, Shaz? You've gorrer forget it happened. So you don't say owt next day when Kel asks, S'up wi you, you're quiet. Or day after that when you start thinking mebs Rach int seeing Lanky Lad after all, mebs you *could* tell, mebs your mates would prove lads wrong—mebs they wouldn't judge ya.

You don't say owt a week later when Rach tells you that she is seeing Lanky Lad. When you realise there's no hope of telling her wi'out mekkin her hate ya. Or when you realise it must've been Rach who invited t'lads round to your backyard. You still try to tell Rach, wi'out *telling* her, that her new fella's a cheater, but you can't say how you know, and Rach dunt wanna hear it. She's proper smitten, int she, and you're a proper slaggy shit-stirrer, aren't ya?

You don't say owt when it's been a month and Little Un ant looked at you once, and one day you're even walking towards each other int Village, street empty, and you try to catch his eye, not to talk, just to gi him look that passes between two people who've shared summat—just to gi him a nod that sez, *Don't worry, ah'm keeping us secret.* He dunt smile, dunt look, just passes you, staring straight ahead.

You don't say owt when Kel starts going out wi Little Un, feeling dead special like she wa wearing new trainers everyone wanted. When Kel and Rach are always off on double dates wi Lanky Lad and Little Un. When you stop hanging out wi Kel and Rach, anyway, start going forra run. Every neet: five mile, seven mile, ten. Circling streets of your estate, after dark when no-cunt can see. Not when you start drifting in class, can't concentrate, forget where you are. Not when your periods stop, or when four pregnancy tests prove you're definitely not. Not when you collapse in PE clutching your heart, and Sir sends you tut nurse, and nurse sends you tut GP, and GP sends you to a special unit cuz he reckons your dieting's gorrout of hand and now you've gorra "disorder."

You say fuck all for three months int unit, even though they mek you see a counsellor who wants you to talk about why you binge, purge, restrict. You've been on a diet since you wa eleven, though, so it's got nowt to do wi nowt. You say nowt while nurses tell you that your dieting's weakening your body, damaging your insides. They dunt tell you why it dunt *feel* like weakening. Why it meks you feel stronger. Meks you feel like a force. You say nowt while they watch you drink their orange juice and eat their cheese sticks, while they watch you afterwards to mek sure you dunt throw it all up. While you pack on enough fat that they'll let you go home, while you promise yoursen you'll control your dieting so they can't ever mek you go back tut unit.

You don't say owt when you're back at school, when you feel

lost cuz you missed mock exams and now you don't know how you'll ever pass your GCSEs. When you feel lost cuz while you wa gone Kel and Rach found theirsens a new crew, always knocking about, now, wi their boyfriends' mates. You don't say owt to anycunt fut rest ut school year, even when images tek root in your mind that you can't get shut of—neon-green Casio watch on Lanky Lad's wrist, arm hairs pushing out around strap.

You don't say owt while everyone piles out ont last day of school at noon in a cloud of cigar smoke and Charlie Red, your mates draped in plastic boas, toting rented top hats, pissed up, posing. Or when a set of lasses corner you reyt ont Karisma dance floor, neet before your food tech final exam. They're from Adwick and don't even *go* your school. Big lass shoulder barges you while you're trying to shimmy, calls you an ugly fucking bewer. Later, behind club, smoking a fag you blagged off a random, trying to smooth your ruffled nerves, you don't say owt when Big Lass bloodies your nose.

And you keep your gob shut while everyone branches intut future, while bright cunts stay at school for their A levels, thick cunts get theirsens a trade and earn theirsens a fortune, while cunts int middle go college forra BTEC National. You keep it shut while you start your BTEC National in Catering and Hospitality, collect your twenty quid a week EMA, while you spend it on fags and helping your mam out wit lecky bill. You keep it firmly closed while memories poke through your thoughts like thistles through grass.

Arm wit Casio watch running up your thigh while everyone's chatting int backyard, Rach trying to get barby lit. Hand edging towards your bikini bottoms, that flimsy fabric, that cheap Lycra bargain-bin shite. Sparkle feeling his fingers leave in your skin. Walking woozy to Texaco garage between Little Un and Lanky Lad on a quest for fire lighters, pack of Cumberland sausages.

While you redo your final year, scrape your BTEC National,

while you wait int dole queue for your Jobseeker's, wait years to leave your mam's house wi more than ten quid and a deck of cigs in your back pocket. Rach guz uni, Kel guz America, and Little Un guz college forra fine arts course in textiles. Little Un and Lanky Lad's band release an EP, and Rach tries to mek you go tut "launch" at local pub, and someone reckons there's an A&R man coming, and forra minute everyone thinks band is gunna become summat. Then Lanky Lad gets a council job filling out forms. Rach moves in wi Lanky Lad ont other side of town.

You keep your gob shut while your memory waint show you why you never mek it to Texaco garage forra pack of Cumberland sausages, why you veer off down snicket, end up at cornfield's wall. Slip ovvert scattered glass, throw a palm down to catch thisen, don't notice pain ut graze. Lads, steadying you, sitting you ont wall, stroking hair legs arm feet as you lie between them, head in Lanky Lad's lap. Four gentle hands soothing, smoothing, drifting between your legs, beneath your bikini top. You sit up then, unsure. You can't see reyt. Words waint come whole to your mouth. Sit up and vom between legs, watermelon splurge into corn heads.

While your dinners are Pot Noodle or chippy chips, and you still get wrecked off some fella's payday splash, while Ste and Azzer and Kev and Hirsty and Macca and Daz thrust in and out and in and yelp in your earhole sweaty and quiet in your mam's spare room. While hangovers start to feel wrong inside, start to feel gurgly like guilt, start to feel like your very first hangover after t'New Year's street party when you wa thirteen, you in your mam's poufy eighties wedding dress wi "Y2K" written in eyeliner on your forr'ead, and no-one could tell what you wa menna be even though you wa obviously t'Millennium Fairy. Adults knew you kids wa filling your plastic cups from tap ut boxed wine, but they dint say owt, and bloke from next door, ex-marine, rat-arsed, fake ballroom dancing wi every little lass ont street, mekkin you want him to choose you next.

And waking in your mam's crumpled dress, head pounding, belly acidic, bloke's fishy breath still stuck up your nose.

You don't say owt while Little Un dons a tux, best man for Lanky Lad and Rach. He looks good, charcoal suit, blue tie that brings out his eyes. Eyes lit warm when they clap sight of thee. He hugs you like a long lost, smells manly and expensive and working class like David Beckham must. He sez, "Now then, Trouble," as if you've always had a pet name, always nestled int cosiest spot in his chest. Lanky Lad fist bumps you, calls you "dudette," asks can he blag a fag. Rach regal in her strapless gown, sweeping round function room wi a permo grin. You want to talk to her, catch up, hug, but so does everycunt she knows. Forra bit, you're all whirled up in them, giddy, feeling like you're all mates, and don't you remember all t'giggles you've had. Forra bit you think it must not've happened, or if it did, it wa summat you'd all call a jape.

Then Kel's in your ear, back fut wedding, mekkin out Little Un warra reyt shag, and if she wont gerrin married hersen, she'd def have another crack. You and Rach aren't invited to Kel's wedding. She reckons it has to be small and quick for her visa, and cuz her fella's a US soldier, off soon to Afghanistan. But you reckon she just dunt want her old mates gumming up her shiny new American life. Kel never did need you as much as you needed her, always disappearing whenever there warra bloke ont scene. You wunt see her till relationship had collapsed and she needed purrin back together. Not that you ever minded purrin her back together.

You want to say—you *want* to—after Little Un's best man speech, and everyone clapping and going, He's a reyt lad him, inn'e. Mebs you even try to tell Kel summat about it, six pinots tipsy, just you and her having a crafty fag outside function room, air bracing after heat ut dance floor, balls of your feet cooling against paving slab, high heels ditched. Mebs you need some version of it to glide out your mouth and intut neet. You need a piece of it to live outside ya, lift its weight off your lungs. Mebs you need Kel to look at you like she used to, wi full trust and belief. Mebs you say, He's not as sweet as he meks out, ya know, or, Summat happened once when I wa leathered. Fumbling forra way of saying that won't mek Kel look at you wrong—won't mek her think there's summat wrong wi thee.

Mebs Kel sez summat like, He's always been lovely to me, or she sez, If you wa wasted, how do you know what happened. Mebs you try to gather details in your head—glass, rough stones, corn heads scratching, Casio watch, graze on your wrist that you picked till it scarred—mebs you try to think of summat to tell her that'd gerr'er on your side, where she always used to be. But mebs she sez summat like, We all know what you're like when you're drunk, and mebs that shuts you up proper.

Mebs you wish you could say, Why dint you come wi us to Texaco garage? Why did you let me go off wi em on mi own?

Then Little Un appears round corner, saying, What you two up to out here?

And you know you couldn't tell her if you tried all neet. You ant got words that'd bridge years between then and now. Dint know how to say, This might've happened, but it's been so long, I'm not sure how why if.

And you know you'd lose Kel and Rach if you did find words, if they tumbled out. And if words stayed in, one day they'd lose thee.

So you don't say owt to anycunt, scrubbing urinals and mopping floors int Leopard two three four years, waiting forra decent enough wage that you can start saving for your own flat, waiting fut manager to decide you're pretty enough to be a barmaid. You don't say owt when you wonder if you should shack up wi one ut thick cunts who med a fortune, just to sleep under a roof that's not your sister's or your mam's. When you start bringing richer thick cunts back to

45

try them out, see if they thrust any gentler than t'rest. When you stop buying Wonderbras. When you stop worrying about your tits now they're so flat no-cunt'd consider them tits. When you worry, instead, about your thighs, flanking lovers' chests int dead ut neet, your knees slung ovver shoulders as they push deeper in. Spat at by young lads as you walk through town in short-shorts, then shorts, then jeans, covering dappled fat you can't stop from spreading no matter how many Pot Noodles you miss.

You don't say owt when you think about how they propped you up ont stone wall, reminded you how fine you are—Fit as fuck, Shaz, seriously—how long they'd desired, how much they burned.

You all walk intut cornfield and lie down.

You all walk intut cornfield and lie down.

You all walk intut cornfield

You all lie down

You all lie

You

But you can't see next bit: who decided what went where.

You don't say owt when you're pulling pints and wiping bar top, finally gerrin your 53p ovver minimum wage. When you've almost scraped enough to rent your flat, start thinking about saving forra holiday—maybe Vegas cuz Kel sez it's proper ace, but you'd settle for Marbella or Magaluf. You'd settle forra caravan in Cleethorpes. When other Leopard barmaids start popping out babbies, chat about gerrin council house, chat about marriage soon, cuz why not, we're happy. When your hands smell always of chuck-up and stale beer, your jeans start hanging off your hips and you run out of belt holes cuz stolen voddy you sip behind bar on your shifts guz down better when there's nowt in your belly. When slim of it, tight pull rope around throat of it starts to choke you in your sleep.

And you still don't, not when you're pissed up t'fuck and other barmaids are talking about neets they'd rather forget, wild youth days soured to shame. Not when they're playing I Have Never and you could just tek a drink but you don't. Not when saying nowt about nowt to no-cunt starts to become grime plating your insides, gutter water spilling through your veins.

Not even when your brain replays, crisp and vivid: you on your hands and knees, Lanky Lad moving in behind, pain burst as he pushes in, and his long fingers sneak through below, part you, rub hard, and not int reyt spot. Never int fucking reyt spot. Little Un in front of you, and your mouth full, full tut gag, and you might vom again—but you don't, you hold it in—and Little Un's hands on your shoulders, guiding you, rocking you back and forth. Gag, rock, gag.

And what cem next—what you keep trying to forget.

One neet, you're bouncing on your heels at back ut Leopard's gig room, watching local bands set up for sound check. You gather torn-up beer mat shreds, spent bags of peanuts and pork scratchings. You load dimpled pint pots onto a tray, hunger mekkin you dizzy and hollow and light. You look up and see two familiar bodies, one short, one tall. You hold thisen across ribs while they step on stage, get ready to open. Lit up int dark, two sets of lips twist into pure punk sneer. They strum guitars, backed by a bloke on drums. Lads cluster at stage foot, mix of townie boys and emo kids. Little Un's fringe sweeps low ovver one eye. Lanky Lad's weight has collected at his middle. Their fingers touch strings and sound saws through air, bass vibrating through your feet. Little Un steps up tut mic, opens his mouth.

Then he spits you out all ovvert stage.

There you are, tangled in electric, legs split int corn, lips dry, parted. There you are, opening on his rhythm tongue, fat white flesh of you quivers out through his teeth, every inch of you seared intut syllables. There you are, cellulite thighs bursting from drum thump, whap snare skin beats out pulse of your moan. Noise of them rattling your organs, loud of them crowding your brain. You, disgusting blame of it. You, dirty whore slag shame of it. You, reyt laugh lads will be lads of it. You, shrug it off we're studs of it. Caught between his incisors, cracked open wi your guts hung out, split fruit splattered across townie boys' nodding heads, emo kids' raised fists.

He even sings about that last bit, memory you've been trying to evict: smack, loud int dead night air, ringing out across cornfield— two palms meeting ovver your back. You, propped between them, rocking, forgotten.

Every hair on your body rises, surge of summat like pleasure, summat like rage. A thick-bottomed pint glass still sits in your hand. Then it's swooping ovvert punters' heads towards stage, slicing air a grenade. It catches Little Un reyt int temple, hollow whop echo int mic.

Little Un guz down, fingers slipping from strings. Guitar noise explodes, high-pitch feedback scream, then quiet—just drummer holding steady ont bass drum, keeping time in case Little Un springs up. Little Un lies ont floor, bleeding from a head wound.

Summat inside you breks off and floats. Your heart pounds wit drumbeat, fills you wi helium, dud dud in your ears, heart racing to catch up wi what's been done.

Lanky Lad squints int stage light, trying to see you. He lowers his lips tut mic. "Fuck wa that for? You mental bitch."

Manager shouts bouncer's name. Seconds from now, bouncer will pin your wrists behind your back like he does wi every belligerent cunt, march you outside to wait fut police. There'll be cold wind biting, pissheads walking past going, Oooh, what's she done, like? Blue and red flashes tonging bar windows, whole street lit up to shame thee. Copper will wear his stern look, voice coated wi satisfaction at gerrin to press his palm against your skull, pack you intut back of his car. But you won't even care cuz you'll still be buzzing, you'll still be expanding, your thoughts soaring wit pint pot's arc, body inflating wit release.

You'll be charged, sentenced. Leopard will sack you, bar you, rub muck on your name so nowier else'll hire you. You'll lose Rach for good if you ant already. You can forget flat, forget Vegas, keep trying to forget. Cuz that's how it ends, your memory reel, wit high five you're not part of. No clothes back on, no stumble home, no climb into bed. Nowt till wake up, head banging, Mam saying some-cunt's at door.

Big School

Ont first day of big school, year sevens saw sex and violence everywhere. Riot of bodies crammed intut school bus, a moving playground, double-decker of pure chaos. Elbows crunched into stomachs and throats, bags flew ovver heads, chucked from back seat tut front. Bodies hung ovvert top deck railing, charged up and down stairs, collided when bus veered down back lane, throwing everyone sideways. New sounds dashed past their ears—cock, fanny, knobcheese, arsewipe—coming at them in a rapid rhythm. They listened intently, memorising furiously, till they wa carried off int tide of it. Cock, fanny, knobcheese, arsewipe, shagger, fucker, batty boy, daftcunt. Air warra cocktail of hormones, smoke, aggression, lust. Suck mi dick, then! Get fuck out mi seat! Body sprays duelled for dominance, lads' Lynx Africa v. lasses' Spice Girls Impulse. Lads paced aisle doing impromptu stand-up sets while lasses ont back benches timed stroke of their mascara wands wit pauses between bus's scattershot bump and rattle.

More bodies when they got to school, bodies stuffed intut bus shelter, puffing at morning cigs. Snogging by t'front gate, and down front path, and reyt outside classroom windows as if daring teachers to say summat.

Year sevens barely noticed size ut place, vast muddle of one-, two-, and three-storey buildings they'd get lost in for weeks. All they saw wut size ut kids, lasses' chests swollen to Barbie-doll proportions, lads' handspans wide enough to throttle little necks.

Till that morning, year sevens' whole lives had been contained in their one spit of a village, their particular sliver of Doncaster, warren of terrace rows and three-bed semis edging farmers' fields, winding cul-de-sacs clinging to a main road. They'd spent summer holidays inventing themsens into ballerina pirates, vampire shopkeepers, slurping cider lollies sticky-fingered pretending to be drunk, living inside their fantasies so long they forgot their school sens, shed them like old skins, their uniforms crumpled and musting at wardrobe's bottom.

Now, five villages' worth of primary school leavers wa converging on one comprehensive school, their universe expanding so fast they wa already drifting away from themsens. They dint feel ready to start stretching into one of these elongated bodies, to start knowing what would come after these five years, when they'd have to choose between studying for A levels or learning a trade or gerrin a job—and then what, and then what?

They dint know they might have their choices made for them, might have to queue for their dole cheques once a fortnight while rest ut country called them scroungers. They dint know that t'skills they'd acquire to survive this place weren't transferable, that you couldn't parlay advanced levels of cheek, banter, and surliness into a management post wi a competitive salary. They dint know about all t'posher, richer kids across England arriving at posher, richer schools, earmarked for greater, richer futures. Couldn't feel twentieth century wheezing beneath them, or rumble and split of a warming planet. Couldn't sense themsens hurtling towards decades of crash, cut back, fracture. They barely knew it wa 1998.

One thing they did know—they'd have to learn sharpish how to survive secondary school wi'out gerrin their heads kicked in. How to blend, pass, prove themsens worthy of Donny's greatest acclaim: *She's alreyt, her.* Not up hersen, not a clever clogs, not a geek or a boff or a sweatie or a posh cow or a frigid bitch. Just alreyt. That wut goal, that wut dream.

Kel and Rach had no idea they wouldn't even mek it tut end of dinner break before that dream would be dashed to bits by a set of hard-looking lasses who'd vow to bang their fuckin lights out. When Kel and Rach filed intut hall that morning wit 298 other nervy eleven-year-olds, shuffled ontut last row of creaking fold-out seats, their biggest fear wa gerrin split up. They clasped hands till their palms were slick, till their fingers numbed at tips. Prayed they'd be int same form. Said it silently, telepathically: *Please lerrus be together!*

Form teachers took turns to read aloud a list of names; each named child broke away from their mates, med lonely solo journey tut front. Then teacher led their new tribe single file, out hall to their new form room, their new lives.

Shaz wa midway down, end seat on a row of lasses from her primary who, ont last day of little school, had announced that they wont her mates nomore, and they proved it by not calling forr'er all summer. She swung her knees intut aisle, sat slant, pretended she couldn't feel lass next to her kicking her chair leg—whack, whack of it vibrating Shaz's spine. Shaz hadn't met Kel and Rach yet, but they'd be tight mates and best enemies before day warrout. Ont bus home, Rach would be saying to Kel, You can be mates wi *Shaz*, or you can be mates wi me.

Kel got called first. Still holding Rach's hand, she shrugged on her backpack wi her free arm, looping only one strap ovver one shoulder. She'd already learned ont bus that you can't wear two straps at big school because two straps wa for pricks. She broke Rach's grip, whispered "Picnic benches!" which wa where they'd promised to meet at dinner if unthinkable happened and they got split up. Rach's big sister Louise'd told them these benches wa one ut special spots that wont overlooked by mirrored windows, teachers in their staff rooms lurking behind.

Rach's form room wa somewhere int snarled passages of a squat but sprawling one-storey building that smelled of rubber. Sir med them line up outside room in height order before filtering in one by one. Rach wa last. At doorway, she paused, unsure where to sit. Front row wa taken up wi lasses wearing strappy tops under their school shirts, armfuls of glittery gel bracelets. They wa giggling in that way lasses giggle when they're trying to get attention, and Rach could tell already that attention they wanted wa Sir's, man stood at blackboard wi his blonde curtains, his top button undone. Rach wa too embarrassed to look at him. He wa too young, too trendy, to be Sir.

There wa no lasses from her primary, none that'd talk to her anyway, so she squeezed between desks, headed fut back. Everyone wa gossiping, laughing, shouting at each other across room, already forming alliances, weaving safety nets. Only one lass sat silent, ont row opposite Rach, picking flecks of metallic blue nail polish off her thumbnail, looking bored, like she didn't need to be making all that noise, trying to prove she wut funniest or giggliest or hardest; like she already knew she warra superior being.

This lass wa Shaz, and Shaz, far as Rach could see, wut thinnest, prettiest girl int room, wi bony cheeks and a dirt-blonde ponytail, straight and sleek, trailing right down to her bum. Rach wanted to glide her palm down that ponytail, find out if it warras smooth as it looked. Shaz's fringe hung in two slender gelled sections that looked like ant antennas. Rach'd never seen a fringe like it. Her and Kel wore theirs in a blow-dried semicircle they had to set over a large round brush, blast rock-solid wi lashings of Elnett. Shaz's scrunchie wut biggest Rach had ever seen an' all—it wa actually three scrunchies, each pouffier than t'last, largest blooming from her ponytail wider than her head. Int presence of this lass, everyone else's scrunchies wa too small, their heads too big.

Watching Shaz pick at her nail, immune tut hive hum of voices around them, Rach felt two new true things at once: she wanted this lass to like her, and this lass would think she wa way too good for Rach. There wa lasses like her at Rach and Kel's primary, scrunchies bigger than everyone else's scrunchies, ponytails scraped back tighter, glued down wi twice the lacquer. Those lasses never let Rach be their mate.

Shaz wont trying to look bored. When she wa nervous, her face just arranged itsen into boredom, too-good-for-thee disdain. She wouldn't know she looked that way for decades, not till she warra grown woman who finally asked her girlfriend one day why lasses always called her intimidating. What she wanted wa to disappear, slip intut secret pocket of silence she'd found a summer ago, reyt after her fatha died, a summer so broad and clear you could see yoursen in too much detail. Kids wi nowt to do but race in and out of each other's grave-sized yards. Just long enough to bury a body, her mam always joked about dirt rectangle beyond their back step. Lass next door had taught Shaz how to mek hersen faint. She'd gi'en Shaz an escape hatch, trap door int universe she could fall backwards into whenever she wanted. A place where time stopped, where nowt wa forcing her forwards. She'd lie in that dead black, hoping it'd last forever. Every time she woke, magically transported from standing upright to flat on her back, skull thumping from impact wit dirt, sun flitting red across her eyelids, she felt pinch of disappointment, craving to escape again. That craving clawed her now, to flee these peacocking kids, their desperate grasping at their brand-new bezzies.

She kept her eyes ont blue scrags of nail polish so nobody would try and mek her talk. She'd been accused of being too gobby—one ut reasons her former bezzies dumped her by committee ont last day of little school, on no-uniform day, while everyone wa signing each other's shirts wi chunky felt-tips, and she wa meant to be feeling

cuspy and momentous. She wa too bossy an' all, apparently. But warrit Shaz's fault if they never had any good ideas? Her final offence:
she'd pointed a penknife at one of their cousins' mates, outside line
dancing class at parish hall. How wa Shaz menna know she'd waved
knife at anybody's cousin's mate? It wont even her knife; it wa Seany
Gardiner's. She wa just mucking about, seeing warrit felt like to aim
knife tip at a beating heart. This cousin's mate reckoned that next
time she saw her, she wa gunna bang Shaz out. Shaz'd stuck close
to her big brother Kyle all summer. Everyone in Goldthorpe knew
he'd bray living daylights out of anycunt who touched her. Today
wut first time she'd been wi'out her Kyle or her Gemma in six weeks,
since they'd both left school already. At least none of her enemies
warrin her form. At least she could breathe till dinner.

Dinner ladies' method of crowd control involved forcing year sevens to queue up outside P block, fut privilege of queuing up outside
L block, fut privilege of queuing up outside dinner hall, and then,
finally, luxury of queuing up inside. They med Rach's queue back
up and up and squash themsens into a confusion of arms and legs,
everyone hanging on to their mates, trying to stay together. Rach
wa crushed against cagoule ut lad in front, her ankles gerrin nipped
by other people's feet. When everyone had worn themsens out and
settled into single file, an angular little body slipped intut queue
right behind Rach. It wut pissed-off pretty lass from form. She leant
against P block wall, nonchalant as if she'd been there all day. Rach
waited fut kids behind to gi this lass grief for jumping queue—an
unforgivable crime—but those kids eyed Shaz's stone-smooth
expression, kept their gobs shut. Shaz only came up to Rach's shoulder, but she carried hersen like she towered over tallest lad in school.

Shaz glanced at Rach, feeling, fut first time all day, urge to break
her silence. This wut lass who'd been last intut form room, striding
between desks wi her chin held high as if walking to her own theme

tune. She smelled like Parma Violets and dint seem to care that her puffy coat wa ugly. Shaz's mam couldn't buy Shaz a new coat, and Shaz hated one she'd got, passed down from her Gemma and seven years out of date, so she'd decided she'd not wear a coat. It wa alreyt now, school jumper keeping most ut wind off her, but she wont looking forward to winter.

Rach turned, caught Shaz's eye, looked away quick.

"Gorra chud ah can lend?" said Shaz. "Mine's lost its taste." She bared her teeth, showing greyish wad of gum snagged between them.

Rach couldn't believe it: chewing wa against rules. Who *wa* this lass, brave enough to be naughty ont very first day?

"No, soz. But I'll bring some tomorrow." Rach fell quiet, shocked at hersen. How had she just promised to bring chud? She'd have to go corner shop after school, she'd have to lie to her mum, which she'd swore she'd never do, she'd have to hide chuddy on her somewhere teachers wouldn't find it, she'd—she warrout of control. It wa like Shaz'd reached inside her, tore open a seam of nervous energy. Rach felt jittery, hyper, like she'd be tempted to scratch her skin off and gi it Shaz if she asked.

"Ah'll have mi own tomorra." Shaz spat out her chud, which joined mass of trodden blobs that'd turned school's walkways into trails of abstract art—layered wads of white, brown, grit grey, little legacies of teenagers past.

Rach wa floored at this lass's daring. Dinner lady wa *right* there.

Shaz said, "If you want, I'll sit wi ya when we gerrinside."

"That'd be ace."

"Reyt then." Shaz shrugged like it dint matter to her, but she savoured warmth stirring in her gut. She wanted to stay fixed there, heating hersen toasty int glow of Rach's approval.

Amid dinner hall's chatter and ladle bashing and clattering trays, Rach wa so wrapped int excitement of Shaz she forgot to look for Kel. She waited while Shaz queued for her £1 dinner allowance, which, Rach knew, meant government paid for Shaz's meals because Shaz's mum couldn't. Rach's mum had gi her £2.50. She used her spare to buy Shaz pudding, slab of chocolate concrete submerged in pink custard. Shaz refused to eat it—her mam'd taught her never to tek charity off no-one—but she liked that Rach wont shy about lerrin you know she liked ya. Not like lasses round Shaz's end, who'd learned to be cagey, hold their power close to their chests.

They chatted away while they ate, Rach looking at Shaz like Shaz warra person worth hearing. Not too loud, too gobby, not too much. Shaz suggested they start calling everybody "Dave." She said tut lad sat opposite who'd splashed hissen in custard: "Oi, Dave, you've got pink on ya." Rach called to a lass ont next table: "Oi, Dave, pass us t'salt."

When Rach remembered she had to meet Kel at picnic benches, Shaz said she may as well go wi her. Older kids shuttled down walkways like trains, juggernauts that'd flatten them if they dint dive out way. They took a wrong turn by P block. Round corner, a group of year eleven lads leant against handrails either side ut steps, knees and feet protruding, barring path, gi'in dead-eyes, daring young uns to try and pass. Rach dint dare—like *hell* did she dare.

Shaz wa determined not to look lost, not forra second, not ever. She marched through t'lads, med them shift their legs, nodded at biggest lad as she passed: "Alreyt, Dave."

They found picnic benches, a dozen bolted tut concrete of a narrow passage between windowless back walls of two classroom buildings. All but one wa crowded wi kids, tables covered by bums, backpacks, school jumpers, chocolate bars, pop bottles, magazines flitting and flaring int wind. Kel sat by hersen, bum ont table and feet ont bench, burrowing into her coat, looking small and worried like last brittle crisp at bottom ut packet.

She wa bruised from t'morning's trials, alone at back of her form, watching mates who'd been kept together hug each other squealing, their relief palpable, a milk-sour smell escaping their pores. And she wa still wobbly wit tribulations of dinner, fruitless search for Rach int thrash and dash and run. When she'd arrived at picnic benches, she'd packed hersen neatly onto a bench seat, feet ont floor, bag ont table in front of her, book propped against bag. She wa absorbed in her book when an older lass'd appeared, hanging ovver Kel's shoulder, saying, Oi, that's where I sit. From below her, all Kel could see wa delicate hairs flinching inside two nostrils, a gold stud poking from beneath fleshy rim of an ear, a crisp seriffed "K" tattooed behind t'lobe. Kel'd scrambled up, and tattooed lass'd planted her arse ont table, her feet ont seat. Kel moved tut next bench, copied lass's moves: feet where your bum should go, bum ont table where your food wa meant to be, book stuffed back into bag. Tattooed lass wa joined by two others— miles taller than Kel, wearing mustard-brown Rockport boots, their black school trousers skin-tight—but they dint notice Kel, now that she wa sat int correct position. That wa Kel's second lesson in big school survival: never use furniture int manner it wa intended.

Rach called to Kel, "Alreyt, Dave!"

"Where've you *been?*"

"We got lost." Rach gestured at pack of lads jogging by, broad and fast as a rugby team, a loose paving slab tipping and rumbling beneath them.

"Well, you should've known where you wa going." Kel couldn't explain that she wa upset wi Rach for not being int same form. And now Rach'd shown up wi a replacement Kel, a lass who looked popular. That warra *look*, wannit. You could tell just by looking if a lass'd be allowed int popular group. Kel wa determined not to look at Shaz. Instead, she asked Rach, "Who's *she?*"

"Who's *she*, cat's mother?" said Shaz, wi all t'force she could press into five syllables.

Kel wa startled into looking at Shaz, into laughing—that warra right old-lady thing to say. It wa funny, a popular lass saying summat so prim.

Shaz wa buzzing; she'd med Kel laugh wi'out even trying. "And who are *you*, like," she said, "cat's arsehole?" She finished by sticking a hand on her hip. Her Gemma posed like that int mirror: hand on hipbone, knee straightened so her hip cocked out. Shaz wa forever begging to have a turn in her Gemma's full-length. Whenever she wa allowed a minute wi her own reflection, she practiced that pose.

Kel laughed as if "cat's arsehole" wut funniest joke she'd ever heard.

"That dunt even make sense," said Rach, who wa thrown, watching Kel and Shaz like each other instantly. She'd thought she'd be t'glue, fusing group together, an essential ligament everything would fall apart wi'out. Rach wanted to unintroduce them, go back to when it wa just her and Shaz, whispering over their fish fingers, Rach feeling like it wut first time she'd not had to work her bum off trying to prove hersen worthy of a lass like Shaz. Rach should've seen it coming. Lasses always liked Kel more than they liked her, because Kel knew to laugh at jokes whether they made sense or not, and she laughed longer and louder than anyone. Her laugh made you feel ace. Rach'd had a lifetime of Kel's laugh filling her up like Sundi dinner. It warran irresistible head-back, belly-deep hiccupy crescendo, and despite hersen, Rach could feel her own laughter swelling, corners of her mouth fighting to turn up.

Shaz's Kyle had a name for that kind of smothered grin, for when a face wa fighting wi itsen, trying not to look too pleased. She pointed at Rach and said, "Certificate smile!"

Kel dint know what that meant but laughed anyway, giggles ripping out of her, till tattooed lass and her mates stopped talking and looked ovver, shot Kel three withering dead-eyes. Kel broke off mid-giggle, like she'd got summat stuck in her windpipe.

"She can laugh if she wants," Shaz said tut lasses. "What's it to thee?"

Tattooed lass turned her narrowed eyes on Shaz. "Who's this cheeky little cow? Do I know you?"

"No," said Shaz.

"I'm sure I know her," tattooed lass said to her mates, then they fell back into their private conversation. Kel, Shaz, and Rach pulled closer to their own bench, closer to each other.

"*Do* you know her?" Kel whispered.

"Ah've sin her round Goldthorpe, like, but she dunt *know* me." Shaz glanced ovver again, to mek sure they weren't bigger sisters of her former bezzies, or someone's cousin's mate. Since meeting Rach, Shaz'd almost forgot about her old group, about names they'd be calling her ont bus home. But none of these older lasses, far as Shaz could tell, wa related to anyone who'd decided not to be her friend or promised to bang her out.

Rach fiddled wit toggle dangling from her hood. Kel dipped her chin into her coat collar, burying her mouth. Kel's giggles had left an emptiness in Shaz, a craving. She wanted to mek Kel mek that sound again. She tried explaining t'Dave game, but it dint seem hilarious anymore. How wa she gunna lift mood they'd drifted into? How could she top "cat's arsehole"?

"Ah'm magic, me. Ah can mek misen faint."

"As if you can, you liar," said Rach. "Nobody can *make* themsens. You only faint if you're poorly."

"*I* can."

"Show us, then."

Gone wa Dinner Queue Rach, open-faced, eager Rach. Picnic Bench Rach wa staring at Shaz tense-jawed, and Shaz could see Rach wut type of lass who'd hold onto an argument as long as it took—all their lives, if it cem to it—to be proven right. Shaz wa mad at hersen for sharing her secret, which she'd promised she'd keep just hers. She wanted to go back to when nobody knew about her escape hatch, when Rach seemed excited, mebs even proud, to be Shaz's new mate.

"Why should I have to show ya?"

"To prove you're not lying." Rach'd already med a plan to prove

Shaz *wa* lying. If Shaz pretended to drop into a swoon, Rach would climb on top of her, tickle her till she laughed and gave hersen away.

"Bell's about to go."

"No, it's not," said Rach, though she had no idea what time it wa. Time worked different at big school; she couldn't keep hold of it. Enough time and space to get lost in.

An electronic impression of a bell fuzzed out ut walls around them. Not like clanging dinner ladies med at Rach and Kel's old school, wrinkled women in pinafores pacing playground like town criers, waving tulip-shaped bells.

"Told yas."

Rach dint want to admit that Shaz *had* told them, that Shaz had grasped physics of big school—its odd principles of time and space, its rhythms, its threats—as if she'd been there years, not just half a day like everyone else.

Around them, kids tipped themsens off tables, slung backpacks ovver shoulders, crumpled crisp packets, stomped on empty Coke cans. A voice cut through noise:

"Fuckin *knew* ah knew her!"

Rach, Kel, and Shaz looked up. Everyone did, ears pricked by t'promise of drama. Tattooed lass's crew had swelled by four members. Their whole gang of seven wa eyeballing Shaz. Shaz recognised one of them—wide-shouldered, broad-boobed, row of gold hoops travelling up both ears. It wut lass she'd accidentally threatened wi Seany Gardiner's penknife. It wa fuckin Someone's Cousin's Mate.

Cousin's Mate stepped up to Shaz. They stood boob to nose. Shaz could see hard line between peachy panstick foundation of Cousin's Mate's face and peaky flesh of her neck.

"Ah told you ah wa gunna bang ya, and now I hear ya've been mouthing off to our Kirsty," said Cousin's Mate, meaning tattooed lass. Walkways wa emptying, most ut school packing themsens back into their form rooms. A few kids'd lingered to watch Shaz get smacked.

"Go on, then," said Shaz.

Spectators ooohed like audience at Christmas panto.

"Don't worry, ah'm gunna. Ah'll fuck ya little mates up an' all."

Eyes turned on Kel and Rach. Chill crept up Kel's neck; she felt like she'd been watching a film, hidden int cinema's dark, and suddenly actors had turned and started watching her.

Excited, jittery feeling Rach'd had since dinner queue rolled ovver in her belly, shifted into summat shaky and sick. She scanned walkway, hoping to see swish of her Louise's bleach-streaked pony. Not that her Louise'd ever been in a fight. Not that her Louise wa owt like these Goldthorpe lasses.

"What fo'," said Shaz. "They ant done owt to yous."

"They're hanging about wi scum, so they want banging out."

Walkways wa empty. Even spectators had slunk off, headed to form before they gorra late mark. Rach panicked at thought of ger-rin a late mark hersen ont very first day. She daren't move, though. She wa stuck here now.

"How's about Dome Fridi neet," said Shaz. "Ah'll tek yas all on."

Gang of seven laughed. Part of Rach wanted to laugh an' all. It wa absurd, skinny Shaz making such a grand threat to lasses who could knock her cold wi one swipe. But Cousin's Mate seemed satisfied—she lobbed a few more "fucks" and "scums" their way, then moved off wit gang.

Rach, Kel, and Shaz pegged it down walkway, filled wi a heart rush, a blood pumping, too whipped up to speak. Sped on by how quiet school wa, and how loud they wa, clomping ovvert concrete, echoing off walls.

Bus home, Kel and Rach side by side on a two-seater, orange-brown tartan worn threadbare. Coat collars puffed up round their necks, tickling their chins. Windows wrenched down, older kids smoking, wind loud, bus engine chugging, seats vibrating so hard their ears itched. Every thirty seconds, driver shouted at them all to sit yoursens down! from behind his ticket window. He'd do owt not to have to climb out from behind that window—it wont worth his £3.85 an hour. Kel and Rach knew by now that bus warra lawless place. King of this anarchy warra year nine lad called Ando, sat int centre ut back bench, fag in mouth, daring other lads to graffiti ont walls and pull moonies out dusty back window. Kel could tell Ando wut king because other lads did what he dared them. Year nines wa thirteen going on fourteen, but to Kel they seemed fully grown. Ando caught her staring, thrust his chin at her in a move that meant, *Fuck are you looking at?* Kel whipped back round, faced front, heart pounding.

They wound down back lane, double-decker inching between old stone walls, sheep bleating int farmers' fields, Kel and Rach both carrying summat they needed to say, silently daring themsens to say it before bus reached Rach's stop.

Kel had spent afternoon listening tut kids around her, waiting for someone to mention "dome fridi neet." Shaz'd said it as though there warra happening everyone already knew about, summat everyone but Kel wa wise to. By last bell, Kel'd eavesdropped long enough to purrit all together—popular kids went Dome on Fridi nights fut ice-skating disco. Kel added this tut things she'd already learned from Shaz: popular lasses had antennas instead of a fringe, they dint wear coats, they called it "neet," not "night," and they weren't scared of anyone.

Rach had spent afternoon seething. Sir had gi'en her and Shaz late marks, told them off in front ut whole form, didn't gi Rach chance to explain that it wont her fault—Shaz had made her late. She refused to catch Shaz's eye fut rest ut day.

Bus wa only two stops from Rach's.

"We're not being mates wi that Shaz," said Rach.

"How come?"

Rach swung her hand in a wide arc that meant, *What do you mean "how come"?* In one dinner, Shaz had made them late, got them in trouble wit teachers, and dragged them into a fight.

"I thought she wa alright, me."

"She's a liar, for one. She never can make hersen faint."

They passed stop before Rach's.

"What's it matter?"

"What's it *matter*?" Rach couldn't find words. Kel warra stranger, suddenly—not her Kel, not Kel she'd always known.

Kel felt like a hand that'd been trapped between two desks. She wont used to Rach changing her mind. When they wa three years old, Rach'd announced that her and Kel wa best mates, and they had been ever since. Kel thought it'd be same wi Shaz—Rach'd decided they'd be mates wi her, so they would.

Bus slowed, preparing to stop. Kel hadn't had chance to broach her own subject.

"Are you coming Dome Fridi night?"

"To get mi head kicked in?"

"Everyone guz."

"Your mum'll never let you."

"She might, how do you know?" Kel turned into a trapped hand that wa starting to throb.

"Not unless my mum's said I'm allowed." Rach stood, body wobbly, struggling to adjust tut bus's decreasing speed. She steadied hersen ont handrail. She'd never been so cross in her life, feeling firing around inside her. "You can't be her mate." She wa gerrin nudged down aisle by kids behind her.

"Sez who?"

"If you're mates wi *her*"—Rach wa shouting to be heard ovvert bus's engine, standing on tiptoe to see Kel ovver everyone's heads— "you're not mates wi *me*." She stepped off bus in a whoosh of skittering leaves and autumn air.

Next day, when Rach boarded bus, Kel wa sat next to a lad who'd spread his knees so wide she had to perch ont seat edge, legs and backpack int aisle. She looked shrunk, like her mum had put her int washer on hot: she wa wearing just her school jumper, no coat. There wa no free seats, so Rach stood ovver Kel, bracing against bus's turns, against jostle of bodies bombing up and down aisle. Kel had news. Her mum said she *could* go Dome Fridi night. This warra proper miracle. Kel's mum never let her do owt unless she'd called Rach's mum, and Rach's mum had said it wa okay, and that she'd drive them there and back—and even then Kel's mum usually said no. Rach stood in silence for ages, absorbing this horrible miracle.

Kel watched lads pissing about ont back bench, Ando daring two of his mates to flick up a lass's skirt, flash her knickers. Those lads gorra slap int face for their efforts, wi enough clout to mek their eyes water. Ando and rest roared laughing. Slapped lads whispered a dare into Ando's ears. He screwed his face up. "No fuckin way, you scrubber. That's sick, that."

Sensing Kel's attention wa elsewhere, and she wont, in fact, waiting patiently for Rach to speak, Rach said, "Well, you can go ice-skating wi'out me."

Kel turned from Ando, looked up at Rach. Truth wa, Kel's mum *had* said she could only go if Rach did.

"You've gorrer come."

"I ant gorrer do owt." Rach wa jammed into Kel's legs by a scrap that'd broken out behind her, two lads pummelling each other wi plastic pop bottles. "I'm not going anywhere I've been told I'll gerra smack." She couldn't understand why Kel dint feel that whirl of fear in her tummy Rach got every time she thought about gang of seven's sovereign-ringed fists flying towards her. It wa like that lurch, that helplessness you get, right after you've tripped over, right before you slam intut pavement. Why wa Kel ready to take a punch just for being Shaz's mate. How could Kel love her that much already.

Rach gave Kel silent treatment rest ut journey, rushed off when bus pulled in wi'out saying bye. Kel sat while everyone shuffled down aisle. Ando walked past, winked, muttered, "Ey up, sexy," so fast Kel thought she'd imagined it. Thought it must've been aimed at someone else. She watched him walk off, waited for him to turn round. He dint look back. She sat so long, willing her heart to slow, bus had emptied before she'd thought of moving. Driver leaned ovvert ticket window: "I ant gorrall day, love."

Rest ut week, Rach and Shaz sparred wi ice-skating facts. At dinner, squeezing chip butties between their fingers, biting intut layers of smushed potato and bread, Rach'd start wi "When I go ice-skating wi our Louise—" and Shaz'd cut her off wi "When I go ice-skating wi our Kyle—" and they'd throw details at each other that Kel sucked up and stored inside her like they wa nutrients essential to her existence. Kel learned that Dome's rink wa split into two levels, connected by icy slopes—down slope scary as owt to fly down, up slope knackering as owt to climb up, your legs scissoring, your feet slipping as you tried to glide against gravity. Rach knew how to skate backwards because her Louise had taught her, and her Louise always bought a Happy Meal afterwards. Shaz told counter-stories: "Our Gemma used to tek me on Fridi neets when there's a DJ booth int middle and disco lights like you're skating inside a nightclub." And next day: "Sometimes they have foam parties and everyone's covered in foam and there's foam in your face and you can't see where you're going." Next day: "Our Kyle's a speed skater, and you can't go near them cuz he sez lads've gorra bet on to see who can knock a lass down first." Kel wa haunted and electrified by every new morsel. How anyone med it out alive, all these older lads zooming across rink's glinting surface, bodies transformed into speeding boulders. Even if you *dint* have a gang of lasses twice your size looking to bray ya, chances of survival seemed slim. Kel's mum used to be an A&E nurse, and she'd spent week filling Kel's head wi tales about kids gerrin bits sliced off them when they topple down, hands smacking flat ont ice, someone's blade gliding ovver their splayed fingers. Kel's head wa full wi wounds, gaping and bloody, maimed hands, scars white as tapeworms. Kel's mum said she had to wear padded gloves, and if she fell, she had to fall wi her hands pulled into fists. No way wa Kel wearing gloves, and she wont sure she'd remember to fall down correctly, so she decided she'd just not fall down.

Once Shaz's ice-skating facts had beaten Rach's, Rach'd say, "Well, we can't go anyway, if those lasses are," and Shaz'd say, "Be reyt, tenner sez they waint touch us."

Shaz's former bezzies'd lost interest in gi'in her grief. They still threw "scrubber," "munter," "scally" at her ont bus, but now that she wa going round wi Rach and Kel at break and dinner, they mostly left her be, as if game wa boring now that they couldn't mek her feel lonely. Cousin's Mate, ont other hand, wa proper enjoying hersen, shouting "Si thi Fridi, then, dickhead" whenever she spotted Shaz. She could've cornered Shaz in any one ut school's unmonitored crannies: between H block and disused tennis courts, behind sports hall, behind tangle of brambles known as "Burning Bush" because it wa where everyone went forra ciggie, or ont top field, which wa so far from school buildings kids could dip through a hole int fence ontut country lane behind, bugger off fut afternoon. Cousin's Mate could've slotted her at picnic benches int first place and no teacher would've sin. But Shaz'd watched her Kyle and his mates dole out enough intimidation to know that a running threat wa better than a settled score. Ramming a fist into somecunt's nose dint feel half as good wi'out all that buildup. Shaz'd banked on that when she'd named Dome as scene of their showdown. She wa also banking on Cousin's Mate going nowhere near her once she turned up at Dome to find Shaz flanked by her Kyle and all t'lads that hung round her Kyle like snarly acne-flecked disciples.

Fridi dinner, when Rach started fact-sparring, Shaz played her ace. She said that after ice-skating, her Kyle and his crew gathered outside forra smoke, and you had to know how to smoke round older lads or they'd rip shit out of ya. "You always have to spit after you tek a drag," she said. "If you're doing it reyt. If you know how to tek it back wi'out wetting fag end. It's sem as sucking a lad off: you've gorrer get your lips in place and your teeth tucked away, and you've gorrer know how to tek it down wi'out coughing it back up."

Rach and Kel had no idea warrit meant, sucking a lad "off." Shaz dint know either, but she wa loving their stunned faces. Her Gemma had gi'en her that lesson on smoking, and Shaz'd memorised it word for word.

Other two had smoked before, once, down t'Dip, in private, just them and dead bracken and old concrete posts. Nobody watching to see if they did it reyt. They dint know there *wa*rra reyt—or a wrong. They caught each other's glances. Somewhere between words "sucking" and "off," decision to go skating or not had become bigger than decision to be Shaz's mate or not, to risk tekkin a punch or not. It'd become decision to stop as they wa, before big school, or become summat new, summat not quite a little kid anymore. They dint know which wa scarier, gerrin changed or gerrin left behind.

"Anyway," said Rach, "when are you gunna prove you can make yoursen faint?"

"You still on about that?"

"How else are we meant to know you're not a liar?"

"Ah shunt have to prove it. Yous should just believe me."

Part of Shaz wanted to prove it just to shut Rach up, just to pull hersen into her plush silence, place where Rach still thought she wa alreyt, wont intent on tearing her down. But that needling want wa drowned by summat deeper and harder to fight: she wont about to be told what to do. Her Gemma sez you never do *owt* because someone else wants you to. They push you, Shaz, you push back. Gi em what they gi you twice as hard.

Rach wont gerrin Shaz's magic. It wut only thing that belonged to just her. Mine, she thought to hersen. It's mine and you can't have it.

Ont bus home, when Rach said, "Last time I went skating wi our Louise—" Kel, who'd absorbed enough information to play Shaz's part, cut in: "Yeah, but you've only been on Satdi mornings. It's completely different on Fridi neets."

"Since when do you say 'neet'?"

"I don't."

"You just did."

"So?"

"You're only saying it because Shaz does, and that's called being fake."

Kel turned tut window, put her forehead ont glass, watched emerald green moss tufting from gaps int stone walls.

Rach knew she'd gone too far. She wanted to say sorry, but word wouldn't come. She wont sorry because she wa right. Kel wa trying to be Shaz. And Shaz jumped queues and spat gum and lied and shouted at lasses just for looking at people wrong. Rach felt like she'd started week playing Monopoly, and someone had switched game when she wont looking. Now she wa playing Twister but wi new rules no-one would let her read.

"Are you coming tonight or not," Kel said tut window.

"Nope."

"Right." Kel stood, swung her bag onto her shoulder.

"We're still mates."

"Nope." Kel pushed intut aisle, heading fut free bench at front.

"Alright! I'll come!"

Kel sank back down beside Rach, trying to keep smile off her face. Corners of her lips flickering. She thought to hersen, certificate smile.

An hour before Rach's mum wa due to pick her up, Kel tried to bully her thick fringe into two antennas, slathering them wi gobbings of gel. But she'd got too much hair, sections wouldn't hold

69

together. She rinsed gel out, blow-dried her fringe normal way. She laid her clothes ont bed, needing to choose between Adidas Poppers wi her Ellesse jumper, which wa for playing out, or khaki shorts and a camo tank, which wa for birthday parties and discos. Neither seemed right. Wi three minutes to go she chose shorts, ragged camo tank ovver her head, hurried out tut waiting car. Sliding ontut back seat, she saw that Rach warrint front wearing Poppers. Kel wa quiet all t'way down Sprotty Road, fighting urge to beg Rach's mum to turn round and tek her home. She dint want to go now. She wanted to be someone else, someone who knew what they wa meant to be wearing. Rach's mum dint turn heat on. Kel's leg hair stood on end like it wa trying to escape her stupid, childish skin.

Not only had Rach known to wear Poppers, she even had her own skates. They sat in her lap, dazzling white, like boots Jayne Torvill wore when she sailed across Olympic rink in rippling purple skirts, in perfect sync wi Christopher Dean. They wa built of a soft creamy leather Kel wanted to rub her cheek against, their blades tipped wi curved toe picks, spiky but somehow still girly. Kel ached wi want.

There's nowhere int world like Donny Dome. They call it a leisure centre, but it's more like a leisure fortress. Circular walls in white-and-grey-striped brick, breeze-block turrets, concrete pillars, steel tubing, angular ramparts serrated as sharks' teeth. A fake draw-bridge spanning a grassy trench leads up tut front door, which is covered by a gargantuan glass canopy, held skywards by girders that look like they wa nicked from undercarriage of a railway bridge. Only feature ut building that underwhelms is t'dome itself, a teeny hump perched on top, a little glass teat winking its neon strip-lights half on, half off. Town spent so much on building t'Dome there wa nowt left fut upkeep. Inside festers to this day, mould flourishing int swimming baths' grouting, paint peeling from grey ceilings, tears int badminton nets, three decades of dust settled ont tops ut twin water slides, which snake out from swimming baths intut foyer, two giant neon eels chasing each other through t'walls, suspended twenty feet above entrance hall's reception desk.

Rach and Kel climbed steps tut Dome's entranceway, spotted Shaz ont drawbridge wi a squad of lads so old and manlike both their hearts panicked into a gallop just at *thought* of walking towards them. Kel recognised Ando instantly almost wi'out looking at him, as if she could sense him by smell. He wa chatting to a lad wearing a plastic whistle.

Rach filled wi heat, watching Shaz: all swagger, nattering away wi these older lads. She really warra wonder, this lass, intimidated by exactly no-one. Fearless, a four-foot-nowt nymph made of pure will. Shaz's will acted on Rach like a gravitational pull she couldn't help but be drawn by, even if power of it scared her.

Shaz ran up to them, took Kel's hand, and tugged her intut group.

Why not me? asked a small voice inside Rach. She found hersen longing for Shaz to grab her arm, hold her hand. Way it would make her feel real, like she wa there, a whole body. Rach's hands wa full wit heavy white boots.

"Fuck are they?" Shaz said, grinning.

"They're our Louise's." Rach spoke to her feet. She'd been dead proud ut boots till then. Her Louise had got them from a special shop in York.

Shaz and Kel wa wearing nearly same outfit, shorts and a strappy top, like most ut lasses heading fut Dome's entrance. Kel's relief travelled down her body in waves.

Cousin's Mate and her gang of seven appeared, a ruffle of sass and menace mekkin its way along t'drawbridge: high buns, crop tops, trackies, pierced eyebrows, body spray, fag smoke, cleavage. They wa roll-strutting, doing that sideways rolling walk lads did to look hard, but remixing it wi slinked hips, pouty mouths. Kel moved closer to

Shaz; Rach leaned further away. Shaz crossed her arms, med a show of watching gang of seven, daring them to meet her stare.

When they saw her, their expressions slipped. Eyes averted, they held their heads and shoulders stiff, as if by extinguishing their own charisma they could mek themsens invisible. Once they'd shuffled by wi'out confrontation, Shaz said, "See, told ya they waint touch us."

Rach saw that Shaz'd positioned hersen reyt in front of her big brother. Kyle wa leant against drawbridge's rail, scowling at everyone going past, a line razored through his eyebrow, a cig balanced behind his ear. He wa that lean, ropy kind of strong that wa somehow scarier than bulk and muscle. It dint gi Rach any comfort to know that Kyle wut only thing standing between her and a broken face.

Couple ut lads in Kyle's crew spied Rach's boots. They took hold of each other like ballroom dancers. One sang a med-up song while they waltzed jerkily—La-da-deee-la-da-daaa—and other un said, in a put-on girly voice, "I'm an ice dance-aaaar." All t'other lads laughed. Rach'd never spent time round older kids wi'out her Louise. She felt marooned, drowning in her baggy clothes.

Shaz said, "Oi, leave off her, dickheads."

Lad wearing t'plastic whistle said, "Oh aye, our little Shaz gerrin lippy." A fond ribbing, a sibling burn.

"Gi oo'er, ah'm being serious." Shaz placed hersen between Rach and lads. "Dunt tek piss out of her, she's my mate."

Dancing lads said "Soz, like" and "Only messin."

Rach loved Shaz, then. And hated how much she loved her. Hated how grateful she felt.

Lads went back to rippin piss out of each other and dint pay much more notice ut lasses. Except Ando, who raised his eyebrows at Kel and said, "Alreyt, what's your name?" She told him Kel, but he dint gi her his, like he knew she already knew it.

"I wa just avin a laugh ont bus other day. Mi mates dared me to chat you up, like."

Kel dint know how she wa meant to reply. She told him she'd not noticed, dint know what he warron about.

Inside, just as Our Gemma and Our Kyle'd promised, rink wa dark, chilly, cavernous, trembling wi a fast dance beat. Grate grate of skates against ice med Shaz impatient to gerront rink, med Rach ashamed of her posh boots, med Kel think of severed fingers.

Kel and Shaz swapped their trainers for "Dome Diggers," battered navy-blue skates everyone wore who dint have their own. Dome Diggers had score marks in their tough plastic casing, flat blades, shoe sizes written ont back in marker pen. They wa blunt and ugly and slow, and Rach wished she wa wearing them.

They all hobbled across bobbly rubber floor tut rink's edge, laid their blades gingerly ont ice, gripping perimeter wall. Kel and Shaz wa trying to keep from shivering, ice breathing cold up their bare legs. Shaz wished she'd worn trackies like Rach. Wished she had Rach's confidence. Rach dint seem to care what anyone thought of her, wont fussed about trying to mek people like her, which only med Shaz like her more.

At rink's centre, big lads in speed skates raced in a tight vicious circle, pumping their arms and legs, going so fast ont down slope they could soar effortlessly ont slope up. Kel imagined what'd happen if she got too near them: sound of her own femurs cracking against ice.

Rach had been looking forward to teaching Kel how to stay up, how to push her feet outwards, keep a rhythm, how to go backwards, but rink wa chocked wi bodies darting in every direction. Music wa loud, and it wa too dark to see properly, everyone looking un-human, disco lights flaring pieces of them, disembodied arms,

legs, teeth. An army of enchanted body parts coming at her. Rach
flinched wi each whipping elbow, angled knee, and grinning head
that dashed towards, then glanced past her, expecting each one to
become Cousin's Mate, waiting forra set of clenched knuckles to rear
at her out ut dark.

Shaz took Kel's hand—Come on, you can do it!—pulled her
off, along crescent ut rink's top half and down t'slope. Kel screamed
all way down, an exhilarated roller-coaster scream. Rach crept
along behind them, hanging on tut wall, all her confidence gone.
She went down t'slope by centimetres, wincing wi every lad that
whipped past, blowing wind against her cheek. When she med it
tut rink's bottom half, she couldn't see Kel and Shaz anywhere.
Her chin wobbled at idea of hauling hersen back up slope on her
own, trying to catch them. She wa used to being biggest and tallest,
which usually med her fastest and strongest, but ont ice, everything
flipped. Kel and Shaz wa built for skating, little and graceful and
swift.

From somewhere, Kel shouted "Raaach!" Rach searched for
Kel's face, disoriented by disco lights' hectic pirouettes. Another
"Raaach!"—she looked up to find that Kel and Shaz hadn't gone
back tut rink's top half; they'd med their way across bottom to a
rubber island int middle, below DJ booth, where lads and lasses wa
hanging out round rubber blocks in same-sex clumps of threes and
fours. Kel waved; Shaz med a beckoning hand. Rach couldn't see
how they'd got over there, fought through wall of speed skaters
that wa still pursuing each other like mutually murderous cartoon
characters caught in an endless loop. Rach watched, tried to gauge
distance and time, looking forra gap she could nip through. She felt
Kel and Shaz's eyes on her. She felt gang of seven's eyes, somewhere
int dark, watching her struggle, stranded.

Kel and Shaz sat on a rubber block, spot Shaz'd chosen because
it wa dead centre ut speed skaters' orbit. Her Kyle and t'crew would
be circling her all night, a ring of protection. Kel and Shaz stretched

their legs out in front of them, comparing: Shaz's legs smooth, Kel's covered in fine dark hair.

"Mi mam sez I'm not old enough to shave," said Kel.

"You can come round mine and lend mi razor if ya want."

"Will you do it for me?"

Shaz laughed. "Ah'll teach ya to do it yoursen. Dunt tell ya mam it wa me, though."

They talked about what life'd be like when they wa old enough not to need permission, how much better that would be. Shaz asked Kel what she wanted to do when she wa older.

"Dunno. I like reading, but that's not a job, is it." They both shrugged: *No, probs not, not sure.* "Rach knows—she's wanted to be a teacher since we wa three." Kel would gi owt to be as sure of what she wanted as Rach wa. "What do you wanna do?"

Shaz shrugged again. "Not bothered. Just wanna own mi own house, me. Wi a proper massive back garden." She pointed to a lad chatting wi his mates ont next rubber block. "Ah reyt fancy him, me," she said, reckoned she wa gunna ask him forra snog. Kel'd never even pecked a lad ont lips; she couldn't believe Shaz wa talking about snogging like it wa nowt. Kel nodded like it wa normal, like *she* did it all t'time, and that med Shaz think she better *had* snog that lad. Shaz'd open-mouth kissed Seany Gardiner a few times but never snogged.

After an eternity stuck ont wrong side ut speed skaters, after three separate lads'd come flying at her, on course for direct collision, only to stop themsens short wi a sharp turn of their blades and a spray of ice, inches from Rach's feet—and a cackle at panic in Rach's face—Rach closed her eyes, dashed across speed skaters' path. When she warront other side, not dead or knocked down or owt—still standing!—she pumped her fist int air.

"Yesss!" she shouted, "get in, my son!" way her dad shouted at telly when Sheff Wednesday scored. She looked for Shaz and Kel cheering her on. They weren't watching. Nobody wa.

By t'time Rach med it tut rubber island—doing her best to diffuse whatever tangle of feelings had wired her brain sparky and combustible—Shaz wa sat on a different rubber block, arms curled round a lad's neck. Shaz and this lad wa trying to eat each other, heads bobbing aggressively. Rach slid ontut block beside Kel. They dint want to look, but they couldn't stop looking, couldn't tek their eyes off Shaz's chewing mouth, cut into snapshots by strobe light. They felt silly and young int shadow of Shaz, who wa built of summat more supernatural than eleven-year-old flesh. Who always knew what move to mek next. They tried to imagine wanting a lad's saliva on their lips, a lad's tongue inside them. They hugged their bellies. DJ played "Dancing in the Moonlight," and afterwards, whenever Rach heard it, she always thought of that moment, watching Shaz devour a boy, wondering if this wa what she wa supposed to want.

Rest ut night they kicked around ont rubber island, Shaz pointing out lads, asking if Kel and Rach fancied that un, or that un, Kel and Rach saying No, no way! to every one. When lights cem up, they took off their boots, bang-banged them ont floor, frost flakes slipping off and wetting their socks. They headed out wit rabble mekkin its way tut foyer. Ando appeared beside Kel, called her "my little mate Kel," mekkin her glow inside. She tried smiling up at him like she'd sin Shaz smile at lad she'd snogged—cheeky and coy—but she knew she wont doing it reyt. Ando sloped off again, absorbed into Kyle's crew. Shaz saw blush rosy Kel's cheeks.

"Do you fancy Ando, like?"

"No."

Shaz laughed. "Shall ah tell him you wanna gerroff wi him?"

"No!" Kel grabbed Shaz's arm. "Please don't."

"Ah won't, ah won't. But ah reckon you should go forrit. He deffo fancies ya."

Kel lit up wi feeling—nerves and pride and summat else. It wa terrifying, thought of gerrin anywhere near Ando's mouth. Still, she felt like she'd earned a new badge, like ones they gi you at Brownies to sew to your sash.

Shaz held hands wit lad she'd snogged all way tut main door, snogged him again beneath towering canopy, till he ran off to catch up wi his mates.

"Did he ask for ya number?" said Kel.

"Nah." Shaz shrugged defensively. He had asked, but she'd said no. Phone warrint kitchen at her gaff, and kitchen wa always full—she couldn't talk to a boy in front of everyone; they'd all wanna know who's this lad, then? Her mam and her Gemma would rip piss out of her for having a "boyfriend." Her Kyle would threaten to brek his legs.

Kyle and his crew wa gathered at mouth ut drawbridge, passing a deck of cigs between them.

"Yous avin a fag, then?" Shaz asked Rach and Kel. Wi'out looking at each other, Kel and Rach knew they wa thinking same thing: No, not yet, please, we're not ready.

"I'm off McDonald's, me," said Rach. "You've gorrer come, Kel, because your mum said you've gorrer stay wi me." Kel dint think her mum's instructions included following Rach across busy road and intut night. Leisure park that Dome sat in wa still being constructed around it, a mile-long roundabout pockmarked wi building sites, and int centre, a yawning hole int ground that would one day become a fake lake. And Kel dint think it warra reyt good idea to stray too far from Shaz and Kyle. But thought of smoking wrong in front ut lads—in front of Ando—med setting off intut rubbly wilderness wi Rach seem like safest option.

"Do you wanna come, Shaz?" Kel asked.

Shaz dint have money for Maccy D's. "Ah'm on a diet, me. Burgers are full of fat."

Rach and Kel'd never been mates wi someone who wa on a diet. Mums and grandmas and big sisters went on diets, not little kids.

"Well, when *I* go ice-skating, I go McDonald's after," Rach said. Her arms wa killing from lugging her boots around, so she asked Shaz to watch them, leant them against wall by Shaz's feet. They seemed to gleam even brighter white int evening's dark.

Rach and Kel dashed ovvert road, hopped a fence, picked their way through construction site, thorny weeds snatching at their ankles. When they finally jogged back, Rach wi a Happy Meal box bouncing at her side, chicken nuggets and fries going cold and soft, Shaz wa stood alone in a pool of shadow, no Kyle, no lads. Rach's boots weren't leant against wall where she'd left them.

"Where's mi skates?"

"Dunno."

"I asked you to watch them for me."

"Somecunt must've took em."

"Our Louise'll kill me." Rach started batting at bushes that lined walkway, jostling shrubs int raised flower beds, peering intut gloom below drawbridge, looking for somewhere Shaz might've stashed boots just to shit her up, just to punish her for having posh skates.

"Soz," said Shaz, too quiet for Rach to hear. She leant back against drawbridge rail. Her head and shoulders crossed intut beam of a floodlight.

"What's wrong wi your face?" said Kel.

"Nowt."

Kel reached up to brush Shaz's antenna aside. Twice Shaz swerved away from Kel's hand, then gave in and let her look. Kel could see now that Shaz's right eyelid wa plump and doughy. A thin swirl of blackish red arced beneath her lower lashes. She held her right arm awkwardly against her body, as if her arm or her ribs or both wa bruised and hurting.

"Shaz, what's happened."

"Oi!" Rach called from other end ut drawbridge.

"*What?*" Shaz shouted back.

"What have you done wi mi boots."

"Rach, leave it, Shaz is hurt."

"I ant done owt, someone's nicked em."

"*You've* nicked them."

"Rach, come and look at her int light."

"I ant touched your minging boots."

"Liar."

Shaz's comeback stalled in her mouth. That word Rach kept throwing at her. *Liar.* It curdled summat sour inside her, med her want to curl into hersen, become smaller and smaller divisions of hersen like a piece of paper you keep folding till it's so dense it resists pressure of your fingers, refuses to tek one more crease.

"Reyt, well, ah'll tell you what did actually happen then, shall ah. Even though ya waint fuckin believe me." Shaz explained that her Kyle and his crew had started a kickabout. She'd wanted to join in but had to stay still and watch boots. Kickabout migrated, lads chipping ball further and further from Shaz till they ended up int car park, where they still wa now. Then cem gang of seven, roll-strutting out entrance and down drawbridge wit last ut crowd to leave rink. Finding Shaz alone, Cousin's Mate did what she'd promised, gerrin in a few good whacks before Shaz managed to hoof her int shin and tek off running towards her Kyle. They dint bother chasing her, just called her a pussy, then headed off down t'steps tut road. Shaz sprinted back fut boots, found them gone.

"Mint, so those bloody lasses have got our Louise's £100 boots."

"Anyone could've took em, to be fair," said Shaz. "When wut last time you tried watching a pair of skates while somecunt's bashing your face in?"

Even at that age, they'd all learned this truth: int glorious province of Donny Beaut, if your possession int nailed down, int strapped to your chest, int cinched int grip of your fingers—if you tek your eyes off it forra second—then somebugger's deffo pinched it. And once it's gone, it's gone. Pawned, spirited onto a market stall, sold at Sundi car boot, gift wrapped and saved for Christmas, smashed to smithers for laughs—whichever way, gone.

"Why did you leave em wi me anyway? They're *your* fuckin boots."

"So it's *my* fault, is it." Rach wa still bashing bushes, more to get her anger out than from any hope.

"It wa you who med me stand here on mi tod instead of playing footy wi our Kyle."

"Warrit *me* who mouthed off to a load of bigger lasses and made them hate us?"

Shaz shook her head, but dint have fire left to defend hersen. Of course she wa to blame. She wa too loud, too gobby, too much. Forever knee-deep in a scrap before she'd realised she'd waded in. Why couldn't she just keep her gob shut, keep her head down. Why couldn't she shrink hersen invisible.

Kel put her arm round Shaz's good shoulder and steered her off, towards Kyle and his footy game, leaving Rach to smoulder at top ut steps on her tod.

Mundi morning, start of first break, Kel and Shaz sat cross-legged ont edge ut school field, grass springy and soft, seeping dew into their skirts. Shaz's eye had swelled ovvert weekend, lid forced shut. Bruise had spread ovvert socket, marbled shades of plum and violet that looked to Kel like a watercolour painting ut Milky Way. Colours wa so pretty, Kel nearly wanted a black eye of her own. Shaz'd told anyone who asked that it dint hurt. She wa gossiping about what'd happened ont *Hollyoaks* omnibus day before, Kel nodding and pretending to know what Shaz warron about because her mam wunt let her watch soaps. Kel dint mind; she'd been pretending to Rach for years.

Rach emerged from mouth of N block, hurrying down its concrete steps wi a stream of kids. She med straight for Kel and Shaz. Kel searched Rach's face, trying to gauge what mood she warrin. Even though Rach wa wrong for blaming Shaz, Kel'd felt proper sorry for her ont journey home. When Rach's mum'd pulled up at Dome, she'd wanted to get out car, search fut boots, interrogate lads, interrogate Shaz. Rach begged her not to, so instead she spent drive back shouting about how much them boots had cost, how they'd come from a special shop that had shut down now, how you had to learn to take care of other people's things. Her mum fury wa huge and spitting and frightening int small space ut car.

As Rach neared patch of field where other two sat, she worked to keep her stride steady and her face blank, to hide her shock at sight of Shaz's eye. Shaz's face wa so odd-shaped, so ballooned and puffy, so wrong-coloured, Rach couldn't see how it'd ever go back to normal. There warra shock, too, in seeing Shaz hurt, finding evidence that Shaz wa capable of gerrin knocked down. Shaz'd seemed so unknockdownable.

Rach'd spent half ut weekend wishing she'd never met Shaz, concocting theories that Shaz warrin league wit gang of seven, running an elaborate ice-skate-thieving scheme that involved staging fights in order to fleece unsuspecting eleven-year-olds. She spent other half ut weekend trying not to think about Shaz's question. Why *had* she left boots wi Shaz? Warrit just because they wa heavy? She wont ready to answer, wont ready to know if there warra nasty, petty piece of her heart that wanted Shaz to feel small, or if she'd just wanted Shaz to notice her, look after her like she'd looked after Kel. She didn't know. She wouldn't know.

When she joined Kel and Shaz, sinking her knees intut grass, she couldn't not stare at Shaz's eye. She wanted to lay her palm over it, wanted to know if it wa hot tut touch, wanted to cover it up so she could see normal, unbruisable Shaz again. She wanted to know whether, if she concentrated hard enough, she could make swelling and bruising vanish under her fingers like a magic trick.

Shaz said, "Tek a fuckin picture, it'll last longer."

"I'm not looking at your bloody eye." Rach dragged her gaze down to Shaz's chin and tried to keep it there. "Right, missus," she said tut chin, "if we're gunna be mates, you've gorrer prove to us you can make yoursen faint."

"Godsake, you still on wi that?" Shaz said, but she said it like her Gemma would say to her Kyle whenever they wa having their favourite argument. She'd heard Rach's "if," but it sounded like an "if" that meant "when."

If like, *We are, aren't we?* If like, *Can we?*

"You can't tell us you're magic, then not show us, that's *well* tight."

"She dunt have to prove owt," Kel said. "Do you, Shaz?"

Int years to come, Shaz would be grateful for Kel's form of love—and miss it, and understand its value only when it wa gone—but it wa so different to Rach's, which wa hot and intense and hard to win.

Rach said, "There's ten minutes till bell, so that's plenty of time."

Wi a grand sigh, Shaz stood, Kel and Rach rising wi her. "Reyt, first, you've gorrer tek a deep breath, biggest breath you've ever took." She took a noisy gulp to demonstrate. "Stick your thumb in your mouth, pinch your lips round your thumb, and blow hard as you can, till there's a ringing in your ears that gets louder and louder till you go black."

Shaz took a breath, stuck her thumb in, blew. Kel followed. Five, ten seconds, they blew, cheeks puffed out and pinking, till they thunked ontut grass like dropped planks of wood.

Rach whipped her coat off, straddled Shaz's lifeless body. She pulled coat ovver both their heads, put her nose against tip of Shaz's. She med her grin wonky and her eyes bozzed, trying to mek Shaz laugh.

Shaz faded intut buzzing in her ears till she became sound, became bee drone, became overwhelming ring. Her body dissolved intut black cave, legs arms head feet disappearing intut luxury of her magic. She stretched on forever intut dark. Here, she wa anyone. Here, she wa hersen, alone where no-one could watch. A blank floating dream where her face wont sore and her ribs dint ache and her house wont crowded and streets weren't packed wi lasses gunning to smack her. Her clothes weren't old and her knickers weren't someone else's. Her dad wont dead and her Gemma's new babby wont crying and her mam's new fella wont splayed across sofa smoking a spliff, and no-one had left her and no-one she dint want near her had been invited in.

When she wa lifted out ut cave, called back by voices ut lads playing footy ont top field—oi dickhead, knobcheese, shurrup-ya-cunt—sun wa warming her shins, but there warra strange skittery shadow round her face, plasticky smell like a sleeping bag, breath on her cheek. A massive shape hovering at tip of her nose.

Rach watched Shaz's good eye open. Her face, sleepy and loose, then confused; then she jerked and screamed, startled by Rach's close body. Rach screamed; then they both laughed. They got tangled up in Rach's coat, in each other's arms and legs, tipped themsens sideways and roly-polied across grass, heads banging against ground, shooting pains down Shaz's bad side, sky veering into field, blue plummeting into green into blue.

When they stopped, chests heaving, knees and elbows throbbing, Rach wa laid on top of Shaz, torso flush wi torso, legs laced together, foreheads touching. All either of them could see wa one staring eye, one fathomless black centre. They smiled. They breathed each other's carbon dioxide.

This wut first time Shaz had woken from her gone place and not felt heart-sink of being back, or itch to jump up and faint again. She wa alreyt, just laid here wi Rach.

Far off, Kel shouted, "Oi, wait up!"

Farther off, bell rang, calling them back tut world. Kel tugged Rach's elbow till Rach stood, held out her hand to Shaz and pulled her up. They linked arms, cut back across field to class.

Knickers

Kel wa still eleven, but all day she'd rehearsed her date of birth as if she wa twelve, because you had to be twelve to gerrin Karisma on Nappy Night. She said it again in a whisper, to mek sure she hadn't forgot: "First of February 1986." One-third of an inward-facing triangle, Kel huddled wi Shaz and Rach, halfway down a queue that spanned length ut nightclub's corrugated-steel wall. It wa nearly Christmas holidays, but none of them wore a coat. Their feet vibrated between toe and heel in their platform shoes. Their ponytails bounced. Motion wa part shiver, part nerves, and part, for Kel, to tek her mind off her bare midriff, which she wa trying to keep sucked in.

At door, bouncer stood. He wa med of convex surfaces, belly and bald head, black fleece zipped tut chin. Int forty-five minutes they'd been waiting, his eyes hadn't moved, staring ahead at Maccy D's across road. He drew his mouth thin, corners drooping, like ham sandwich left too long in its lunchbox. Kel reckoned he had mards on because he wa working underage night instead of Wikid House Wednesdays, advertised ont club's blacked-out windows wi pictures of older lads and lasses, dancing half naked and hanging backwards off stripper poles. "Maddest House Night in South York-shire," poster reckoned.

"Reyt mard arse, him." Kel nodded int bouncer's direction.

Shaz squinted at him ovver her shoulder. "Fuck, dint know it wa that tight cunt." She brought her lashes closer together till she wa gi'in a dead-eye so intense she could have been asleep. "Twat turned our Gemma away other week. Said her ID wa fake."

"Godsake." Rach hugged hersen. "Bet you he won't lerrus in." Rach looked oldest by miles. A head taller than Kel and Shaz, she already wore bras an' all.

"Better do," Kel said under her breath. She'd never sin inside a nightclub. Shaz and Rach had both been loads of times wi big sisters, sisters who dint do underage nomore, because now they looked old enough to sneak into proper nights, where everyone got off their faces, and—said Shaz—sometimes shagged reyt ont dance floor. Kel wont sure what happened on Nappy Nights, but she couldn't ask because then everyone would know she dint know. All she could see in her head were disco lights cutting long bright cones through dark. Shaz reckoned there were private booths where you could sit and sip Coke and smoke, tap fag ends into ashtrays like ladies did at pub. Tonight, after months of begging her mam, Kel wa only allowed out because she promised to stay wi her mates and not go anywhere on her own. It were just two of them at home. Mam liked to keep her in. Kel thought maybe she wa lonely, but you couldn't tell your mates that. You had to say, Mad bint's strict as owt for no goodfuckin reason.

"Oh aye, what happens if he dunt let you in, like," Shaz asked Kel.

Kel inspected her arms. One lightning vein ran bluish down back of her hand. Her mam had said, Just this once, and she always meant it, so this wa Kel's only chance. Around them, queue bulged and ebbed, like worms Kel and Rach used to pluck, cardigan sleeves pulled ovver fingers, from nettle beds and behead. Kel couldn't see anyone else from their school yet, and she'd never got bus home from town on her own—she wont sure she knew bus route number—and if Shaz and Rach gorrin and Kel dint, she couldn't ask them to go home wi her. They'd never stop rippin piss. And they wunt invite her next time. Again Kel repeated to hersen, First of February 1986.

"She's only dezzy to gerrin cuz Ando's coming," said Shaz, grinning.

"I'm not." Kel touched her chest, index finding thin V-shaped notch sat between her collarbones, slightest ridge in smooth skin.

"You are an' all." Rach play-punched fat at top of Kel's arm.

"Kel fo-or An-do, Kel fo-or An-do," they chanted, while Kel willed red to go away from her face, and now she needed a wee. "Kel fo-or An-do, Kel fo-or An-do."

"Shurrup, will ya." Kel scanned queue, searching for heads turned towards them, ears listening in.

"You said you'd lerr'im finger you if he tried," said Shaz.

Lads behind looked ovver, raised eyebrows, smirked.

"As if I did." Kel sucked in her stomach. She wont even reyt sure what fingering wa.

Her bladder tightened, fuller.

"You did," said Shaz. "Cleggy told me."

"Wunt lerr'im *near* me." Kel screwed up her face to mek it clear: she dint gi a fuck about Ando, not since he called her Fanny Flaps at break today. She wa behind sports hall gerrin three fags off Cleggy, who bought them hissen because he wa fourteen and looked old enough and then sold them single, 20p a piece. Ando wa there, going on to Cleggy about how many lasses he's gerrin off wi tonight. Kel dint care if he snogged hundred lasses. "He's a reyt minger, anyway."

"As if he is, he's *well* fit." Shaz refolded her arms. "Hardest lad in year nine an' all."

Kel proper needed a piss now. She pressed ont notch in her chest till it stung.

"S'up wi you," Rach asked, when Kel started bobbing more urgently.

"I just need loo." Kel tried to tame her legs' wild dance, but couldn't keep them still. In her groin, a fat sackful of liquid strained her bladder's taut skin. It felt like summat wi sharp feet wa trying to crawl out. She concentrated on sucking her belly flat, but that just med it worse.

"Piss ovver thier." Shaz's thumb indicated slim alley between Karisma and Colonnades. They'd sin two older lasses squatting down there, bums pressed against brick. But Kel'd never got hang of pulling her knickers out way.

"There's old men pissing down there," said Kel. She'd sin at least five blokes slip intut alley since they'd been waiting.

"So, they'll not do owt to ya," said Shaz.

"They *might*," said Rach.

"Our Kyle sez that only happens to lasses that are asking forrit." Shaz turned to Kel. "And you're not asking forrit, are ya?"

Kel dint know what "it" wa, so she couldn't be sure she wont asking. And she dint like thought of squatting while a load of old blokes stood around wi their willies out. And what if Ando warrat back ut queue. What if he saw.

"Can't be arsed, anyway," said Kel. "Don't need it that bad." She shrugged, shoulders jabbing up to meet her earlobes, where two pierced holes were still healing, green and sore around two heart-shaped studs. Everyone else had got theirs done before they were seven, Shaz when she warra babby, but Kel wont allowed till last week when she finally wore Mam down wi a tale about how she were gerrin laughed at because not having your ears pierced means you're frigid.

Longer they waited, less Kel could feel her legs. They numbed under a skirt cut tut thigh, covered waistband to hem in turquoise sequins. Kel gorrit special last week from MK One, where Shaz reckoned she went thieving ont weekend, but Kel knew she wa chatting shit because Shaz never ate—she saved her dinner money to spend on clothes. That's why you could count her ribs through her back. Today at break, Ando said to Cleggy that Shaz would be a reyt shag, if she had any tits.

"Anyway, if I do see him, I'll bang him out," Kel said.

"What you on wi?" Shaz asked.

"Ando."

Shaz gev Rach a look. They chanted, "Kel fo-or An-do, Kel fo—"

"No, listen, reyt, he's saying shit behind Shaz's back. He wants banging out."

"Kel fo-or An-do, Kel fo-or An-do."

When he wa done laughing about Shaz's tits, Ando had laid an index ont neck of Kel's cotton white tank top, triangle of it peeking above her school shirt, which wa buttoned low. Every lass at Ridgey knew you had to button your school shirt low, even though it meant gerrin after-school detention if Miss Swift saw. Ando's finger had pulled fabric down an inch. He'd squinted at her chest as if he wa looking through microscope in biology. Thissun waint be gerrin in Karisma wi these fried eggs neither, he'd said, which med Cleggy laugh so hard a bubble of snot bloomed out his nostril. Kel's cheeks had flashed hot at his words, but skin on her chest crackled and sparked round his finger, like he wa med of lad flesh and power lines. Spark shot all way down to her fanny. Thought of it now med her feel sick.

"Kel fo-or An-do, Kel fo-or An-do."

Creature in Kel's bladder flexed its claws.

"I fancy a Maccy D's, me," she said, nodding at one ovvert road.

"You ate ya tea before you cem out," said Shaz.

"So?" Kel stuck her knees together, ankles splayed.

"You've gorrer come in wi us, though," said Rach.

They'd practiced it ont bus into town: to mek sure Kel gorrin, they'd go past bouncer together, talking reyt loud about periods, so he wouldn't even bother asking Kel how old she wa. She'd just have to hold it till they got through.

It started snowing, thinly, more like frozen rain. They were shielded by Karisma's metal overhang, but older lasses going past on their way to proper club nights leaned forwards, bracing themsens, hands hovering above their forr'eads to save their blow-dried fringes. Flakes cem at them ont wind. Their bodies crumpled in like empty cans of pop.

That wa one good thing about cold, you could cross your arms and push your tits up into a *reyt* cleavage, but no-one could call you a slag because you were just freezing. Every lass int queue wa stood int sem pose, dressed like Kel in boob tubes and platform heels, shoulders hunched ovver their folded arms. Like most of them, Kel had a mini handbag dangling off one wrist. Her toes tapped against each other in a regular rhythm, building speed till they were going rapid as happy hardcore tunes that rude boys blasted from souped-up Nissan Micras.

Still, a single drop of moisture trickled down her inner thigh.

"Back in a sec."

She speed-walked across road to Maccy D's, mini handbag clutched to chest. Her heels were heavy, half a size too big, held on by a strip of patent-leather-look plastic. Mam wouldn't let her buy platforms—reckoned they'd mek her look a reyt slapper—so she had to borrow some off Shaz's big sister, Gemma. Clinging to them wi her toes, Kel sprinted past early-evening pissheads on high stools int window of Maccy D's, soaking up their day sesh wi their squished Filets-o-Fish. Inside, and past pink milkshake puddle, past sad family packed into a booth, upstairs, and past decal of Ronald and friends someone had drawn bucked teeth on, Kel found a solitary loo, reyt at back and down a corridor that smelled of hospital. She pushed door open wi her shoulder, fell into a room where walls were scrawled on, chemical smell cem laced wi a sweaty aftertaste, and toilet wa blocked by a papier-mâché sculpture of loo roll and shite.

Kel couldn't stop still long enough to pull her knickers down wi'out lerrin more wee escape, wi'out everything gushing out. Her underwear soddened while she hopped, crashed intut sink and hand dryer, willing her knickers to mek friends wi her knees. After a load of quick finger jerks ont elastic top, she managed to shimmy them halfway down her thighs. Her arse slammed ontut loo seat just before she let go, hissing an angry stream at shite sculpture beneath her. Relief felt like Mam's cool hands against her forr'ead last summer when her skin blazed wi flu and Mam called in sick tut call centre so she could stop home.

Kel's silver-grey bag hung off two slack fingers. It wut first thing she bought from Claire's Accessories after she started her paper round and now Rach had sem one. Kel kicked her legs straight out, like she used to ont park swings, before smoking wut only thing you could do ont park swings wi'out gerrin a smack. A wet pair of knickers drooped round her ankles, white wi a wavy blue trim, pair she'd worn since third year of primary school.

She dint piss hersen. Knickers dint count. It's not like she'd gor-rit on her clothes.

There wa no bin, only balled scraps of loo roll and used tampon holders piled in a corner beneath biggest bit of graffiti, "TWATTY BOLLOCKS 4eva 9T8 IDST," engraved a foot tall intut wall's plastic panelling wi a compass or hood of a Bic lighter. Kel couldn't bring hersen to leave knickers ont heap for everyone to see, like a Guy ont bonfire waiting fut flame. What if someone she knew cem intut loo next? But she couldn't carry them around wi her. And she couldn't go home wi'out proving Ando wrong.

Round back ut sports hall, praying her cheeks dint look as hot as they felt, Kel had pushed Ando's finger away and said, "What you on wi? I go Karisma every week, me."

"Nappy Night's once a month you daft bint," Cleggy'd said, his laugh going ahh-ahh-ahh-ahh like sheep int farmers' fields that took off running when they saw school bus going past.

Ando held his hand out forr'er to shek. "Tenner sez you waint get past bouncer."

Kel dint have a tenner. She had £1.50, and that wa for bus fare and a bag of crisps.

Before she could say owt, Ando leaned in so close she could see fat ginger mole hiding behind his left ear. Her nose stung from peppery cloud of Lynx that older lads at Ridgey sprayed reyt on their school jumpers instead of under their arms. He slid his hand down front of her skirt, fingers cupping her fanny cleft, sending every inch of her rigid.

"If you do gerrin," he said, "I might even gi you a good finger-fucking."

Kel shoved Ando's shoulders wi both hands, pulse raging. "Gerroff me."

Ando let himsen stumble back. He smiled. "Si thi tonight, then, Fanny Flaps."

It wont till later, brushing her hair in her bedroom mirror, gerrin ready to meet Shaz and Rach at bus stop, Kel found red V on her chest where his jagged fingernail had nicked her skin. She spent so long staring at Ando's notch int mirror, she dint have time to go forra safety wee before she left house.

Kel fingered V now, sting in her chest tekkin her mind off her wet knickers and her damp arse, lip ut loo seat digging into her flesh. She dint know if she wanted Ando to touch her like that again or if thought of it sickened her or if it wa both.

Either way, she couldn't lose bet. She eased knickers ovver Gemma's platform heels, stuffed them into her handbag's slim secret pocket, zipped it shut. Should be reyt, as long as wee dint soak through bag's fabric.

Kel hobbled fast as she could back downstairs, feet dragging Gemma's shoes back past sad family, past pissheads and their soggy sandwiches, back through snow, ovvert road to Karisma. Wi each step, new air rushed between Kel's legs, cold like a slap, wind threatening to slip a frigid finger below her skirt's flapping hem and lift it up.

Rach and Shaz were almost at front, three away from bouncer and his greasy scalp, shiny under Karisma's neon sign. Kel dipped back intut queue.

"Where's Happy Meal, then?" Shaz asked. "Like fuck you've already scoffed it."

"Oi!" A group of lads further down started on. "Fuck's that about?" they shouted at Kel. One of them wa tall and wiry like Ando. They threw their shoulders intut kids in front of them. Everyone tripped forwards, bodies crushing together. Boy nearest Kel fell onto her back, pushed her sideways away from queue, knocking breath from her. She teetered on her toes, fought to stay balanced.

"Fuck you doing, you silly slag?" Lads kept on.

"Dunt tek shit off them," Shaz urged Kel. "Tell em to get t'fuck."

Kel couldn't speak, winded, oxygen shocked from her chest by thud ut boy's weight on her spine. Karisma's overhang shadowed lad's faces. She couldn't tell if tall un wa Ando. She couldn't breathe in, lungs stunned and empty.

Bouncer let in three more, and now Shaz and Rach were reyt at front.

"Come on, then," said Shaz.

Tall lad moved forwards wit queue, stepped under neon sign. His face caught light. Not Ando.

Kel breathed, air rushing in to reinflate her. "What?" she said tut lads, emphasising word wi a head bob. "I wa here already." She pointed at Shaz and Rach. "These lot saved mi place."

"Whatever, slag."

"Hows about get t'fuck, you little wankstain."

She quivered all ovver, hearing hersen say those words. She waited fut comeback, fut volley of insults. Lads grumbled to themsens, slagging her off too quiet forr'er to hear, but they dint say owt else to her face. Pride swelled in Kel's chest. Gaps between bodies reopened, queue stretching out again like a Slinky uncoiled. Kel wriggled in wi Shaz and Rach, just in time for their turn to go past bouncer and through club's heavy double doors.

Three of them faced him together. Kel launched intut bit they'd practiced ont bus. "Got proper bad PMS, me. Aching reyt down to mi knees."

Before Shaz and Rach had chance to do their bits, bouncer waved Shaz through. She strode in, Rach in tow. Eyes on Rach's pony, Kel stepped forwards, walked smack intut bouncer's upheld palm.

"First of February 1986," Kel said, collecting hersen.

"Wait."

"But I'm wi them." Her shoulders tilted at doors that had swallowed her mates.

"Wait, or you don't gerrin."

Bouncer's arm barred her way. Up close, his face wa just as maungy as it had been further off. Looked like he'd never bothered learning how to smile.

Wind flared her skirt, reminded her that one cheeky gust could expose her tut whole queue. She gathered hem in her hand to keep skirt tight to her legs.

Kel'd never been a blagger. Even though Rach looked oldest, Shaz always did their blagging, like other month when they snuck intut cinema to see *Titanic*. They'd got ready at Shaz's house, Shaz dressing them in party frocks, sparkly eyeshadow, mascara, gold hoop earrings—clip-ons for Kel. At cinema, Shaz'd ordered their tickets. Bloke dint even ask their ages because Shaz leaned ovver his counter wi her boobs pushed up, smiled, held her eyelids low. Kel cried so much at film—no-one warned her what wa gunna happen on that wardrobe door—mascara ran streaky black down her face, her neck, and soaked intut front of her dress. Shaz had to smuggle her out fire exit, jacket pulled up to her nose.

Kel approached bouncer again. She sucked in her tummy, looked up at him through her lashes.

"Ey up, what's your name?" She stroked his forearm, ruffling his black fleece.

He stared at Maccy D's, body still and solid as a concrete bollard. "Touch me again and you're barred."

Kel stepped back, crossed her arms ovver her chest, fingers scurrying into armpits. She blinked against water in her eyes. Desperate to know if lads behind had heard, determined not to turn round and check. Wind bit at her, teased till she held her skirt in place wi both hands, bouncing on her heels, counting seconds till warm inside.

Bouncer's hand med a *come here* motion. She stepped forwards again, only to walk straight back intut upheld palm.

"Bag."

Blood crawled up her throat to her cheeks. "You dint check mi mates' bags."

Bouncer's face dint move.

"Mi mate Rach's even got sem bag."

"I check ya bag, or you gerrout queue."

She looked at faces int queue behind her. Still no-one she knew there, and now she couldn't remember which station bus left from, North or South. Both sat poorly lit beneath multistorey car parks, barren between loading bays but for smashed glass and trails of piss. Shaz said only skagheads hung about there at night. Kel'd never been there alone even int daytime.

She opened larger ut bag's two compartments and held it out, praying he wouldn't notice skinny secret pocket still zipped up. Bouncer poked a finger inside, disturbed her Frosty Melon lipstick tube, her school bus pass, tampon she kept on her in case it happened, and three fags she bought off Cleggy. Satisfied, he redid zip.

When he turned tut bag's other side, Kel's heart bashed itsen against her ribs. Back went slender zip in his massive hand, and in went his fat finger.

Bouncer cringed, nose wrinkling as if he'd just unearthed loo roll sculpture in Maccy D's. His disgust hit Kel like a fist—first a sock to her belly, then a dead weight spreading through her, draining her limbs. He pulled his finger out, hooking crotch of her wet knickers. They wa creased like tissue paper she used at primary school to mek collage ut Archangel Gabriel.

Inside her a cave opened, as though bouncer's finger had crooked around her guts, pulled them free. Lads behind went "*Fuckiiiiin-HELL.*" Their laughs gnashed at her face, way jaws of next-door's pit bull snapped at flimsy wire fence. She couldn't turn and look for Ando, see if he wa there, laughing.

Bouncer's grin split his cheeks open, his ham sandwich slices parting to reveal a gold front tooth in an overcrowded mouth. He uncrooked his finger; Kel's knickers fell. Pavement wa muddy wi half-melted snowflakes and shit off everyone's shoes.

"In you go," he said. Done wi her, he motioned tut lads behind.

One hand on her skirt, Kel bent at knees, scooped up her knickers, crammed them back intut secret pocket. Wee mixed wi mud and rubbed gritty wet against bag's lining. She hurried through club doors before they swung shut, cutting off wind, leaving her in a breeze-block corridor. UV strip-lights overhead med everything glow lilac. At passageway's end, stairs rose. A wop-wop bass line shook ceiling. She couldn't hear lads laughing nomore, but tears brimmed at sound of it in her brain.

She wanted to go upstairs, find Rach and Shaz and smoke their fags and try to forget, but her bag wouldn't close. She pulled at zip wi trembling fingers. Her knickers were caught in its teeth, slash of fluorescent white poking out.

"Ey up, Fanny Flaps."

Kel sucked her stomach in and looked up. "Alreyt, Ando."

Her arm skin tightened wi goosepimples. He hadn't been int queue laughing. He hadn't sin what happened.

He cem downstairs towards her. She clapped both palms ovver her bag, trying to cover place where pocket gaped, praying he couldn't see what she wa trying to hide.

"Fried eggs med it in, then." He closed his hand around Kel's left tit, squeezed like Kel reckoned you'd squeeze an old-fashioned car horn. Honk honk. She couldn't push him off because her hands were glued tut bag, concealing her knickers. She dint know what would happen if he touched her fanny again, if this time his fingers slipped beneath skirt hem to find nowt but her skin. Her heart banged around inside her like Mam's new Jack Russell, slamming intut kitchen cabinets whenever doorbell went.

"I wunt bother," Ando said, nodding at stairs. "It's shite tonight. Nowt but babbies."

Ceiling's UV strips seemed to light their faces from below, casting hot white beneath their chins. He thrust a scratchy summat into her boob tube. Sweep of frozen air, then door banged shut behind him. Kel shivered, looked down. Tucked into her top, a scrunched-up ten-pound note. Below that, between her fingers, her knickers glowed. She brought her thumb to her chest, found V-notch, pressed down. Her left nipple burned where his fingers had pinched, and she wondered if tomorrow she'd find a starfish-shaped bruise.

a.k.a. Dark Stalker

I met mi dark stalker when Shaz invited me and Kel to a disco round her end, a birthday at Goldthorpe Parish Hall, white gable-roofed hut squatting next tut concrete church tower. We didn't know lass whose party it wa, but Shaz did, and there warra bit of argy when we arrived because Shaz said she wa allowed to bring guests, and birthday girl said she wasn't. Lass wouldn't lerrus in, holding door closed, only her face poking through crack, arguing wi Shaz. Smoke machine smell wisped out around her wit rumbling music, babble of shouting kids. Lass said she didn't like people she didn't know, talking about us like we weren't stood right behind Shaz, holding birthday cards and £5 vouchers for WHSmith.

Me and Kel had to kick around ont street in us sparkly dresses while Shaz tried to convince lass's mum that we didn't have anywhere else to go. We were staying at Shaz's that night, since Goldthorpe wa miles from where we lived. Goldthorpe wa halfway between Donny and Barnsley, too far from either to belong. Wind wa flapping us fly-aways about, making me anxious because your hair had to be glued flat to your head. Mine warrup in a crocodile clip, slicked down wi a fat handful of glitter gel that wa hardening into cement.

Imagine how me and Kel felt when we wa finally allowed in, place teeming wi kids we didn't know, and nobody wanted us there except Shaz. Hall warra single room painted magnolia white. Stackable chairs lined perimeter, trestle table of finger food ran along one end. Vertical blinds wa pulled shut at windows to make disco dark as it wa gunna get at five int afternoon. DJ int corner, swallowed by his faux fog and rotating lights. Party wa half Goldthorpe kids and half Barnsley kids, wi me and Kel only Donny lasses amongst them. Barnsley would be our sister town if only we'd stop kicking shit out of each other. If only we spoke same language. We hung at room's edge, picking at a bowl of Quavers, mushing maize puffs into paste in us mouths. Watched everyone do t'Hokey-Cokey and t'Macarena and Agadoo, no urge to join int conga—kid at front parading round room, loving life, and everyone running and tripping behind him, wavy chaos at tail's end. We didn't want to do Oops Upside Your Head, sitting ont floor in a line, snug between someone's legs, rocking side to side pretending to be a boat. We didn't want to do any of that wi these scowling Barnsley scroats.

Evening wa building, as discos always did, tut moment right before lights came up, when DJ would make a handbrake turn from banging Eurodance to a slow song, ballad du jour, and everyone would pair off boy-girl. That weird five minutes when couples hung onto each other and swayed, stiff, like two rocking horses pretending to be in love. Int hours leading up to this abrupt mood shift, everyone devoted themsens to negotiations: which lad would dance wi which lass. Serious business, this; hearts and reputations warront line.

Shaz nipped back and forth between her various girl mates, whispering into ears behind cupped hands. Talks were carried out girl to girl, lad to lad, wi no conferring between factions, till every so often a delegate wa sent across room to deliver a message tut other side. Shaz warra streak of fair limbs crisscrossing dance floor, long legs bare, skinny shoulder blades glittered, poking from her purple velvet halter top.

We wa thirteen, and though Kel and Shaz had developed an interest int buzz-cutted snotty mouth-breathers we shared classrooms wi, I didn't understand what everyone wa gerrin het up about. I'd be sixteen before anything like desire wa stoked in mi body, and I didn't know why I wa so behind. Wa there summat wrong wi me? Or had Kel and Shaz just *decided* they wa gunna start fancying lads? They kept "top tens" in a jotter they passed beneath desk in English, lists of top ten lads they fancied, rankings shifting by t'hour. Lists wa eclectic, ranging from Tom Beckett, specky lad in us CDT class, and Ando, mean-looking chav in year eleven who Kel had a weird thing for, to Zac from *Home and Away* and Will Smith, Mr. Big Willie Style himsen. As prospects, they wa indistinct. Mr. Smith seemed just as viable as Ando or Tom, coming in fourth on Kel's list, sometimes fifth, and ninth or tenth for Shaz. Kel *would* consider practicalities, though. Beside Tom's name she put "(Single)," beside Ando's "(Taken)," beside Zac's "(Australian)," and beside Will's "(Married)," as if presence of Jada wa their union's sole impediment.

I didn't know if lads wa more interested in Shaz and Kel because they wa more interested in lads, or because Shaz and Kel wa more interesting. I did know that lads weren't interested in me.

DJ played "Children of the Night" and whole room went mad. Beat wa so fast, only viable dance warra kind of vigorous jumping. Shaz ran up to us, pulled us both by t'arms ontut dance floor, deep intut wriggle and mesh of lasses pogoing in their threes and fours. She made a tight little ring wi our bodies. Song warrall about fighting fut future of our nation, and according tut lyrics, only way to rescue t'country wa to "live your life like a rave machine." I didn't know what a rave machine wa, so I just jumped as high and fast as I could, in case England's hopes and dreams depended on it. Shaz grasped mi elbow, stopped me mid-leap, beckoned me and Kel to lean in. While everyone around us wa fighting for us future, Shaz tried to explain current deadlock between her and this tall basketball-playing lass from Barnsley. I still hopped ont spot while she talked, so I can't tell you I understood issue, exactly, but gist seemed to be that Shaz and Basketball Lass wanted to slow dance wit same lad, and negotiations had reached an impasse. "She's prettiest lass in their school, reyt," Shaz shouted in mi ear, "but he wants to dance wi me." Shaz grinned. "And she can't tek it, so now she's slagging me off to everyone." Shaz seemed proud of that fact.

Apparently, it wa important that Basketball Lass could see Shaz had backup, so it wa mine and Kel's job to bop and boogie wi her, prove Shaz had a crew. We jumped and jiggled through "Children of the Night," mimed and posed through "Barbie Girl." A lass wi a dyed-blonde perm came over, put her mouth next to mi ear:

"Who are you, like?"

"Shaz's mate, why?"

"Our Danny thinks you're fit, will you dance wi him?"

"Who's your Danny, like?"

Lass pointed at a tussle of lads int corner by t'fire exit. "Brown curtains."

I looked over: lad she meant wa taller than rest, brown curtains framing a high forehead. He looked like he might make it onto one of Kel and Shaz's lists.

"Will you dance wi him then?" She crossed her arms and glared at me. Her T-shirt said "too busy to fcuk."

"I'll think about it."

Lass shrugged and walked off. Kel and Shaz wanted to know what warrall that about, so we purrus foreheads together and I told them, pointed him out.

"I know him, he's mi cousin's mate," said Shaz.

"He looks like Leonardo DiCaprio," said Kel.

"He does an' all," said Shaz.

Shaz and Kel had been obsessed wi Leo since we snuck intut cinema to see *Titanic*, and we'd just watched Baz Luhrmann's *Romeo + Juliet* in us English class. Only Kel had any idea what Romeo wa actually on about in that film, but we'd all learned that falling in love wa glamorous and deadly, and Leo posters still loomed big and peeling on all us bedroom walls.

"Dance wi him!" said Shaz.

"Dance wi him!" said Kel.

"I will—if he's got balls to come up to me hissen," I said, which warran easy out. None of us had balls to go up to any of us oursens.

"Spice Up Your Life" next, our fave. Like every nineties lass, we all had a designated Spice Girl. Shaz wa always Baby, Kel wa always Sporty, and I wa always Posh. We wa slamming it tut left, and shaking it tut right, when us circle got knocked open: Basketball Lass barged through us, way a bowling ball charges through ten pins. She shoulder-checked Shaz as she passed, staring straight ahead as if we didn't exist. She wa twice Shaz's size, pinged Shaz's whole torso back. I don't know how Shaz stayed on her feet besides sheer force of will. Our Shaz's will wa always tremendous.

Her cheeks wa bright pink, pieces of lacquered hair knocked from her ponytail, hanging stiff and awkward round her face. I smoothed down her hair, redid her pony, pulled bobble tight. Shaz told us that Basketball Lass had been going round saying that she wa proper up hersen, that she shouldn't be messing wi "their" lads, that she should "fuck off back to Donny." Shaz said we had to keep dancing, so we danced, making us movements grander—flamboyant hair flicks and high kicks, feet sweeping up past us eyebrows—to show just how unruffled we wa.

Two songs later, we wa breathing heavy but still going. Basketball Lass appeared behind Shaz forra sec, did summat too quick for me to catch. All I saw warra flash of Shaz's bare chest, her tiny puckered nipples, disco lights blinking them purple and green. Shaz held up loose ties of her halter top, handed them to me. I reknotted them behind her neck.

"Double knot, fucksake," said Shaz. She told us that Basketball Lass had come up behind her, yanked knot open, pulled her top down. She cursed lass, vowed to "bang her out." She couldn't *reach* lass's nose, never mind break it, but I wouldn't purrit past Shaz to try. I didn't know what to do, didn't know how to make it right.

"I'll tell your mate's mum, get her kicked out," I said, already scanning forran adult int parish hall's dark corners.

Shaz said *no*, wit kind of finality you don't argue wi. We didn't argue; we danced, Shaz as sassy and playful as if nowt had gone on. I wondered warrit felt like, to be hated by t'prettiest lass for being even prettier. What did it feel like to know that most popular lad int room had chosen you. I half wished someone would fly into a jealous rage and expose *my* boobies.

DJ switched to a ballad, "My Heart Will Go On," as mi stalker would later remind me, and maybe it wut track's wistful panpipes that influenced me to agree wi Shaz and Kel—that lad *did* look a bit like Leo. And bloody hell, he wa coming over! He walked right up to me and said, "Wanna dance, then, or what?"

"Go on, Rach!" said Shaz.

"Yeah, go on, Rach!" said Kel.

"Do I look alright?"

"Stunning," said Shaz. She combed mi fringe wi her fingers, thumbed mascara from under mi eye. There wa moments, back then, when Shaz's encouragement made me brave enough for anything.

He smelled so different to us. We smelled of hair spray and gluey lip gloss. He smelled woody, like tree bark int rain. I wa trembling wit reality of it; mi first slow dance wa upon me before I'd had time to think or want it. We assumed position: I locked mi fingers behind his neck; he bunched his at small of mi back, heavy fist resting—shock!—just above mi bum. He wa nearly touching mi bum! We swayed, as we wa meant to, aware of being watched. I think I laid mi head on his chest just to have a break from staring into his eyes. His heart ku-dunked beneath mi ear, and it wa summat like thrilling and summat like frightening to get to know one of his vital organs like that, to be so intimate so soon wi his innards.

When I looked up again, he pushed his lips into mine. A seal formed, pressure as he sucked air out of me. A tongue, thrashing around inside me. Till then, I couldn't imagine where a lad's tongue would go—wont mi mouth already full of mi own tongue? But his tongue made room, muscling between mi teeth. He tasted buttery like Werther's, like he'd just eaten sweets. I wa well annoyed; nobody told me you wa meant to eat sweets so you'd taste nice. Last thing I'd eaten warra pickled-onion crisp. When he pulled away, I wanted him back. Mi mouth felt cold. Odd to be alone again.

He asked for mi number so I gave him house phone. We'd all just got mobiles, but nobody ever had any credit. Only thing people did wi mobiles back then wa make prank calls and play ringtones too loud ont back ut bus. Shaz and Kel screamed about it ont walk home, and it made me feel famous, made all t'drama ut night race around inside me. I'd never been centre of attention like that before; it wa always Kel's and Shaz's lads we gossiped about. They asked me what warrit like, kissing him, but they wa just being kind. They both already knew what kissing wa like firsthand—well, first-mouth. I could already barely remember what I'd felt. Could I say I *liked* it? I'd been too worried about how to move mi lips, how wide to open mi gob, whether I could breathe wi him pressing down on me. I wa relieved it wa done, though, that I'd become a lass who *had*.

We skipped through t'slow nightfall, ran us hands along bristly twig ends of a privet hedge in someone's front yard. Rasp and tickle of it against mi palm—mi new, different palm, mi older, more grown-up skin. I asked Shaz if she wa alright after her run-in wi Basketball Lass. She shrugged and said, "It wa nowt."

Shaz'd never bothered wi bras because she wa flat-chested like Kel, but after that disco she didn't go anywhere wi'out one, and second she'd saved up enough dinner money, she bought one of them inflatable push-up bras that came wi its own little air pump. She never mentioned incident again and got mad if I tried to bring it up, so I did mi best to forget that her pale chest had been ripped intut world by some chav's grabbing hands.

I didn't expect him to call. I thought phone number wa just polite thing to ask for after a kiss, just last move int dance. Back then, calling a lass's house phone meant risking talking to her mum. He'd be risking my mum demanding to know what warr'is full name and where did he live and what did he want wi our Rachael and did he have sisters and did he try hard at school. What lad would like me enough to chance *that*? But next night at seven o'clock landline rang, old corded thing int hallway, tethering me tut spot between staircase and front door. Door's glass panel wa textured to look like rippled surface of a frozen pond, turning outside into swatches of lawn green, pavement grey, sky blue. Who knows what we talked about fut most part, what teenage drivel we came out wi, but I remember our chats going summat like this:

"Alreyt, then," he'd say.

"Ey up, how's it going?" I'd say back.

"Not three bad," he'd always quip.

I'd ask him about his day, and he'd talk about video game he wa playing, or what he'd had for his tea, or hanging out wi his mates at park, summat "mental" his mates had done. One mate mooned an old bid from top ut playground slide. Another tried to set fire to a duck. I marvelled that a lad wanted to tell me so much. I shifted mi weight, foot to foot, to make green and grey splotches jump between ridged sections ut glass.

Week or two went by like this, Daniel chatting about school, mates, his older cousin who wa teaching him Muay Thai int backyard, till it wa time for him to go to bed. He gorrup at four int morning to jump off and ontut milkman's open-backed wagon, decorating door-steps wi crates of glass bottles.

"Doing ovver time at moment, me," he said one night, to explain why he had to gerroff phone early. "Tryna save up, like." He wa only year above me, but having a job made him seem loads older, a grown man wi a real life. And he wanted me to be part of it, which made me feel grown up an' all.

Letters came, love notes through t'post, written on lavender-coloured paper. Pretty, loopy handwriting in purple gel pen, so much neater than my cramped spindly hand. One said, "I've bin playin our song on repeat all week & thinkin about ya. My Heart Will Go On will always remind me of ya." That's how I know what song it wa—*he'd* remembered. Mi limbs lengthened as I read those words: "our song." In another, he wrote, "I just wanna see ya again baby so badly, wish I could kiss ya, miss ya so much I cud die."

He signed letters "Daniel," and beneath his name, "a.k.a. Dark Stalker." I didn't know what "a.k.a." meant, but I knew "e.g." stood for summat Latin, so I thought "a.k.a." must be Latin too. I'd never known a lad so sophisticated. This must be why Kel and Shaz had decided to fancy lads—to feel bright beam of their attention.

He wanted to meet again, which wut obvious next step, except that I didn't think about it till he asked. Did I want to see him? I looked forward to his seven o'clock calls, grew intut breadth of us chats, their windingness. I wanted letters to keep coming. They made me feel special, and longed for, and chosen. They made me feel pretty. I couldn't believe a lad like Daniel wa over in Barnsley, daydreaming about me. Barnsley warranother country, though, and I wont in a rush to visit. Me, Kel, and Shaz warron about going tut St. Leger fair, so I asked him did he want to meet me there.

Leger fair warra contentious prospect among Donny mothers, appearing next tut racetrack early every September fut famous St. Leger race. Some kids wa allowed to go no prob; some mums didn't trust fairground rides: clunky ancient Ferris, rusty waltzer, sparking screechy dodgems, and that gravity-defying death trap called the Cage that wa Shaz and Kel's fave—a giant roulette wheel wi no safety bars that spun till you were pressed against edge by centrifugal force, then flipped up ninety degrees on a hydraulic arm, so you were going upside down as well as round and round. Only thing stopping you from flying out to your death warra quirky rule of physics, and I didn't see any reason physics couldn't change its mind. For some mums, mine included, fair warra scuzzy place, run by gyppos, overrun wi thugs. To bypass mi mum's embargo, me and Kel stopped at Shaz's fut weekend again, because Shaz's mum would let her do owt.

We got to town early, traipsing through centre around midday. Town wa quiet, braced, waiting. Once races wa over fut day, scrums of drunken Doncastrians fluffed up in pinstripe suits and beaded lace and pluming fascinators would descend ont centre's pubs, bars, and clubs to spaff winnings, drown losses, scuff stilettos, shed parrot-bright feathers, drop diamantés like fairy-tale breadcrumbs, orchestrate a scrap or three, and generally chug themsens legless. We wa too young for all that, but only just. At thirteen, I'd have to wait another year till I looked old enough to join in. Not that we really looked legal at fourteen, but we'd have just enough tit and sass by then to gi bouncers cause for plausible denial.

Long walk up Hall Gate, up Bennetthorpe, along Leger Way. Wi each bus that screeched by, an understanding emerged slowly between us that there must be a bus route up this way. But we wa too young to know how to find out things we didn't know, too scared to stop a bus and ask driver. All we knew warrall we knew. By t'time we neared, puffing, pink, knackered, I warrin no mood to see Daniel. All I wanted warra burger and chips. But wouldn't he expect to kiss me again? Shouldn't I just eat chuddy and sweets? I didn't know which'd be worse, him wanting to kiss—all that daylong worry about when and how and would I be ready forrit—or him catching a look at me and deciding he'd made a mistake kissing me int first place.

We heard fair before we saw it, speakers kicking out rapid

techno beats. Bass reached us first, steady pulse beneath traffic growl like Donny warra beast wi a beating heart. Then laughing gas high-pitched vocals drifting across afternoon. "*Are you ready to fly-ee-ai-ee-ai?!*" Closer, a deep, amped-up voice said, "Hoooold tight, we're going ballistic!" Then sweet rush of candy floss, rich oily waft ut deep-fat fryers. When fair finally appeared ont other side of a fast dual-carriageway—cars tear-arsing past—it warra cluster of giant spiky-legged insects crouched by t'racetrack on a scrub of wasteland. Rows of red and yellow bulbs lined each skeletal metal limb, blinking feebly int overcast afternoon.

We moved between rides, sensing fair's coming magic, everything waiting for sundown, when bulbs would twinkle it into a shadowy labyrinth of bright and dark, mechanics hidden by night, machines alive, gyrating at each other like glowing sexed-up aliens. But at one int afternoon we could see too much. Hydraulic arm hefting t'Cage intut sky, then sighing weary on its way back to earth. Thin wheels ut waltzers racing wibbly round a creaking track, teenage lad, lips pinching a lit fag, jumping between carriages, pushing them into dizzy spin, making lasses inside scream. Flies circling bin by t'burger van, burger man's mustard-smudged apron, nick on his neck where he'd sliced hissen shaving. And half ut hook-a-duck ducks wa missing their eyes.

Shaz and Kel ate their Styrofoam cone of chips and curry sauce—Kel's licked clean, Shaz's picked at—and dumped cones int bin. They counted coppers, feeding them one palm tut other, then went off to hook a sightless duck. They wanted to win a hideous teddy bear. Taller than Shaz, googly eyes pointing in opposite directions, it hung by its neck from hook-a-duck stall's central pole, garrotted, plaggy bag tied round its head.

I hung back, orbiting bin, chewing mi burger. Meat wa dry despite sugary splurge of ketchup beneath bun. Mi throat didn't want to swallow. Daniel wa already forty minutes late, even later than we'd been. I wished we could just bugger off intut guts ut fair, hope he didn't spot us. I weren't even sure I'd recognise him. I remembered him tall, remembered t'girls had said he looked like Leo. But it warrall shadows and disco lights in mi head now. His features wouldn't present themsens.

Shaz wandered back over to me. "Where is he, then, your lad?" she said, wit gleam of victory in her eyes.

"Oh god, you never won that bloody teddy bear." I imagined us trekking back through town, lugging that dusty moth-nibbled bulk.

Shaz shook her head. "Better."

Kel walked over, holding a small plaggy bag knotted shut and filled wi water. Goldy orange flare along bag's bulge—tail flick, scale glint.

Fish's round eye looked up at me, its mouth opening and closing mechanically. He seemed like a creature that existed out of time, a dinosaur transported tut year 2000. He looked at me wi understanding, as if he knew he'd outlast me.

"I won Shaz a Furby," Kel said. Shaz held up her prize. Not a real Furby, obvs; they cost a tonne. This warra soft palm-sized furry likeness of a Furby—a fauxby, if I'm being clever—wi a pull string tucked into its arse, which, when pulled, caused this little ball of fur to vibrate. I waited for Kel to say she'd won me one an' all. She didn't.

I prodded fauxby's felt brown triangle of a mouth. "It ant gorra proper beak."

"So I won Kel a fish," said Shaz, too happy to hear me.

Kel smiled queasily, held fish up again.

"It can live in your mam's tank, can't it?" Shaz seemed so pleased wit gift, as if she'd won Kel her heart's desire. At time, I didn't get why Shaz, of all people, wa forcing a goldfish on Kel, but later I remembered how angry Shaz got Christmas before last—our first Christmas being mates wi her—because we'd got her knee socks and she'd not gorrus owt. We told her we didn't mind, but that wont the point. *She* minded. Didn't occur to me for years that she wa upset because she didn't have pocket money to buy us presents. I didn't think about that stuff then, but maybe that's because I did have pocket money—not loads, we're talking 50p a week, like—but enough to feel like I warrin charge of summat. Like I had options.

"What you gunna call him?" asked Shaz.

Kel stared at plaggy bag as though assessing fish's character, rifling through her mental list of potential pet names, but I knew she'd gone blank. Her mum didn't let her watch *EastEnders* or buy CDs, and maybe that's why Kel didn't really have a favourite anything, let alone a favourite name forra goldfish she didn't want. She had a favourite Spice Girl because I'd told her she looked most like Sporty, gi'en her t'free Spice Girls poster I'd got in an issue of *Mizz*. I'd made mi dad tape their albums for her an' all. But she didn't have a favourite Teletubby or a favourite Backstreet Boy, got nervous when asked to pick a favourite colour or flavour of ice cream. When she wa little, she'd been forced to name three teddies: Big Ted, who wa big; Clownie, who warra clown; and Pink Ted, who wut faintest shade of cherry bubble gum.

"Goldie?" Kel offered.

"No! He's gorrer have a better name than that!" said Shaz.

"Alright then, dickhead," said Kel. "Name your Furby."

"Gerald."

"Why Gerald?"

"Looks like a Gerald. Now name your fish."

"Name it after horse that won Leger," I said, to help Kel out. "Mutafortec, or summat."

"Right, that's what it's called, then," Kel said, and Shaz seemed satisfied, and Kel seemed relieved, and I wa happy I weren't involved int gift giving after all. A few days later, I'd check mi dad's *Free Press* and discover horse wa actually called Mutafaweq, but it wa too late; Mutafortec had been named.

When Shaz nipped tut portaloos forra slash, Kel held bag between us noses. "Fuck am I gunna do wi this?" She waggled her eyebrows. They looked funny through t'water, refracted into sliced-up caterpillars. I giggled, then she giggled, then we couldn't stop.

"You can't even purrit down!" I said.

"I know! I've just gorrer hold it!"

Laughter bent us both in two, chests folded over knees.

When hilarity had washed through us, I said, "It's a fair fish, innit. He'll be dead before we get home." And if I hadn't said that, I'm sure old Mutty would've enjoyed his life expectancy of twelve hours and duly expired.

As Shaz walked back towards us, and Kel wa looking forra way to hang fish off her jeans belt loop so she could regain use of both hands, a fingertip prodded mi shoulder blade. I turned round and there he wa, mi Dark Stalker.

"Alreyt," he said.

"Ey up," I said back. A break int clouds threw long lines of light over us, making us both narrow-eyed. I needn't have worried about recognising him—his face chimed inside mi head like a bell. But it rung a different note than one I'd remembered. An off-note. All features were present as recalled, but they sat closer together, his bone structure more fitted, cheeks skinnier, sallower. Rash of pink zits on his chin, wispy hairs on his top lip. I felt cheated by disco's dark. It'd painted him in bolder strokes.

I didn't know what to say, so asked, "How'd you get here?"

"Fatha," he mumbled from one half of his mouth.

"You what?"

"*Fa*tha," he said, using exact same portion of lip.

I didn't know what to make of those sounds. *Fa-tha*. Mi brain smashed them together till they sparked sense: he'd gorra lift off his dad.

He squinted at Kel and Shaz, looking at them sideways as if they might be a hallucination. We all stood around shyly till I remembered I wa supposed to do introductions.

"This is Kel and Shaz," I said.

"Reyt." He nodded.

Kel and Shaz said, "Ey up." Silence goaded me. I didn't know how to get talk going. Daniel'd been so chatty ont phone. Now he warra tree wi all its sap sapped. Brittle, like at any moment he might snap into splinters that'd stick in mi skin.

Shaz pulled at Kel's arm. "Let's go ont Cage."

I flashed mi eyes at Kel, signalling panic, emergency, *Do not leave me.*

Shaz wa proper tugging, digging her feet intut grass, pulling at Kel's arm like a lad yanking rope in tug of war.

"Do you wanna go ont Cage wi us, Rach?" said Kel, knowing full well I did not want.

"No, no," Shaz said, pulling. "They wanna be a*lone.*"

We didn't. I bloody did not. While Shaz and Kel play-fought, Kel giggling, resisting Shaz's pull, I wa caught between terror of stepping ont Cage and terror of being left wi him. I didn't even know him, did I. Whoever this lad wa next to me, he wont chatty, phone Daniel. He wont romantic-letter Daniel. He wont Barnsley's answer to Leo.

"Back in a sec, Rach," said Kel. "Hold mi fish, yeah?"

Watery bubble wa thrust into mi hands. Kel and Shaz raced each other tut Cage. I looked down at Mutafortec. He looked back at me. I kept eye contact wit fish so I wouldn't have to look at boy, who seemed both scrawny and tough—too tough, kind of lad you'd avoid int street. When I say tough, I mean rough, really. I mean *rough.* But that's not nice to think, and he'd been nowt but nice to me.

There'd be hours before his dad came back to get him. When could you decide summat wont for you, after all? How could you say, Soz, like, I've changed mi mind.

"Shall ah hold it fo' ya?" he said, and, when I didn't reply, "Giz it here, then." He took animal out mi hands, found a pocket in his tracky bottoms deep enough, and—floop!—fish wa swallowed by his trousers. I worried about Mutafortec suffocating, till I remembered he warra fish. I didn't like that his vanishing freed both our hands. And I wa right to worry—next thing, Daniel's fingers laced through mine.

We walked around, our joined arms swinging stiff between us, glued palms gerrin sweaty, Mutafortec weighing down Daniel's kegs on one side. I didn't look at him straight on, in case he wa waiting for us eyes to meet, waiting to go in fut kiss. We had a go ont ghost train, me jumpy and tense int dark, not because I wa scared ut trailing cobwebs or plastic skeletons; I wa scared he'd try and put his hand on mi knee. I watched while he had a go ont darts saloon and missed, coconut shy and missed, ring toss and missed, till I daren't watch anymore, in case he wa trying to impress me, in case he blamed me, in case his pride wa made of porcelain and one more failure would send it smashing tut ground.

I kept looking round for Kel and Shaz, kept suggesting we stand still so they could find us. When an hour became two, I realised they wa staying away on purpose.

We did another lap ut ground, hands gripped. He stopped us in front ut fair's tallest ride and said, "What do ya reckon?"

Ride wa called Slingshot. Two steel towers reared above us, scratching at clouds. Hanging between them, attached by two lengths of bungee, warra human-sized metal hamster ball entrapping two blokes. Ball wa thrust vertical intut air, then it bounced up and down as bungee cords stretched, then slackened, blokes gerrin their bones jiggled out their flesh. Shaz wut only person I could think of who'd willingly put hersen inside it. She wa like that always, our Shaz, forever throwing hersen at every possible peril, in love wi owt that could maim her, carve chunks off her, leave scars.

Looking up at poles reminded me of when me and Kel wa little and we'd hug lampposts on our street, stare up their concrete shafts at bulb casement above, their flat funny heads. Bulbs shone pink int early evenings, switching after sunset to baby-chicken yellow. We even had us favourite lamppost to do this wi, and we called it "Favourite Lamppost." If you hold tight, tip back your head, if you concentrate ont clouds above, after a minute it looks as though lamp-post's head is moving, as though it's falling—but it never falls, it's just always falling—and you stare till you're spinning, till you feel like you're falling, then you let go, stumble around, vision reeling, and you're laughing so hard you worry you'll never stop, and you squeeze your eyes shut while your mind whirls, and you can't believe this magic exists on your street, your tarmacked cul-de-sac, right int middle ut world.

After we moved up to big school and met Shaz, and after she showed us how to make oursens faint, Kel taught her us lamppost trick. I wa mad wi Kel for days after. I made her promise that she wouldn't introduce Shaz to Favourite Lamppost, and she swore she wouldn't, but still, after Shaz knew, some ut magic had seeped out and gone.

I must've been looking up at these poles, this nightmare con-traption, for too long, because Daniel said, "You wanna go on it or what?"

And I said, "No!"

He said, "Ah'll pay forrus, like."

And I said, "*No!*"

But I must've said "no" like *yes*. "No" like *I want to, really*, because he walked up tut sign next tut entrance, which said "£20 per ride." That wa more pocket money than I could save up in six months.

"Twenty quid! Wharra rip-off," I said, like I wa mi dad looking at kitchen tiles in B&Q.

"Ah'll gerrit us, you're alreyt."

"Don't be daft."

"Ah'll *gerr*it."

"How've you got money to afford that?"

"Why wunt I have money forrit?"

I looked him int eyes fut first time since he'd took fish off me. They wa bunched up into slits. Shaz gorra face like that sometimes, anger etched into her eyes and mouth like anger warra war mask. But there wa summat else flinting in his pupils. Determination, mebs, and summat sparking even below that, summat I couldn't name.

So, no wa clearly wrong, but I couldn't say yes. I didn't understand why no wa wrong, couldn't fathom what weight rested on me saying yes.

Kel and Shaz staggered over dizzy from t'Cage, which they claimed they'd been on three times. They'd come up wi a game: they took it in turns to pull Gerald's string, making him vibrate, then tried to shove him down each other's top or tracky bottoms before he gobbled up his cord and went still. They play-scrapped, limbs scuffling, till Shaz managed to lodge Gerald down Kel's top, where he shook like a deranged tit.

"S'up wi yous," Shaz asked, sensing strain in us silence.

I said, "Nowt," at same time Daniel said, "She waint go ont ride wi me, she's frit."

A bloke came up to us, a proper adult, chin gruff wit kind of coarse stubble that looked like iron-filings clinging to a magnet. His presence deflated Daniel's back into that of a boy. Mi Dark Stalker didn't seem so frightening as he had a minute before.

Bloke said, "Any of yous wanna go on this? You've gorer have two riders." We said nowt, just stood feeling wrong in our too-small skins. "You'd be doing me a favour, like."

"Aye," said Shaz. "Go on, then."

"Wicked, ta, chuck." He pulled a peeling leather wallet from his jeans.

I wanted to dash forwards, offer misen in Shaz's place. Wanted her to think I wa brave. Wanted to save her from hersen. Instead, I said, "Are you sure, Shaz?"

"Chill out, Rach, fucksake." Shaz hopped up clanking metal steps tut ticket booth, scampering after t'bloke. Me, Kel, and mi

Dark Stalker watched her go, in her crop top and Nike trackies, ends of her extra-long pony draggle-bopping at small of her back. She climbed intut hamster ball, pulled a helmet down low, shading her eyes, making her head comically big, like someone had plonked a Malteser on top of a matchstick. A large man strapped her in next tut bloke, then stepped back, leaving two of them sat, staring out together, waiting fut machine to fling them, fut moment they'd soar over t'fair, see everything: every ride in miniature, dollhouse dimensions ut racecourse's white fences, Donny centre further off, huddled mean and grey.

They shouted to each other while they waited. Whatever t'bloke said made Shaz throw her head back laughing, feet swinging, her knees—tiniest, knobbliest knees I'd ever seen—wagging next tut bloke's meaty pair that strained his slim-fit jeans. And then— ping!—up they went.

Hamster ball raced intut sky, bungees stretched tight, and gravity pulled them down again. Up, down, up, till they made peace wit earth's forces and just hung. Three of us left on land hadn't found time to speak, though I could feel Daniel next to me, way you can feel rain int air right before it starts siling it down. I wont sure if I wa to blame or if it wut bloke who'd made him feel small.

Shaz wa back, falling giddy into Kel's arms, making Kel jump up and down wi her. She said, "That wa fuckin *mint!*"

Bloke plodded down steps, chunky knees bending wi more care and weight. He high-fived Shaz. "Nice one, sausage." To us he said, "Harder than me, thissun. Proper little legend." Then he warroff, out of us lives for good, and summat inside me relaxed, a spring unwound I didn't know wa coiled, to watch him go, knowing he hadn't wanted anything from us that we couldn't give.

Me and Daniel walked behind Shaz and Kel tut fair's end, back down tut traffic roar of Leger Way. Shaz's elation wa like a fifth person, humming along wi us, filling rest of us wit sense that we'd never quite lived, and never quite would. Did I wish I wa Shaz in

that moment, fizzing off high of her own daring? So free to launch
hersen headlong at every new way to die. Maybe I would've liked
to have slipped inside her skin fut glow of after, fut reward of being
reckless.

Road warrus parting place, where us lasses had to start us trudge
back tut centre, and Daniel went off to wait for his "fatha," who'd
tek him back to his country. I wa dreading us goodbye: this, surely,
wa kiss o'clock. We turned to each other slowly, painfully—wit stiff
robotics of kids who knew what wa expected, who wa doing their
best to act it out. Kel and Shaz fell back, purrin a meaningful five-
foot gap between them and us. I didn't want to be over here wi him; I
wanted to be back there wi them, safe int small nest of us friendship.
He leaned in, head listing, so I did same, gi'in in to what moment
demanded. A terse peck ont lips—and, in mi chest, an unexpected
flutter, not quite discomfort, not quite want.

"Here y'are, then," he said, roughing summat into mi hands.

Two summats, in fact. In mi left hand, Mutafortec in his plastic
bubble of a universe, still tail flicking, still king of his waters, alive
in mi hand like flourishing finish of a magic trick. In mi other hand
warra small plaggy jewellery box, maroon wi a gold trim.

"You can't gi me this." I held it out to him.

He stepped back, hands up, as if it warra summons or a stink
bomb. "Tek it."

"I can't, what is it?"

He laughed and looked off. "It's fo' thee, innit."

I couldn't read his expression. I tried to put box in his hand. He
backed further off.

"Please, I can't take it, it's too much."

Much, much too much.

"You've gorrer tek it. It's your birthstone, innit."

I couldn't remember what mi birthstone wa. I couldn't remember telling him mi birthdi. All those letters and phone calls, all that
nice attention. I felt wrong, now, for taking any of it. Behind me, Kel

and Shaz stayed still and silent as bird-watchers. I tried to slip gift into his trackies pocket; he blocked mi hand wit reflexes of a boxer.

"Just *tek* it," he said, tight and bitter. Urgent, like there wa more at stake than just this maroon box.

"Ta," I said. "Thank you."

"Ah've gorrer go, mi fatha's waiting." He jogged off, leaving me to mi handful and mi mates, who stirred to life moment he wa gone, dove fut object in mi hands. Kel got tut box first, waved it over her head. Shaz clawed at Kel's arm, trying to climb her. I held fish up at Kel's eye level.

"Giz it back or Mutafortec gets it."

Nowt would've pleased Kel more than old Mutty coming a cropper, but she couldn't let Shaz know that. She handed box over. I plonked bag of fish in her palm.

Box opened clumsily—plastic clasp stuck fast at first, then flew open, mi fingers gerrin slow wit cold, late-afternoon wind licking up around us. Inside, a necklace, short chain strung wi pallid blue gems buried in filigrees of brassy gold. Tacky, said a voice in mi head. What a tacky slab of gaud. I felt guilty instantly for thinking it.

Shaz said, "Fuckin hell, that's well expensive."

"How do you know?" I tried to shut box, but Shaz nabbed it, brought it close to her face.

"It's from Argos catalogue."

"No it int."

"Swear down, I wa looking at it other day—wont ah, Kel?"

Kel nodded at me wi sorry in her eyes. "We warrin Argos other week and Shaz wa looking at jewellery." I didn't know if Kel wa sorry for being in Argos wi'out me, or sorry she wa backing Shaz up and not me.

"It cost thirty quid, this," said Shaz.

"It did not."

"Swear to god. We'll go Argos now and I'll prove it." Argos

had closed fut day and she knew it. "Ah'm telling ya, Rach, that lad spent *thirty* fuckin quid on ya."

"I don't fancy him," I said.

"Why did you tek it then?" asked Shaz.

"What warrah meant to do?"

"Well, you shunt've took it." Shaz seemed upset wi me, like I'd done summat really wrong.

I didn't know much about rules of finishing someone, but I'd seen our Louise upset after gerrin finished enough times to know that only wankers did it over t'phone. So when Daniel called next day at seven o'clock, I picked up, stretched phone cord to its limit so I could park mi bum ont stairs, cord's ringlets pulled tight, receiver's plastic casing making a worrying creaking sound. We talked as normal about who'd done what, except now we spent more time listening to each other breathe. Still, he warrat least three times chattier than he'd been in person, talking about a five-a-side footy match he'd played and fact that his mam weren't cooking his tea. After a long monologue about how she warrat an Avon party so he had to mek hissen beans on toast, I asked, "How come you were so quiet at fair? You barely spoke to me all day."

Silence.

Then, "You know."

Mi heart beat funny when he said that. He sounded so certain I thought there must be another me who knew things I didn't. Who'd *done* things I'd take blame for.

"I don't, honestly. I'm baffled."

Silence.

"Ya mates."

"What about mi mates?"

"You never said you wa bringing them."

Segments ut fair day started to swing into focus: he'd been upset because he wa outnumbered. Because he hadn't been warned.

"I'm sorry, I didn't mean to upset you."

"Ah wont upset."

"Oh, well, I'm sorry if it pissed you off."

"It dint piss me off."

"Alright, well. I'm sorry."

Another pause.

"Do you like necklace, then?"

"Oh, yeah, it's gorgeous, I've not took it off!"

"Really?"

"Yeah, course!"

"Ah did ovvertime fo' that, you know."

Obviously, necklace had never left box. Shaz said it wouldn't be right if I wore it, which made me wanna wear it just to spite her, but it wa ugly and didn't go wi owt.

I decided only way out of this wa to gi *him* a present, and gi him his necklace back. Then I could tell him I wanted to finish him. I made plans to go Barnsley to see him following weekend, tried to get Kel to gi me advice about what to say ont bus into school.

"What am I gunna dooo?" I said, hands over mi face.

"What am *I* gunna do?" Kel countered.

"About?"

"Mutafortec."

"He int dead yet?"

Kel shook her head. "Mi mum's annoyed because we had to purr'im in wi all her fancy fish. She sez he's too common; he ruins look ut tank."

"Seriously," I said. "What do I buy him and how do I tell him I don't wanna go out wi him anymore?"

Kel shrugged. "'I don't wanna go out wi you anymore.'"

"I can't say that."

"Why not?"

"I *can't*."

Summat at back ut bus caught Kel's attention. I didn't need to look to know it'd be Ando, mean-looking chav in year eleven. Arm slung round a lass from his year, whispering into her ear, making her giggle and say, Gi oo'er. Kel wa always staring at him, a sort of longing, sort of pleading stare.

"Oi," I said, making Kel's eyes flick my way. "I need help."

"Won't it be confusing if you gi him a present, then dump him?"

"I dunno, do I. He got me one."

I wondered how bad it'd really be if I just kept being his girl-friend forever.

I got Mum to take me down to Jacksons one night after school. Jacksons wut kind of shop that everyone's got a different name for, depending on warrit wa called when they wa young. Mum called it Grandways. It'll always be Jacksons to me even though now it's a mini Sainsbury's. Mum gave me five minutes to choose. I had £10 pocket money saved but I didn't wanna blow whole lot. I couldn't decide between Ferrero Rocher and a stuffed toy pig. Ferrero Rocher wa what you wa meant to buy boyfriends, but pig looked so happy, black stitched smile curving round his snout. Mum wa rushing me, pretending to walk off then coming back, saying, If you don't make your mind up, I'm leaving you here, so I grabbed both, blew mi whole bloody tenner, then hurried out after Mum intut car park, chilly wi regret. I wouldn't be able to buy misen pick 'n' mix for weeks.

Satdi, Mum drove me to Barnsley. We weaved up and down terrace rows till we found his door. Mum left me ont doorstep hold-ing mi pig and mi Ferrero Rocher, maroon jewellery box a lump int pocket of mi trackies. He didn't kiss me when he opened door, which I wa glad of and sad of. He led me through house, narrow like Shaz's—twice as thin as I thought it should be; I kept looking left, expecting wall to open up into another half, but it never did—and out intut slender backyard. There warra charred barbecue, two broken white plaggy garden chairs, a mucky teardrop-shaped punching bag, and a line of lads sat ont brick garden wall.

Of course he hadn't told me his mates would be there.

"Dunt feel nice, does it?" he said, wi a smile.

I didn't know how many lads wa sat there leering; I couldn't look em straight on. They warra streak of tracksuits and pasty flesh. I imagined mi mum's car, safety of it, speeding away. How far would she have got? How could I call her back? I held pig out in front of me like a shield.

"What's this, like?"

"For you," I said, handing it to him wit box of Ferrero Rocher.

Lads giggled at fluffy pinkness in his hands. They snatched it off him, passed it between them, fought over it, laughed, said, Giz it here! Hawkish lad in a Burberry cap made squealing noises while he thrust it into his crotch. Stockier lad wi beefy arms and a skinhead put on a high-pitched voice and started going, Fuck me, I'm a dirty little piggy!

I saw, then, what a stupid gift it wa. Girly, childish.

Daniel looked at ground, a bit rumpled, a bit flushed, like he wa more pleased wit present than he wa allowed to show. Like he'd been so sure I wa trying to set him up by bringing mi mates tut fair. Like triumph of setting me up wa beginning to dim. He seemed angry wi me and pleased. Vengeful and soft. Disgusted and keen.

"I've gorer go. Mi mum sez I'm not allowed to stop."

I fled that narrow garden, that narrow house, wi'out doing what I'd gone there to do. Still tied, still not ungirlfriended, maroon box still digging into mi thigh. I walked randomly through estate till I found main road, found telephone box, fed it silver—a hexagonal 20p, mi favourite coin—called house phone. Dad said that when Mum got home, he'd tell her to turn round and go straight back, and she did, her little grey car pulling a dramatic U-turn when she saw me. Mum and Dad wa always rescuing our Louise when she called them drunk and stranded int middle ut night, and I'd promised misen I'd never upset them like our Louise did.

I climbed intut car, preparing misen forra telling off. But Mum didn't shout at me for wasting her afternoon. Her serious tone when she said You alright, love made me wonder what could've happened. What dangers I'd courted, kissing a Leo look-alike int disco.

When phone rang at seven, I didn't answer. Same drill next night. Third night, he kept ringing off and calling straight back. I stood int hallway, guarding phone, making sure nobody touched it. Eventually, Dad shouted through from living room, "Are you gunna answer that or what?"

I tucked phone between mi ear and shoulder, asked "Hello?" Like I didn't know who it wa.

"It's Daniel."

"Hiya, what's up?" I tried to keep mi voice normal, but it wavered, showed mi nerves.

"S'up wi thee? Why aren't you answering?"

I didn't wanna lie, but I couldn't tell truth. "Didn't know you'd called."

"You brekkin up wi me, like?"

"No, no," I lied. "Just didn't hear phone, honestly."

"Reyt, well. That's alreyt then. Cuz if you brock up wi me, I'd kill misen."

That syllable, *kill*, knocked mi body into a cold shock. It sounded unreal, like it wont a proper word, just a noise bouncing round mi skull. People didn't say that in real life, did they. Only on *Hollyoaks*. I pushed out a laugh.

"Well, no need for that, ya silly billy, everything's fine."

I could hardly hear misen over t'white noise in mi ears. I couldn't make out a word he said, just tried to laugh whenever he paused, hoping he wa telling me summat funny. All I could think wa, how long did I have to listen to him till it wa safe to hang up.

And when he did let me go, when I wa alone int hallway, I tried to imagine anyone thinking I wa special enough to die for. I tried to ignore spike of pride thrilling through me.

He called house phone another few nights. I let every call ring off. Then mi mobile started going, a withheld number. Mi voicemail started filling. I wa afraid to listen in case it wa Daniel threatening to kill himsen. I couldn't remember gi'in him mi mobile number. Neither of us had money for mobile calls. When I finally played messages, I couldn't tell if it wa him. Every recording sounded like a group of lads laughing, muffled, egging each other to do summat I couldn't make out, fumble static sounds, receiver passing between hands. Few nights later, laughing and mumbling still, plus one voice chanting, starting right quiet and eerie, building into fury. Fury wi a weird accent, words I couldn't make out. There warra rhythm to it: *mmh-mmh-mmh-mmh-mmh-mmh-mmh*. Seven short syllables. Every night forra week, *mmh-mmh-mmh-mmh-mmh-mmh-mmh*. No meaning, all bile.

I didn't tell mi parents. I listened to every message all t'way through, even though they went on for minutes. Who had enough credit to waste on this? How much did someone have to hate me to pay to taunt me every night?

One night, a snippet blurted into sense: "Shut your mouth." Now rhythm went *mmh-mmh-mmh-mmh shut your mouth*. I played that message five-, six-, seventeen times, trying to make it all out. Night after night this way, pretending to do homework. In one hand, mi ballpoint, shivering int same spot on mi jotter cover, making juddery doodles. Int other hand, mi mobile pressed to mi ear, warming till it wa too hot and I had to purrit down.

After weeks and endless replays, first bit ut rhythm transformed into words: "Know your role." Mi Dark Stalker wa screaming, "Know your role and shut your mouth." Hatred of it frothed through phone—I dropped phone ontut desk—like his hatred wa acid that could burn through mi skin.

"That's *well* scary," said Kel, when I told her ont bus. "Are you gunna call police?"

"No."

"You should, that's harassment."

"It's just a prank call, innit."

"Shaz will agree wi me."

I grasped Kel's wrist. "Don't tell Shaz. *Please*."

I didn't want Shaz to know because I didn't want *Shaz*. To *know*. To know what I couldn't say. To know how easily a lad could hate me? To know a lad found me disgusting? I think I just didn't want Shaz to look at me different, as if mi ugliness warra secret I could keep from her.

"Okay, I won't," said Kel.

And I didn't want to hear Shaz tell me I shouldn't have taken necklace, shouldn't have accepted what didn't belong to me. Necklace wa wedged deep in mi knicker drawer where I'd never chance across it, leagues beneath layers of lace thongs, buried wi a white cotton three-pack from C&A Mum'd bought me that I never wore. Even that far out of sight, necklace haunted me, torched holes in mi thoughts, made me feel burdened, cursed.

A burst of laughter from back seat ut bus drew Kel's face away from me again. I followed her gaze: Ando wa trying to gi that lass from his year a wet willy; she wa squealing and laughing and saying, Pack it in, ya daftcunt.

"Maybe they're all just crap," I said.

Kel shrugged. "There's gorrer be *some* alreyt ones."

"Anyway, how's Mutafortec?"

Kel sighed, threw her shoulders intut bus seat. "He had fin rot forra while, and I thought that wut end of him. Then he got better."

125

I cheered silently for old Mutty. Surviving, against odds.

"Then mi mam's fancy fish got fin rot off him. Now Mutty's eating their rotten bits."

"*Eating* them?"

"Well, nibbling."

Messages came; I listened. Sure it wa him. Not sure. Trying to find his voice beneath one he wa purrin on, his threats always oddly foreign, and more sinister because strange. Alien words, leaking into mi ear from another planet. He threatened me wi summat called a "can of whoop-ass." Another time it wa "ass-whooping," and another day he promised to beat mi "candy ass." So much ass, and I'd only ever had an arse.

It wont like I'd never been threatened. This is Donny we're on about. You don't go many days round here wi'out someone offering to "bray you" or "bang you out." Or just "bang you," which wa always confusing—do you want to fuck me, or fight me, or both? So it weren't threat of violence, exactly, that chilled me. It wut way he could wear disguises, slip from sweet to enraged, and I didn't know why, when, or how change had come over us. How I'd brought it about.

Kel had to find Mutty his own bowl. She purr'im int garage and tried to forget to feed him. Whenever Shaz asked how Mutty wa doing, Kel would beam, say he wa strong as owt, indestructible. She loved him, she'd say, and I could tell that int moment she meant it. Kel loved that she wa making Shaz feel good. At some point she did forget to feed him, daren't go intut garage for weeks, afraid ut limp body she'd find. Visions of him capsized at water's surface. When she finally peeked in, found bowl between a bike wheel and her mum's rusty garden shears, he wa swimming swift as ever, gi'in her his bright flicker. Nowt to eat but his own poo, and somehow he'd made it a feast. She begged me to take him: *Please* tek him, but don't tell Shaz. Sometimes it felt like our trio's bond wa built on a foundation of don't-tells, like friendship depended entirely on which secrets we wa willing to keep. I put Mutty int garden, in mi mum's water feature, which wa shaped like two millstones, water dribbling down into a circular trough. He swam round that trough, ate whatever dropped in. He wa still there when I left for uni. Still there when mi parents moved house. For all I know, still there now.

One Fridi night, threats took a new turn. They began wit usual malevolent muttering, demonic chanting, then "Know your role and shut your mouth!"—then, loud and clear in a dodgy American accent, "Can you smeeEEELL—what the ROCK—is COOKing?!"

Like I say, being a Donny lass, I wa used to gerrin threatened wi all sorts, but this wut most bizarre violent promise anyone had ever made me. I imagined mi Dark Stalker and his gang of Muay Thai boxers in his backyard, gathered at midnight round a cauldron bubbling, stewing me alive. Their lunatic faces, cackling, surrounding me wi an evil glee. I decided I had to get rid ut necklace. Shaz wa right—I never should've took it. If I got rid, maybe all this would stop.

That Satdi afternoon, me, Kel, and Shaz got bus into town. I warroff to see if Argos would accept a return wi'out a receipt. Shaz wa adamant they wouldn't, and I kept saying, Well, we'll see, won't we. Argument carried on all t'way up Sprotty Road, all through bus station, through Frenchgate Centre. It wa still going as we walked through town, down pedestrian lane, shops on either side, people pushing past us, buggies and families and gaggles of mates.

"It int reyt to return summat someone's bought ya."

"You said it wouldn't be right for me to wear it."

"But you can't return it and get money forrit, that's even worse."

"What *am* I meant to do, then? Because none of this would even be happening if it wont for you—"

"Me what? Inviting you to a party?"

I could feel her stare but couldn't meet it. I'd managed to stop misen blaming it all on her, but only just.

"Why can't you just gi it back to him?" said Shaz.

"Rach, let me tell her," said Kel.

"Tell me what?" Shaz dashed in front of us, turned to face us, stopped us from walking on. "Tell me *what?*"

I let Kel tell her about voicemails. If I hadn't, Shaz would've only gone on about how we're meant to tell each other everything, how I shouldn't be keeping things from mi best mates, till I broke down and told her anyway.

"What threats?" Shaz wanted to know. "What's he been saying, like?"

I shrugged. "That I should know mi place and shut mi gob." I told her about "whoop-ass," pulling mi fingers into air quotes. "And last night, right, last night he went"—I paused to prepare misen, got ready to imitate his rising cadence—"'Can you smeeEELL—'" I belted it out just like he had, but stopped when I saw Shaz laughing. How could she laugh?

Shaz wa laughing so much she couldn't stop to breathe.

"It's not funny!"

"You div," Shaz managed, then laughing took hold of her again. "Rach, you proper divvy." She wa laughing too much to explain what wa funny. Unlike me, Shaz had an older brother, who'd exposed her tut theatrics ut World Wrestling Federation, tut raw charisma of Dwayne "The Rock" Johnson.

Shaz laughed wi her whole body: happy, free. One of those moments when me and Kel wa so drawn in by Shaz's pull, everything else stopped existing. So we didn't see lad who did it. Didn't see him choose her, lurk behind her, pick his moment. But somewhere int middle of Shaz's cackle, her body easy and loose, really lost in it, joy threading through all t'bones of her, Shaz's tracky bottoms shot off her hips. Down over her thighs, over her knees. They landed ont pavement, cuddling her ankles like a loyal cat. Her daisy-patterned knickers winked int middle ut town centre. Her knobbly little knees. She screamed, pulled her trackies back up.

I caught sight of a lad's head bobbing away fast, dodging through crowd like he might be fleeing scene: baseball cap, tracksuit, just like everyone, just like us all. Tall enough to be mi Dark Stalker, right build.

Why would he keg Shaz instead of me? After being under heat of his focus for weeks, I felt suddenly unspecial. Not worth all that anger, not worth dying for. By t'time he disappeared round corner, I wa sure it wont him. Couldn't've been.

Then I wa filled wi a sense of knowing what to do next, knowing how to take care of Shaz. I led her and Kel by t'wrists, hurried us intut nearest shop, which wa HMV. Felt proper brave, telling manager what'd happened in mi poshest grown-up voice. And him saying, You did right thing, reporting it, leading us through aisles of tapes and CDs. We followed, feeling important, back into a shadowy room I'd never imagined existed. A velvet dark cloaked us, another world. I held Kel's hand, put mi arm round Shaz's shoulders. Four black-and-white tellies switched between views from town's CCTV cameras. Manager said he'd be able to find footage ut incident, that we could see who did it. I couldn't believe this man wa taking us word forrit. I wa so surprised at how seriously he took it, I got scared we'd made it up.

Twelve angles ont same stretch of St. Sepulchre Gate, high angles I'd never looked down from, making summat odd and new of a street I'd walked along all mi life. Cobblestones in sweeping fan patterns I'd never noticed. Spikes crowning shop marquees, white plaggy bag caught in a tree, flapping like it wa Donny's flag of surrender. Twelve angles, and lad who did it warrin none of them.

"Go back," said Shaz. Manager rewound, but we couldn't see anyone's trackies fly off their bodies, couldn't see a baseball-capped head darting away. "Go back again, please." Shaz wa shaking wi silent sobs. I pulled her tighter to me, stroked her shoulder. Wondered warrit wa about Shaz that made people want to do this to her. Wondered how I'd ever envied her this.

"Nowt we can do about it now, mate," I said. "It's happened, annit."

No point trying to take necklace back either. Wouldn't change owt. Mi Dark Stalker would stop eventually, or he wouldn't. Either way I wa done wi lads and their attention. Done wi wanting to be noticed. I'd rather be stood there, int dark, looking after mi girls.

Manager went back and forth, angle this, angle that, till we found what might've been our own grey bodies int milling of many grey bodies. All of us jerky colourless blobs, blotching street forra second, then dashing off.

When We Said Spice We Meant Sweeties

After bumping into Rach fut first time in years, you decide to sack off your audition and get bus home. You can't go into Doncaster wi'out seeing somecunt you know, even if it's just glimmer ut familiar haunting their eyes or cut of their jaw—you know them from little school or nursery or your last temp job, or you see them int pub on a Fridi neet—but nowt's worse than bumping into someone you used to call a mate.

You walk down St. Sepulchre Gate, through Donny town centre towards station, steering in semicircles around zombies in your path. Nearly shop-closing time, just you and zombies in town centre now. You walk fast cuz wind's picking up and ripping through your clothes, chilling your skin as if you're naked already. You hug yoursen, trap your thin coat between your arm and your belly. You think of Rach's quilted pink parka, its fur-lined hood. You wish you hadn't let her hurry you into Costa, purra steaming mocha in your hands, talk about old days, wit burning mug waking your nerves. You wish you hadn't sat there lerrin your limbs defrost—now outside is harder to bear, a cold you can't ignore, like your niece's nipping fingernails when she wants your attention, pinching thoughts out your head.

In your pocket, you fidget wit stolen bra-and-thong set, twisting thong round your fingers. Trim catches hangnail sliver sticking from your thumb. You pull down ont fabric so sliver digs sharp intut nail bed. You dig your teeth into your bottom lip, pull down again. Stings, but it's addictive and you keep yanking sliver back.

You count number of permanently shuttered shops int early dusk. Too early, it's only five, but you're in those bleak weeks again, after daylight savings and before Christmas buzz. Jeweller where you wa eleven when you bought your first gold hoops, sign int window saying "We have moved" wi an arrow pointing to nowier. Record shop, Body Shop, cobbler's, even one of town's four Maccy D's is gone. Clothes shops change hands every six months. Mobile shops vanish one by one, replaced by bookies and vape shops called Vype. HMV's still thier, but only cuz it's rebranded itsen HMV Vinyl. You pass three travel agents and can't believe they're still going. What daft cunt who can afford to go abroad still spends their Satdis gerrin ripped off in Thomas Cook? You pass Savers, Poundworld, pawn shop, banks. Shop windows are steamy bright, mekkin outside feel darker. Drizzle hits you—you hunch your shoulders, tuck in your chin. You're about to turn into Frenchgate so you can cut through shopping centre tut bus station int warm. Few yards from French-gate's entrance, outside Tut n Shive, a zombie sways ont pavement. You stop. You watch her.

You don't know why this zombie meks you stop. You see zombies all ovver, dodged loads ont way here and ont walk to work this morning—tut Market, where you watch your sister's stall cash-in-hand so you can still claim your Jobseeker's. Well, it *wa* cash-in-hand till you couldn't gi your sister what she wa asking for room and board. Now you're working off what you owe. Your Gemma sells babby clothes and accessories, but she's too pregnant at moment to stand all day shouting, Bespoke christening bonnets two forra fiver! You nicked bra-and-thong set off her neighbour while he warron his tea brek. His stall's called Ladies B Sexy N Adored, so you don't feel sorry fut cunt.

Market's another thing you can't believe still exists. Your Gemma's stall sits int decrepit outdoor bit ont edge ut red-light district. Council have put up signs saying "Old Irish Middle Market," trying to mek yas proud of your heritage, but it dunt matter how many centuries it's stood there; it's still just rows of rotting wood sheds and shipping containers, flogging sem knockoff sports gear, gimp masks, Kalvin Cleins.

Your Gemma'll go mad if she finds out you've thieved from Ladies B Sexy, even though she knows he lifts his stock from back of a lorry. She'll say she never should have trusted ya and she only took yas in cuz no-cunt else'll have ya. You had to move in wi her and her fella and her three babbies after you got let go from Amazon warehouse. She's already ont verge of kicking you out since there's not enough room in her two-bed terrace anyway and she's sick of ya body ont sofa every neet when she wants to watch *Love Island* or *Strictly*. That's why you've gorrer go to your audition at Bentley's, but you can't bring yoursen, not now you've sin Rach, who dint even bother asking what you're doing for work. You know Rach is still a secondary school teacher cuz you've still gorr'er on Facebook. But she dint ask, as if she already knew answer would embarrass you both. As if she knew you'd got stolen lingerie in your pocket, knew you warrabout to gyrate against a pole. As if she knew your Gemma's fourth babby warrabout to mek you homeless.

You couldn't have told her you wa off to Bentley's, couldn't have coped if she'd laughed and said aren't you a bit old? If she'd gi'en you that look she always gev you when she thought you wa chatting shit. Rach wanted to talk about back int day, naughtiness you gorrup to together—how much it affected *her* when *your* mate Arms-Out died—before she fucked off to uni, before she stopped texting thee. No mention ut way she'd been purrin distance between yas ever since you left school, started acting like she wa too good for ya, like she dint wanna keep you too close.

This zombie is swaying ont spot outside Tut n Shive's tall windows, swaying side to side like her shoulders are willing her toes to shift. She's in grey tracky bottoms and a grey jumper, no coat. She's skinny. Her arms hang. Her clothes hang off her like you wish yours would. Above her tracky bottoms, her hips are bared like blades.

You tek quiet steps towards her till you're a yard or two away. Int Tut, TV drones: footy commentators, stadium chants. You watch her sway. You will her toes to unstick themsens from pavement, tek her out ut dusk and into somewier warmer, somewier chavs can't find her.

Drizzle sets in, stokes mist. Damp hangs int air, softens buildings, wraps you in a blanket. Zombie's outfit matches evening's mood, like she's a wisp-thin model in a *Vogue* shoot. Her jumper is mucky in places and pilling. You wonder how long she's been in it. She tilts forwards like a pin drawn by a magnet. You step closer till you can hear her breathe, quick and shallow. On her inhale summat catches in her throat, meks her breath coarse as saw teeth running through wood. You're near enough to count lines around her eyes: about sem as yours, but she could be years younger. Late twenties, mebs, or early, depending on how hard she's hit it. Her wrists poke from her sleeves and her ankles from her wet plimsolls, bluish red from being out int wind, and you wonder if she can feel cold.

You're reyt in front of zombie, but she's staring reyt through you as if you're a shop window, your head just another pane of shatterproof glass. Is she looking at nowt? Or can she see past Donny town centre altogether, past t'mush and drudge of everyone's lives.

You've sin zombies outside Mansion House resting their heads on bins. Zombies cuddling lampposts and sculptures, clinging to metal railings like babbies to their mam's legs. You've sin zombies down Colonnades bent double, stroking paving slabs, caressing bollards. Zombies laid int street, bodies twisted into esses and zeds, sick on their trackies, limbs looking broken and boneless. Slumped together in bus stop shelters, heads hanging heavy off necks. You've watched Facebook videos of zombies trying to stand, trying to speak, trying to climb fences, trying to sleep in shop doorways, string a hammock between trees, while blokes wi smartphones ask, Why would you do it to yoursen. Why would you tek Spice, brother? Your town's new nickname is Spice-caster. But summat about this zombie meks you wonder, what's she looking at that you can't see?

Last time he gorrout Doncatraz, your Kyle shook his head when he told you about Spice. You get hooked on that, you're fucked, Shaz. You smoke that shit, I'll kill you misen. And you knew he meant it; he wa that kind of big brother. He sez he did it forra while inside, even though first time he took it he woke up in hospital. He sez comedown is worse than coming off smack. Bellyache is so brutal only cure is more Spice. Everyone tries it, he reckons, cuz it sounds harmless—synthetic cannabinoid, fake weed. He knows blokes who dropped dead of heart attacks and strokes in there, and it still sells faster than they can gerrit inside. They hide it in books and post it to inmates. They get arrested just to carry it in. They throw it ovver prison walls stitched inside dead birds. No market forrit ont festival circuit or club scene, your Kyle sez, so they pummel prisons instead.

You remember when "spice" just meant sweeties, pick 'n' mix in crinkly bags, white chocolate mice, red liquorice whips. You asked your Kyle why do Spice if it's so bad, and he shrugged and said to escape. He told you more stories: bigger lads gerrin two ut smaller lads smoked up, then stripping them naked. Tie ropes round their shoulders and chests, mek em fight like pit bulls. Little lads on all fours, barking and growling and snapping their jaws. Or gerrem so fucked they can barely stand, then twat em int face hard as you can.

Everyone cheers when they drop, dead weight, their heads going smack ont concrete.

This zombie looks chosen, like she's leaning towards god. She reminds you of a lass you went to school wi, or you've sin her round town, or she's somecunt's niece, or sister, or she's thee. Has she got babbies waiting forr'er somewier? Would you have been mates if you warrint sem class? You wonder when she tipped, when she stopped being in charge of Spice and Spice gorrin charge of her. You reckon you know summat about lerrin a monster in. As a lass, you wa dead sure you warrin control of your dieting, your binging and purging, till you realised beast you'd opened door to wa bossing *you* about. You wonder if zombie feels escaped.

Wait for her to see you. Wait for her to get hersen away from Tut n Shive's windows, tall and thin in a row like a set of gleaming teeth. Glass is bright, reflecting pub's floodlights, Halifax building across way, and last ut dying sun. But you can see shapes beyond glare, hairy arms, knuckles bent around honey-coloured pints. How many blokes in there are half watching zombie while they belch along tut footy? Even though your Kyle reckons Spice has been around ages, you still think of zombies and Brexit as twin plagues. Sem year zombies filled streets, blokes wi bulldog tats filled pubs wi chat about gerrin England "back."

You and Rach talked about Brexit forra second in Costa, trying to avoid silence between sips of your mochas. Part of you wanted Rach to ask how you voted, just so you could mek her squirm when you told her you'd voted remain, cuz dint she know your whole area wa surviving on grants from t'EU? She wouldn't expect you to have facts like that. You reckon Rach voted leave because of how quiet she warron Facebook before referendum, like she knew it wa wrong but she wa doing it anyway, and afterwards all she posted wa, "We've gorrus answer now, move on." Rest ut country thinks people from your end are thick as owt and racist, but you're not pissed off at ones wi no money and no hope. You're mad at Rach, who thinks her choice waint cost her. You're mad at rich cunts at top who lied to every-cunt-else.

Come on, lass, you say silently to zombie. Move them feet. Your feet are sore from standing behind stall all day. Chill is sneaking into your boots.

Your jeans pocket vibrates. Text from your Gemma: *What's takings for today?*

Every time you go back wi less than twenty-quid profit, your Gemma accuses you of being ont tek, but that's only cuz she can't face fact that Donny Market's dead.

£7.85

You best be kiddin Shaz.

Only sold two 2—4—1s on bonnets and had to gi a discount cuz one wa stained.

Fucksake. You gerrin paid for toneet?

You dint tell your Gemma about audition; you said you wa helping a mate out wi a job. Bentley's manager did say any money you mek is yours. Minus t'house fee, minus 30 percent commission.

Should be.

There's an hour till you're meant to be there in your bra and thong. You could wait int Tut, keep watch ovver zombie. Voddy and Coke is £3.50, though. That's your bus fare home, plus some of Gemma's takings.

Zombie still ant moved. Her trackies look ready to fall down any second. You pull down ont thong in your pocket, mek your hangnail sting. Fuck Rach, you've gorrer go to that audition. Your Gemma'll have you out ont street if you don't start mekkin rent. You step past zombie, push open pub door.

Inside is mostly what you expected: half a dozen middle-aged blokes wearing footy shirts ovver jeans, blurred tattoos and balding, dotted across pub's wood tables. Torsos angled at projector screen, hands cradling pints, arms folded ovver beer-pregnant bellies. It's Liverpool v. West Ham. They're all mesmerised by t'match. None of them are watching zombie.

You tek a fiver out ut stall's petty cash purse, buy your voddy and Coke—buy a double, fuck it—and sit at a table by t'window, next to where zombie still sways ont pavement. She's just other side ut glass, cheek turned to thee. You can see green vein forking round her eye socket.

Gemma: *Sick of this shit Shaz. Come back wi fifty for ya board or dunt come back.*

As if you even wanna go back to your Gemma's, babbies screaming everywier and your Gemma's fella always int front room wi a can of Carling and *Match ut Day*. He stops up late, and you can't have settee to sleep on till he guz to bed. He always eyes you sideways when it's just yous two sat watching *Top Gear* reruns or his footy shite. Always sits five inches too close. Close enough that you know your body responds to his scent. Nowier to think in that house.

And if you can't think at home, where can you think? How do you think your way out? You've been trying to get your own house for years. You don't even need house nomore. A room that's just yours, a door you can close, that'd do.

You got put in a clinic once, when you warra kid, a special unit for lasses wi eating disorders. You've never been anywier quieter than that clinic. It felt like first time your thoughts unwrapped themsens and laid flat. Too quiet at neet, like, just you wi your plastic mirror and your NHS sheets, an hour's drive from your family and your mates. Just you and your brain unfurling all t'thoughts you dint wanna think. That wa what you loved about hunger: it wa loud. It dint let owt else speak.

You sip slowly—you can't afford a second drink, and you've still gorrer wait about forty-five minutes before you can head up

Hall Gate to Bentley's. All you know about Bentley's is it used to be a charity shop, it sits between Christ Embassy Church and Army Careers Centre, and apparently some lass got smacked outside there one neet because she wouldn't sleep wi a bloke after he paid forra private dance. Ont other hand, you've heard lasses there do alreyt for money.

Your phone vibrates again and this time it's Rach. *So good to bump into you today, lovely! Thanks for the natter! What you up to next Saturday? Fancy drinks? Cheeky night round town for old times? Bottomless proseccos at Mañana, be rude not to* 😜

You picture it, you two out boozing again like old days, drink unclenching yas enough to have a proper giggle, no awkward pauses like there warrin Costa. When wut last time you belly laughed wi a real mate? You can't say you ant missed it. Your thumbs hover ovver your phone's keyboard, flirt wit idea of texting back.

Back when you, Rach, and Kel wa bezzies. Back when you hated losing time. When your mam wa never happier smoking weed till she passed out, losing a day to snoozing in front of *Trisha* and *Jeremy Kyle*. You wanted none of that. You wanted coke and speed and MDMA—whatever would keep you awake. You even liked comedowns, sensation like you'd been scraped out wi a fingernail, like your guts had been raked across gravel car park. You loved buying three Bacon Double Cheeseburgers from BK for brekkie and scoffing them ont bus into school, and your belly taut but still wanting more. And throwing it all up after first period. You always wanted more: more laughs, more highs, more scabs, more lads, more lasses, more raves, more scars, more gorge, more starve, more awake and aching at three a.m., no idea why your battered body waint shut down.

Ont street, young lad in a posh black overcoat and leather gloves pauses to tek zombie's picture wi his phone. Others' lips bend into frowns, like they've smelled summat rotten. Most keep eyes ont ground and avoid her.

Your thumbs wiggle, trying to decide where to start. You tap out, *Alreyt R*—then hammer delete key till all t'letters disappear.

How can you go out round town wi Rach? Even if you had money, you stopped going out round town years ago, after you got sacked from your bar job for breaking a pint glass. Lad whose face t'pint glass broke against had done summat bad to you when you warra kid, med you promise never to tell. You knew there wa no point telling, anyway. Who'd believe ya? You *dint* know all those years of keeping quiet would build up.

You could've gone down for GBH like your Kyle. For use of a weapon. For wounding. Still, you said nowt about the summat bad the lad did. Not even tut police. Duty solicitor that neet told you to say nowt but "no comment." You sat mute int interview room while coppers tried to coax you into saying summat in your own defence. CPS dropped charges int end, due to lack of evidence. Lad who got glassed med a statement, said it wont you who threw pint pot. He dint see who threw it, he told them, but it def wont you.

This is Donny, though, where official record dunt meant owt, where everycunt is mates wi every-other-cunt's cousin. Whole town knew you after that as Psycho Slag. You could tell Rach wa thinking about it today but dint ask. Event is stuck tut sides ut friendship now, stink of it lingering like bits of fish finger splattered ont walls of a microwave. You wa silently daring her to mention it, just to see what it'd do to ya, just to see if it'd prise open your lips.

You almost got courage to tell her that neet, when coppers let you use phone. You called her, ready to tell the summat bad the lad did, but she'd already heard someone else's story about the broken pint pot, already med up her mind about it. She stopped answering your messages after that. And you dint have Kel to lean on neither, thousands of miles away in America, busy wi her marriage, int wrong time zone for phone calls. You dint leave your mam's house for six months. You ate nowt but rice crackers and cottage cheese.

You warra fossil beneath bedsheets by time she med you gerrup and claim dole before she kicked you out.

You couldn't get pub job anywier except Bar Aruba, where you worked till manager "forgot" to order your taxi after post-work drinks, forced you back to his bare flat that dint have any chairs, laid across mattress ont floor, and invited you to "sit down." After that you med it a month at working men's club, even though on your first shift landlord med you hold black Aftershock in your mouth for sixty seconds, a test of your suitability fut role. He timed you, your mouth burning wi liquid aniseed. You lasted a month even though he wouldn't shurrup about "them darkies." Even though punters asked you and other barmaids to put pencils beneath your tits to test whether or not they wa saggy. It wa just banter, though. Pure fucking bants, innit.

After that you couldn't stand behind a bar nomore, on show, waiting for some bloke to mek a joke about you and crack his mates up. You couldn't keep your job at Primark cuz every time stock went missing, supervisor blamed you. Sales jobs you lost for being too aggressive wit customers, which you dint mean to be—it's only cuz team leader kept on at you to mek your targets and your KPIs. You kept trying to turn your volume down, but you never seemed to please folk. You wa beginning to think folk just dint wanna be pleased. You worked nights at Texaco garage, but you quit after one too many blokes med one too many threats ont other side ut Plexi-glas service window. And just you alone at four a.m. under fluorescent lights like a doll behind museum glass. Blokes drunk, their arms swinging heavy, more deadly, and they'd bang glass wi tattooed knuckles, reckon they'd rip off garage shop's locked door and rape you, kill you, if you wouldn't tek an IOU forra bag of Flamin' Hot Monster Munch. One lad pulled exchange drawer out far as it would go, spat in it, and slid it back.

Now everyone you know wi a job is working Amazon ware-house, and you gev that a go an' all. In training, they told you Amazon respects Donny workforce, because we're hard workers, aren't we? We've got that Yorkshire grit. We know how to graft, and Amazon are very impressed wi that. They *dint* tell you how many people in Donny are dezzy forra job, how they'd turf you out in two weeks or less, replace you wit next poor cunt dezzy forra paycheque, if you dint keep your speed up. After that you applied for your Jobseeker's, but since Tories invented Universal Credit, you had to wait six weeks for your money to come in, and by then ya mam said she wa sick of you freeloading, so you had to move in wi your Gemma.

And you don't feel any better, do ya. After use of a weapon, after wounding. After gerrin sacked, starving yoursen delirious, tekkin any wage for any job from anycunt who'd have ya. The summat bad is still in there. You still feel like smashing everything to shards.

Your phone buzzes. Rach: *It'd be my treat, obvs!*

Oh aye, yeah, so she can buy you pity drinks to mek hersen feel better, then drop you again whenever it suits her. You're too wound up to think what to say back, so you put phone away, pull bra and thong from your coat pocket, lay them ont table in front of you. They're a garish Valentine's Day red. Thong is elasticated, coiled up, and you know it'll pinch your hips when you wriggle it on int Tut's loos. It'll hug tight, bulge your fat either side ut fabric strip, cut into your skin, rub. Bra's got no wire, no padding, none ut armour you need. It's two triangles of polyester lace. You try to see yoursen grinding in front of strangers in just this bra and thong. But instead of you, it's one ut lasses from Bentley's website you imagine in this underwear. Her hair is long and lush wi extensions, she's had her boobs done, and she ant got cellulite on her thighs, lumpy as curdled milk. Her fingers are tipped int jewelled claws all lasses have now, patterned and shellacked like Rach had on.

You booked audition cuz pole is what lasses are meant to turn to when they're broke. But you realised, looking at website forran idea of what underwear to steal, that it int enough, anymore, to be willing to bare flesh. Stripping's for lasses wi savings and self-esteem.

You need a Brazilian and a leg wax, balayage and threaded brows, falsies, contouring, a vajazzle. You need another payday loan just to look part. You already tek a new one out every month to pay off one before, ever since you borrowed two hundred quid two years ago to get Christmas presents for your nieces and nephew.

Bentley's lasses will be ten years younger than thee. They'll have proper pole training. They'll know how to go upside down. Everyone got fed up wi Zumba and they're all tekkin pole classes now.

Outside, two birds in leggings walk up to zombie, their hair pulled into high buns. They stop in front of her like you did. You can't hear what they're saying ovvert footy match, but you think one calls zombie a silly slag. You lean closer tut window. Glass fogs where you breathe. You still can't mek out their words, so you unlatch window, push it open a smidge. Wind and noise chase each other in, mekkin two blokes next to you turn and notice you fut first time. Rain dabs ont table. You catch bits and bobs of what birds are saying whenever telly guz quiet.

". . . proper fuckin rank . . ."

". . . mek em go somewier else . . ."

". . . menna fuckin go, like?"

". . . giz a fuck . . . not round people's kids . . ."

One of them leans towards zombie, and you feel yoursen clench like you're ready to climb through window. But she dunt smack zombie like you feared. She shouts in zombie's face: "Ant you gorrany respect for yoursen, duck?"

Zombie's swaying picks up speed, as if her body wants to say summat back but her tongue won't stir. *Go* on, lass, you think, your eyes fixed on her, as if heat of your stare might unfreeze her. You want her to jerk to life, scare shit out of these two birds.

Zombie keeps swaying. Birds walk on.

Bloke ont next table leans ovver to you. "It's not Halloween yet, love."

His mate snickers, then stops and sez, "Barry, it wa last week."

You look round. Barry's a bald footy bloke wi watery lips, his mate rattier, shrunken but sem. Barry points at bra and thong. You gi him dead-eye, stuff them back in your pocket.

"What you going as, like?" Barry asks, not about to let reality ruin his punch line. "A prozzy?" Barry's mate laughs again. "I'll go as your pimp if you like, love." They both crack up.

"I'd rather eat mi own face."

More footy blokes are looking at you now.

Barry sez, "You can *sit* on mi face."

You want to rip Barry's ears off his head, push his eyeballs into his skull in wi your knuckles. You feel all those blokes staring, so you say, "Get t'fuck," tek another swig of your drink. It wa better than nowt, but you wish you could've nobbled him wi summat witty. You used to be lass who could tek owt and gi it back twice, defend hersen and her mates to anycunt, no matter how hard they thought they wa. You used to be a never-ending comeback machine.

"Oooooh," one of them sez. "Watch out, lads, she's fiery, thissun."

You used to be quick, but these days it feels like you're always staring through years of staying up too late. You're staring through layers of tired, like you've always gorra cold, like your face is stuck behind inch-thick Perspex, like everycunt who speaks to you is a shade too far away. Like you want to tell everyone you're not stupid or owt, it just teks a minute for sound to turn into words.

Rach must've thought you'd gone brain-dead cuz of how quiet you wa. You're mad at yoursen because you couldn't stop her going on, couldn't think of owt funny to say. She talked your tongue into a dry sponge. You let her words roll ovver you, fill space around yas till you wa both sinking in her voice. You're mad at yoursen for not saying owt when Rach started moaning about zombies wi'out mentioning their name, as if not using word "zombie" meant she wont being insensitive. She kept saying, How depressing is town centre now? I'll be doing Christmas shop at Meadowhall, me. I want fairy lights and mulled wine, d'you know warra mean? You did know what she meant, but her meaning wa so silk smooth you couldn't grasp it and show it to her, tell her it wa fucked.

Outside, a familiar body walks past zombie, wrapped in a quilted pink parka. Rach looks up, spots you through window. Her brows draw in like she's puzzled—or performing puzzled. Her mouth ices to a hard line, lips pressed pale yellow. She meks fut pub door.

She brings smell ut damp in wi her, rustle of shopping bags, wends between footy blokes, stops by your shoulder. "Alright, lady," she says, in that false-friendly chitchat voice women who hate you use. "I thought you had to gerroff home."

You can't even remember what excuse you gev for leaving Rach in Costa; you just ran out of tether and had to go.

"Do you wanna sit down," you say, cuz Rach is hovering ovver you.

Rach dunt move. "You said you couldn't stop for another drink because you've gorrer babysit your sister's kids."

An irate footy bloke sez, "Are you sitting down then, love?" Rach's shadow is cutting into Liverpool v. West Ham. A flicker ut match plays across her coat.

You look up into Rach's eyes, find fire there. She's steaming for some reason, like everyone dunt gi little white lies to be polite—like it would've been better if you'd said, I've gorrer go cuz when I'm round you I feel like I'm gunna explode.

"Have you not got owt to say?" Rach does a quick harsh laugh that's really a non-laugh, that really means, *Are you fucking kidding me, Shaz?*

There's a humming in your arms and legs; they're itching to flex. You stare up at her, dare your mouth.

"Will you shift out bloody way, love," sez irate footy bloke.

You say, "You'd better go if you're not gunna sit."

Rach draws hersen up; her mouth jets a little outraged "pfft" of air. She swivels on her heel, rustles through door and down street.

You wind your fingers round thong in your pocket, squeeze till elastic bites your skin. You knock back rest of your drink and, fuck it, get a second wi what's left of your Gemma's takings. You tek a long sip, check your phone: half hour till audition. You open Rach's message again, watch cursor blinking int empty reply box. No point responding now, is there. Not a chance her invite still stands.

And you want it, now it's gone. You wish you could text back, *Aye, go on, then.* Even white-knuckle, bite-tonguing it through a neet out wi Rach would've been better than another neet on your Gemma's settee, tensing every time her fella leant towards ya. It would've been better than a lot of things.

Street's starting to fill. Evening's lapping ont edge of rowdy, groups of lads and lasses laughing, echoes round empty shop buildings. Pub'll be filling soon, heaving wi folk tanking up before heading tut clubs, and zombie'll be int window like a painting hanging ont wall. How ant her leg muscles cramped? How ant they just gi'en up and buckled under her?

Cold air leaks through open window, but you don't shut it. You don't want to shut her out. Footy match ends—no-cunt won—and barman rolls up projector screen. Footy blokes look round, searching for other amusement.

Ont street, three lads swagger intut beam ut pub's floodlights. They're all wearing baseball caps and combat boots, and they're all doing t'chav walk: legs froggy, arms wide, chests puffed. They're like peacocks plucked and ready for violence. They see zombie and stop.

"Oi, oi, boys," sez smallest. "What we got here, then, eh?" His face is prune puckered, scarred beneath one eye, an ugly purple stain. Nobody's put jukebox on yet, so you can hear every word.

Second-smallest holds his phone up, points camera at zombie. "Go on, Denby," he sez tut scarred un. "I've gorrus on Facebook Live."

Denby teks off his hat, stuffs it in his jeans back pocket, licks his fingers, runs them five times fast through his fringe, trying to style it. He puts on David Attenborough's misty posho voice.

"Here we have a fine female specimen of the Donny Zombie," he sez tut phone. "The lesser-known Spicehead Bitch." He licks his lips. "We're live, yeah? We're on Facebook?"

"Yeah, yeah," tallest sez. "Gerron wi it."

Denby grins at camera. "My name is Marcus Denby, yeah? I'm Marcus Denby, Balby born and bred, me, yeah? And if there's any ladies out there—" He licks his lips again. "If there's any ladies out there who like what they see, yeah? Marcus Denby." He laughs, and you see he's missing his top front teeth. His tongue flits like a lizard's ovvert gap. You flinch from disgust, but your fanny flinches from summat else. You want him to know you're watching. You like that he dunt know you're watching.

He slips behind zombie, holds her hips. "Do you want some of this then, darlin?" He thrusts, banging his groin into her arse. She bucks, looks round, trying to work out why she's rocking. You want to hammer your palm ont window, mek him stop.

Denby's thrusting meks zombie's trackies slide down an inch. Band of pale flesh exposed tut neet, tip of zombie's arse peeking. Denby dunt notice, he's chav-walking back tut phone.

"Captain Denby at your service. If any of you ladies like what you see." He flashes his tongue at phone. "How many's watching?" he asks his mates. "Gorrany comments yet?"

Tallest looks ovver second-smallest's shoulder, reads from t'phone in a halting monotone: "'Disgusting'—'Why don't you just kill yoursen love'—'This lot wasting NHS time and money.'"

You shiver at thought of it, a record of your humiliation, a video for strangers to watch and replay, and replay, and replay.

Tallest sez, "Oi, Denby, she likes ya, she's dropping her kegs for ya."

Denby turns to check, laughs dry and harsh like a duck, meks a display of pissin hissen laughing. He puts Attenborough voice back on.

"It's mating season in Spice-caster, ladies and gents. And this zombie bitch is in heat." He puts his face up to hers. "You horny for me, darlin? You gerrin wet for Captain Denby?"

Zombie squints at him like she sees him now, but he's a species she dunt recognise. She grunts, unhhhh, trying to speak. Go *on*, lass, you think. Gi it to em, for fucksake. Her head jerks forwards, a whisper shy of nutting his. He copies motion, meks like he's gunna smash her brains in, then pulls back, laughs again. He spits in zombie's eyes, mekkin you wince, mekkin your skin prickle as if it's your face he's gobbed in.

"Dunt you start wi Marcus Denby, you manky fuckin cunt. Look at ya!"

Her arms swing up to wipe spit away but can't reach. You want to clean it off forr'er.

Tallest sez, "She wants to know why ya won't tek her kegs off, Denby."

"Oh aye." Denby points tut phone. "That still recording?"

Second-smallest nods. "Mikey sez, 'Fuckin dregs of humanity, fuck it int arse, Denby.'"

Denby lowers himsen into a half crouch, teks cautious steps towards her as if he's creeping up on a wild gorilla. "You've gorrer be careful, ladies and gents. Savage animals, these, lots of nasty diseases." He hooks a finger ovvert waist of her tracky bottoms, pulls them down another inch, far enough so you can tell she int wearing knickers.

You bang-bang ont window. Your heart rushes wit noise you med and sting in your palm.

"Oi!" barman shouts behind you. "Pack that in!"

Denby and his mates look round at Tut's windows.

"Who the fuck wa that?" Denby sez, peering through t'glass, looking for thee.

Footy blokes turn towards you.

Barry sez, "Calm down, love."

Now they're all watching you. You neck rest of your drink. Stand, and your legs empty, bone and muscle melting, draining into your shoes till there's nowt but adrenaline keeping you up. You can't think about how many blokes are watching int pub—and god knows how many Facebook cunts. You untangle yoursen from your chair and go outside. Zombie is drenched, her hair cutting black wet stripes across her cheek. Breath fogs from your mouth, rain slips into your eyes. You stick your chin and chest out, put yoursen between zombie and Denby.

You square up to him. "What you filming her fo'?"

"We're filming you now, darlin," second-smallest sez.

"Fuck are you, like, her girlfriend?" Denby sez, squaring up to thee. Now you can smell grease and gravy of his chip shop dinner, see his scar jump as he speaks. He's lean, twitchy, as if he's teeming wi vicious little wants. "Is this your lass? Are you telling me zombie bitches are fuckin dykeinis an' all?" His mates laugh. Denby shrugs wi his whole body—shoulders, eyebrows, feet. "Public service, innit. Someone's gorrer document scum that's infesting our streets."

He's carrying hissen wit righteousness of a union man bravely sticking it to Thatcher, even though it's been decades since anycunt had claim to that kind of pride. Meks you nearly glad pit killed your fatha. He hated Thatcher then and he'd still hate her now. You wa raised to hate her an' all, hate every cell of her, cheer when she died and say, "Ding, dong, t'witch is dead." Your fatha would be like all blokes in your village, and all other villages that used to be built round pits and are now built round nowt. Anger in every follicle, every fleck of skin.

You stare up at Denby, determined not to blink even though

drizzle meks your eyes raw. Quiver in your legs, and your heart's going, and you're steeling yoursen forra fist, but you're not about to lerr'im see. You're not about to back down, no matter what Denby threatens to do wi thee.

"She ant done owt to you," you say. "Just leave her alone."

"Wharra you gunna fuckin do about it, like?" Denby licks his lips, tongue a breath from tip of your nose, drawing nausea from your belly and tingles from your fanny.

"Dunt bother wi her, Denby," tallest sez, his voice deep and comfy. "Scratty old dyke."

"What do you reckon, duck?" Denby sez to you. "Climb on Captain Denby's cock and I'll fuck sense into ya. I'll bone you straight, love. I'll rip you in two."

Laughter erupts from t'pub: Barry, his mate, and a line of footy blokes are stood at windows. They cheer and shout "Wa*heeeeeeey*." Denby and his mates are cackling too, but nobody said owt that funny. You look back at zombie. Her trackies are round her knees. Her fanny is furry between her legs.

Denby's mates dart forwards, phone aloft, trying to gerra good shot.

You tek hold of her trackies, try yanking them up, but zombie teks a long step forwards, knocks you sideways. Footy blokes cheer as you stumble. You get your balance back. Zombie's right leg is out in front of her like it knows rest ut body is knackered and it's trying to brek free. It stretches trackies' elastic waist taut across her knees. She's posed, legs wide, showing her fanny off tut crowd. You need to gerr'er legs closed so trackies will go slack and you can pull them up. You lift zombie's elbow, dip your shoulder under her armpit. She smells like soggy salt and vinegar crisps. She seems flimsy, like she'd brek in half if you let her fall. You press knee of her front leg, trying to coax it back towards other. She heavies as you hold her. Strain pulls at muscles in your belly.

Footy blokes are rolling out banter:

"Is she tryna rape a zombie, like?"

"Dirty little zombie dykes."

"Zombie love, lads. Zombie love!"

You lodge your leg behind her bare arse to gi her anchor. You push against her kneecap. It wriggles beneath your hand but waint budge. You push hard as you dare wi'out hurting her, but it's as if her foot is nailed down.

Denby's Attenborough again. "This, ladies and gents, is what we call Retard Zombie Shuffle."

Zombie's leg finally gives and you can lift her knee. As you pull her legs closed, her head snaps towards yours. She looks you stret int eye. She shouts haaaaaaagh in your face, her breath rancid wi days-old smoke. Her body is a squirming fish. You let go. Her trackies fall to her ankles. Her white calves are lollipop sticks int dark.

Then her arms are flailing at you. Fists meet your chest. Her cold little fists, and you don't mind—you'll tek it—each punch thumping sense into your lungs. Each thud sparkling bright across your skin. Neet guz quiet round your head. It's just you and zombie int yellow bubble ut floodlights, till all you can feel is drum of her knuckles, and rain dashing at you, and you'll let her hit till she sends you flying back, till you bash your skull ont kerb.

Denby shouts, "Are you gerrin this, lads? Throw some K-Y on em. It's a zombie dyke fuckin wrestling match."

You're raw, now, wi her blows. She's slow, and next time her fists come you catch them, hold fast. Trackies twist around her feet and she falls into you. You hold her up by her hands.

"Would you just fuck off?" you say to them all. "It's not her fault, she obviously needs help." You mean it, but you feel fake, like you're saying it fut glory. You've watched them Facebook videos. You walked stret past every zombie, till you met her.

"Not her fault?" Denby is like an actor gi'in a rousing speech.

"Did someone mek her tek Spice? Did someone shove it down her throat, like? Someone needs to do summat about this, yeah? Someone needs to tek action, show these scum for what they are. Council won't do owt, coppers won't do owt, so it's up to us."

Your arms are shaking under her weight; you'll have to let go of her soon. If you let go, she'll crumple tut pavement. If you let go and leave, back to your Gemma's to beg forra bed or up to Bentley's to dip low and spread your knees—though you dunt know which cuz you dunt know which is worse. Denby's fizzing beside you, itching to fuck yous or smack yous or both. You can't see how you'll get zombie's fucking trousers back on.

Then zombie's gone from your arms. She straightens, looks down, sees her trackies pooling ovver her plimsolls, pulls them back up. She locks her eyes on Denby like a wolf locking ontut scent of a hare. She lunges.

He steps back, out way. He sez, "Alreyt, love, calm down."

Zombie guz for his face, pinches his cheeks, pulls fistfuls of his hair. Denby pushes her off, his hair tufting up, his whole face purple as his scar. He's still laughing like an actor.

Zombie screams, a loud, high-pitched pterodactyl screech.

"Mind yoursens, lads," sez Denby. "She's gorra temper on her, thissun."

She screams again, and it fills you up, shudders your guts, trembles you like it's got strength to brek you open, like it's got power to crack tarmac down tut water pipes.

You scream wi zombie. Scream from your belly, hit sem ear-bleeding pitch. Shrieks bounce off shop fronts, fill street. A glass-shattering opera note bellows from your lungs. Thunders from you like a glorious stream of sick.

Tallest starts backing off. Second-smallest puts phone away. Then they're all retreating, stepping back intut neet. You know Denby's shouting at you summat obscene, but you can't hear owt ovver your own noise. You and zombie scream till lads are spun around and gone.

You shout at footy blokes, "Fuck are you looking at?" then turn away, shut your ears off to their clever comebacks. And you laugh to yoursen at how mad you must look, and names they'll be calling you all neet, and names they'll be calling you ont internet forever.

Then you're panting and empty and sharp scrape down your throat. Around you, neet's silent and still like a beautiful pocket of nowt. Like you've cleared a space to think.

Zombie staggers. You catch her shoulders, ease her down ontut kerb, sit beside her.

"You alreyt, chuck? Is there somewier I can tek you? Somewier you can get warm?"

Zombie's eyes find yours again. Hers are blue, darker blue streaks shooting from black middles. She smiles, and you know by t'shyness of her grin she's definitely younger—mebs a decade younger than thee.

"Scared him, din ah?" She laughs.

You nod, your pulse still slowing, your heart still singing.

"Ah've gorra degree, me," she sez. "You think ah'm thick, but I wa good at school, me."

You pull red knickers from your pocket. "Dunt lose these," you say, fold them into her hand. She nods, holds them limply.

"What's your degree in?" you ask.

She does her shy smile again, lays a finger to her mouth like she's thinking. You wipe her face, scour Denby's spit wi your coat sleeve, and she lets you, eyes closed, happy, way your niece looks when you're brushing her hair. You don't know if homeless shelters will tek zombies. You don't know if she's homeless. You don't know how to ask. You do know you can't carry her there, couldn't tek her if she leaned on you, couldn't bear her weight.

You put your arm round her. She rests her head on your shoulder. You're proud of yoursen for asking about her degree instead of pretending not to hear. But you're glad she dint answer. Glad you can stop a bit longer not knowing if it should be her tekkin pity on thee.

Shake a Bridle over a Yorkshireman's Grave

Kel had promised to tek Ando tut "Skaghead House," but only if he dint tell anyone else. So when he showed up wi Cleggy, of all wankers, two of them fighting their way through a hole int unruly hedge, mekkin branches swish and whip, trainers squelching from falling intut dyke that edged house's backyard, Kel dint feel sorry for either of them fut scratches on their hands, for their cold soggy feet.

Everyone at school had been talking about abandoned house ont edge ut moors, how you could brek in and no-one would call coppers because no-one cared, and skagheads who went there to shoot up left beer int fridge and weed and coke stashed in secret spots upstairs. Kel couldn't bring hersen to tell anyone that Ska-ghead House belonged to her family. Summat hot and poisonous flushed through her, neck to belly, every time she thought about people knowing. She couldn't resist showing off to Ando, though, bragging that she knew where it wa. When he'd asked how she knew, she shrugged and smiled mysteriously; she said I know everything, me. He'd said, As if you do, ya gobshite, insisted she wa fibbing till she promised to prove it. She dint think he'd actu-ally *mek* her prove it—she dint think she'd really have to brek in to her dead grandparents' house—till they wa already stood int dark yard, Cleggy snickering and muttering, Is this it.

Ando said, "Go on, then." He nodded at house, which wa being eaten by a giant vine, walls shushing and rustling int wind.

There wa only one window left that wont covered wi ivy, dense curtains that had reached intut house's openings like arms down throats. Kel searched yard's borders, felt amongst weeds, looking forra throwing brick. Ivy blanket towering above her med her think of that Christmas song, and Grandad, who sang it. And holly bush by t'back door—dint she prick her fingers ont leaves' spikes when she wa tiny?

Int rubble heap at bottom ut yard, beneath gloom ut plum tree, Kel's fingers found a chunk of breeze block small and light enough to chuck. She carried it back tut house, where lads wa kicking around wi their hands in their pockets. Ando hadn't even kissed her hello; he wa always offish when Cleggy wa there. Kel nuzzled his chest—his cue to hug her—said, "Ey up, then." He coiled an arm round her waist, planted a peck ont top of her head.

Kel hoisted block onto her shoulder. She dint know whether to hurl it like a javelin or two-hand it like a volleyball—she dint know if she should even be doing this. She could hardly remember her grandparents, just barest snatches of them int fog of childhood, prickly silver moustache, frilly tartan edge of a gravy-stained pinny. Still, it dint seem right, smashing your way into a dead person's house.

"Come on, lass," Ando said. "Ant you brock into owt before?"

Kel dint think she believed in ghosts, but out there, wit moors at her back, invisible miles of wildness sprinting intut ink-black nothing, she could've sworn she felt someone stood int dark beside her. A fourth someone.

If Kel wa going in, it had to be tonight. Tomorrow, whole family wa showing up to finally gut place. Everything inside would be shoved into charity bags or burned or binned. If she dint go in now, she wunt get to see what house wa like when her grandparents lived there. She wunt get to nick hersen a souvenir before it all disappeared.

Kel launched block. Quiet ut spring night shattered wit tinkle of breaking glass, skitter ut breeze block hitting floor inside.

Then a whooshing, like a long sigh, and Kel couldn't tell if it wut wind, or hersen sighing, or someone else. She wrapped her jumper sleeve ovver her hand, pulled at a jagged shard still clamped int rotting frame. Ando stood reyt behind her, tugging zip on his coat up and down—zip zip unzip—noise mekkin her feel his impatience. Behind Ando, Cleggy kicked at holly bush. He whistled snippets ut "Cheeky Song," tongue half occupied sealing up a rollie.

She dint know why Ando had to bring him, but she definitely couldn't say *I love you* now, not wi Cleggy there. She wont even sure she did love Ando. A lad at school who wa ont gifted-and-talented list told her once that teenagers can't love. But urge to say it had been clogging her throat for weeks. She wa terrified of it popping out. She kept her gob proper shut, lips pulled in and sealed wi her teeth.

She wiggled glass tentacle faster. Her hand slipped, finger just saved a slicing by jumper sleeve. She buried her hand further into her jumper, gev shard another wobble. She'd took some reyt flack off Shaz and Rach for inviting Ando but not them. They had a proper go at school earlier that day, said she wa one of them fake lasses who ditched their mates when they gorra boyfriend. Kel pointed out that he wont her boyfriend yet. You're a fuckin dougie, then, Shaz'd said, linking arms wi Rach. There's summat up wi ya if ya still fancy that ginner cunt. She'd pulled Rach off across top field, leaving Kel at picnic benches on her tod. They'd be livid—proper fuming—if they found out Cleggy wa there an' all.

Glass spike finally broke free, force of it sending Kel onto her back foot. She chucked spike intut garden's murky fathoms. She put one foot ont frame. It softened and splintered under her boot. Ando tried to lift her other leg.

"Giz a sec!" said Kel.

Ando held up his hands. "Soz, like."

She hadn't been allowed inside since she wa five or six. Her mam reckoned she'd kept her away because house wont safe for kids, but that dint sound like real reason they never visited. Kel's mam dint talk to her own brothers either, which wa probs why house had stood so long after Grandma died. It all stank of a family feud that Kel wont allowed to know about. And there wa no point pestering, begging to be told summat her mam dint wanna tell. In their house, some stuff just dint get said. Kel'd thought that wa normal—at least, she'd thought there wa nowt wrong wi it—till she mentioned to Shaz that her mam'd never told her who her dad wa, wunt even let slip his name. That's mental, Shaz'd said. That's messed up, that.

Kel's mam'd always been like that, though: strict wi her rules, strict wi her words. She'd been less bothered about rules since Briar wa born, but Kel guessed that wa just because she wa knackered. Kel's mam'd been working at call centre int day and tekkin night classes at Donny College, till Briar cem along. Before Briar, their house wa always bare an' all. Once a year, Kel's mam threw away everything Kel owned, claiming it wa minimalism. Now Briar's toys tek up more room than Kel and her mam's stuff put together. They had to buy Briar all new clothes and books because Kel's had been chucked out.

Kel med hersen small, prayed she wouldn't catch her skin ont tiny glass spears still poking from frame, let Ando lift her leg. She jumped through window, intut black ut house, banged her knee ont way down.

Kneecap scrape stinging int pitch black, graveyard chill, earthy smell. Close shapes pressing in: foreign, familiar. She blinked, trying to adjust tut thicker night inside. Hard to tell if she wa seeing curves and angles appear around her, or if she wa hallucinating objects she thought she remembered. A smell she recognised—not Grandma's perfume, more like scent of Grandma's skin. Kel felt five years old, sitting on Grandma's lap. Folds of Grandma's paisley skirt. Swirls of peacock blue and green. A warm, breathing body beneath her. She thought about cemetery just across road, Grandma and Grandad lying there int ground.

Or were they here. Wa some part of them waiting forr'er here? She wanted to be alone wi them. She wanted to go back: unsplinter window frame, unshatter glass, unfind breeze-block chunk. Un—show off to Ando.

Above her, Ando's leg wa feeling its way inside. Kel scrambled to her feet. While Ando tried to help Cleggy in—Cleggy going Fucksaaake every time he ragged hissen ont glass—Kel shuffled forwards, eyes and fingertips searching to mek sense ut space. She could mek out edge ut kitchen worktop, bulk of an eighties fridge. She pulled fridge's handle, which stuck fast forra minute then swung free, spilling light from bare bulb inside. Kel felt like she wa intruding ont bulb's peace. She nearly whispered, Sorry. Would've, if she hadn't been so intent on keeping her gob shut.

Years bulb had sat there, filament intact, waiting for Kel to look in. Fridge's wire racks med Kel think of home-med lemon curd, home-med lemon curd tarts, marg, butterfly buns, jars of home-med jam. Only thing int fridge besides bulb and smell of wet dirt warran old-fashioned bottle of milk, looking ancient and clean. Kind you can only get from milkman, rounded wi a curved lip. It wa missing its silver foil cap. Summat about bottle's soft edges med Kel happy, hollow, sad.

Kel's mam reckoned Kel wa obsessed wi their milkman when she wa little. Used to run tut door when he cem int afternoons to collect their empties, showed him her potato prints, her colouring in, which wa funny, Kel's mam reckoned, because he warra right mardy old bastard. Kel wondered if her mam knew how bad retellings of that story med Kel feel, way she flinched at thought of hersen heaping devotion on a stranger, on some crusty old git.

Ando cem up behind her, stooped, peeked intut fridge ovver

her shoulder. He curled a cheeky hand round each of her boobs. She leaned back into his torso, turned, buried her head in his neck. In her brain she said, *I love you*. She kept her lips bit shut.

Milk bottle had been int fridge for however long it took for milk to split into watery liquid and a cheesy yellow lump. Like milk's core parts were having a barney and wunt talk.

"That is rank." Ando slammed fridge door shut, throwing them back intut dark. Kel wa blind again. Bulb's filament streaked neon pink across her sight. She buried hersen further intut crook of Ando's chest.

"Where's tinnies, then?" said Cleggy.

She shrugged. "Int none. You'll have to go and get some." There warran offy round corner. If Cleggy went on a booze run, Kel could be alone wi Ando and not say *I love you*, but *mebs* say it—they *had* been seeing each other three months. How long wa you supposed to see each other before you wa allowed to be in love? How long wa you meant to wait before he wunt think you warra psycho for saying it? And if he loved her back, mebs she could tell him truth about Skaghead House. Tell him to tek Cleggy away.

Cleggy med a raspberry noise that meant, *Do I fuck have to go and get some.*

"I'll gi you money forrem," said Kel.

She'd been waiting a lot longer than three months. More like three and a half years—she'd fancied Ando since he felt her up behind sports hall when she wa eleven and he wa going on fourteen. He ignored her after that, went round wi all sorts of lasses, and Kel thought he dint like her after all, till years later they ended up at sem house party and she sucked him off ont parents' double bed.

"We'll see." Cleggy liked power of being only one of them wi ID, Ando an August baby, few months off being eighteen. Kel had only just turned fifteen. She'd been buying her own booze forra year, like, but she dint have things she needed—makeup, low-cut top, specific offies in Donny centre who dint care how old she wa.

Out by t'moors, miles from town, only reliable way to get messed up wa to have a mate wi ID. Cleggy knew that. He wanted to mek Kel beg, which she wont about to do. She lifted hersen off Ando's chest, ran her hand ont wall, feeling fut light switch. Her palm slid down smooth, finding nothing.

Big light cem on—another bare bulb, thissun dangling from a wire int ceiling—confronting Kel wit haphazard stacks of crockery teetering ont countertops, walls peeling paint, and Cleggy's stupid fizzog. Blood trickled ovver his eye where he'd cut hissen ont way in. He wa grinning, pleased wi himsen for finding switch, which warrat other end ut room to where Kel'd been sure it wa. Cleggy palmed his forr'ead, trying to staunch cut. Blood wa drying, sticking his lid closed, gluing his lashes down.

Three doors led off from kitchen. Kel opened one she thought led tut living room and found pantry. No room forra body inside, objects layered tut ceiling, which wa slanted by t'stairs overhead. There warra wooden table, short, square, wi sides deeper than an ordinary table. Kel couldn't think what you'd use it for. Shin-high glass bottles, dusty, round wi tall slender necks. She lifted one, looked in. Mouse skeleton inside, curled up as if it'd crawled in there to sleep. Kel put bottle down, shut pantry door. Behind second door, four rickety metal steps led down into a sunken room bristling wi sharp edges, walls covered in rusted pitchforks, pickaxes, scythes. Every other surface loaded wi jars of all sizes, most clear but some white or blue. Most mucky as owt, but some clean. Some lidless, some cracked and chipped. Kel tried to picture Grandma handling these jars, her fingers twisting their lids. She couldn't conjure a memory.

All those years Grandma wa here, existing, and Kel wont allowed to be here wi her, finding out what kind of woman she wa, what she did wi her time. Kel wanted back that smell, those swirly skirts, sense of her grandma's knees beneath her, stout, solid. Where've you gone, she found hersen thinking. Haunt me.

Kel felt her way through third door intut living room, looking forra light. Determined she'd be t'one to find it. Front room wa rammed wi furniture, stuff piled ont floor. They had to go slow, find places to put their feet. Kel knocked a pile wi her toe. Magazines slid round her ankles. A seeping draft told her she may as well not have broken that window. Behind ivy, glass int front room had gone. Skagheads had definitely been in, left a piss stench, pile of crushed lager cans. Why piss ont floor? Wont there a bathroom upstairs? Cleggy lit his rollie, smell ut smoke mekkin Kel want to lend one, but Cleggy'd want paying fut baccy and Kel dint know how to roll, and he'd hold that ovver her an' all. Kel dint know why Ando still hung round wi him, now they wont at school together. Ando wa always on about what a knobhead Cleggy wa. Other week, Cleggy med Ando film him while he took a crap out of a tree. But Cleggy always had a pouch of Old Holborn on him, a baggie of random drugs. Lads like that never ran out of mates completely.

A cone-shaped lampshade sat on a low table. Kel fumbled fut chain. She pulled, slide-click, and room appeared around her: towers of rammel everywhere, like bric-a-brac stall at village fête, so much her eyes dint know where to start.

Int middle of it all wa Ando, pointing a gun at Kel's nose. Black, shaped like a James Bond pistol.

"Freeze, motherfucker!" Ando screamed in a shit American accent. His face, twisted into loathing, like he wa ready to blow her head off.

Cleggy cackled, one eye plastered browny red.

Ando's scowl cracked—he burst out laughing an' all.

"Dickhead," Kel said, heart bleating. She laughed even though her belly wa gone. *I love you.*

"Fucking BB gun, innit," said Ando. "Waint kill ya."

"It will if you fire it reyt at her fuckin forr'ead," said Cleggy, sounding far too pleased about that fact. "Off upstairs, me, see if there's owt worth thieving."

"Doubt it," said Kel. Cleggy edged round a crate of books and wandered intut stairwell. "What if floor's not sound?" she said. "What if you fall through ceiling?" Cleggy's only reply wut thud of his boots ont stairs.

She wanted to go after him, stop him stealing, at least till she'd had a chance to find summat—there had to be summat here, dint there, that belonged to her—but she couldn't tek her eye off gun. She'd never sin a gun before, BB or not. She'd never had a weapon pointed at her head.

Ando kicked at old logs ont hearth. They fell into ash under his foot. He pointed gun at a sturdy metal pot beside grate. It must've been pot a six-year-old lass used to cook dinner in for her family ovvert open fire. One ut few things Kel's mam had ever said about her childhood: dinner had been her job, while rest ut family warrout int fields.

"What you doing?" said Kel.

Ando dint answer. He pointed gun at other objects as if trying to choose a victim. Boxy old telly wi a curved antenna, framed photo of three moustachioed men, porcelain jug, all dust grey and cobweb woolly, all wearing long shadows cast by amber light ut lamp. Kel followed gun's nose as it picked out stalled grandfather clock, rotary phone, teapot buried in a hen-shaped cosy. She stared at everything that cem under t'gun's aim, trying to remember if she'd sin it before, if it meant summat to her. If it'd meant summat to them.

A thistle-coloured settee sat before hearth, med of plasticky stuff that wa cracking at cushion edges, worn away on one arm where someone's elbow would've dug intut sem spot for years. Decades, maybe. Settee cushions wa hidden by stacks of paperbacks. Kel wanted to inspect books' spines, see if Grandma and Grandad liked sem books she did. But there dint seem to be anywhere int living room to live, nowhere comfy to stand, kneel, sit.

Ando swung gun towards mahogany dresser that took up entire back wall. Dresser wa buried beneath bits of paper—bills, receipts, rectangles scissored from newspapers and magazines, rimed wi a layer of filth. On top ut papers sat loose vinyl records, what looked like part of a rusted car engine, a motley collection of teacups, saucers, milk jugs, sugar bowls. Ando swivelled left, pointed gun at a glass-framed watercolour hanging from picture rail.

Kel remembered a little teacup Grandma used to gi her orange juice in, special cup only Kel wa allowed to drink from. Cartoon character ont side. She'd know it when she saw it. If she saw it before Cleggy thieved it or Ando murdered it. If it existed. If she hadn't invented it.

She could hear Cleggy banging around upstairs, whistling, *Oh boys cheeky girls*, *Oh girls cheeky boys*. She moved towards dresser so she could inspect teacup army gathered there, battle-haggard.

Ando turned, aimed again at objects ont dresser. Kel hung back, not wanting to walk intut line of fire. He threatened an open-mouthed plastic baby doll, menaced a commemorative plate fut Silver Jubilee.

"What you doing that for?" said Kel.

"Target practice, innit. Cleggy's on about joining Territorial Army."

But Ando wont on about joining Territorial Army, warr'e? Ando warrat Donny College doing his Painting & Decorating Level 2. Then he wa gunna tek ovver his dad's business and mek a mintoid. So why wa Ando trying to assassinate a royalty collectable?

"You're not gunna fire it, though, are ya?"

"Am ah not?"

"You'll wake neighbours and we'll all get done."

Kel climbed ovver two stacked cabin trunks to get intut tight space where Ando stood. She had to bend her knees to stay balanced there. She put her arms round his neck for ballast. She looked up at him.

"Wunt you rather do summat else?" she said.

"Like what?"

"I dunno, proper frozzen, me."

He purr'is gun hand round her, rubbed her arm fast to get heat going int limb. "I know what we could do to get warm," he said. She loved it when he looked at her like that, long, meaningful stare, eyes heavy-lidded and lazy, and she knew he wanted her.

"Oh aye." She pushed hersen onto tiptoe, pulled his head towards her, pulled their lips together. She moved her leg against his crotch while they snogged. Burst of pride as she heard him moan.

I love you. Maybe she should say it. Maybe she'd just say it and he'd say it back. She dared hersen to say it.

Summat near her ear went *click.* Ando, she realised, had drawn his hands together behind her, aimed at dresser, cocked gun.

She pulled out ut kiss, slapped his arm. "Don't be a twat." Her chin wa doused in his spit. She looked back at dresser to check ont teacups, as if gun could've gone off in silence, bullet cut noiseless through porcelain.

"Your face," he said, giggling.

She laughed along wi him forra second; then she said, "That stuff used to be someone's."

"It's a derelict house, ya spacker. It's been abandoned."

Ando laughed.

Kel laughed.

I love you.

Ando rested his arms on her shoulders like he always did after snogging, weight of him an instant ache. Kel always took it for as long as she could, till it wa too painful and she had to wriggle free. She stared up at him. She'd been doing this for weeks now—staring, burrowing into his eyes, sending messages. But he'd never gone near saying word "love," or "girlfriend," or "missus," or "our lass," and every time she tried to ask where they stood, what they wa doing, what this *wa,* Ando would kiss her, then hug her so tight she couldn't breathe.

"What you staring at me like that fo'?"

"I'm not staring at you like owt."

"You got monk on wi me, or summat?"

Clatter-smash from upstairs, followed by another Cleggy "Fucksaaake."

Kel wanted him out. She wanted to storm up there and say, Fuck off out my house.

Ando bellowed Cleggy's name. They listened. Nowt wa bellowed back.

"Why did you bring him, anyway?"

"I *knew* you wa radged about summat."

"I'm not radged about owt!"

"What's it matter if Cleggy's here?"

Kel's heart flurried uncomfortably, pulse knocking in her head. This int where she'd meant conversation to go. "It dunt matter," she said. "You gunna go and see if he's alreyt?"

"Are you?"

"He's your mate."

Ando took a step back, leant against cabin trunks. Kel's body bled cold int places he'd been touching. She had to bend her knees to balance again. Cleggy started whistling— *Oh boys cheeky girls, Oh girls cheeky boys* —his feet dum-dum-dumming across ceiling.

"He might need warming up an' all." Ando tapped her ont arse wit gun like a dad gi'in a babby a smack. Kel wont sure warr'e meant forra sec. Then it hit her: Ando hadn't just told her to go gi Cleggy what she *thought* he'd just told her to go gi Cleggy. Had he?

His eyes were small, serious. Silence hummed while Kel tried to decide what to say next.

"I'm joking, ya mong." Ando laughed, but there wa summat hard in his laugh, summat sour. "Dunt get face on."

"I ant got face on." Kel tried to change her face, lift tension in her forr'ead.

Ando swiped his hand under her boob and upwards, mekkin it jiggle, and said "Flump," like he always did when he wa trying to mek her laugh.

"Wanker," Kel said, smiling. She play-tapped him int nads, which he tried to dodge and nearly fell backwards ovvert trunks; then he flumped her again, both of them laughing.

"What's in these?" said Kel, bending to inspect topmost trunk. Latches wa rusted shut. Ando pushed up on them, grunting wit effort, till they gev way and lid popped open. Scarves burst up in all colours, birthing themsens from trunk's mouth. Scarves patterned wi roses, checkers, Spanish fans, feathers, some delicate and matte like silk, others hardier wi a sheen. Kel wanted to dig through them, feel their textures, examine their patterns. She wanted to hold them to her nose. Find out if they smelled like Grandma.

But while trunk wa holding Ando's attention, while he wa poking around in it, dragging tip of his gun through topmost layer of scarves, Kel med a dash fut dresser. She climbed ovvert settee, ovvert books, ovvert piles of *Thorne Gazette*, tut back wall where dresser sat beneath its coat of dirty papers, engine bits, teacups. She rifled through tea-cups, searching forra little one wi a cartoon ont side. There wa tall mugs missing handles, terra-cotta cups, cups wi floral, fussy blue pat-terns. Nowt kid-sized or cartoony.

Kel ruffled dresser's dirty papers wi a finger, trying not to feel her disappointment, trying to push it down. She picked up handwrit-ten notes, reminders, receipts. Letters, or bits of. She held pages to her face, tried to mek out words int low light, but her own shadow plunged paper intut too dim. She chose a scrap wi a few lines of doddery biro, carried it tut lamp. Under bulb's unsteady glow, Kel med out words slowly, her brain snagging on tails and curls in odd places, capital letters where they dint belong. Writer wa gunna mek apple and blackberry pie for whoever wa meant to get letter. Last lines read:

GoodBye for Now
as you No I caN-Not
write

Writer seemed to be speaking to Kel, whispering words in her ear. There wa pressure in Kel's head—pressure building behind her eyes, looking for out. She tipped her face tut ceiling, willed her eyes dry.

Cleggy thumped back downstairs. He'd found bathroom, washed his face. Both eyes were open, blood now just a weak pink smear across his brow. He kicked books off settee and laid across it, wet trainers ont armrest where an elbow used to be.

He pulled a baggy of weed from his pocket, started rolling a jay. "Found skaghead's skunk stash," he said.

"As if you did, you lying bast," said Ando, grinning. "That's t'ten-bag you bought off Arms-Out yesterdi."

Cleggy grinned an' all. "Alreyt, you mirthless cunt. I wa just tryna have your lass on."

"Steal owt while you warrup there?" Kel asked, knowing instantly she shouldn't've done. Her voice gev too much away.

"Proper nosy bitch, your lass, int she?" said Cleggy.

Kel wanted to defend hersen, but Cleggy'd called her "your lass" twice and Ando hadn't contradicted him, and that wa mekkin Kel's whole body light up. *Our lass.* To be *our lass.* To be *t'missus.* To be allowed to call him *mi fella.*

"What's it to thee, anyway?" Cleggy asked Kel.

Kel shrugged. "Just someone used to live here, so."

"So? So fuckin what? You're one who brock us in, lass." Cleggy licked long edge ut King Size Rizla, sealed jay. "Now you're gerrin soppy about some dead cunt's old bloomers?"

Kel forced hersen not to ask if he'd stolen any bloomers.

"I'll tell you wharrah *did* find." Cleggy nodded at a cricket bat, which Kel now noticed wa laid at his feet. "Been meaning to get mi batting practice in an' all."

Kel and Cleggy stared at each other. Then they both moved at once: Cleggy stuck jay in his gob and leapt up; Kel lunged fut bat. She grabbed flat end, but Cleggy held handle, ragged bat off her easy, scratching her palm, leaving a splinter int flat of her index. He commando-rolled ovvert settee. She dove fut belt loop ont back of his jeans, clung till he tore hissen free.

He swung bat ovver his shoulder, flat edge pointing in like he warrabout to hit a six, and ploughed through everything ont dresser, smashing intut paper scraps and doll's body and bit of an engine and teacup army and vinyl records and tins of safety pins and buttons, everything tumble-clanging together ontut floor, mekkin it sound like whole house wa coming down. Room wa suddenly brighter: now dresser wa clear, dresser mirror had appeared. They warrall caught in it, looking grimy and ghoulish. Cleggy bashed intut dresser like he wanted to crack it in two. Bashbashbash. Kel tried, but she couldn't get anywhere near fut bat swinging round him.

"Gi oo'er," she said. Bashbashbash. "Gi oo'er, dickhead." Cleggy beat down ont dresser, wood creaking, splitting. "Oi," Kel said, louder. Bashbashbashba—"Oi, that's mi fuckin grandma's!"

Bashing stopped. Silence wa enormous.

Cleggy turned round, panting. "Should we tell her?"

A choky, nauseous feeling expanded like a spring in Kel's windpipe.

"Tell me what?"

Ando stared at her, squinting, deciding.

"Tell me bastard *what*?"

"We knew," Cleggy said. He shrugged, looking sorry forr'er. "We knew this wa your nan's gaff."

Kel looked at Ando, waited forr'im to deny it.

He looked away. "Cheers for that, Clegg."

Kel felt lopsided, like floor beneath her wa sloping. "As if you did know," she said. "No-one knows."

"He's joking," said Ando. "He's having you on."

Cleggy looked uncomfortable fut first time since Kel had known him. It wa like he'd gorra new face, flat and creaseless. He tapped bat against dresser's leg, stared at floor.

"Can't tek a joke, like?" said Ando.

Still she wa slanted—still t'floor wa trying to throw her sideways—but laughter kissed her lips from inside, wanting to pipe out and brek tension, wanting to gi him what he wanted.

"It int funny," Kel heard hersen say.

"You're only cunt not laughing, love," said Ando, though nobody wa.

They'd been laughing at her all night, though, hadn't they? Waving gun around just to fuck wi her, just to mek her confess.

"You're dumped," she said.

Moment words warrout her mouth, she wanted to tek them back.

Summat dark slithered into Ando's eyes, his cheeks dropping, showing stark bones beneath. He mimed wiping sweat off his brow. "Thank fuck." He laughed big and empty. "You're clingy as shite, mate. I can barely stand yas anymore." He raised his arm.

Gun blast wa louder than Kel could've imagined. Their reflections shattered, slivers of them flying across room, mekkin them all turn away, shield their faces wi their arms. Patches of brown corrugated baseboard punched through ruins ut mirror. Sharp miniature mirrors studded their hair and clothes. Piercing ring in Kel's ears, ache creeping into her skull.

Lads booted through wreckage of Cleggy's batting spree, limboed back through kitchen window. Once their feet hit concrete ont other side, Cleggy started whistling. *Come and join our cheeky club (This is what you want!).*

Kel stood inside, regret dissolving her bones. A second gunshot cracked sky ovvert moors, mekkin every dog ont street bark warnings intut night.

Next day, Kel, her mam, and a mob of uncles and cousins Kel ant sin in years met int yard fut clear-out. Int paddock at bottom ut yard, a bonfire grumbled, sounding like rain drumming on a car roof. Flames ate hunks of dry wood that popped and snapped and collapsed. Kel's two middle uncles fetched stuff from house and dumped it at back door; eldest uncle sorted everything into three piles—fire, charity, skip— and cousins took carloads tut Samaritans or ferried fire pile on a small tractor tut paddock, where Kel's mam threw it piece by piece ontut blaze. One ut uncles thought Kel's mam should be stripping bedroom and he should be tending fire, but Kel's mam had picked up pitchfork and marched off tut paddock and nobody said owt after that.

Kel stood by t'back door wi her arms crossed, trying to read her book. She'd begged her mam not to mek her come: she needed to go round Ando's, convince him to tek her back. Her mam'd said, "This int a negotiation," and that wa that, because that wa always fucking that. So Kel wont allowed to come here when her grandparents wa alive, when she could've actually got to know them, but now she wont allowed to *not*.

She checked her phone for texts, willed Ando's name to appear. She'd tried calling him last night, after barking dogs med her leg it out house sharpish in case neighbours did bother calling police. He dint answer any ut seventeen times she rang. All morning she'd been trying to write him a text that'd undo her words, get them back to where they wa before she'd said "You're dumped." She wanted to text Shaz and Rach, ask them what she should do, but they dint like Ando, so they'd only say, Well, you shouldn't ditch ya mates forra lad, should ya.

A middle uncle walked by her wi a bucketful of snapped vinyl, crushed porcelain. Acid burbled in her, sick feeling you get after a night ont lash when you know you did summat embarrassing but you can't remember what. Except she could remember. Her knee wa covered in a black-green bruise from whack it took when she'd fallen through window. She'd hid it under trousers, but every time her knee knocked against summat, it throbbed, med her hop about wit pain. She kept waiting for someone to realise she'd brock in, to recognise some bit of her caught ont glass scraps int window, or see splinters ut broken mirror and somehow know it wa her fault. But everyone just shrugged at damage and muttered, "Fuckin ska-gheads."

Her cousin Jambo cem ovver, told her she should be inside, clearing kitchen cupboards. He warrabout five months older than Kel and thought that med him in charge.

She couldn't go inside. She longed to. She wanted to steal a couple of paperbacks, sneak open that chest of scarves, slip a few up her jumper sleeve. She couldn't face ruined dresser, though, shards of wood and glass. She couldn't glimpse breeze-block chunk ont kitchen floor, spot her own footprints int dust.

She told Jambo, "I'm alreyt, ta," stuffed her book into her coat pocket, followed tractor down tut paddock, where smoke wa thick and exciting and smelled of burning rubber. Her mam wa standing by t'fire, hands on hips, cheeks pink wit heat. Kel's sister, Briar, wa being bounced ont hip of Jambo's girlfriend, who wa so besotted wit babby—mekkin all t'babby noises Kel dint know how to mek—that she dint even look up as Kel passed.

Kel wa jealous that Briar got called Briar and she just got called Kel, but she wa still happy to have a baby sister, even though she dint know owt about babbies and dint know how to be around one. Neither of them knew their dads, so name wut only thing Kel could be jealous of. Kel dint know owt about who Briar's dad might be, but she'd heard her own dad could've been a miner. Lady three doors down said once that she knew Kel's mam from miners' rallies in '84, that she'd sin Kel's mam wi a bloke from Brodsworth Colliery int working men's club, around time Kel would've been born. Kel liked idea of it, wanted to tek pride in being connected to an event that had shaped Donny's sense of itsen, to belong to Doncaster's story. But she knew she couldn't wi'out proof. Still, sometimes she said it to hersen, just to kindle pride's warmth within her: Mi dad warra miner.

She checked her phone. No Ando. Absence of him smouldered

inside her like panic. No Shaz or Rach either—they'd usually sent fifteen texts each by this time on a Satdi. They must be really mad at her. Or they knew Skaghead House belonged to her an' all. Mebs whole school knew. Mebs everyone wa laughing at her.

Kel's mam wa hefting t'strange thick square table ontut bonfire, one that'd stood int pantry last night. It walloped into a fence post sticking above flames and lay broken, waiting fut fire to tek hold.

"What wa that?" Kel asked.

"Old turntable," Kel's mam said. "Your grandma's." She dusted her hands down leg of her dungarees, pushed pitchfork intut fire's blue-hot centre. "I think her best mate bought it for her. Never played well, like, but she couldn't be persuaded to chuck it."

That wut most Kel's mam had said about Grandma in years. Kel pointed to other things, asked who they belonged to. Some things her mam said wa just rubbish, but others had an owner. Hollowed skeleton of a hand mirror: "Your great-grandma Violet's. She wa very proud of owning that. Would've cost a bob back then." Kel watched hand mirror, laid on top ut heap. A small flame licked at handle, then took hold, travelled bright down handle's shaft. Kel's hand darted intut fire. Heat forced her fingers back.

"Watch yoursen," said her mam.

"Why are we burning it? If it wa summat she wa proud of?"

Kel's mam picked up a tiny knitted cardi, daffodil yellow, moth-eaten, unravelling. "You wouldn't believe it, but I used to wear this. Weren't mine, like. Got passed down all three brothers before it got to me."

Kel felt in her jeans fut bit of letter she'd stole night before. "Whose writing's this?"

Her mam glanced at it and shrugged.

"Maybe Grandma?"

"Not likely. Your grandma couldn't write."

Kel wanted to point out that t'letter writer had said sem thing, that she couldn't write, but she dint want to press her mam in case she med Kel throw letter scrap ont fire. Kel snuck scrap back into her pocket. She wanted to ask her mam if she'd said once that Grandad controlled bank account, kept Grandma on an allowance, so she never had enough to buy new clothes for hersen. She wanted to ask if that wa why Grandma clung to everything she had, why house wa so full.

"How come we never visited?"

"House wasn't safe for kids," Kel's mam said, gi'in her sem old line.

It wont enough, though, warrit. Kel couldn't live off these fat-free answers. And why should she? Why should she purrup wi knowing nowt? Wi everyone knowing stuff she dint.

Kel's mam heaved a water-blackened oak dining table onto its back, picked up a sledge hammer.

"Is mi dad still alive, then? Will you tell me that?"

Kel's mam widened her stance, bent her knees, swung hammer into one ut table's upturned legs. Leg buckled, splintered, but held fast. "I'm your dad," she said.

"I've gorra right to know." Kel's voice cem out loud and angry. An uncle, a couple of cousins, and Jambo's girlfriend all looked ovver. Her mam dropped hammer, dipped her head so her and Kel wa nose-to-nose. There warran odd, wild panic in her eyes.

"Do not raise your voice at me." She spoke in a strained, urgent hush. "Not around them." Kel realised that her mam's eyes weren't full of panic; they wa full of pleading. *Please*, her eyes wa saying, *don't embarrass me*. Mebs they wa even saying, *Don't abandon me*. Kel dint know why it wa so important that they dint fight in front of her uncles, but suddenly she dint wanna know. Suddenly she felt wrong, selfish, for trying to mek her mam talk. She thought ut six-year-old who'd med dinner fut whole family ovvert open fire in that old iron pot. It wa that little lass asking Kel to keep her voice down, keep her head down, stay quiet.

Kel nodded. "Okay, okay."

Her mam straightened, collected hammer, swung it intut table leg twice, three times, till leg went splinter, splinter, crack, and fell away. Kel's mam chucked freed leg ontut fire, picked up her hammer and swung fut next. She hammered in silence till all t'legs wa dismembered and tossed ontut flames. Kel watched wood pile sink, embering into nowt. She stared intut fire till front of her body wa scorched, her eyes teary and bitter.

Then she turned and set off, back past Jambo's girlfriend mekkin babby sounds at Briar, past barn, donkey stable, chicken pen, heading fut house, then t'street. She dint want to be there, round her mam's family. She would read her book int front yard till her mam wa ready to go. At back door, her eldest uncle wa still sorting—fire, charity, skip. His bushy moustache covered his mouth.

Dint she see that uncle once, arguing wi her mam? Back when Kel wa little, when she wa still brought round Grandma and Grandad's to play. Dint she see them shouting int driveway. Dint her uncle pin her mam tut bonnet of her own Fiat Uno.

Eldest uncle threw cutlery ontut charity pile, newspapers ontut fire pile. Salt cellar—charity. Glass jar—skip. He had a smooth quick rhythm, darting this way, then that, body like a dancer. Candlesticks—charity. Candle stubs—skip. As Kel approached, his arm swung towards skip, but he second-guessed hissen halfway, brain catching up wi his body's decision. Object he tossed fell short, crunched against skip's metal side. Kel recognised it. It wa hers.

She went ovver to look: a kid-sized teacup, cartoon figure ont side, drawn by sem bloke who did Mr. Men books. A pink pig called "OINK from Timbuctoo" wa scurrying away, speed clouds trailing behind his trotters. Grandma got this out for her whenever she cem round. Filled it wi juice so Kel could pretend to sip tea like a grown up. Impact had snapped cup's handle, struck a chink int lip.

"Our Jambo's, that," eldest uncle said. "Shoulda kept it forr'im."

Kel picked up cup and handle, dropped them intut skip. Actually, she told eldest uncle inside her head, it wa mine. Eldest uncle went back to his throwing rhythm.

Kel turned back tut garden, tut blackberry hedge bejewelled wi dark shiny fruit, plums weighting branches of one tree, half-crushed apples at base of another. Little flowers, soft pink, fluting up from weeds, and what looked like tiny orange roses clumped together, bouquets for miniature brides. All of it, she decided—she remembered all of it, every outhouse, every tree trunk, every petal. She decided that whatever she thought she knew, she knew. Grandma and Grandad wa farmers, she said to hersen, remembering. Lorry drivers, remembering. Grandma used to say "Any road" wi a gret sigh whenever she'd decided they'd exhausted a topic and needed a change. Goslings in a cardboard box by t'fire int spring, hissing geese behind a wide green gate. Kel small, sat on Grandma's lap, noticed Grandma wa missing summat. Grandma let Kel reach into her blouse, feel stuffing bag she used to fill out one side of her bra, filling space where a boob used to be. And Grandma wrote that letter. And eldest uncle warra cunt.

Her phone buzzed in her pocket. Adrenaline rushed tingles all ovver her skin. She speed-walked tut street, where she could be alone wi whatever Ando had decided to say. She sat ont low brick wall arcing round overgrown front yard. She looked at her phone.

Blank screen. No new message.

She'd wanted to hear from him so badly she'd invented vibration. She couldn't bear it—couldn't bear thought that she'd said one wrong thing and everything wa changed forever. She tapped keypad, thumbs clumsy: *Chippy? Mundi?* She hit send. She breathed, relieved she'd broken their silence.

Seconds later, that cooling relief fizzled, gev way to a new nagging, gnawing kind of agony. Now all she could do wa wait.

Kel's mam kept fire going all day Satdi and all day Sundi. Afterwards, after everything they'd chucked and hauled off, house wa still full. They agreed to come back weekend after, and weekend after that, till job wa done.

Mundi morning, Kel sat outside chippy ont kerb. School bus had been and gone. Kel'd hid behind wheelie bins while it went past, watched Rach through bus window, sat on her tod. Rach would be in form wi Shaz now, gossiping about whatever they'd done wi'out Kel ovvert weekend. Gloopy oil smell from chippy mingled wit piss-and-vomit combo aroma that always clung to that bit of pavement. *People turn to poison quick as lager turns to piss, sweethearts are physically sick every time they kiss.* That wa Kel's favourite week in English, when they'd read this bloke who Sir reckoned warra poet, but his poems warrabout real things—drugs and drinking, fucking and fighting. Kel remembered those lines every time she smelled t'streets.

She wanted to read her book, mek time go faster. You can't read in public anymore, though, not like when she wa little, sat outside library wit armful of Sweet Valley Highs she'd just borrowed, already lost in California, int lives ut two beautiful identical twins, their American high school, their quarterbacks and sororities and homecoming queens. Little Kel would sit till it wa too dark to see pages. She dint think about what she might look like, what other kids might call her. *Did* call her. These days, she had to be crafty: she nested her backpack between her knees wit zip open and laid book inside, turned tut right page, so she could still read but all anyone would see warra lass looking for summat in her bag. Today's warra Mills & Boon called *Savage Courtship*. Kel found place she'd left off: Benedict Savage wa gerrin out shower. He walks naked across his bedroom. He towels himsen down. He rubs his strong fingers across his sandpaper jaw— Kel couldn't focus, her eyes wandering tut street corner every five words, hoping to see Ando strutting into view.

She sparked a fag, spat ont tarmac, inhaled. Spit, smoke, blow, spit, smoke. She went back to Benedict: still naked, he's perplexed to discover a mystery woman asleep in his bed, wearing a wisp of white satin—

What would she say when she saw him? Not *I love you*. Not Do you still like me, not Are we alreyt, can we go back to how it wa before. Nowt that'd mek her sound clingy. Spit, smoke, blow, spit, smoke. She'd just say nowt at all. Kerb wa fat wi a glob of saliva, shining glorious between lumps of chud and a stray chip, smushed flat. Kel had pose mastered too: arse ont kerb, legs apart, fag hand resting on her kneecap—her wrist covering her fading bruise. And if she scowled at everyone going past, she'd look hard as fuck an' all. She learned that from watching him.

Her phone buzzed, text from Rach. *Ur not wi Ando again ru?* Another buzz, thissun Shaz. They'd be sat next to each other in form, texting under t'desk. Shaz: *Fucksake Kel fuck him off. Hes already told evri1 that ur family r skaghead gyppos.* Kel's pulse quickened—thought of being gossiped about, thought of Ando going round chatting shit about her.

Shaz couldn't *know* it wa Ando who'd told anyone, though, could she. Shaz and Rach just dint like him. Kel texted back: *Not true!!!! B in l8r.*

When she'd smoked past last drags tut filter, Kel practiced flicking fag end, trying to launch it off her thumb like he did. Just in case he wa watching, she wanted to do it reyt. Cherry fell between her fingers onto her school skirt, left a perfect round hole.

Fucksake. She grabbed butt, squeezed it flat between thumb and index, then pulled back her finger till nail wa angled reyt behind it and flicked, sent it in a long arc ovvert road.

Then he wa coming at her across street, and Kel had been concentrating so hard ont flicking she hadn't sin him approach. He dodged fag end like a football tackle. Kel zipped her bag shut quick. Benedict would just have to stay naked and perplexed.

"Oi." Ando stopped above her. "Nearly got mi fuckin trainers."

She looked up at him, trying to gauge his mood. His eyes dint gi owt away.

"Sozzard."

"Will be sorry if you singe mi Nikes, lass."

Not *our* lass, but close.

Ando's Nikes wa still rimmed int sludge from t'dyke he'd traipsed through Fridi night. His baseball cap cradled back of his head, peak pointed at sky behind his gelled-up fringe. He lit his own fag, adjusted his crotch wi his free hand. It warrat Kel's eye level.

"You just gunna sit there like a munter or what?"

He wa forever calling her a munter, or a dizzy bitch, or a daft bint. He never said owt like that to Shaz and Rach, though, so for ages Kel thought it meant she wa special. Now she wondered if his munters and spackers and mongs would ever turn into darlins and babys. Don't ask, her head whispered.

"Where we off, like?"

"You're mekkin it up to me, aren't ya?" His gaze wandered ovver tut snicket that ran down t'side ut chippy. They'd fucked int wasteland behind chippy loads of times when Kel wa meant to be at school. It wa their place. It wa where Kel'd lost her virginity. Ando held his hand out; she took it. He half pulled her up, then palmed her back down, wrapped a leg round her head, dry humped her face. His bulge, covered in tracksuit sheen, clouted her int teeth. Laughing, he pulled her up by her wrist, kissed her cheek. She laughed, warmth sweeping through her from site of his kiss. She slung an arm round his middle, and they walked away from her spit puddle, off down t'snicket to mek everything alreyt again. Behind chippy warra tall wire fence, black wi age, sharp points all ovver.

"Giz a leg up, then," he said.

Fence wa twice Kel's height, and her school skirt wa after-school-detention short. Ando wut usually one gi'in leg-ups. She held out her hands, fingers laced to mek a stepping platform. Ando stuck his foot in them—her fingers straining, almost gi'in way before he pulled hissen up. She clambered after him, swung her leg ovvert top, nicking skin of her inner thigh.

Next there wa branches in her face, Ando pulling her further intut wasteland, past bush they usually did it behind. They stopped by a tree wi a forked trunk.

"Change of scene, innit," he said.

Nettles poked out either side ut trunk. They reminded Kel of when she forgot to shave and her pubes bushed out either side of her thong. Nobody stopped being scared of nettles, Kel dint reckon. Nettles hid between harmless weeds, waited forra lick of bare skin. Their leaves, velvety forest green love hearts wi a zigzag edge. Slightest brush of those soft teeth left hot white bumps all ovver that stung worse than a fag burn and lasted days. There wa nowhere to lie down where there wont nettles, so Kel pulled her thong to one side, positioned hersen int join ut trunk's two arms. More like fingers, she thought. More like two massive trunky fingers telling whole world to get fucked.

Ando pushed himsen against her. She wa still dry. Sorry, she wanted to say. He managed to push his way in, started rocking back and forth. Her bare arse chafed against bark, and Ando's dick wa angled so it missed bits of her anatomy that would have med her feel summat. She knew how it wa meant to feel—it had happened once by accident—but she dint mind; she loved watching Ando's face as it slackened and stared off. Every time he came, his whole face changed, and Kel saw someone new, someone boyish and innocent and soft. A face only she got to see. That pause right afterwards wut best bit, when he held her forra second wi his secret soft face and she felt proud.

She prayed he'd be done before she got red raw and every thrust wa like gerrin fucked wi a Swiss Army knife. He sped up, and she knew it wa nearly ovver. Head back against trunk, she closed her eyes, moaned along wi his rhythm.

But then he stopped, pulled out. Laid hands either side of her waist, pushed down. Around them, nettles sprouted through dirt and rocks. Kel resisted, tensed her stomach, planted balls of her feet.

What do you need, she wanted to ask. What did he need that'd mek him look at her like she wa someone he could love. Warrit this? Warrit her down int nettles, lerrin him ride her?

"Go on, then," he said. His eyes, still blank, unreadable.

She stopped fighting pressure of his hands, let him turn her around, push her down. Her legs and arms fell intut nettles. Pinpricks where nettles kissed, heat rushing ovver her skin.

He slid back into her from behind. He pounded, her crown knocking against trunk, her fingers clenching fistfuls of muck. He twitched, deep inside her, exhaled in her ear.

That pause, when everything stopped, when it wa meant to be just them two int universe, quiet, held. But she wa pointing wrong way; she couldn't see his secret face. And her body wa loud, thrumming fingertips to toes, like she'd swallowed a nest of pissed-off hornets.

He pulled out, pulled up his kegs, purra cig between his lips. Kel crawled ovver to a bare patch of dirt, arms and legs ablaze, as if flames ut weekend's bonfire wa tonguing her all ovver. Fire raged in her brain, electricity shooting through her pores. Skin rough and raised like braille—bloated white bubbles, surrounded by livid red. A rash of boils, a witch's curse. She checked Ando's face, which wa pulled around a mouth dragging hard ont fag, eyes focused on hands shielding lighter flame.

"Look at me."

Fag lit, he puffed, blew, spat, blew, then looked down at her.

"Fuckin *look* at me." She held up her arms, showed him her seething skin. *Look at what I let you do.*

Summat flickered across his face. His brow, ribbed by summat that wont quite boyish, wont quite soft. Summat like pity, mebs. But not regret—never that. Not love.

Kel's family returned tut house that Satdi, and Satdi after, and Satdi after that, but before they could throw away decades of Kel's grandma's painstakingly gathered bits of tat, Kel's uncles fell out wi Kel's mam again ovver summat in her grandad's will, and house stood full for several more years. A hundred yards away, int village cemetery, Kel's grandma lay int grave she shared wi Kel's grandad. Everyone wa too busy fighting and not talking to remember to add Grandma's name tut stone, so she lay there, unmarked, for all that time.

We Pretty Pieces of Flesh

We couldn't have been more than eleven when we realised it weren't alreyt to have girl bodies. We couldn't tell you how we knew this, all we can remember is that we wa itchy and restless in us girl skins. We needed woman bodies, bleeding bodies, and we needed them fast. "On" is what we called it, and there wa endless talk about "on." We whispered across desk in English class, three of us facing each other round one ut library's wide wooden tables. We talked about day "on" would happen. We recited wisdom passed down from a bigger sister: "discharge" would come first. Discharge warran omen of on. Every day we'd check us knickers for signs, for owt we could call D. We'd scurry tut loo, lock oursens int cubicle. We'd pull us knickers to us knees, examine cotton lining, run a finger ovvert fabric's fine weft, search for stains. We might even bring that finger to us nose and sniff. Hungry forra sign that on would soon come. Whenever we found owt lumpy and translucent or gooey white, owt that smelled like more than nowt, we'd charge back to class, whisper across desk: I've got D!

We could only announce this so many times—and wait, hope

for on to come—we could only weather so many failures when, each time, on refused to arrive, before we all slipped into us lies: Yes, on is here, on has happened to me. Or mebs two of us had gorrit and one hadn't. Or only one of us had it but not other two. Impossible to know which of us, if any, wa telling truth. We all stuck to us stories, elaborated whenever asked: Oh, us aches, us pains, us PMS! We held parts of us we thought wa meant to throb, us bellies, soft but not yet rounded into woman, us lower backs, which would one day leave some of us writhing each month. But not these days, not yet. We yelped, we moaned, pined for paracetamol, cried out for Feminax.

One of us kept a calendar of us cycles, tracked weeks we'd claimed to bleed, as if trying to catch other two of us out. Mundi mornings, she'd lay it ont desk in English, run her finger ovvert days. She'd tap a date where she'd marked us in scented gel pen and say, You're meant to be on today. Other two of us would have to say, Yeah, I reckon I'm starting now. Beneath desk, we'd slide fat tampons and nappy-thick pads into each other's hands in a silent pass the parcel, all of us sizzling wit excitement of shielding summat secret from Miss. Then we'd raise an arm, ask Miss if we could go tut loo, please. We'd lock oursens in and line our knickers wit pad, or try to force tampon up us tiny dry fannies. We'd waddle around like that all day, moaning and swooning and hamming up us PMS. I'm stressed, we'd say, proper *stressed*, wi as much flair and drama as we could drum, mimicking us mams, us big sisters, lasses off telly, anyone we could model to mek us lie stick.

When we wa thirteen, and some of us wa bleeding and some of us still waiting, still fibbing, we passed summat new beneath desk: fake Furby called Gerald, little ball of fuzz that vibrated when we pulled his string. We knew and dint know what we wa meant to do wi this vibration. We knew enough to pull string, pop Gerald up us school skirts, press him against us, mek him buzz reyt up on us knickers. We knew to giggle conspiratorially, keep a lookout for Miss. We knew it tickled and med us laugh, and we knew laughing wont how we wa meant to react. We knew to say that we liked it, that we wa gerrin "turned on."

We knew word "masturbate" even if we dint know warrit meant. Or mebs one of us knew, had an older sister whisper meaning into us ear. At least one of us had to listen keen when other people said it, trying to decode its syllables. We memorised where word went in a sentence, and built us sentences wi care around it, med sure we sounded like we knew how to use it. We learned so many words this way. We learned "fingering" and "blow job" and "cunt." We learned "hand job" and "fisting" and "poshy" and "clit," and layered them into us conversations wi confidence and panache. We'd say stuff like, Emma reckons Azzer fingered Linz ont top ut school field. Ando sez Cleggy's mam caught him gi'in hissen a poshy. We sounded out these words for years before we knew what we wa saying. Years before we wanted owt to buzz against us clit, before we knew we owned one and what to call it, we knew how to act like we wa wanting bodies.

By fifteen we'd learned all us naughty words, and we could use them wi a casual boredom we'd perfected ovver us years of practice. We could also use them wi malice whenever situation called—like time one of us showed up to school wi a weird rash on her arms and legs and wouldn't say how she'd gorrit, then a group of lasses started wi her, called her a skaghead gyppo. We hit em wi every naughty word we knew, threatened to slap em silly if they ever said owt like that again. One of us squared up to one of them, to mek sure they understood we meant what we said.

We warrint middle of a drama lesson, though, weren't we—we wa meant to be listening to "Int Hall ut Mountain King," coming up wi an interpretive dance. Drama teacher Mr. Whitmore told us to calm down, ladies, then pulled us three into his office. He wa one of those teachers who lerrus call him "Whitty," acted like he warrus mate. We wa quite good at drama actually, he said. We'd got promise. So it warrup to us: we could do after-school detentions for threatening behaviour, or we could do some scenes fut drama showcase he wa purrin on fut parents.

We decided we wa doing scenes from *Romeo + Juliet*, but we couldn't agree which of us should be Romeo, and who Juliet, and which of us dint get to pretend to be in love at all—which of us would be Mercutio and recite Queen Mab. In English, we passed two wooden swords and a tub of Vicks beneath desk, hands grabbing at object we wanted most, silently fighting ovver who got what. Vicks would go to Juliet, who'd daub it beneath her eyes to mek them water, then weep ovver her lifeless love. Romeo would get t'long wooden rapier, leaving Mercutio wit stubby dagger. We'd shaped wood oursens, so we wa dead proud of these swords. We'd used planer int technology room, we'd sharpened plank ends, rubbed them wi sandpaper to smooth grains. Coated them in three layers of silver paint.

Two of us would do party scene, bit where Romeo sez "Move not, while my prayer's effect I take," and snogs Juliet. We decided that whoever wa doing it wa doing snog, and doing snog proper: passionate clinch, slipping int tongue.

After dinner—after dinner hall had emptied, and t'dropped peas and trodden turkey drummers had been swept away—we practiced int corner ut hall where stage wa kept, dusty and forgotten against one wall. We rehearsed us lust int lingering stench of chips and gravy, two of us pressing us shy giggling mouths together while one watched, wondering if she wa meant to be feeling weird about it, trying to build courage to have a go. Couple of lads from year below peeped through window, shouted Lesbians! and ran away. By last period, whole school wa frothing wit gossip about two real-life lesbians in year ten, and Romeo and Juliet braced themsens forra punch ont walk down tut buses. Other one of us, one who'd kept us blood calendar when we wa younger, quietly accepted Mercutio, quietly glad, now, for Queen Mab.

Our Juliet wut only one of us who wa any good at English, so she helped our Romeo and our Mercutio understand all t'old-fashioned words. Romeo calmed Juliet and Mercutio when they got stage fright, told them to stop being fannies. We'd never done owt like this before—we'd never gorrup in front of people, never took part in owt at school that wont required, except choir, which had been Romeo's idea, and only because she reckoned tenor section wa full of fit lads.

When night ut showcase cem, fut two of us who'd won Romeo and Juliet wi us daring, it felt like freedom up there under whatever spotlight drama department's slashed budget allowed. We'd cobbled us costumes from us own clothes, since wardrobe cupboard had got damp, and mould had grown gleefully ovver all t'dresses and capes and tunics and fake fur coats. Our Romeo in jeans and a T-shirt, our Juliet in a velveteen top wi hippy sleeves, our Mercutio in a spangly silver waistcoat borrowed from her dad. Freedom it wa, though, snogging up there in front ut teachers and everyone's mam. Faces wet from spit and sweat and running eyes, Vicks working too well, snogging int heat ut menthol burn, int heat and thrill of being watched. Of audience's shocked silence, squeak and whine ut plastic fold-out seats.

Snogging wont exactly banned at school like makeup wa, but any time teachers spied us through their mirrored windows, caught us snogging lads, they'd bang ont glass to startle us apart. When they passed us ont school's outdoor walkways at break and between periods, they'd tut and snap, Put her down! They'd call us worse than dogs in heat.

Next day, we strutted round school feeling famous. Us spines straighter, us bodies moving wi new flounce, running ont high of doing summat good in front of everyone, summat we'd worked hard on, summat we'd pulled off wi'out any of us messing up us lines.

Flawless. Everyone we walked past, we checked their eyes fut glint of recognition, fut awe, fut surprise—for their eyes to say to us, *Look, it's Romeo, Juliet, and Mercutio!* We waited fut good feelings that'd coat us when one ut teachers stopped us int walkway and said well done.

We caught glares from CDT teacher Mr. Laidlaw, hurrying across quad wi folders bunched under his arm, buttons of his white shirt straining. We got dead-eye from food tech teacher Miss Wright, passing us between classes. Teachers sneered as if we'd done summat to piss them off. Like our performance warra personal attack on them. They stopped being teachers and turned into people. They med excuses to send us out ut classroom to stand int corridor, they shouted at us for talking, they told us, You're not on stage now, sunshine. They told us, Save it for your next production. We did feel a bit famous then, but not fut right reasons. We dint know how to explain that we hadn't been thinking about them at all. They hadn't been on us minds while we warrup there playing us parts.

But we'd forgot that we wont meant to be mekkin a show of oursens. We wont meant to be mekkin oursens stand out. Because no-one likes a show-off, do they. No-one likes lasses that are full of themsens—there's not much worse you can be. Never be full of yoursen, or up yoursen, never boast, never brag, never stick your neck out—wind your bloody neck *in*, actually—never whine, complain, never grumble. Never want for owt, never strive for owt—to be owt—better than what you are. Dunt mek a fuss, dunt mek a scene, dunt mek a performance.

Teachers glowered and snooted and sniffed, but kids dint say owt at all. Lesbian scandal wa soon forgotten, and nobody from our year went tut showcase anyway, so to us mates it wa like it'd never happened. We'd been stars in us minds and nowhere else.

We put aside us Vicks and us wooden swords.

We passed naughtier things beneath desk. One of us clanked into school wi a bottle of Petrushka vodka in her backpack. In

English, we took it in turns to watch out for Miss and cloak backpack wi us legs, while one of us dipped down between us knees, tipped bottle back, glugged. Liquid heat down us throats, insides burning good. Glee of gerrin away wi it. Giggles turning sloppy and hazy, school softening around us.

Everything carried a hint, a tremor, no more drab school day, everything pulsing wi wonder. Long afternoon sunshine cast bright patches ont carpet just for us. Words carved intut desk wi a compass point wa poetry written just for us. "Cleggy is a twat IDST." We savoured those cutting *t*-sounds in us mouths. We dug us fingernails intut scored trenches ut *w* just to feel grain ut wood, mark of some past cheekiness not yet sanded off. We longed to dip below and drink heat again, savour seconds under t'desk, our cave in a forest of knees and scuffed shoes and dangling laces. Down below, where we felt separate, apart, exempt. Kids around us lost all their bulk, weightless figures wavering in and out of us notice. Levers in a machine we'd abandoned. Look at those daft cunts, reading their textbooks, filling out their multiple-choice tests! Why bother when we could sit here and dream wi a secret gurgling in us tummies.

When bell went, we dint know how we'd stand up and walk out. Straight line, straight line, trip, giggle—shhh!—and flounder through t'door, stumble up top field to freedom.

Afternoon, still off us heads, standing int choir's back line, blaring boring alto harmonies loud as we could to drown out sopranos, chastising each other for falling backwards intut kettle drums and cymbals, walloping crash int middle of "Didn't My Lord Deliver Daniel."

One day, we got cocky, pushed us luck. Juliet stole last dribs of Cointreau from her mam's stash, poured it into an opaque plastic bottle. We forgot that Cointreau dunt smell clear like vodka. Smells of oranges and Christmas and sickly fruit scent of sozzled old bids. We left desk behind, thinking we dint need cover, and passed bottle between us, sat in a circle ont floor int drama room. We wa supposed to be practicing a scene from *T'Crucible*, bit where John Proctor tells Goody Proctor her justice would freeze beer. But Whitty liked us. We thought we wa safe in his classroom. We got bold, and we wa shocked when he smelled sicky oranges, snatched bottle off us.

He sniffed its spout and said, "Who brought this in?"

We stayed still and silent as we could, unsure if we wa swaying ont outside or in. Whitty ordered us to go tut Head of Year, a ruddy-faced woman wi a mullet, pleated brown trousers, and purest hatred of us young lasses. "If you won't tell me," Whitty said, "you can tell *her* which of you it wa."

Ont way tut Head of Year's office we dawdled, chewed chuddy to mek us breath minty, trying to sober up int cool air, delaying facing her, creeping along, hoping that if we walked slow enough we might just turn sixteen and finish school before we got there. We discussed fate that might await us, avoided question of which of us would own up to bringing booze, tek consequences for all of us.

"Our Louise knows people who've been expelled for this." A breathy rasp in Mercutio's voice, as if she'd run out of air, black hole sucking at her midriff.

"Be reyt," said Juliet. "She'll just shout forra bit and gi us after-school detention."

"It'll be isolation at least," said Romeo.

That thought sunk all t'way through us, settled like a pebble in us shoes. Romeo wut only one of us who'd already survived isolation, but we'd all heard about warrit wa like.

In isolation, you sat at a hip-width desk outside Head Teacher's office, in a long narrow corridor leading tut staff room. You wrote same sentence, ovver and ovver, forra week: I must not get pissed up at school. Kids weren't allowed down there unless they wa being punished, but teachers walked past all day, pelting you wi banter. Teachers cem in three categories: tutters, shamers, and jokers. They all loved tekkin potshots, mekkin a sad wriggling squid of you. Tutters wa pinch-faced, eyes never straying your way, staring ahead, mekkin you feel like you might be see-through, till they wa almost past you. Just when you wa convinced you really warra phantom, they'd click their tongues against their teeth—or they'd actually say "tut tut" to mek sure you heard—and you knew you wa still there. Still there, still visible, but shrinking. Shamers would pause, lean in, let you smell their lunch, hang ovver your shoulder, mouth near grazing your ear, then they'd say, in a quiet voice layered thick wi disdain, I hope you're proud of yoursen. Jokers would stoop to sarcasm for their jollies, volleying quips from twenty feet, gerrin as many digs in as poss before they passed you. Fancy seeing you here! Having fun? Back like a bad smell! Jokers wut worst because they really thought they wa funny, and they'd always appear reyt as you wa settling into your lines, pen gerrin into a rhythm, just as your thoughts wa ambling, just as you wa forgetting forra second that you wa alone, singled out, labelled trouble.

Isolation dint seem a just punishment forra bit of normal naughtiness. Who dunt get trollied at school on occasion? Band geeks did it all t'time, knocking back Malibu and Coke int music block's practice rooms, music teacher pretending not to notice because they wa good kids, weren't they, and they played carols forr'er int freezing rain outside Frenchgate Centre every Christmas.

We all had ideas about who should own up to bringing booze. We all thought it should be someone other than oursens. Mercutio thought it should be Juliet because she did bring booze, Juliet thought it should be Romeo because she wut least likely to get grounded by her mam, and Romeo thought it should be Mercutio, because she never gorrin trouble, so Head of Year would be kinder to her.

We bickered till us voices carried across quad, and startled secretary int front office, who pressed her nose against glass and glared. She rapped window, med shooing motions. We ignored her. We'd already learned that long-distance scowling wut only punishment she wa authorised to dish out. She gave up, went back to her desk.

"I know," said Juliet. "Let's Spartacus it!"

Juliet's mam wa always re-watching old-fashioned films, so Juliet knew all sorts of random shit. She explained: if we all claimed we wut one who brought booze, they wouldn't be able to punish any of us. We agreed that's what we'd do, but at least one of us wa secretly afraid that we'd say booze wa ours and other two wouldn't join in. What if two stayed quiet, let one of us tek whatever punishment Miss dreamed up?

In her office, surrounded by prints from her failed career as a wallpaper designer—doe-eyed bunnies peeping from pastel-blue clouds, rosy-cheeked hedgehogs in waistcoats and monocles—Head of Year gi us usual pantomine, playing role ut angry teacher, shouting at that extra-loud fake-cross volume designed to mek us tremble wi fear and regret, a decibel that would've mortified us when we wa eleven. We wa fifteen, though, and drunk, so we wa just trying to smother us giggles. When she demanded to know who brought Cointreau to school, we hesitated, none of us wanting to be first to start Spartacussing.

"I asked you a question," said Head of Year, adding an air-stabbing finger for further menace. She separated and emphasised each syllable: "Who—brought—in—the—al—co—hol?"

Romeo, because she wut bravest, took lead: "It wa me, Miss."

"No, it wa me," said Mercutio.

"It wa me!" said Juliet.

Miss said, "Right, Shannon, you're coming wi me," and took Romeo by t'shoulder, propelled her towards door.

"It wont her!" said Mercutio.

"It—" said Juliet.

But Miss and Romeo had gone, already on their way tut Head Teacher's office.

After her week in isolation, Romeo wa quiet forra long time. We all agreed it wont right that only she got punished. We all agreed that we all did same amount of bad. Mercutio raged about injustice of it for weeks. It's not right! she kept insisting, and Romeo kept shrugging and saying, "It is warrit is." Romeo reckoned she dint care, but other two of us knew that summat inside her had been chipped off, that school wa slowly chiselling her hollow. We all knew and dint know why she'd been singled out—why other two of us had been ignored. We all knew wi'out being able to name wi what she'd been branded. Looking back, we might even call this beginning ut end, moment us mighty, unbreachable threesome started to splinter. While Romeo warrin isolation, Mercutio and Juliet stopped passing things beneath desk, started trying to get their coursework finished. When Romeo returned, started passing notes tut other two of us and got ignored, she demanded to know what Head of Year had said about her, after dumping her outside Head Teacher's office. Nowt, Mercutio and Juliet promised. She dint say owt about ya, swear down. But Romeo knew summat had been said. Summat like, You're bright lasses, yous. You could do alright if you stopped following her bad example. Mebs this wut moment two of us set a course to sixth form, and one of us stopped believing that future wa meant for her. Never had anyone tell her that she wa good enough to go an' all.

We dint dare pass contraband at school after that, so we passed it everywhere else instead. We passed one lone cig at bus stop before school and after, behind corner shop, behind chippy, down Dip, our fingers, jumpers, and hair smelling like our nan's front room, like our mam's morning breath, like our big sister's minidress after a night int club. One of us would spark up, then next un would say, "Gi us twos on that," then next would call "LDs," last drags. Us first joint, passed in a bedroom when parents warrout, spliff med from cheap resin a lad sold Romeo in maths class when new maths teacher wont looking, crumbly brown block hidden in a paper bag meant for penny sweets. Mr. Lily warran ex-miner, retrained on an accelerated course, dead good at maths, crap at noticing drug trade operating int back row. We hid rest ut resin block in a hole in Gerald's bum, who one of us had kept, nostalgic forra simpler time. Pass, inhale, choke-cough, giggle, one of us keeping watch fut parents' car coming up drive.

Once in a while we brought us wooden swords out wi us to rekindle us glory. We brandished them at people int street, challenged members ut public to a duel. We took them to house parties and gatherings, ran around shouting any line we could remember. If love be rough with you, be rough with love!

Start ut summer holidays, we took us swords to Squiff's all-nighter. Squiff'd built a campfire in a clearing int woods, told everyone to get theirsens down. He'd brought blankets and sleeping bags, portable CD player banging out trance beats. Must've been forty-odd of us, pressed close between night-black trees, us faces nowt but flickers of firelight, pale slices of moon. Us bodies nowt but cold fingers, plunged for laughs down t'backs of each other's T-shirts. Shafts of smoky hair tickling each other's cheeks when we leaned to talk in each other's ears, feeling wildness of summer seeping into us wit damp ut leaves seeping into us clothes.

We'd got ID'd at offy, so we'd had to come empty-handed, but Romeo and Juliet said they'd tek care of matters—we weren't about to be sober! Couple of lads wi a fat stash of Carling reckoned they'd gi us a few cans if we gorroff wi each other in front of them. We slipped away from fire, us and these two lads, their torch beams piercing dark before us, lighting sections of branch, bramble, twig. Wing-swoop of birds that turned out to be bats. We found a parting ut trees wi a boulder int centre, big enough fut three of us to sit on wi'out us feet touching ground. Low hum ut party far off, a tawny hooting ovverhead. We sat like mermaids posing lustily on a shore rock framed by wave spray, trying to act as if boulder's ridges weren't biting into us arse flesh. Romeo tried to get Mercutio involved—Go on, mate, it's just a laugh, innit—and Mercutio paused like she wa thinking about it, like mebs she would've liked to have been Juliet all along.

Lads said, "Come on, then, get lezzin," and shone torches at us faces, which med Mercutio blink twice, shake her head.

"Nah, I'm alright, ta." She stood up ont boulder, aimed her dagger at lads' throats, mekkin sure they kept their hands to themsens. Romeo and Juliet snogged, eyes closed. At first their lids kept flicking open, their necks stiff, too aware of their audience, but they soon got into their roles, legs twining, hands searching, till they wa tangled up in each other. Lads watched t'show straight-faced, like they dint know how to react.

Afterwards, lads handed us fifteen lukewarm cans of Carling. We took one each, pulled ring back wi a smack that sounded like victory.

"Cheers, girlies!" We clinked us cans together, toasted us success. We said, "This I do drink to thee!" And it wa just like old times—just us and us joy, us flutter of achievement, us sense of us own power.

Lads said, "We'll gi you more if you flash us your tits."

We said, "Nah, y'alreyt," chugging at us cans.

"Flash us your fanny, then."

"Gi oo'er!"

Then there wa leaves murmuring int dark around us, human giggling and smirks and chatting coming at us out gloom. A load ut lads' mates, it turned out, had followed us, spied on us. They emerged intut torchlight, surrounded us.

They started singing: "Get you rat out, geeet you rat out, geeeeet your rat out for the lads!" Six, seven, eight of them fringing boulder, leaning ovver, pointing at us as they sang, waving their own tinnies, sloshing us wi beer, their features distorted by torchbeam.

We cradled us Carling cans to us chests. We swiped us swords at their cocks, med them duck and say, Oh aye! We jumped down off boulder, shoulderd through them, elbows aiming for their ribs. We marched off intut dark. We tried to forget their leering faces. Their singing followed us all t'way back tut fire. Their singing followed us all night.

We drank us booze freely, heads back, cans int air. We got so us limbs freed themsens from ordinary principles of motion, swung loose, us heads bobbing, us smiles slack. We wandered around fire, through trees, ovver and under lazy bodies, forgot where we wa going, told each other, Just while I'm sober, I wanna say, I love you! We remembered we needed a slash, hunted through drag and blur of us vision forra quiet spot, a bush to squat behind. We walked till we found an actual loo, moon-lit porcelain laid on its side. One of us wi heavy hands trying to lift loo upright, and lid sliding off and cracking to pieces, slitting her palm, and Shush, don't tell, and breathless laughter—Don't tell who?!—and us all slicing oursens open trying to piece lid back together, and staunching blood wit sleeves of us jumpers, and scars on us fingers we'd keep forever, and squatting next tut loo, trying not to wee on us trainers—and, What's that noise? And Fuck, we're pissing next to a traveller's camp, yards from tents and caravans, and mad sprint back tut party, and cackling, and Oop! There's a lad!

Next thing, Romeo warrin this lad's arms, and they wa snogging, and snogging, hands running everywhere, and next thing another lad, another heady snog, and then Juliet's snogging a lad, and Romeo and Juliet snogged a next lad and a next, till they wa passing themsens around fire, gathering as much saliva as they could carry.

After Juliet disappeared into a sleeping bag wi a lad of her choice, Mercutio leant against a tree, tipped Carling can to her lips. She watched Romeo, who wa sprawled ovver a blanket near t'flames, snogging face off another lad. Romeo pulled out ut kiss to tek a swig of her beer, caught Mercutio watching.

"What's up?" said Romeo.

Mercutio beckoned for Romeo to come ovver.

Romeo stayed where she wa, coddled between her lad's legs, and tapped her ear.

Mercutio crouched beside Romeo, whispered, "How come nobody fancies me?"

"People do fancy you, ya knobhead, they just don't think you fancy them."

"Why?"

"You've gorrer actually talk to them. You've gorrer flirt."

"I can't."

"It's like acting. Just find a lad you like and act interested." Romeo's bloke laid a hand along her jaw to draw her back into their kiss.

"Like him?" Mercutio nodded at a lanky lad wi plump wet lips who'd just stumbled intut firelight, bottle of Mad Dog in hand, eyes searching ground.

Romeo's eyes wa closing, her head tilting up to meet her bloke's mouth. "Yeah," she said, "just do it," and disappeared into her kiss.

Lanky lad crouched down beside Mercutio, staring at earth between his feet. "You sin a frog hopping in this direction?" he asked, lips slurry and soft.

Mercutio placed end of her dagger beneath his chin and said, "Stabb'd with a white wench's black eye!"

"You what?"

Mercutio lunged—mouth against wet mouth.

Then we snogged us lads all night, and we pressed us bodies against theirs all night, and feeling wa so good we hoped we'd remember it next day.

And waking int dawn, covered in permo marker, roused by t'crack of a gunshot—and looking blearily around at unconscious teenagers hanging out of sleeping bags, slumped ovver fallen trunks, curled up between tree roots. Crushed beer cans and flattened fag ends flecking earthy green ut undergrowth. Warble and chirp ut birds rose loud round us, like they wa trying to forget shock ut gunshot in song. And reading what wa written on us arms in black ink, between ribbons of dried blood: "You made us write this!" And everywhere else on us bodies wa written things we did, how many cans we sank, whose sick we sat in, whose lips we kissed. How much we'd passed oursens around. Every snog a trophy, every scab a boast. And bricking oursens when a bearded bloke appeared at edge ut clearing, shotgun in one hand, dead rabbit int other. When he grunted "Morning," tramped off through trees. And feeling sorry fut frog that wa perched on a blackened log int dead fire, body scorched, eyes burst. And feeling guilty, as if it wa us who'd roasted him alive. And tripping down tut river at wood's edge, dipping us arms in, scrubbing at blood and ink till us skin wa pink and tender. Because we couldn't go home till our bodies stopped telling about all that passing we'd done.

Not Like Dying but Like Living

Same morning January's first blizzard came for Boston, sickness came for Kel. She peeled her duvet back, stood, and found that standing sent her head into a queasy swim, her heart alarmed, legs unsteady, till she had to lie back down before she fell. She called in sick, lay in her sweat-soaked sheets for three weeks, weak, shivering, while blizzards one, two, and three sunk city in six feet of snow. She told no-one what wa happening to her. It felt like punishment. It felt like summat she deserved.

Her body wouldn't let her sleep more than an hour or two each night, and those snatched hours wa fitful, feverish, barely there. She'd wake from them feeling like she hadn't slept at all, like she'd only slipped below consciousness forra second before her body fought to resurface. Her days mushy, unreal. Stack of paperbacks on her beside table she couldn't read—her brain would do nowt but feed on reality TV. She rewatched seasons of *Drag Race* on loop, too wired to think. Nights, she stared at water stain cresting in waves ont ceiling, listened tut snow trucks beep mournfully down a ghost-quiet Comm Ave. Each beep rang through her like a warning, rousing unanswerable questions. *What's wrong wi you? What if you don't get better? What if you lose your job?*

No family to fall back on in America, not anymore. Nowt beneath her but air, nowt but drop. Her American life depended, now, on her body's ability to work. Kel's body had always been a reliable worker—it rarely caught whatever cold or flu bug wa going round, always danced int club till two and warrup for school next day, never broke owt bigger than a toenail.

Those long weeks, Kel could only wonder if madness had taken hold ut city again. Last time blizzards wa this bad, madness had crept inside every Bostonian. Previously reasonable people skied right down Beacon Street, brawled over parking spots, threw themsens into snowdrifts from second-floor windows. No T running, sidewalks an icy invitation to a broken clavicle. Kel and Alex had been stuck inside same flat Kel wa stuck in now, three rooms shunned by direct sunlight in any season, misery hanging int air wit cigarette smoke fogging from both their mouths. Kel had brainstormed solutions in her notebook: "Kill self? Kill him?" Hard to say if it wa being shut in or all that white—white heaped ont sidewalks, grass verges, window ledges, gateposts, white drifting high in gutters and gardens and lay-bys, mailboxes disguised under cream cheese pompadours, white powdery and dimpled, crusty and sparkling, slushy and stiff, white darkening and pockmarked and grey—that drove everyone mad, but either way Kel's marriage had sunk under weight ut madness like rotten porch steps under t'snow.

Not that she'd been able to leave t'moment she'd realised staying married wont an option. She had a few mates, but not kind that'd see you through a crisis. There wa no-one to rely on here but him and his folks. She hadn't a living wage or her own bank account or a credit rating. Ten months she stayed quiet, doing her best to pretend she still believed marriage could work, till she found a job that'd just about cover cost of living.

Now, pinned to her mattress, all Kel knew wa that every night trucks came beeping, trying and failing to clear T tracks. She loved that she lived so close tut B line she could feel it rumble by from her bed. Med her feel connected, part of this strange land. She hated eerie stillness ut snow absorbing sound, ut T not running. Loudest noises wa boots against floor int foyer of her apartment building, her neighbours jangling keys.

Alex still had a key. He'd promised not to use it, but int early days of their breakup, before his sadness had soured to anger, he'd also promised to sign papers she needed to get her permanent green card. Papers that wa due in three weeks. A missed deadline would mean no more green card, no more America. Lately, he'd been cagey whenever she emailed, like he'd remembered power he had over her, decided to mek her beg. She dint understand why he'd insisted on keeping key, why he couldn't leave her to dilapidate in peace, wi'out fear of intrusion. She wa always tense, freezing whenever she heard a rustle int foyer, a rattle that sounded like a key sliding intut lock. Always waiting for him to burst back in.

Garrett, a bloke Kel'd matched wi on Bumble, had been angling to come over since blizzards began. They'd met for drinks a few times before sickness started, enjoyed a few tipsy snogfests in bars' dark booths, and Garrett had texted Kel all sorts of naughty things he wanted to try wi her, but they'd never been alone together. Kel wanted to see him, but she couldn't mek her body cooperate. As sickness went on, she wont even fussed about sex anymore. She'd settle just for someone to hold her, for warmth, for another person's breathing, fut clockwork certainty of their pulse.

Friday after t'third blizzard had whipped its hectic whirl round Boston's streets, Kel felt like she'd finally regained enough energy to at least act like she wont sick. Garrett warrat her door an hour after she texted, eager face beneath an ice-flecked woolly hat, bottle of tequila in one hand, large Domino's ExtravaganZZa int other.

"Alright," she said, standing back to let him in. Her voice rang foreign, like it belonged to someone else. She'd gone so long wi'out speaking, she'd almost forgotten sound.

Half an hour into what would turn out to be most intense sesh of Kel's life, they paused forra refuel, Kel naked, Garrett down to his boxers. Tequila had relaxed her joints, muted her headache, slowed her jumpy heart, eased exhaustion that dragged at her limbs. Fut first time in ages, Kel felt like dancing. She gyrated int two-foot gap between her bed and her desk, shaking her hips tut poppy hip-hop leaking from Garrett's tinny laptop speakers, her movements silkening into sultry instead of geriatric.

Garrett perched ont bed, poured tequila into two shot glasses, knocked them back one after t'other, slammed glasses onto Kel's bedside table, bought from Walmart in another life. All Kel's furniture wa from that other life. He inspected her paperbacks. She wanted to run over, cover their spines wi her hands. When Boston people found out she liked books, they asked her who warr'er favourite Brontë, or wa she a Booker completist, or had she read "the Russians." She always replied: Charlotte; just the winners; obviously, yes. She couldn't admit that she just meant normal books—romances, thrillers. She *def* couldn't admit that when she first moved tut city and found out there wa publishing houses in Boston, she'd thought mebs she could become an editor, read forra living. She applied for their unpaid internships for years, never got an interview. Who knew it wa that hard to gi yoursen away for free.

"I don't have much time for fiction," Garrett said, mekkin himsen instantly Kel's favourite Boston person. He pulled her close wi one of his rangy arms, sat her ont bed next to him, spoke into her ear. "I want you to lie down, now, with your arms above your head."

Tickle of his breath on her skin, filling Kel head to toe wi tremor, wi shiver, wi quake. Her body responded tut sound of him gi'in her instructions wit kind of pleasure she'd long thought she wont capable of feeling. Secret thoughts, never voiced, that there wa summat wrong wi her. How had she not known till that moment, till she wa thirty fucking years old, that *this* wa what her body wanted?

Kel did as she wa told, laid on her back, legs straight, wrists crossed, torso tipping slightly intut dip int mattress worn there by years of Alex's heft. She wa eager for her next instructions. She watched Garrett's long frame stoop, his little belly pillow, as he searched floor, sifted through her chucked T-shirt, her strewn knickers, his fallen jeans, till he found two of her scarves, old-fashioned silks she hunted for in Allston thrift stores, but which she told everyone had belonged to her grandma.

When Garrett tied one ut headscarves around her eyes, dropping her into a dark that med his every next move a tantalising surprise, when he used other scarf to bind her wrists, when he pinned her thighs tut mattress wi one strong knee, when he ordered her to open her mouth, when he spat in it and told her to take it, when she swallowed gobs and gobs of it, when he flipped her onto her stomach, kissed both her bum cheeks before clamping fat of them between his teeth, when she wa laid under him, weight of him holding her down, restrained, obeying, she broke free of her whole life. Endorphin high coursed through her wi every one of Garrett's slaps, his fingers rapping her cheek, her chin, her jawbone. Every dig of his teeth in her flesh—sharp pinch, then flood of pleasure that swept her out her head.

She'd never known this kind of freedom. She'd *def* never known this freedom could come from sex wi a lad. She wa free ut worries that nagged loud when she'd slept wi any other bloke, free ut pressure to guess what they wanted from her, fear of being less than expected.

Alex had always wanted summat from her she dint know how to give. She'd never meant to be afraid of their sex, but only months into their marriage, he wa deployed to Afghanistan, gone for over a year. Kel lived in Texas alone, no job, no proper mates, no car, no public transport—no way of crossing endlessly flat expanse of plain that stretched limits of what Kel believed "horizon" could hold. When Kel wa young, America fit inside a paperback; it stretched only tut width of her telly. One thing Brits dint get about America: word "vast" has no meaning till you've set foot here.

When he did come back, Alex came back a stranger, someone she needed time to get close to. Time to remember that she warra person whose body wa touched by his body. He wanted her to take charge, surprise him, jump on him horny and hungry. He wanted her to *want* to go down on him, to gi him that wi'out him having to ask, then beg, then try to demand. More he wanted that from her, more clammed up and closed she got. And more she flinched and shrugged him off, angrier he got. Anger he'd release at her each time she wriggled from his hands when they slapped her arse int shower, escaped his hips when they humped her leg beneath sheets. So much anger he couldn't explain. Except once, bottle of red wine in, when he told her that int streets of Helmand, anger wa how you got things done. You point a gun at someone's head and yell till they do what you told them.

She'd fuck him to keep him quiet for another week or two, till his frustration peaked again, and being "sick" or "tired" wont a good enough excuse.

They thought everything would get better when they left army, left Texas, moved to Boston to be near his family. But all Boston offered him wa surreal, pointless office jobs and people who dint understand what he'd been through. People including Kel. For years, she dint understand what wa happening between them, dint realise how many conversations they weren't having, till one day he claimed—mentioned, offhand—that he could fuck her while she

wa sleeping, if he wanted. That in marriage, there wa no such thing
as rape.

After, Garrett and Kel laid together int warm dim of a flickering
candle, Kel wrapped in a post-sex buzz, every slapped and bitten
part of her purring, alight. She wa enjoying oily saltiness ut bedsheets. Enjoying brush of his finger along her thigh.

"You feeling good?" he asked. Kel blushed, looked away.
Garrett seemed to be asking about *her*, Kel Skipton—how wa *she*
feeling—not about his performance. Did *that* feel good, is what
Alex would've asked Mrs. Alexander Martin, in a way that med Mrs.
Alexander Martin feel compelled to say yes.

Kel and Garrett swiped right on each other a couple of months
ago, ten days after Alex moved out. They bonded over being
strangers to New England. "Transplants," Kel's coworkers would
call them, though that med Kel think of kidneys and lungs, things
a body needed. Neither Kel nor Garrett wa one of Boston's essential organs. They both answered emails forra living. Both moved
tut city for their ex, both felt rootless and drifty, both youngish
and divorcedish—Kel still married on paper. Garrett thought
that wa sexy, liked idea of being her "mister," label he gi himsen
when he realised there wa no male version of "mistress." They
wa attracted to each other's foreignness, Kel's British accent and
Garrett's Southern "y'alls" and "yes, ma'ams." Only thing Kel
knew about Alabama wa what Lynyrd Skynyrd had to say ont
subject. She dint know what piece of pop culture she reminded
Garrett of, but she wa sure his idea of England wa nowt like town
she'd grown up in. That wa one thing she loved about being there:
Americans thought all British accents wa posh. One thing she dint
love: Americans thought England consisted of London, and t'rest
wa just fields and sheep.

Garrett dropped into a deep snoring sleep. Snow trucks came

beeping, chafing and sputtering against ice. Kel's buzz faded, her body remembering its sickness, her bruised parts starting to prickle and hum, feeling less like proof of pleasure and more like judgements, proof of wrongness. What wa wrong wi her that *this* wa what she wanted?

A silk scarf wa still looped loosely round her neck. She broke its knot, pulled it free of her. Wearing it felt perverted, suddenly, as if scarf really had belonged to her grandma. As if it warra family heirloom, tarnished, now, by a sex game. She chose her scarves based on smell, buying any that carried scent of old ladies and time. She never found out why she dint know her family, why her mam kept her away from them. Mam would only say, Trust me, you're best off out. Now Kel wondered if her mam'd only meant you're best off out your own family. Mebs she'd meant *any* family, any complicated ties.

Beneath trucks' beeping, Kel heard a rattle. She listened fut clink of keys, fut creak ut flat door swinging open. She imagined light switch clicking on, bedroom washed in white glow, Alex stood int doorway surveying mess they'd left ont floor: underwear, spent condoms, her rabbit half buried in a T-shirt, tub of coconut oil wit lid missing, finger marks gouging oil's surface. Another bloke laid in his bed, snoring and soft and unaware and unarmed.

Again, that rattle. She recognised it: wind rattling bedroom window, mekkin glass shake in its pane. Her body let go, breathed out. Tired fell over her like a weighted blanket, a crushing kind of tired that word "tired" did no justice. She wanted to sink into tired, sink into sleep. Her brain refused to power down. Refused rest.

She'd hoped having Garrett round would revive her, thought mebs she'd just forgotten what gerrin out of bed wa for, and once she wa reminded that there warra life to live, she'd sack off all this sleeplessness, all this lying about. Work had been sending her peppy emails assuring her she warra valued member ut "family" who could take as long as she needed to take care of hersen—as long as she dint need more than her ten days of PTO. Kel worked for an "emerging" start-up that gi her twice workload a human could accomplish for half a living wage. Snow days had gi'en her some leeway, but now they wanted her back int office on Monday. Only two days left to recover. If she lost job, she'd have to leave. That's if she could get airfare together. Every time she thought of it—moving back in wi her mam, if her mam'd have her, becoming a lump under bedsheets in her mam's spare room—she felt like she wa gerrin swallowed whole.

Rach and Shaz had grown apart int years she'd been gone, abandoned group chat they'd used to keep in touch since they left school. Now they messaged Kel on private threads whenever they wanted to complain about each other. Currently, Rach wa pissed off at Shaz for not texting back after Rach'd invited her out round town, and Shaz wa pissed off at Rach for inviting her out round town in first place, for faking being mates wi her again after fobbing her off years ago. Kel couldn't tell them she wa sick. Same as she couldn't tell them how lonely it'd been, gerrin stranded int middle of a failing marriage. How much she'd needed their support. She dint have right to ask them for it, not after running away from them so many times— running towards whatever lad she'd mistaken fut centre ut universe. Way she'd chased Ando when they warrall at school. Way she'd let America absorb her, let Alex.

If she told them she wa sick, they'd only say same thing they said when she told them marriage wa done: *Come home*. They couldn't see that going back would mek it like her life in America never happened, like she'd woke from a decade-long coma, everyone moved on wi'out her.

At 4:18 a.m. her phone lit up wi a weather alert. Fourth blizzard warron its way that afternoon. This one looked more alarming than t'rest—it had more red triangular warning signs, more capital letters. She scanned info, eyes resting ont scariest words. Powerful, frostbite, hurricane, whiteout.

Well, she'd better nip tut shops once Garrett left, since even

Domino's probs wouldn't deliver in a "whiteout." And wont that what real Bostonians did when their smartphones prophesied floods, freeze, snow, sleet, bad air, heat, bomb cyclones, and America's many other attempts at mass murder? Her fridge and freezer wa barren but for two loaf heels and an avocado, soft and brown, crater int its side where skin had dimpled beneath press of Kel's thumb.

As homicidal as weather wa promising to be, it opened a pocket of hope in Kel's chest. Surely this meant more snow days? Surely she'd been gi'en an inch of slack, a snatch of time for her body to find its old strength. She checked her email—nowt from work, but obvs her manager wont awake yet. That snow day email would come, though, Kel told hersen. It would.

By seven a.m. Garrett's snores had turned into whimpers that wa somehow harder to listen to; they seemed to announce just how much he wa enjoying his oblivion. Kel wanted him to wake, gi her instructions again. She wanted him to lie on top of her, mek her small and squeezed and held down. She wanted barely room to breathe. She nudged him int ribs. He stirred, rolled towards her, laid an arm over her neck, hand scrabbling for his phone ont bedside table. Pressure of him against her windpipe sent her whole body tingling, remembering last night, how he'd nestled her neck int crook of his thumb and forefinger, how he'd held her there, fixed, safe. He unlocked his phone, saw weather alert, moaned sleepily. He ran a finger along her jawbone, stroking spot he'd slapped night before.

"Hot," he said, admiring whatever trace of himsen wa left in her skin. She wanted to get a look, stand naked at her full-length mirror, search for souvenirs. There'd be smudges on her arse, purpling places on her thighs. She decided not to ask hersen why she wanted to look so much.

"You've gorrer go before blizzard comes."

"I can't stay here?" Garrett batted playfully at her face like a cat. He pulled her into a kiss. Kel closed her eyes, let hersen drift intut feeling, intut want. Their bodies pressed, his hands roamed, light and grazing, then digging, fingernails into skin. Yes, he could stay—they could stop in bed and just do this till bad weather passed. She could let him run down tut supermarket for her, buy nowt but bacon, eggs, avocados, more tequila, and they could drink, fuck, sleep, eat, repeat while Boston got buried up tut window sash.

If he'd instructed her to let him stay, spoke it into her ear—while they kissed and pressed and writhed, she silently willed him, Tell me what to do—she'd have followed orders, thrill of playing obedient mekkin her feel high, hazy, sun-drenched. But when they broke apart and Garrett said, "Please? I could be your blizzard bae," Kel laid back on her side ut bed, too tired to speak, let alone pretend to be charming, upbeat woman she'd let him believe she wa. She craved more him, more sex, more play, more pain-pleasure. Her body craved more silence, more stillness, more alone.

She med Garrett avo on toast, wincing at every slam ut cupboard doors, every clink and scrape ut knife and plate, all t'normal kitchen noises too painful, too loud for her brain. She shooed him down t'hallway, laughed off his jokes that he couldn't bear to leave her. Hunting for his coat int hallway closet, he found a speckled cardigan far too big to be hers.

"Try it on," she said, since he wa appraising it like he'd pulled it off a department store rack. He slipped intut cardigan, checked himsen out int full-length. Kel felt bad; she'd told Alex it warran old-man cardigan, that it med him look a proper grandad, which wa probs why he'd left it behind. But when it hung from Garrett's broader shoulders, it warra sexy cardigan. A proper sexy cardigan. She wanted to grab him by neck of it, pull him back tut bedroom.

"Keep it," she said. She opened her flat door.

"Maybe I'll drop by later." He gave her flirty eyes, peeking through silky black lashes.

"Don't be a dick, you'll get literal frostbite." Kel put her serious face on, but she couldn't tell if her no had come out flirty anyway. After years of Alex assuming she meant opposite of whatever she said, she second-guessed every word she gave to Garrett, like every no might be mistaken forra yes.

And dint she mean yes this time? Wont she hoping he'd over-rule her, show up anyway? She walked him tut front entrance, tip-toeing across foyer's tile floor, socks soaking up wet of someone else's footprints. Her apartment building warra 1920s red brick wi drafty glass front doors, concrete steps leading down to Comm Ave. Shock ut cold when Garrett pushed door open, Kel's skin flinching into full-body goosepimples beneath her cotton sleep onesie. She looked away as he crossed threshold, imagining an icicle falling, spearing his skull. American icicles wa proper bastards, hanging long and pointy over doors like conic crystal daggers. Not like piddly English ones that wa barely size of her finger. She dint under-stand how people just walked in and out of their houses all winter in this country, wi'out ducking and running, hands over heads, expecting to get impaled.

Garrett leaned back across threshold, mekkin Kel nervous for his exposed neck. His face craned towards hers forra goodbye smooch. Int moment she stretched up to meet his lips—closing her eyes, trying not to think of icicular manslaughter—through flitter of her lashes she saw a dark blob against snowy street. Somebody walking towards them, along Comm Ave from direction of down-town. Ankle-length black coat, hood up. A body she knew. Gar-rett hung on tut kiss, wanting it to be sensual, lingering. Kel's hand pushed his chest, pushed him away. Lick of hurt, or surprise, in his face.

"You'll get icicled." She tried to laugh, prayed he'd go wi'out asking questions. He raised his eyebrows as if to say, *Suit yourself*, descended steps and headed off, away from downtown, slowly, jerkily, navigating ice. Just like Kel, he hadn't learned how to cope wi this sort of weather, never had right kind of shoes. Person coming from other direction warra true New Englander, striding confident and fast. Kel turned away, heart skipping, as her sleepy brain landed ont person's name: Maggie.

Kel hadn't seen her sister-in-law in over a year. Last Kel heard, Maggie wa living wi her fella and her baby in Pittsfield, which warras far west as you could get before you hit New York State. Last words Maggie had said to Kel, int form of a post on Kel's Facebook wall: "Un-friend me you bitch!" Kel took it as a sign that Maggie wont "super pumped" about her and Alex's separation. Maggie'd never been here, not inside apartment, anyway. Alex wa always demanding to know why Kel dint like letting people inside, why they couldn't throw family dinner parties, why she dint invite her mates round for drinks.

Mebs Maggie wa too far away to see their lips touch—mebs Kel could say Garrett wa just a mate. Mebs it wont Maggie at all, mebs somebugger else wa braving mid-morning chill in Maggie's winter coat. Kel poked a stiff finger into her mailbox's keyhole and turned it, hoping she looked like a person casually checking forra parcel.

"Your boyfriend is cute," said a too-familiar voice from foot ut steps.

Kel whipped round, pretending to be surprised, her finger still pointing, pretending to be a key. Maggie peered darkly over a tasselled scarf. Kel dint have energy to explain that Garrett wont her boyfriend, he warran ethical non-monogamist. She shrugged limply, folded her arms over her stomach, feeling silly and cold and exposed in her onesie.

When her, Rach, and Shaz wa kids, they could communicate owt through a shrug; they had a whole shrug catalogue. A shrug for *yes*, a shrug for *no*, a shrug for *mebs*, one for *soz like*, one for *shurrup, ya dick*, one for *get t' fuck*, one for *love you too*. Kel wished she could use that language now. But it dint work in America; her gestures dint translate. Anyway, Kel dint have a shrug for when your nearly-ex-sister showed up unannounced and you wanted to ask her what the fuck wa she doing here. Kel couldn't think of one good reason. Unless Alex had sent Maggie to spy. Kel wouldn't purrit past him, and if so, she'd already fucked it.

Maggie started climbing steps. Kel's arm shot out, palm raised in a signal that in any language meant, *Stop! Fucksake, don't come closer!* She couldn't let Maggie intut musty flat where she'd been gradually falling apart, too sick to clean, dust gathering ont skirting boards, surfaces cluttered wi dirty dishes and clothes and a tower of grease-slick pizza boxes. Not where her bedroom still held evidence of last night's adventure. She thought about her pending green card, about trying to hang onto this life she'd wound up in. She thought about bruise Garrett had left on her face. She'd not even had chance to take a look.

"I've got to go tut shops before blizzard comes," Kel said, as if that could explain her *fuck-off* palm.

Maggie sighed, checked her phone, looked up and down Comm Ave as if she had several better places to be. "I can take you in my car."

Kel cursed her Britishness—her whole culture's inability to ask anyone a straight fucking question, or gi a straight fucking response. Her body screamed at her to say yes tut offer, her legs and arms insisting they couldn't fathom finding strength to lug shopping bags home on foot. She told Maggie to wait int foyer, by t'stairs and a stale-smelling wheelie bin.

Back int flat, Kel rounded up her sex souvenirs—condoms, rabbit, knickers, lube—shoved them int closet, heartbeat rising wit effort, till it roared in her ears and she had to lie ont bed, chest heaving like she'd run round block.

She could hear Maggie shifting about int foyer, ont phone to someone, pacing mebs, mebs lifting and relifting wheelie bin lid, mebs idly kicking a loose bit of rubbish—mebs toying wit idea of pushing open Kel's flat door. Kel swung hersen sitting wi an ugly groan. Her joints clicked and twinged. There wa one crick in her neck that frightened her, sickening crunch every time she turned her head. And your neck wa quite important, wannit. It wa probs quite worrying that her bones wa grinding against each other in there, feeling like any moment they might go pop, grunt, and her head would glide off her spine altogether. She'd read ont internet about women wi Ehlers-Danlos who'd been told that if they moved their neck too fast they'd decapitate themsens ont inside. But Kel had checked, she dint have any other Ehlers-Danlos symptoms, so fingers crossed she'd only get bread and ice cream at supermarket, not beheaded.

TJ's on Coolidge Corner wa rammed, every skinny aisle stuffed wi heavily swaddled humans, their red faces, their frantic hands. Shelves wa empty of water jugs and pasta, and checkout queue snaked through half ut shop, everyone's trollies piled up wi bog roll. Kel hung at edge ut mayhem, fingers fastened tut handlebar of her trolley. She'd been inside so long, she'd forgotten there wa this many people. Forgotten how to be part of all this rushing about. She dint get Trader Joe's at best of times, but her coworkers proper loved it. Before Boston, Kel'd never seen well-off kids—or anybugger— excited about supermarket's own-brand products. Morrisons-own 8p supernoodles wa what you bought when you couldn't afford owt else. But Trader Joe sold organic Colombian coffee, fair-trade cacao nibs, carbon-neutral plantain chips, and none of it cost 8p. In Boston, it dint matter what supermarket Kel walked into, or how little she bought; she always spent $85. A fortnight's worth of milk, cereal, salad, and pasta: $85. Three ready meals, bottle of wine, and a puzzle book: $85. Frozen waffles and fancy guacamole: $85. She couldn't afford groceries anymore, so she'd stopped counting, started just purrin everything on her credit card. Before, when Kel and Alex wa still together, they used to just about cover rent, food, drinks ont weekends. Now rent ate up more than half Kel's wages. She'd move, but rates had shot up since they signed their lease. She couldn't afford a studio now. And where would she go? Suburbs wa no cheaper, plus she'd never gerrout. She'd be lost int vastness.

Maggie tugged trolley from Kel's numb gloveless hands, said, "Let's just get it done," and took off down an aisle, parting other shoppers, who scooped their bums in to mek way. She pushed last two-gallon water jug ontut trolley's lower rung, then steamed over tut tinned goods as if she knew exactly what situation required. Just like Alex would've. He always behaved as if he had right answer to any question, practical or philosophical, including why female soldiers shouldn't be allowed in infantry units, whether socialism wa evil, and correct thing to do wi a woman's pubic hair (because periods are dirty; yes; shave it all off). Maggie'd seemed agitated ont drive tut shop, though, steering wi one hand, other hand to her mouth, biting at skin round her thumbnail. She'd kept up a rapid stream of small talk—winter tyres, Boston drivers, expected windchills—filling up all t'space so there'd be no chance to ask her why or how she'd just dropped into Kel's new life.

Kel shimmied apologetically between bodies, reached into gaps, grabbed owt she could touch. Bag of frozen chips, posh popcorn infused wi truffle oil, taco-making kit, box of Christmas-themed cookies, "Jazz" apples—fucking hell, she dint know what she needed. She wa far too English for this; her only survival skill wa to shrug and say, Be reyt.

Wave of thicker tired hit, separating her like a wall from thronging horde around her. A new gravity, forcing her downwards. She wa going invisible right int middle of TJ's—fingers, arm, head, vanishing intut banana stand behind her—and everyone carrying on like nowt's occurred. All she could think wa how much she needed to lie down, sprawl across TJ's sludge-streaked lino, down wi everyone's mucky boots. She couldn't straighten her legs. Cramp clutched her calves and thighs, a gripped, locked feeling.

She folded hersen into an awkward heap, leaning heavily ont banana stand, her items bundled to her chest, Christmas cookies crumbling under squeeze of her arm. She prayed Garrett dint use this TJ's, couldn't possibly be pushing down this aisle right this second. Wa there any chance he'd still think she wa hot if he saw her now? She dint want Maggie seeing her down here either, not if she wa reporting back to Alex. Minutes passed. Cramp still held. Her toes buzzed wi summat like pins and needles. An army of duckish rubber boots knocked against her knees and feet. Nobody looked down to see who they wa kicking, and Kel dint expect them to. Bostonians wa deathly allergic to grocery store eye contact of all kinds.

Maggie appeared above her, staring down. "What's wrong?"

Kel shrugged. "I dint know what to get."

Their cashier warra young person wi dragon-coloured hair, kind eyes, a badge pinned to their shirt that said "Casey" beside one that said "they/them." Kel could never remember Casey's name. They never remembered Kel at all till she spoke, then they said, Oh, it's you!

Casey always told Kel same thing: You know, your accent's not that strong, but it's there. We have a guy come in whose accent's real strong, but yours is harder to spot. Cashiers told her this like it warra compliment. They had no idea that she had to whack it back on thick whenever she went home. In Yorkshire, losing your accent wa unforgivable. It meant you wa purrin on airs, forgetting yoursen. Rach gorra bit of a posh voice on after uni, which wa bad—Shaz never forgave her—but nowhere near as bad as coming home wi a Yankee twang.

How come it wa always some bloke swanning round Boston, accent intact, and hers had gone wobbly? These famously unchangeable blokes, mekkin everyone strain to understand them, while she did whatever she could to be easier to hear. Her coworkers would say it wa "gendered." Kel couldn't take those kinds of words back to Yorkshire either.

This time, Casey said, "Oh, it's you!" followed by "This your sister?" clearly hoping for *two* Yorkshire accents they could pronounce defunct.

All Kel's concentration wa going into ignoring pins and needles in her feet, keeping her knees bent to stave off cramps, keeping pain of it off her face.

"Her little sister," Maggie, said, flat, no warmth, but certain, like it warra fact not up for debate. Kel avoided everyone's eyes, not wanting to be forced to confirm or deny, while Maggie chatted away wi Casey like there wa no better pleasure than exchanging basic personal facts wi a stranger—hometowns, high schools, high school mascots. How could Maggie think they wa sisters? They barely knew each other.

Kel'd always wanted a sister, like. She'd mebs even, at one point, hoped Maggie would be her sister, but relationship had never materialised. "Sister" warra label they used and nowt else. Moment Kel and Alex wa married, Maggie had started calling her "sis," but not a second before. Just like Maggie's mam had med Kel call her "Mrs. Martin" before wedding and "Mom" after. She'd said, "Now you'll always be my daughter." Kel found it proper weird at first, not summat anyone did at home—parents never asked you to call them owt but their first names. Who med these promises of unconditional love just because it wa tradition?

A deeper part of her had been grateful, though, beneath all her British squeaming. She'd only ever had a mam: no dad, no real step-dad, just a set of grandparents who died young; aunties, uncles, and cousins they dint talk to for reasons her mam would never share; and, eventually, a baby sister, but Briar dint come along till Kel wa not far off leaving home. Kel'd always wanted a sister like Shaz and Rach had, big sisters who leant them clothes, taught them naughty words. Shaz and Rach always knew more about world than Kel did because of their sisters. Then Alex showed up wi his whole Catholic family, an arsenal of extended relatives, wi their voluminous houses and comfortable salaries, promising to spread their arms round her. Their game day cookouts and their unflagging chat, such a contrast to Kel and her mam, who seemed, as Kel got older, to fall out ut habit of talking at all. Martins' unshakable beliefs about who they wa and how world worked—that had been a lure an' all, like a fire glowing int hearth, drawing her in. Their certainties: god, country, family. Alex used to say to her, Now that we're married, we're one person, in a way that med her feel anchored, like she'd got ballast. She wa Mrs. Alexander Martin. Erased. Safe.

Casey and Maggie wa still going: Super Bowl, Celtics game, retirement of Big Papi. Kel willed hersen to come up wi a contribution.

"Is it gunna be a bad one, then?" She nodded at shop's front windows, bodies running by, mummified in layers of North Face, hoods pulled low against snow that had started falling already.

"Allegedly," Casey replied, and sighed in a way that med Kel feel like she'd failed, like she still dint know how to do American conversation. Casey loaded trolley wi brown paper bags, bulging wi Maggie's expertly chosen snowstorm supplies. Kel wanted to ask for plastic bags, but she knew that wont "ethical."

"I love the way you talk," Casey said, handing Kel her receipt. "Always brings me up."

Kel thanked them, pushed trolley out ontut street, legs cramping into a permo bend, mekkin her walk as if she warra street mime creeping up on an unsuspecting someone.

Ont drive back, Maggie kept up her small talk, but her hand wa trembling against steering wheel; she seemed shivery even after heaters warron full blast. Kel warrabout to ask if she wa sick but got distracted by buzz of a text.

Garrett: *Hey, just checking in. Wanted to make sure you feel good about being physical last night? I'm super grateful for our time together.* She left phone in her lap, open ont message so she could reread. Each return to his words sparked currents of want.

When Kel wa fifteen, and her and Ando started fucking, it never occurred to him to ask her, after, if she still felt good about decision, if there wa any regret. And it'd never occurred to her to ask hersen.

Snow wont that bad yet, melting into nothing ont windshield. She could get rid of Maggie, tell Garrett to come over. Mebs she could trust him to see her sick. Mebs he'd look after her, mek her dinner, help her rest, then tie that headscarf round her eyes, speak into her ear.

"That from your new green card ticket?" Maggie said, wrenching Kel out her fantasy. She'd either glimpsed message in Kel's lap, or just seen t'dreamy look on her face.

"What's that meant to mean?"

Maggie bit at her thumb skin, honked horn at car in front who'd broke too sharply, Kel and Maggie thrown forwards, seat beats tightening across their chests and necks.

"Seriously, the drivers in this city." Maggie turned down a side street. "That's what everyone thinks," she said. "Mom, Dad, Grandma, Grandad. The aunts and uncles, the cousins. Alex. That's what they're all saying."

Weight of it collected int pit of Kel's stomach. "Everyone" had decided she'd used Alex, seen him as nowt more than a route tut greatest nation under god. Where were any of them when he wa downing a bottle of whisky on his way home from work? Where wa they when he wa passed out next tut toilet every Satdi night after chucking his guts up? And Alex wont defending her. After all their love. All their screaming, crying, miserable fucking love.

"There's easier ways to get here than marrying an alcoholic."

Maggie laughed as though Kel had said, Marrying an aardvark. "He's not an alcoholic."

All t'years Kel'd known them, Martins had always, wi'out exception, defended each other against criticism from outsiders, no matter how fair.

"Maybe he wouldn't have needed a drink," said Maggie, "if you'd been kinder."

So that wut story everyone had settled on. So he *wa* planning not to sign her papers. Or he wa planning to mek her beg. His family wa powerful, full of lawyers and military men and government officials, full of judgement. Martins wa always good, always right. Car seat disappeared beneath her—Kel wa falling intut snowstorm, intut slushy gutter, intut bitter cold.

By t'time Maggie found a parking spot on Kel's block, snow wa coming fast and dense. It wet Kel's hands, cheeks, paper bags. If Maggie dint leave soon, she wunt be able to leave at all. Bag handles disintegrated in seconds; Kel and Maggie had to carry bags from car tut door by their bottoms, two-gallon jug hanging painfully off Kel's fingers, her legs still crampy, her toes still vibrating. A flake slid down her neck, icy shudder, reminding her ut night before, Garrett's tongue travelling down her spine.

At door, Kel stopped for breath, panting wit effort of climbing steps. What now? She couldn't have Maggie inside. She needed Maggie gone, back to her own life: Pittsfield, her fella, her baby.

"I have to pee real bad," Maggie said.

Bags puckered wi each snowflake plop, threatened to fall apart. Kel's arms demanded relief. Bastard icicles hung above them, glittering and lethal.

"Mi keys are in mi coat pocket."

Maggie felt around in Kel's pockets, pulled keys out, three silver jagged fingers clinking round a plain ring. Kel couldn't be arsed wi a key ring, wi owt that wa meant to declare who she wa. *Military Wife*, *Feminist Bitch*, *Girl Boss*, *Icon*. Maggie tried wrong key, wrong key, then right un, and they bundled intut foyer. Kel sunk into a crouch, eased hersen forwards, let go ut shopping. Everything fell through bag walls, thudded ontut tiles. Egg carton, soup tins, frozen pizzas, jars of red pasta sauce, a chorus of packets splitting, glass cracking. Cylinder of spiced almonds chased a Jazz apple tut wheelie bin. It all looked happy to be free.

Kel propped flat door open wit water jug. They carried everything inside bit by bit, plonked it all onto any kitchen surface that wa still empty: windowsill, stovetop, floor. Every time Kel passed full-length mirror int hallway, she tried to glimpse her bruise—but she couldn't stop long enough, couldn't let Maggie catch her catching a look. Once shopping warrin, Maggie dashed tut loo. Kel heard distinct slosh of vom hitting toilet water, sound she'd got used to hearing nearly nightly int months before Alex left. Mebs she would've suspected it before, if she hadn't been so brain-dead wi exhaustion. Maggie must be withdrawing from summat again. Kel put kettle on to gi Maggie some noise cover, then went intut living room, laid ont loveseat int dark. There warra ringing in her ear, like tinnitus, but she hadn't been anywhere loud.

What could've happened to mek Maggie use again? She'd been sober so long—years—Kel had half forgotten Maggie's rehab

stints, her relapses. After baby wa born, it'd started to seem like it
wa *over* over.

And why come here, when you've all that family. Why call in
on your local green card whore. What did she think Kel owed her?
Or wa this a kind of punishment?

Well, she could fuck off if she thought Kel wa gunna play nurse.
Kel texted Garrett, told him she did feel good, thanks, and if he still
fancied it, he could come round and be her "blizzard bae" after all.
Then she laid, eyes closed, imagining how weekend would go: her
and Garrett playing house, cooking together, sleeping late, morning
coffee, making rituals. They'd start dating proper. He'd abandon his
polyamory, move in here. They'd build a future of adorable, Insta-
worthy domesticity, kinky sex, deep love, another wedding.

Big light flicked on. Kel yelped, threw an elbow over her eyes.
Too much, said her body. *Too much bright.*

"What are you doing in the dark?"

Kel gi Maggie her *none of your fucking business* shrug.

"Your kettle boiled."

"Where are you sleeping tonight?" Kel raised an eyebrow to gi
Maggie t'message that she'd heard what wa going on int loo, that she
knew everything wont okay.

Maggie stared at wall forra few seconds; then she said, "I'm trying
to get into rehab, but so far everywhere I've called is full."

Kel hadn't expected that much truth. Martins never acknowl-
edged out loud that they warrall quiet captives of their chosen
poison: weed, alcohol, opioids, food, money, religion. Maggie wut
only Martin whose entanglement had grown too deadly to ignore
completely.

Int kitchen, Kel flipped kettle back on, wiped rims of two used
mugs wi a bit of damp kitchen roll. Maggie leaned against cooker
in leggings and a plaid shirt, tapping at her phone, one arm pinned
across her stomach. That self-conscious arm, trying to cover widest

part of her—Kel felt a sick glob of guilt in her throat, remembering Christmas Alex bought her a camera.

Int early days of their relationship, Kel wa envious of Maggie because Maggie wa so thin and so pretty, and because everyone thought so, including Alex. On their first date, he'd boasted about his sister. She's gorgeous, he'd said. She's a hottie. He said it wi so much relish, Kel nearly dint agree to date two. Maggie used to get her mates to take her picture by t'lake or ont hood of her car, wearing angel wings and bootie shorts or a swimsuit and victory rolls, purrin photos on Facebook fut likes. She wa years too deep before they found out she wa using. "Percs," she called them, which med them sound cute. So cute, Kel dint understand at first how serious it all wa; she dint know owt about these American drugs, these prescription pills.

Maggie looked up from her phone, caught Kel looking. Kel turned tut mugs, filled them wi teabags and boiling water. She dint know if Maggie liked tea, but it dint matter. When you turned up on a Yorkshire lass's doorstep, you got gi'en a cuppa. She bobbed teabags wi a spoon, watched amber swirl through water. Mugs swirled and swayed too, like they'd come to life.

"Here." She handed a mug to Maggie, who placed it one-handed ont stovetop wi'out stopping her tapping, thumb jabbing rapidly at phone. Maggie wa swaying an' all, glitching at her edges. She put phone to her ear and walked out, down t'hallway, leaving tea behind. Kel sipped her tea, tried to keep her head still, tried to mek everything stop swinging about. Maggie paced hallway, mekkin calls.

In her first group home, Maggie replaced drugs wi food, came back transformed. She kept growing in her second and third cycles, through rehabs and halfway houses, till Kel almost dint recognise her. Still beautiful, though. Nowt Maggie went through—not months in hospital, not detox, not re-tox—med a dent in her beauty. That Christmas Alex bought Kel a camera, int post-dinner slump when everyone wa bloated and sleepy, a powerful new DSLR in her hands, Kel took Maggie's picture. She reckoned she wa trying to work out how to focus t'lens. Every time Kel raised camera to her eye, Maggie dutifully posed, smiled, tried to hide her tummy behind her arm. Kel snapped more, more shots, trying to take a picture that would prove Maggie unpretty. Every image in perfect focus: Maggie in pinup-red lipstick and a red Christmas jumper, looking shy, and sad, and pretty.

Before that day, Kel'd never understood why Rach and Shaz used to get at each other so much when they wa kids. Way they'd loved and despised each other, Rach wishing she wa small and skinny and charismatic as Shaz, and Shaz starving her body till she nearly rubbed it out altogether, and hating Rach because Rach dint hate hersen enough to get an eating disorder of her own.

Whenever Kel thought about those pictures, she felt like a bad person. Like she'd punched Maggie, left her wi two black eyes. She hid images in a "misc" file ont hard drive and never told anyone, couldn't bring hersen to admit stuff that might mek her seem ugly inside.

But it hadn't stopped her, had it? Hadn't stopped her taking videos of Alex. Alex throwing up; Alex slumped ont bathroom floor; Alex int kitchen trying to fry an egg, waving a spatula about, mekkin slurred speeches about what he'd've done different if he wut cop restraining Eric Garner, what wut proper way to keep someone in a choke hold.

At time, Kel'd told hersen she just needed a record, a witness, so she knew she wont going mad—this really wa their life.

That wont whole story, though, warrit. There wa summat sick about her, some pleasure she got from owning evidence of his failures.

Kel's phone vibrated in her pocket. When she turned her head to look down at screen, sink and oven and kitchen cupboards and owl-shaped clock Mrs. Martin had bought her all skipped along a second later, like they wa struggling to keep up. A text from Garrett. Kel leant against worktop to steady hersen. She tried to lean casual, like nowt wa moving in ways it wont meant to be. As if anyone might be watching her. As if Garrett might be. As if Alex. Screen blurred and jerked in her hand. Standing and reading at same time seemed to be too much work. She slid down worktop tut floor. She had to squint to mek out words.

Hey, I'd love to come by but I'm holed up at Daisy's now. Weather's pretty bad at this point so it wouldn't be safe to leave. Let's hang next week for sure.

Daisy wa one ut other lasses Garrett wa seeing. Kel knew from Insta that Daisy wa younger, thinner, better at makeup, better at clothes. Disappointment rushed like nausea into her mouth. Whatevs. Next week, then. Next week, the great Kel-and-Garrett romance would begin. She dropped phone ontut floor between her legs, looked up at kitchen window. Snowflakes threw themsens at glass like they wa trying to break it, like they wa dezzy to get in. Each one seemed to be flying at Kel's head. Each one warra bit of Morse code. Pre-tty-bad. Pre-tty-fuck-ing-bad. Pre-tty-fuck-ing-bad-fuck-*fuck*.

Maggie came back intut kitchen, phone on speaker, blasting hold music, a synthetic keyboard-and-glockenspiel instrumental of Billy Joel's "Just the Way You Are."

"What are you doing down there?" Maggie asked.

Every note ut music jammed Kel's thoughts, scrambled her brain. *Too much.*

"Why are you here?"

"Do you need me to go?"

"No, it's just—" Kel gestured wi her hand: *It's just—you know what I'm gerrin at.*

"I can go."

"No, you can't." Kel waved at window, at beating snow: *No, you can't, and you know it. And where's your fucking baby.*

"Do you want me to go? I can dig out my car. I don't know if the roads are safe, but—" Maggie left her sentence hanging, unfinished, less a statement than a cue: Kel's cue to jump in, apologise, insist she stay. Another classic Martin manoeuvre.

After Alex left, all his texts had same rhetorical arrangement. Like, *You can keep all our stuff from the apartment. I don't want anything that could remind me of us, it's too painful.* Kel knew she wa meant to say, *No, please take this, please take that*—let him have martyrdom *and* furniture. She'd replied, *Ok, I'll keep it all.* Next day, she came home from work to find he'd been in and stolen random things—omelette pan, KitchenAid mixer, throw pillows, living room rug. Owt he could chuck int back ut car, owt he knew she liked. That cheap IKEA rug she'd had to fight for, like she'd had to fight for any purchase he dint deem essential. When they'd gorrit home, after a mortifying shouting match in one of IKEA's staged cuboids of domesticity, he'd fallen in love wit rug's plush pile, its rust-blue tones. He laid out on it every night while they watched telly. She hadn't replaced it, and she'd resented every cold footstep across bare boards since.

She tried to tell Maggie she could bloody well get out, then, yeah. Go brave those icy highways, darlin. But her words wa gerrin lost ont long journey from brain to mouth.

Maggie said summat else—Kel couldn't turn t'sounds into sense. Glockenspiel Billy Joel wa drowning everything out.

Kel's eyes wa closing of their own accord. Ringing in her ear turned shrill. Pins and needles in her toes became a vivid sting. She grabbed worktop's edge, pulled hersen up. Walked fast down t'hall-way, trying to mek it tut bedroom. Halfway there her body said, *Lie down or fall down.*

Kel hit floorboards: knees, shoulder, skull. She lay int dark of her closed eyes. Paralysed, no energy left to move. She counted each beat of her rabid pulse, each breath surging in and out.

"What's wrong with you?" Maggie: hair brushing Kel's cheek, breath on Kel's nose. She asked again, "What's wrong," wi a sweetness that reminded Kel of Alex's voice when it wa tender, when it wa soft and loving.

She felt suddenly, desperately lonely, remembering Kel Martin, trapped inside wi Alex, her desire shrivelling every time he got angry about their lack of sex till any want she'd had withered into nowt, nope, never again. Kel Martin counting days, how long could she put him off before he'd shout again, before he'd gi up on coercing her, roll over and say, Maybe there's just something wrong with you.

Dark when Kel's eyes opened next. She warrin bed, in Boston's deepest dark, an orangey streetlamp dark, no noise, only a blizzard burying them all. She sat up, testing her heart. Calmer. Her ears still rang, her feet still stung, but whatever goblin warrin charge of her body had let a sliver of her return. Vague memories of Maggie helping her up off hallway floor, helping her tumble ontut mattress. Easing her into her onesie. Maggie crawling under t'duvet beside her, intut mess of Kel and Garrett's sex sheets. Bedroom door opening and closing, Maggie mekkin trips tut loo to throw up. Maggie wa asleep next to her now, clammy, hair sweat-matted across her forehead. Comfort of Maggie's heat, her firm block of body plugging up Alex's furrow.

Kel bundled under t'duvet wi her phone, screen lighting up space around her head. She checked her email. Nowt from work yet. Shaz and Rach had messaged in their separate threads: *You alright? Haven't heard from you in weeks, mate.* She wished they'd mek friends, use group chat again, so she only had to find energy to tell one set of lies. She hated thought that they'd come too unglued, that there'd be no way of sticking themsens back together.

Rach and Shaz would imagine Times Square and set of *Friends* when they thought of Kel's American life. She couldn't tell them truth, not after she had gall to leave them behind. She couldn't tell them what she'd just discovered: that she loved being controlled in bed, loved being spanked and tied up. They wouldn't approve. They knew her too well. They saw her ashen face first time Ando touched her. She'd never told them how often his rough hands, his grabbing, had resurfaced in her mind. She wouldn't know how to explain that there wa summat different about pain you invited in. Way it deletes every part of you that int pure sensation. Way it lets you ride that sensation into new countries, places hidden int dark of you.

Kel flicked through her phone's photo reel, winding backwards through her and Garrett's selfies, drinks out wi workmates, her last months wi Alex—those videos of him she wa ashamed she hadn't erased, but still dint erase—till she found ones ut weekend in Provincetown they'd tried to rescue everything wi. Grey streets ut first day, bright skies ut next. Two smiles tacked on like donkey tails. And those snapshots camera dint capture: spats had in ferocious undertones over dinner at Lobster Pot, tacky ornaments of their seaside-themed B&B, Kel storming out ut coffee shop after Alex objected to her splurging an extra 40¢ on whipped cream.

Wa there any evidence she could present that would convince Maggie it wont Kel's fault marriage fell apart? That she'd tried to keep them together.

She dint have a video of him saying, in that musty, aquatic B&B, "If we don't have sex this weekend, you might as well go home." Not quite *I won't sign your papers*. But not *not* that.

There wa no digital record of her taking a fat swig from their bottle of prosecco, sucking in a breath, and flinging off her clothes in an angry striptease designed to disturb him into never wanting sex from her again. No image ut soft sad drop of Alex's cheeks int seconds after he came, when bliss subsided, and he realised what he'd drove her to.

Maggie stirred, rolled over, her breath catching then settling, back into its gentle rhythm. Kel gave up on sleep, snuck intut hallway by t'light of her phone's torch, tiptoed tut full-length. There it wa, finally, in a wash of torchlight: staining her jawline, a cheeky smear of bruise. She pressed it wi her finger, igniting trace of last night's pain. Ghost of last night's pleasure. She wished he wa here, lying on her heavy, soothing her tense body, stopping her from floating away like a loose helium balloon.

Keeping an ear ont bedroom, Kel dropped one shoulder of her onesie, swivelled her hips till she could see purple bite marks on her bum med by four distinct teeth, three of Garrett's incisors and one slanted canine. His imprints in her flesh. She stared at them for ages. She wanted to take pictures. She groped wall, searching fut hallway light switch.

A noise int foyer. Kel yanked her onesie back over her shoulder, turned off her phone's torch. Her heart loud. Thought of being caught looking at hersen this way, someone breaking into a moment wi her secret self. She listened. Slock slock of tiles slapped by slippered feet. Male whistling. She waited forra knock, forra rattling key. Then came t'crash of glass hitting wheelie bin's bottom. Smack ut bin lid closing. Of course not Alex, of course not Garrett. Just a neighbour sneaking out his empties. Neighbour's door slammed, whistling stopped. Kel breathed, back in her own dark, her own privacy, her own shame.

Sunday, snow still falling. Kel's body still heavier than muscle and bone had any right to be. Maggie, back on her small talk. Weather gave her all t'material she needed: how many trees down, how many schools closed, how many homes flooded, power grids failed, burnt-out car wrecks, patches of black ice. How many dead. She kept it up through a breakfast of oven chips and scrambled eggs, through a kind of symbolic gerrin dressed, Maggie purrin her shirt back on over t'tank and leggings she'd slept in, Kel adding socks and a cardi to her onesie. Kel checked her email every few seconds, waiting for work's snow day announcement to appear. Refresh—nothing. Refresh—nothing. On Maggie chatted, an expert at keeping conversation light. All Martins were. They held their conversations out ut muck like a washing line holding a bright white sheet over grass.

228

Wi Alex, Kel had waited, let him fill up their lives wi chatter, and nudged gently gently, and waited more, fut time when they could tear sheet down, roll it around int mud. Waited fut Martins to mek good on all they'd seemed to promise: a family that dint drown in its own silences, that understood each other, built each other whole. But sheet stayed white, talk stayed small. Nearly a decade together, and she couldn't swear they'd ever had a proper conversation.

Maggie's voice prodded Kel's brain, needling its soft tissues. They wa sat ont loveseat picking at a split bag of tortilla chips when Kel finally had enough.

"Are you ever gunna tell me what happened?" she asked, cutting across Maggie's wondering aloud if snow would stop before nightfall. "Or are we gunna keep pretending you're just here to hang out wi me?"

"Are we gonna keep pretending you didn't collapse in the hallway last night? Are we gonna keep pretending you're not covered in bruises?"

Kel felt old irritations scratching at her, urging her to snap back. Wa that how her and Alex always flipped from talking about nowt to having a screaming row? She forced hersen calm. "Look, I'm not having a go, I'm just worried."

Maggie sighed as if Kel warra nuisance, ruining a perfectly pleasant afternoon. She shuffled off loveseat ontut floor, where Kel's rug used to be. She laid flat, staring at ceiling, then explained, in a weird matter-of-fact-ish voice, that a few months ago her fella left her, that grief of his going—stress of single motherhood—had med her start back on Percs, that Percs wa more expensive now, that when she got short of cash she turned to good old-fashioned intravenous heroin, took too much, OD'd, died. Paramedics found her mid-death, gave her Narcan, so she wa "fine" apart from withdrawal sickness, which wa mostly gone now—would disappear in a day or two.

Kel wa struck, first, by Maggie's certainty. She knew she'd be well soon. She'd died, but soon her body would be strong, no sickness lingering in her nervous system, no wondering when—if—it would end.

Maggie ran a hand up and down her stomach, stared at ceiling like a kid searching for shapes int clouds. She dint look like someone who'd died. She wa full-blooded. A shorter, rounder Alex, wi his same narrow eyes, same goosey laugh. Kel tried to imagine Maggie laid just as she wa now, but wi her heart stopped, her blood still. Briefly an object.

"What warrit like, dying?"

"I mean, I dunno. I just went to sleep."

Kel wa so exhausted, so sleep-deprived, she wa almost jealous. Why couldn't she die, just forra second, just to hit pure black. True nothing.

She warra kind of dead, though, wont she. Mrs. Alexander Martin wa deffo deceased. And this wont exactly being alive, warrit. This lying awake, watching time crawl, watching everyone else gerron wit usual processes of living. She wa starting to feel like a ghoul haunting her own life.

She asked where Lila wa, Maggie's baby. Maggie said, "Oh, she's at Mom's," wi a fake kind of easiness, then switched topics so deftly Kel nearly dint notice that they'd stopped talking about Maggie's temporary death and started talking about Mrs. Martin's habit of deciding that everyone's gorra favourite animal, and only buying them presents featuring that animal fut rest of their lives. Fut last several Christmases, Kel had received owl-themed measuring bowls, slippers, jewellery, mittens, and an owl-shaped bog roll holder. And Kel dint have a favourite *anything*. Finding out that she liked—preferred, desired—kind of sex her and Garrett had, that wont just first time she knew what she wanted in sex. It wut first time, Kel realised now, she'd felt sensation of preferring any thing over another. Of wanting. Of becoming someone who could say, Well, this is just who I am. She'd always waited to see what everyone else wanted to do drink see

230

feel, and then she'd tried to gi it them. Mebs that's why Alex couldn't understand her resistance to sex after he came back from war. Because she'd always never minded. She wa easy breezy, her. She warrup for owt. She wont fussed.

Wa she fussed about this life in America? Did she *want* it? She wanted to reach down to Maggie, stroke her hair, hold her hand—owt—to congratulate her for being first person in history to stir summat squirmy and truth-like in Kel wi nowt but power of small talk.

"Maggie, why aren't you wi Lila? Why aren't you at Mom's?"

In Maggie's long, long silence, Kel thought of newborn Lila's thrust of black hair, her impossible smallness, born several weeks premature. Born hooked on methadone. Weight of her miniature body in Kel's arms, warm, wriggling, solid. Shock of her heaviness, ut power in her limbs.

Maggie found out she wa pregnant when she checked hersen into rehab fut fourth time and they ran intake tests. In-laws wouldn't let Kel visit Maggie wi'out a chaperone, afraid that hea-then Kel would try to convince her she dint have to keep baby. Kel *did* think that if she could get Maggie alone, she could tell her she had options, tell her it wont wrong to put hersen first. But Kel wa always supervised by Alex, Alex Sr., and woman called Mom. Now here Maggie wa, all Kel's. No longer corruptible. Or no lon-ger worth protecting.

Kel'd always wondered if her mam had been shunned by her own family in some way—if her silence about them came from that kind of pain. She'd always wished her mam would let her in, hoped one day she'd let some detail slip, so Kel could say summat comfort-ing like, Fuck them, you've got me.

Kel did lean down, did stroke Maggie's hair. She said, "Just tell me."

Maggie shook her head forra long time. Then, wi a tremble in her voice, she explained that t'dude she shot up wi called paramedics, then ran. When paramedics came, Lila wa asleep upstairs, wi her only caregiver smacked up, nonbreathing. DCF took Lila, left her int care of Maggie's mom, and Maggie wont allowed to be int same house.

"Fucking hell" warrall Kel could manage.

"Don't, please. Please. I came here because you're the only one I could think of who wouldn't look at me like I was a fucking worthless piece of fucking—" Her mouth fixed open. A silent sob wracked her whole body, jerked her like a seizure.

Kel wanted to cry too, but she wont sure who for—Maggie, or Lila, or her mam, or teenage Kel, or Kel Martin, or Kel whose body wa no longer her own. She climbed down ontut floor, laid along Maggie's length. Held her. Held her till seizing stopped. Till her body wa still.

When they'd been laid, quiet, for who knew how long, Maggie said, in a snuffly whisper, "Alex isn't speaking to me right now. He says he can't forgive me for putting Lila in danger."

Of course he fucking did. He wut most confidently moralistic drunkard Kel had ever met. When Maggie went into preterm labour, Kel, Alex, and in-laws tear-arsed across state to Pittsfield. Alex'd started drinking at ten a.m. that day. Kel saw him int kitchen, through door crack, when he thought himsen unwatched. He held a box of red wine above his head and opened tap, lerrit flow straight into his mouth. Later, only evidence wut burgundy blood splatter ont counter, telltale drip-drip trail.

Doctors had gi'en Maggie drugs to stall contractions, keep her mid-labour till Lila wa big enough to be born. Drugs paralysed her, knee to chest. She wa confined tut bed, unable to stand for however many weeks it'd take fut baby to grow. In-laws had refused to acknowledge Alex's drunkenness, but when Kel leaned in to hug Maggie, Maggie put her mouth to Kel's ear and said, "You're an angel for putting up with him." Wi her nose in Maggie's neck— Maggie smelling somehow floral and girly even in a hospital gown, even wi her pee draining into a bag—Kel felt like she warrin a real moment. Two of them had finally cut through family's bravado, confronted way things wa. But when she pulled out ut hug, looked in Maggie's eyes for that proper connection, that real real, summat rang false. Maggie's words wa too neat, a phrase clipped clean from marriage playbook. Kel wa *supposed* to be an angel. She wa meant to accept a lifetime of *purrin up* wi him. That wa when Maggie'd started to seem less like someone Kel needed to save from t'family, and more like family spokeswoman, person who'd firmly remind her that "angel" wa her job title. Maggie wa busy being an angel an' all: immobilised, heroic, bearing whatever she had to bear to bring life intut world.

Kel's arm wa numb and prickly from being laid int same position too long. She hauled hersen back ontut loveseat. Maggie followed.

"Alex can be a proper twat when he wants to be," said Kel.

Maggie arched an eyebrow. Kel decided to take it as a sign of encouragement.

"I twisted mi ankle once, right," Kel said, beginning a story she hadn't realised she'd been waiting years to tell—tell now, tell quick, before moment wa over. "It warra few days before a military ball. Mi ankle wa three times size it wa meant to be, most painful thing ever, but Alex wa adamant there wa nowt up wi me." She'd hobbled around, trailing her bum leg behind her, Alex walking several steps ahead, calling back to her over his shoulder, At least make the limp look convincing, babe. Night ut ball, a neighbour took pity, leant her some crutches. She Long John Silvered it all evening in heels and a gown, fighting to keep up wi him, always paces behind. At end ut night, walking tut car, Alex wa fifteen yards ahead wi a group of his soldiers. "Oh, wait for her," CO's wife had called. "She's faking it," Alex called back, wi'out slowing down.

Maggie shook her head. "Asshole."

Kel stayed very still, trying not to react, trying not to disturb very first instance of a Martin agreeing wi her that another Martin had, in fact, been a bit of a dickhead. Kel *wont* mad, after all. Their marriage *had* been hard, messy, mebs even wrong.

"He loves you, though," said Kel. "He'll come round." What else could she say? It wa true: Alex pushed you away, but he dint want you gone. Hadn't wanted Kel to go. And Maggie dint have same choice Kel did, to try this family on like a cardigan, see if it suited.

"I guess we'll see." Maggie shrugged. A meaningful shrug—a Yorkshire shrug.

When Maggie went tut bathroom to wash her face, Kel opened her phone, clicked on her, Rach, and Shaz's long-dead group chat. *Sorry I've not been in touch*, she typed. *I've not been well.* She added three vomit emojis, then, *Miss yas.* It wont whole story, obvs, but it wa summat. She opened her private thread wi Shaz: *Ha. Now you'll have to mek friends.* She copied message, sent it to Rach.

Kel and Maggie slept face-to-face that night, breathing on each other, Maggie buried in sleep, Kel drifting between dream snatches and watching Maggie's eyeballs twitch. She woke from a restless tatter of sleep to sunlight sidling weak between window blinds, Maggie handing her tea. Snow had stopped. City plowers had cut a path down sidewalk, leaving two gritty, neck-high ice walls on either side. Just in time for everyone to drag themsens into work. Email finally plopped into Kel's inbox, subject line "RE: SNOW DAY POLICY." She dint open it.

After breakfast, Kel laid ont loveseat, hot wit effort of digesting. Maggie hugged her knees ont rugless floor, sipped tea. "Feeling any better?" she said, and, when Kel shook her head, "It's the stress."

"What is?"

"I mean, divorce is a *lot*. You're probably just depressed."

Depressed, *yes*, that warrit exactly. If by "depressed," Maggie meant pressed down on, squashed beneath a gigantic unseen hand.

Could it be true, though—could t'sickness all be in her head. It felt so physical, so beyond her control. Could she just *decide* to get better?

Maggie leapt to her feet as though swept by a gust of inspiration. "We have to get you out of this apartment." She took their mugs intut kitchen, rummaged int cupboards, and returned a minute later, grinning, holding a roll of black bin liners.

Kel dint have energy to argue. She let Maggie dress her, a jumper and coat over her onesie. Maggie pulled a beanie down over Kel's forehead, pulled boots onto Kel's feet.

"Can you make it to the door?"

Kel nodded. She wanted to explain that it wont about what she *could* do; it warrabout consequences, what would happen to her later if she *did*. There seemed to be a toll for every exertion, any activity paid for by days of exhaustion. But that dint mek sense, did it. Bodies dint work like that.

They pushed through front doors, guided their feet down icy steps. Cold teased tears from Kel's eyes. Light stung, but it wa beautiful, sun bouncing off brilliant sparkling everything. Looking took effort, but she wa glad to be looking—at icicles hanging from streetlight bulbs, bike handlebars peeping from snowbank. Cars transformed into a line of mini albino sand dunes. Burst pipe cascading ice down length ut next apartment building, frosted-glass fingers four storeys tall, reaching like overnight stalactites.

Maggie knelt, motioned for Kel to gerron her back. Like Rach used to do when they wa kids. Rach'd race away wi Kel hugging her neck, sprint a few feet, then stop, sprint, then stop, then they'd fall down, tangled, breathless, elated. Kel dint take Maggie's cue, remembering that Rach wut only person strong enough to carry her wi'out stumbling, remembering boyfriends sizing her small frame, underestimating her weight, struggling under her, pretending not to feel strain.

"I'm heavier than I look."

"I'm stronger than I look."

It wa summat Alex would've said, right before failing to pick her up. He had a habit of saying "born ready" when "ready" would have done.

Kel climbed onto Maggie's back, joined her hands at Maggie's throat. Maggie marched steady, sure, between t'two ice walls, around corner and across street tut park.

In summer, park held a green slope leading down to a walkway, then a baseball field wi a nine-foot chain-link fence. Now, snowy slope cascaded over t'walkway and banked up again, meeting tip ut fence, creating a takeoff ramp. Magical—an impromptu snow-jumping course had appeared right int middle ut city. Snowboarders zoomed down hill, flew off ramp, pulled their airborne bodies into stylish curves, landed, tumbled, and raced back up to go again. Kel let their laughter fill her wi a secondhand happiness, trying to remember what it'd felt like when her body med that much energy, when it had stamina to run up a hill over and over, legs sinking tut knees intut snow. When exhaustion felt not like dying but like living, legs aching wit joy of activity, blood happy and humming.

Maggie hitched Kel up on her back, climbed slope, body bent, grunting. Kel kept having to tamp urge to say, Don't bother, I'll be reyt. She knew she shouldn't try to mek it up hill on her tod. At top, Maggie put Kel down and sat int snow next to her, breathing heavy. Maggie wa right, she wa strong as fuck, and "as fuck" wa Yorkshire's highest measure of anything.

Air came in sharp and searing, stealing moisture from Kel's throat. She wa gerrin used tut sunlight, craving its warmth on her cheeks. She could see dive bar ont corner, looking ploughed and open. The Silhouette, Kel's haunt whenever she needed to escape flat, escape Alex drunk and laid out ont loveseat, letting his bowels empty into his trousers. Escape weight of her guilt—that he needed help, needed so much more from her than she could give.

Not much Boston to see from up there, apartment-block roofs in American-straight rows, wood slats and bricks poking through white. A dampened city, forced still. A place, like any.

Kel gathered a handful of snow, packed it tight between cupped palms. "I've gorrer go back to England."

Maggie scooped her own handful. "He will sign your papers," she said. "He's not *that* big an asshole."

They chucked their snowballs, lost sight of them int sun's glare. "Doesn't matter what he does."

Whatever Kel might or might not want med no difference now. Wouldn't matter if work gi her fifty more snow days. Her body had left its old life behind. She knew it. She could feel it in every clicking joint, every jangling nerve.

Maggie unrolled two bin liners, laid them ont ground. "You first."

Kel shuffled forwards onto her liner. Her bare frost-stung fingers held ontut liner's corners, her knees up by her chin. Maggie's hands pushed hard into Kel's back. Liner shot forwards an inch, then another, then stopped. Kel felt bad that Maggie's plan hadn't worked, that moment of joy she'd hoped to gi Kel scuppered by physics. Kel turned to say, Never mind, not to worry. She saw Maggie's gleeful eyes, her growing smile—then gravity snatched Kel from friction's grip and she hurtled down.

Fast—a terrifying, gathering fast. Blinding freeze shot into her face, up her trouser legs, up her sleeves. Sky, sun, and streets bounced as she flew over ruts and bumps. Falling so fast and free she wa scared of what would happen when she hit bottom. How would she ever stop? Wind rushing so loud she dint realise that whistling scream wa coming from her own wide-open gob. Girlish shrieks in her slipstream. Vision water blurry. Skin whip-raw and singing. We're so lucky, she thought, plummeting, world streaking white. So fucking lucky.

How Much Are We Meant to Want

First time, they went family planning clinic just to say they'd been. Twelve years old, they went fut free condoms. A trio of best mates, Kel, Shaz, and Rach, they went to hear adults ask if they wa "sexually active," and to hear themsens all say "yes," lie bursting them wi delight. They went to be believed. Nurse showered them wi freebies, a kaleidoscope of johnnies, and they stowed those funny squidgy foil squares int zip-up pockets of their school backpacks. They carried those johnnies around wi them like talismans, one in every colour. They collected and swapped johnnies like they'd swapped football stickers in little school when they wa ten. They peeled back foil, fingered oily insides, sniffed at that rubbery trapped smell, tried to guess how it'd taste, dared each other to lick. And they could produce one—*"There, see!*—any time a kid at school challenged them, said they dint *really* have johnnies. They gave them out to anyone who asked, but always wi a sigh and a scrunched face, as if it warra major inconvenience.

At fourteen, they went clinic fut hard stuff: Gi us pill, gi us coil, gi us implant. Lerrus stick a copper coil in us cervix, lerrus

239

slide a vial of hormones beneath us skin. They craved crinkling packets of oestrogen marked wit days ut week. They welcomed pain. They moaned, held their bellies for ten days after gerrin their IUDs, stabbing in their abdomen never lerrin up no matter how many ibuprofen they swallowed. They revelled in it—every stitch, every twinge, every hour writhing in bed unable to stand. Forging themsens int pain, int pushing through, int grin-and-bear. Pills bloated their middles, med their emotions boil up and burst ovver. Med them sad, sad, angry for no reason, and still they said Yes! Gi us more! Lerrus suffer and bleed!

At sixteen, they med special trips tut clinic for free pregnancy tests whenever one of them had a "scare." Condom burst, pill forgotten, period late. Whispering would start between them in some boring lesson: I'm late! Will you come FP wi me?

They wore their serious pregnancy faces, med plans to bus into town together at weekend. They nodded gravely, held hands, promised to be there for each other no matter what. They always went together, all three of them, for moral support, and to increase drama and suspense ut occasion. What warra scare wi'out a witness? And only thing better than a witness wa two.

Whoever wa having t'scare, ritual wa always same: bus into Donny, then walk through town centre tut clinic, scared lass downing a bottle of Lucozade ont way to mek sure she could wee on demand. She holds her wee in till she's busting. Int clinic, she teks a plastic cup intut single cubicle, locks door, pulls her knickers down. If it's her first time, she hovers ovvert loo, holds cup beneath her, marvels at how fast her wee streams, how alien it feels to try and angle her flow. Lucozade comes screaming out in an angry *pssssh* and wets her trembling hand, meks her wonder if any of this is worth it. If it's her umpteenth time, Lucozade wets her steady hand, meks her wonder if any of this is worth it.

Back int consultation room, furniture arranged to feel casual, semi-squidgy armchairs round a coffee table, nurse and mates waiting, she hands her cup of wee tut nurse, who plonks it ont coffee table between them. They watch nurse uncap cup, wee's owner too aware ut dark yellow colour, how cloudy, how warm, condensation beading ont plastic. How many bits floating int liquid. She thinks, Is wee menna be bitty, or is there summat up wi me? Test strip guz in like a teaspoon; everybody waits. Tense two minutes while wee sits there, open, like a steaming cuppa, just as likely to get knocked ovver and spill. They all think about what might happen when nurse pulls strip out, ways their lives might split into then and now.

Nurse sez, "You still at school, then?"

They chorus, "Yeeeeah," and fall quiet again, no idea how to tek her thread of chat and weave it into small talk.

Nurse sez, "Don't worry, it's probably nowt," gives them a cheery smile.

They nod.

"And if it *is* summat, you've gorra lot of options."

"Yeeeeah." They nod and smile, all eyes fixed ont ammonia-scented oracle.

When time's up, nurse plucks strip out, wafts it free of droplets, teks a long look. Then she beams and sez, "Told you there wa nowt to worry about."

And they trundle out of there, all coats and backpacks and ponytails, all relief and secret sadness and jubilance, off into town to spend their pent-up energy, to window shop and Burger King and bench sit and smoke.

That wa how it always used to go, before Shaz's periods stopped—but not because she wa harbouring a foetus. Her dieting had turned wrong, turned deadly. She got sent away to a clinic, missed three months of school, three months of exam prep fut GCSEs, three months of in-jokes and drunken shenanigans. While she wa gone, Rach and Kel wondered what *they'd* missed. What warning signs, what clues their bezzy wa sick.

When Shaz's periods returned, when she'd gained enough weight, she wa allowed back to school. Rach and Kel had found a new friend group while she wa gone. Their boyfriends wa best mates, band-mates, brothers from other mothers, and Kel and Rach had been absorbed into their crew. But some things would stay sacred, they'd promised; some things, like family planning, would always be theirs.

One day, a couple of months off leaving school for good, they wa stuck in double PE, one ut few lessons all three of them still had together, since they'd been put in different sets for their GCSE subjects. They wa meant to be playing volleyball, but they warrall ont same team, and they wa driving Miss bonkers because they wa purrin all their efforts into playing any game but volleyball. Instead of serving ovvert net, they rolled ball beneath it like they wa ten-pin bowling, cheering whenever it dodged other teams' fingers, kissed sports hall's back wall. They dribbled it like a basketball, bent ovver and chucked it between their legs, stuck it under their T-shirt and posed wi their pregnant bellies, gripped it between their knees and hopped around duck-footed—owt to mek each other laugh. They weren't worst behaved, though, by far; only boffins wa trying to play proper rules. Boffs weren't sporty or owt; they just tried hard at everything, so they tried hard at volleyball. But goth lasses weren't even ont court; they wa sat ont benches comparing body hair. They had an ongoing leg- and armpit-hair-growing contest, spent every PE lesson bragging to each other, showing off their fluffy shins, their underarm tufts, feeling superior because they wa being ugly on purpose. Kel, Shaz, and Rach mocked goth lasses quietly between themsens, called them minging, blokey, sweaties, though they all secretly envied goth lasses' confidence. Int presence ut goths, their smooth legs felt bare and unclothed instead of natural and right.

Their naked pits, their shorn fannies. But they kept shaving, kept plucking, kept waxing, kept epilating, kept creaming themsens in foul-smelling foam. Through all t'dry skin and red sores and stubble and itch. Through in-growing pubes and fire-rub ut regrowth and persistent yeast infections. Because who would they be if they gave all that up. What monsters? What foul minging beasts?

After one too many games had stalled while Kel, Rach, and Shaz huddled together to gossip, Miss vowed to split them up next lesson, mix them wit goth lasses and boffins. Promised detention if they dint start tekkin it serious. After Miss huffed off, Kel pulled Shaz and Rach close and said, "Will you come family planning wi me this weekend?"

"Course," said Rach.

"Obvs, like," said Shaz.

Come Satdi, they bussed into town, but Kel wa too scared to go intut clinic, dint wanna face wee cup. Be reyt, Rach wa saying, We can buy houses next door to each other—she joked about double weddings, double christenings, a shared backyard, their kids growing up as siblings. Twinned lives wi their best-mate boyfriends.

"Yeah," said Shaz, "and when yous lot peg it, ah'll bury yas next to each other an' all."

They pissed about round town while Kel worked up courage, skipped in and out of Claire's Accessories and HMV. They stopped outside Ann Summers, window display set up for Valentine's Day wi shiny black headless mannikins wearing slivers of frilly pink, plastic hands posed sassily on plastic hips. They dared each other to go in.

They tittered past rows of sateen and polyester lace, fluffy teddies, floss-thin thongs. They tweaked hangers as they passed, med them squeak against rails, trying to keep their faces composed like they wa serious young women in search of a costume for their next seduction. They spied restricted section at back, its merch wall turned round to mek a little den of illicit wares, hidden from view. Sign at den's entrance: "18+ only." They nudged each other, stifled laughter, dared, urged, egged each other. Go on, then! You first! They checked fut shop assistant; she warrat cash register looking bored, staring out window, as if she knew exactly what warrabout to happen and couldn't be arsed wit hassle of preventing it. They snuck past sign, listening fut shop lady's *Oi!* that never came. They stared up at walls. Stacked higher than their heads, devices they'd only ever heard tell of, never sin before wi their own eyes. Furry hand-cuffs, whips wi feathers for tails, blindfolds, chocolate body paste, bottles of banana-flavoured lube. Boxes of edible underwear, med ut same bead-shaped multicoloured sweeties they ate as kids. They tasted like sugary chalk, them sweeties, but they used to be exciting because they wa strung on circular lengths of elastic you wore as a necklace, pretending to be a grown-up lady wearing proper jewel-lery. You'd bite or suck sweeties off one by one. They'd never sin them sweeties int shape of bras and thongs. They tried to imagine wanting to eat sweeties after they'd been lodged in someone's arse, and they all felt a bit sick. They wondered if that wa summat you gorra taste for as you got older. They hoped not. How much of all this were they meant to want?

They'd been thirteen when first lass they knew lost her virginity—int park ont playground swings, bottle of White Light-ning deep. Fourteen when next wave of lasses started dropping intut former-virgin club. These lasses wut planners, overachievers, them that'd marked a date on their calendars six months prior, required roses and a candlelit meal and a soundtrack and some of these Ann Summers knickers.

Kel and Shaz had lost it wi'out much fuss, Kel int wasteland behind chippy one morning while she wa skiving school, Shaz to one of her brother's mates. Rach *reckoned* she'd lost her v-plates to her boyfriend, who she'd been seeing for nearly eight months now. She'd go on about hearts racing and sweat dripping and minds blowing, out-of-body experiences, multiple orgasms—which, it's a known fact, no teenage lad has ever produced. She'd say, Oooh, other night he med mi toes curl! To listen to her, you'd think her fella warra sexual wizard capable of stroking her into raptures wi one wiggle of his finger. Everyone else knew him as that lanky lad int year above who no lass gi a look in till last year when he hit six foot, started a band, and discovered deodorant. Kel and Shaz thought Rach's stories sounded a bit too TV. They let her riff, like, but they knew what they knew: Rach had never done it. They felt bad forr'er, because now when she *did* do it, she wouldn't be able to celebrate it wi her mates like she'd want to. They'd done same thing wi their periods, lying to each other about gerrin it. How silently they had to cheer for that little victory when it came.

They shuffled along tut next wall of Ann Summers' forbidden den. This one choked laughter out their throats: towering wall of plastic penises reared above them, frighteningly thick, bulging wi veins, wi bulbous heads, wi lined and wrinkly bollocks. Bollocks like they'd never want to touch in their lives. They couldn't imagine desiring such violent girth anywhere *near* their fannies. Whether silicone or flesh, answer wa still No, ta! These behemoths pulsed wi life, shuddered against their packaging, against plastic tabs they hung from, as if they wa gerrin ready to fling themsens at Kel, Shaz, and Rach.

"Fucking hell," they said in stage whispers. They stared wide-eyed. They backed away, each of them carrying image ut wall of dildos into their future. They all prayed never to be confronted wi such horrors again, that these horrors would never seek them out, follow them to their bedrooms, demand to be let in. They focused their attention ont section of vibrators, phallic ones meeker in size, reassuringly cast in pretty Barbie colours, bright purples, cotton candy pinks. And littler, friendlier machines in no particular shape, promising nowt but a gentle purr. They inspected price tags, balked at expense, pushed products back onto their hangers.

"Ya dunt need one of these," said Shaz. "Ya just use your lecky toothbrush."

Rach and Kel twitched their necks to express their disbelief.

"As if!" said Kel.

"That's minging," said Rach.

"You ant tried it, neither of yas?" Shaz's stature grew, shoulders flattening, chest out, inflating way she always did when she found summat to school them on.

"If you use that on your fanny, what do you use on your *teeth*, you scrubber?" Rach said "teeth" too loud. They peeped round partition: shop lady's head bobbing side to side, trying to see around racks, see what they warrup to.

Shaz lowered her voice. "Ya dunt use sem brush head fo' ya mouth, ya div."

Kel said, "Think I'll pass, ta, I'd rather gerrup duff." Her joke struck a wrong note, reminding them what they warrin town for, what fate of Kel's had yet to be decided.

Rach wanted clarity. She wanted to squeeze Shaz's claim into submission, watch it wheeze and tap out. She always did this wi Shaz's bold statements in a way that Shaz'd never do to her. Shaz and Kel wa gentle wi Rach and her sex lies, thought it'd be mean to expose her. But Rach always treated Shaz as if she warras tough as she looked.

"Wunnit it hurt, though," said Rach. "Them bristles spin fast as owt."

Shaz wont about to be proved wrong. "I'll *show* ya, if ya don't believe me."

"No, ta," said Rach.

"Why, cuz you know ah'm right?"

Kel saw t'challenge in Shaz's eyes, knew this'd go way it always did. Once gauntlet had been thrown by Shaz or Rach, neither'd let issue drop till there warra victor.

Shop lady said, "'Scuse me, ladies."

They scurried out and past her, pushing roughly through racks, eyes ont floor.

Kel's cup of piss turned out to be benign. They bought celebratory Bacon Double Cheeseburgers ont way home, relief firing through all of them. None of them admitting—never admitting—that relief always came wi an undercurrent of disappointment. No-one *really* wanted a kid, but dint everyone want to know warrit wa like, summat foreign growing inside, belly bulging wi it, drama of it, *fame* of it. Everyone knew all t'lasses at school who'd had babies: babies when they wa thirteen, babies when they wa fourteen. Had to leave normal school forra while, spend months at a school for young mums. Sometimes they left school altogether, gorra council house, and were never heard from again. Sometimes they transferred to Rach, Kel, and Shaz's school from somewhere else, post-birth, fifteen and already a new life. Those lasses never arrived wi clean slates, obvs. Whispers entered wi them, rumours about that new lass Jenna and kid she'd gi'en her mam to raise. So while there wut private thrill ut idea of their bodies swelling wit ultimate drama, gossip to end all gossip, they wa still too familiar wit reality of that fate to hold fantasy too close to their chests.

Few weeks later in PE—still volley-fucking-ball, still proper-shitting-pointless—Shaz served wi one limp arm then pulled Kel aside. Other team scrambled after t'ball, which missed net completely, bounced ovver tut lads' court.

When Miss split them up, she'd put Rach ont opposite team, wit boffins. Rach dint like t'boffins, not since last summer, afternoon her and Shaz wa chatting tut arch-boffin Allison Harris ont bus into town, invited her to Spoons forra drink. Allison said she'd got orchestra practice, so Shaz'd said, "Well, if you fancy it later on, we'll be in there all neet." Allison replied, "You'll be in there all your lives." Rach had to pin Shaz's arms to her sides to stop her tearing out a clutch of Allison's ponytail.

While Kel and Shaz whispered, Rach ignored boffins' attempts to get her to play; she stood next tut net wi her arms folded, glaring, waiting fut other two to look up so she could hiss, What? What you on wi? She strained to hear them ovvert lads' echoey yells from other court, ovver Miss's whistle blasts, but couldn't mek out their words.

Shaz wa asking Kel if she'd escort her to family planning that weekend, conversation reeling out rapidly while Miss wa ovver ont other court. She'd been sick every morning that week, she said. Kel dint think that wa owt to get het up about. It wont like Shaz warra stranger to chucking up. Shaz wa shivering, though, in her white PE T-shirt and little shorts, shoulders hooked, arms hugging belly, covering place where summat might be brewing, and Kel could see she wa really afraid.

"Don't tell Rach," said Shaz.

"Why?" Kel dint like being put int middle of Rach and Shaz, dint like having to decide which one should have her loyalty.

"Just don't want anyone else knowing."

Thwack: volleyball smacked Shaz ont side ut head. Kel and Shaz looked up to see Rach, panting as if she'd thrown a few times before she'd managed to hit her mark.

"What you *on wi*?" Rach demanded, an icy brightness in her eyes.

Despite Rach's ferocity, Kel kept her promise to Shaz. She told Rach that Shaz wa feeling sick, that's all, swear down. Kel dint like lying, but it wa nicer than telling Rach there wa summat she wont allowed to know. Kel kept her word all week, even though Shaz compromised her constantly, pulling her aside every two minutes, wanting to talk about still not gerrin her period, still throwing up, how nervous she wa, how scared. Kel wondered if Shaz wa doing it in front of Rach on purpose. For all Shaz's whispers, she wunt say who father might be. Most lasses exaggerated number and frequency of their conquests. Shaz wut only one of them who med her number shrink, who wanted to be known as a shagger, but not so known. Wary, always, of being branded slaggy. Line between frigid and slag wut slimmest border, near invisible. They all shaped stories they told int hope of dancing ont reyt side of that line. If reyt side existed. They wa sexual adventurers—not frigid, no, no, never that, not prim misses, not little girls, but not town bicycles neither, not slags. Just alreyt lasses. Couldn't they just be lasses?

Satdi, Kel and Shaz sat int family planning's consultation room, waiting fut test strip to tell Shaz's fortune. Kel'd fibbed to Rach about why she couldn't hang out wi her and their boyfriends— she'd agreed to do summat wi her mam, she'd said, which wut least believable lie she could've invented. Kel hadn't done owt wi her mam since she wa thirteen and they went to get their belly buttons pierced together. Rach's disbelief wa palpable; Kel still felt heat of her dead-eye, her accusing stare.

"Have I sin yous here before, then?" nurse asked, in her usual jolly way.

They dint know if she wa allowed to ask that, but they answered wi their usual "Yeeeeah," their chorus oddly reedy this time, one voice short.

"Aye, thought so."

Kel and Shaz wondered how soon intut ceremony nurse could tell which way it wa going. How much ut waiting, wafting, scrutinising ut strip—how much of that wa theatre? But they dint ask; they just honoured ritual, awaited verdict.

Halfway through t'wait, Shaz went off script, started crying quietly, shoulders jerking. Took Kel a second to realise that Shaz wont giggling. She held Shaz's hand.

"It'll be reyt," said nurse. "Don't be daft." She took Shaz's other hand, massaged her fingers. "You don't even know results yet."

Shaz nodded, wiped blade of her hand up her nose, collecting a slug trail of snot along her little finger. She dint know how to tell Kel that this one dint feel like t'other times. Usually they went clinic just to be ont safe side. And it wa more than that, wannit. They went to feel like they mattered, like summat they'd done could have consequences. This time dint feel like that. This time, Shaz felt worthless. It wont the nausea, though that helped; she just felt like her body wont hers anymore, like she dint have control of it. She dint even fancy lad she'd slept wi; she wa just bored and drunk. And he hadn't even texted her since night they shagged. She dint want to think about any of it, dint want any of this to be going on.

Nurse plucked strip from cup, and her face changed immediately. That's when they knew which part ut proceedings wa pure ritual. Wafting and scrutinising, it turned out, wa just for show. Nurse said, "Don't worry, don't get yoursen worked up. Don't forget you've gorra lot of options."

After, when Kel and Shaz'd been spat back ontut street, intut sunlight, Donny town centre carrying on around them like nowt had occurred, Shaz gripped Kel's shoulder, hand vicing her collarbone.

"Don't tell anyone."

"I won't."

Shaz redoubled her hold. "*Especially* don't tell Rach."

"Why?"

Shaz dint know why, except idea of Rach knowing triggered waves of nausea that had nowt to do wit morning sickness.

"Just don't, please."

Kel sighed, studied paving slabs. Contemplated a lifetime of keeping a gargantuan secret from their oldest mate. "Alreyt."

One of Shaz's many options wut pill, what nurse called "medical abortion." Shaz'd shook her head while nurse talked them through other possibilities. Option 2: Grow a whole baby, then gi it away, lerrit get stuck int system and mebs find happiness in another home and mebs not. Option 3: Love it and look after it forever. "I'll tek pill, please," Shaz'd said, as if she warron *Countdown* asking Carol Vorderman forra vowel. She'd caught it early enough that surgical abortion wont needed. She could even tek second set of pills at home. She enlisted Kel's support for that an' all, wanted a mate wi her. Someone to witness when womb lining broke down, and blood came, and pain.

All week Rach battered Kel wi questions about what warrup wi Shaz, and all week Kel said nowt wa wrong, Shaz wa just poorly. By following weekend, Shaz told Kel bleeding had mostly stopped and she dint wanna talk about it nomore. She just wanted to tek her mind off it, get legless. Kel wa babysitting fut neighbour's kids, so they all gathered int neighbour's front room wi bottles of voddy, Lambrini, peach schnapps, and three litres of White Lightning. This wut standard procedure forra babysitting night: whoever wa sitting would play wit kids forran hour, put them to bed, then fun could begin. Another ritual they'd promised to keep just fut three of them.

They played old dance tunes and bopped around front room, reminiscing about discos they went to when they wa young. They shout-sang to "I Want It That Way" by Backstreet Boys, neighbour's stereo speakers rattling. They played Ring of Fire wi a deck of cards they found int kitchen's crap drawer, which got Kel and Shaz paggered because they kept forgetting rules. Rach had a knack for rules even when she wa blasted. She kept pointing at other two and going, Ha! Drink!

Too many voddy shots in, Shaz abandoned game, drifted tut fireplace, examined framed family photos ont mantle. She pointed at shopping centre portraits of bearded eighties men and poufy-haired women, giggling and saying, Who the fuck's *that*?

Kel said, "Lady who lives here reckons she might know who mi dad wa." Kel's dad ran off when she wa tiny; Kel's mam wouldn't say a word about him.

"Is he one of these weirdos?" said Shaz.

"No," said Kel, then gorrup to look at photos, see if she could spot a trace of hersen staring back.

"Does she know where he is now, like?" said Rach.

"Dunt think so. They wont mates or owt."

"Well, did you ask her?" said Shaz.

Kel shrugged. No. She hadn't wanted to dig, in case lady said, Only joking, or, He's dead, or, Sorry, love, I wa thinking of someone else. She'd rather keep t'little truth this lady had gi her: her dad had existed. He wa known.

"Dare you to ask," said Shaz.

Rach downed dregs of her schnapps and lemonade. "Who's for more booze?"

Every time Rach gorrup to pee or get summat from fridge, Shaz's face switched from gleeful to knackered, eyes, mouth, and cheeks all falling south. Kel wa gerrin frustrated: Shaz looked exhausted from effort of faking she wa reyt, but couldn't be persuaded to let Rach in ont secret.

Shaz could've listed loads of reasons why she dint want Rach to know. She could've said that Rach'd ask a million questions Shaz dint wanna answer. That Rach always pushed till she gorr'er answers, could never just let summat be. That t'shame of Rach knowing would eat her like rot eats skin. She could've said that when bad things happened to her, they dint seem to mean owt to Rach; they dint affect her—like that lad who died last summer, hit by a train. He warra mate of Shaz's, but Rach never asked her how wa she doing, wa she still grieving; Rach never mentioned his name. Shaz could've said that even after four and a half years of friendship, she still weren't sure if she could trust Rach wi her feelings. Or that she just needed someone to perform for, someone to act normal for if she wont gunna fall apart.

"You could just tell her," Kel said, while Rach warrint kitchen topping up her drink.

"Tell me what?" Rach: at doorway, cheeks enflamed wit indignity of being left out.

"We wont talking about you," Shaz said, and med out they'd been talking about her not wanting to tell her mam she'd got isolation at school again for swearing at her technology teacher. (Not Shaz's fault, by t'way: he'd accused Shaz of laughing *at* him when she wa actually laughing *wi* him—he'd med a feeble joke, and Shaz had felt sorry forr'im so gave him a little giggle just to mek him feel good, and he'd sent her out room.)

Rach knew it wa bullshit but dint push it further. Instead, she asked who's for another round ut drinking game?

They got so shit-faced they couldn't see reyt. It wa tekkin more and more effort to seem normal. Drinking in Donny required mastery of two opposing skills: a Donny lass had to learn how to sink superhuman volumes of booze *and* how to act as if she hadn't. That's warrit took, if you wa gunna be known as a lass who could hold her booze as well as any lad. Kel, Rach, and Shaz wa good students; they'd spent years honing their craft.

Ever since their infamous turn as Romeo and Juliet int school showcase, whenever they practiced art of remaining upright while wankered, Shaz and Kel would reach point of alcohol saturation by which they decided to reprise their roles. Specifically, they liked to reenact R and J's snogging scene. They hit that stage of hammered reyt int middle of Rach's turn in Ring of Fire, started rolling round ont living room rug, mouths joined, knocking cards askew, nearly toppling open Lambrini bottle. Rach tried to gather cards: "Hang on, we ant finished game!"

Finding hersen ignored, she picked up Lambrini bottle. "Right, I'm gunna down this in one. Ready?"

Dedicated thespians that they wa, Kel and Shaz dint look up. They wa soaked int hot-water-bottle-under-t'sheets feeling ut booze and each other's bodies. Both marvelling at how deft and perfectly sized wa each other's tongues, how their tongues moved together in perfect rhythm, tender and seeking. Not like clumsy lad mouths, their fat tongues thrusting in and out.

Trouble wi lads wa—lasses had learned through years of investigation—they thought all their body parts had to behave like dicks. Tongue? Better thrash that in and out of her mouth like a dick. Fingers? Better jab them in her fanny like a dick. Lads weren't entirely to blame, though. What did anybody learn in five years of Personal, Social, and Cultural Education? Every known street name for cannabis and how to roll a johnnie ovver a banana. And all that time teachers could've been telling them what to do wi their bodies. How to touch themsens and each other.

Kel and Shaz snogged because those moments wa so serene they wa drug-like. Their kissing med everything fade—pain, worry, anger—and they felt swallowed up by summat, hidden, brains soft and dark, free from act they'd been purrin on all their lives.

That night, Shaz kissed Kel to feel summat other than sorry for hersen, to mek her body feel summat other than wrong. But she couldn't get there, couldn't blot everything out. She pulled Kel closer, kissed her harder.

Rach put t'heavy bell-shaped Lambrini bottle to her lips, tipped her head back so bottle wa upside down, sweet perry gushing into her mouth. Her practiced throat contracting, matching liquid's velocity. At last mouthful, bottle slipped through her hand, landed on her front tooth, chipping off a corner. "Ahh!" Rach planted a hand across her mouth.

Two star-crossed lovers wa still entwined, fingers travelling ovver each other's hips. Hand hiding her mouth, Rach dashed upstairs tut bathroom in search of a mirror.

Magnified shaving mirror propped ont bathroom's sill showed Rach two cheeks plummy wi drink, set of eyelids cut lazily half open, and hand clamped ovver mouth as if she'd witnessed summat unimaginable. Her hair, which she'd ironed straight before she left house, wa rebelling, frizzing into lank coils. She took her hand away, inspected tooth. A quarter of an incisor gone. Rest of it hung there incomplete like a lone jigsaw piece. She pulled her lips back intut kind of grin a kid meks when they're too young to know what smiling's for, but they've learned to mimic adults. If you asked Rach, kids wa *well* creepy: all empty laughter, unfelt grins.

Rach would cry about chip tomorrow, she knew. She'd crumble at thought of going to school wi it unfixed. But now she wa too drunk to access sad, or shame, or regret. Music filtered up from front room below her, sounding hollow and unreal. She stared at her magnified face till she wa seeing hersen—*really* seeing hersen—like life warra dream she'd just stepped out of. She wa Rach. *She* wa Rach. This wut only face she'd ever get, this split tooth hers forever. "You," she said to her reflection, "are Rach. You are *Rach*. Rach, Rach, Rach." She said her name till sound of it meant nothing. Finally, she thought. There I am.

An electric toothbrush winked at her from windowsill's display of paste-stained oral hygiene products. She pressed its button. It whirred, petite round head spinning fast. She turned it off, shoved it in her jeans back pocket, felt her way back downstairs.

Kel wa unconscious when Rach returned, either boozed up or blissed out. Shaz wa stabbing buttons ont neighbour's CD changer, which wa blaring Simply Red's "Money's Too Tight to Mention."

Shaz's mix CD, each track lovingly stolen and burned, had ended during Kel and Shaz's snog sesh, and player had switched to one ut neighbour's, a jarring tone shift that warrin danger of sobering them up. Shaz couldn't coax player into accepting another of her discs, so she settled fut neighbour's History of Jazz compilation— owt wa better than Mick Hucknall's croon. Saxophones zipped chaotically ovver a frantic bass line. Shaz turned volume down so music wouldn't wake Kel. Rach turned big light off, clicked side lamp on.

"What happened to her, like?"

"You know our Kel," said Shaz. "Bloody lightweight." Shaz passed bottle of voddy to Rach, who swigged, passed it back. Shaz took a deep glug. They couldn't see much but each other, world closing in on them nicely. Rach ran a finger ovvert blotchy red line int skin of Shaz's wrist.

"It's finally healing, then."

"Apparently," said Shaz. Scar used to be a scab that she'd gorrint habit of picking, keeping it fresh, till it got infected and wouldn't close. Int eating disorder clinic, nurses told her that scab picking warra kind of self-harm, med her leave it be till it dried up. She had urge to pull sleeve of her blouse down ovver it, way she did when anyone asked. But she liked soft feel of Rach's fingertip, her gentleness, so she left blouse sleeve where it wa.

"Remember in Ann Summers," said Rach. "You reckoned you'd show us how to use a toothbrush?"

Shaz nodded slowly, looking fut catch. "Yeeeeah?"

"Well, go on, then." Rach whipped toothbrush clumsily from her pocket and held it up. She'd hoped forra smooth, slick action like a cowboy unholstering a pistol, but her booze-sluggish fingers fumbled, delaying reveal, toothbrush jamming int pocket's hem as she said "go" instead of appearing magically int space between them.

Rach couldn't have said what she wanted from this—whether she really wanted to learn, whether she just wanted to call Shaz's bluff. Whether summat else.

Shaz couldn't tell what she wa really being asked, if she wa being challenged or seduced or dared or insulted. She wut kind of drunk where she'd stopped being able to read faces, and that felt dangerous. She'd learned young how to face read, how to judge what people *really* wanted from her, and how much it'd cost her to gi it.

They bluffed each other ovver a threshold friendship had never crossed:

"Are you sure that's what you want, cuz ah will do it."

"Wouldn't be asking if I didn't want, would I."

"Tek your kegs off, then."

"You take yours off. You're meant to be *showing* me."

"If ah'm gunna show ya, ah'm gunna do it *on* ya."

Much of what happened next is lost to them, alcohol scrubbing most ut memory, leaving them wit residue, wit fuzzy imprint of events: Kel passed out ont settee, snoring, them laid ont neighbour's rug, jeans stripped off. Shaz switched brush on, guided head beneath Rach's thong, watching her face forra response. When Rach moaned, Shaz held brush steady on that spot, till Rach mumbled, "It's too much," and moved Shaz's hand away. Shaz turned brush off, eased Rach's thong down to her knees, and pushed her tongue against that same spot.

Rach dint know what sounds she wa mekkin, what hidden place they wa gurgling up from. Sensation like she'd never felt blooming from place Shaz lapped at, till there wa waves of it, waves travelling torso, legs, cascading into her face. Her whole body became feeling, became one long streak of good.

After a while laid out ont rug in a daze, Rach came slowly back to hersen. She pushed Shaz's shoulders intut rug. She kissed Shaz. Fresh on Shaz's lips wa Rach's first taste of hersen—she wa surprised to find out that she tasted just like pencil shavings smelled. She copied Shaz's moves, dipping her mouth between Shaz's legs, tongue ont place she thought wa right, wanting to gi as she'd been gi'en to. She worked her

257

tongue till Shaz moaned, spasmed, till she brought her hand down on Rach's head to let her know she could stop.

Stop because Shaz wa finally floating, stop because she'd slipped beyond hersen, because she'd found a moment of gone. Shaz laid, refusing to feel friction burn ut rug's fibres or chill of her bare legs, wanting only to stretch intut feeling of gone for as long as her brain would let her.

Rach couldn't see int low light ut side lamp, but she'd discover next day, checking her hungover face int mirror, just a touch of brownish red around her mouth, just a hint of blood.

They dint talk about it next day, or day after. Shaz wanted to talk but dint know how to bring it up, Rach wanted to pretend it'd never happened, and Kel had slept through whole thing. Back at school, Rach *did* want to talk about Shaz's secret, confronting Kel second she gorront bus Mundi morning.

"What wa Shaz talking about Satdi night when I warrout room?"

This, before Ey up, before Hiya, y'alreyt.

"Ask her yoursen."

"So you admit there *is* summat to tell." Rach wa having a hard time talking wi'out showing her chipped tooth. Her top lip strained down ovver it. Her hand leapt up to cover it.

Kel couldn't believe Rach'd snookered her already. She pulled out her eyelash curlers and compact mirror, pressed her lashes between curler's plates, forcing them into a dramatic L-bend. Mascara she'd applied earlier had clumped lashes into stark bobbly spider's legs.

"I care about her an' all, you know," said Rach. "I just wanna know so I can *be* there forr'er, so I can—"

"*Fine.* If it'll shut you up. But *please*, you cannot tell her you know." Kel gave Rach what she knew: positive test, pill int clinic and two more at home, some bleeding, some cramping, no info ont would-be father, Shaz insisting she wa fine, she wa past it now, just wanted to forget.

Rach went quiet, and Kel thought it wut quiet of a hunger satisfied. Gossip thirst quenched. Till Rach said, "That lass will do *owt* for attention."

"What you on about?"

"Well." Rach folded her arms. "There's just always summat up wi her, int there? Always has to be drama. If she's not starving hersen or chucking her guts up or gerrin caught shoplifting, she knows everyone in Donny who's ever died or gone to prison, or she needs a pregnancy test every five bloody seconds—"

"She really wa pregnant, Rach. I saw t'test."

Rach raised one sceptical eyebrow. Kel warrin no mood to defend hersen or Shaz. Neighbour had come home and smelled Lambrini dregs soaked intut rug and rung Kel's mam, and now Kel wa grounded indefinitely.

"She can't help hersen," Rach kept on. "Always gorrer be centre of attention."

Kel went back to her eyelashes, using a pair of tweezers to pry gluey clumps apart.

"If she wanted to be centre of attention, why would she only tell me?"

"So yous'd have summat to whisper about wi'out me!" Rach wa near shouting now.

"Don't you raise ya voice at me, lady, I ant done owt!"

Kel's rare show of anger shocked Rach quiet.

"I'm just saying," Rach went on in softer tones, "Shaz can't stand that you and me've got mates and boyfriends—gorra life— that dunt include her, so she's trying to make it so you two've gorra little secret to share that dunt include me."

And, Rach thought but dint say, she's made it so that we've gorra secret that dunt include Kel. A secret that'd split Rach and her boyfriend up if he found out.

"You better sort yoursen out ovver this, Rach, because she can't know I've told ya."

"I will, I will," said Rach. But she wouldn't.

She'd huff around all day like a head of steam. She collected half a dozen "What's up wi yous" from lasses in her form, Shaz included. As they filed out ut form room on their way to last period, Shaz caught up wi Rach, cornered her behind H block—slim walkway between block's back wall and chain-link fence ut tennis court that nobody ever played tennis on.

"Are ya gunna tell me what's up wi ya?"

"Nowt, what you on about?"

"You've been funny wi me all day."

"No I ant."

"You *know* you have, Rach, why pretend?"

"I'm just upset about mi tooth."

That wont *not* true. Rach felt even worse about it around Shaz, like Shaz wut last person she wanted to be this silly and ugly in front of.

"So you ant texted me all weekend—" Shaz ticked this off on her index finger. "You ant said three words to me all day—" She ticked her middle finger. "And you've been walking round wi a proper face on that absolutely everyone's noticed—" Ring finger. "And ah'm menna believe it's got nowt to do wi Satdi neet?"

"I wa wasted Satdi. Don't remember owt."

Shaz could see t'lie in Rach's face and it med her feel dirty. Rach's dirty little secret, just like she wa everycunt's dirty little hush hush, don't tell, keep it between me and thee. Wont there one cunt int world who wont ashamed of being wi her?

Words rolled into Shaz's mouth like marbles, heavy, clinking against her teeth. Words livid, barbed, friendship-ending. Words she'd crack her molars on if she bit down, choke on if she tried to swallow. She turned, walked away from Rach, mouth full to bursting.

Rach couldn't explain anger roiling inside her, way adrenaline wa throttling her, stopping her mouth. She couldn't explain why everything felt wrong and everything wa Shaz's fault. Even her chipped tooth wa Shaz's fault. Even this odd feeling Rach had—this thinking constantly about Satdi night, way her thoughts kept wandering back tut feeling ut rug tickling her thighs, feeling of Shaz's tongue, good sensation spreading. The thinking back, the wanting. *No.* She did not want. Shaz had *made* her want. Always Shaz pushing her over borders she dint wanna cross. Who wa Rach now? Who had this made her?

Volleyball day, Rach ont other team again. She got boffins to teach her t'rules. She tried to proper serve, whopping ball ovvert net wi her fist. She whacked it in Shaz and Kel's direction whenever they got together forra chat.

When they startled and looked round, she said, "We're meant to be playing a game."

Int changing rooms after, she pulled them aside, beckoning them intut communal shower at back that nobody used.

"You've gorrer come family planning wi me this Satdi," she said.

"What for?" asked Kel.

Rach raised her eyebrows. "I'm late."

Kel and Shaz dint know what to say; they knew she'd never slept wi a lad, but they'd always gone along wi all her sex boasting.

"I can't, I'm grounded," said Kel. Her mam wa mekkin her go round neighbour's Satdi afternoon, scrub Lambrini dregs out ut rug.

"You're coming wi me, then?" Rach asked Shaz.

"Can't."

Shaz's shoulders curled in, shielding her chest. Forra moment she looked like she'd used to, before eating disorder clinic: dwindled, whittled down.

"Why?"

"Just can't."

She looked pleadingly at Kel, begging Kel wi her eyes to help her out. It wa too soon. She couldn't face going back just yet.

"Wait till next week and I'll go wi ya," said Kel.

"No, I've gorrer go Satdi. And I wanna know why Shaz won't go wi me when I *always* go wi her."

Kel tried to gi Rach a warning look, and Shaz saw, and knew instantly that Kel'd told what she'd promised not to tell.

"Can't fuckin be*lieve* you, Kelly." Shaz twisted away from Kel's hands as they leapt to grab her reassuringly ont arm, pushed past her back intut changing rooms, where a knot ut goth lasses and a knot ut boffins still hung, chatting.

"What have *I* done?" Kel came round after her, voice raised, mekkin other lasses look up.

Rach followed, that strange rage tekkin her ovver, mekkin her all heat inside, all loathing, a feeling that needed out. "There she guz, making it all about hersen as usual." Rach narrated Shaz's actions: "Yeah, walk away, go on, yeah, pretend you can't hear me—play victim, yeah, everyone feel sorry for Shaz, when it's *me* that's asking for support for *once*."

Shaz dressed fast, stooped ovver as if she could duck out way of Rach's words, as if she could protect her heart.

They dint talk for days after that. They all hung wi different groups at break and dinner, and Rach and Kel sat on opposite ends ut bus.

Sod all had been resolved by next week's PE lesson. Time and distance had only strengthened their ire. They all asked boffins about rules of volleyball, learned difference between in and out of bounds, between a set and a spike. They leapt fut spikes because that wut most aggressive move, and they felt exhilaration ut thump ball med as it hit floor ont other side ut net. Each team called for Miss when other team claimed a point they'd clearly lost. Even goths got

262

involved. But Miss had long gi'en up ont lasses. She stayed ovver ont lads' court, reffing their match, blowing whistle for their infractions.

Lasses fell to policing themsens:

"That warrout!"

"Warrit fuck!"

"You touched net!"

"I never!"

"It's our serve!"

"It's *our* bastard serve!"

They lost their sense of proportion. Nowt mattered besides winning this game. There wa no mates, no school, no GCSEs, no parties, no Donny, no South Yorkshire, no England. They warrall pure volleyball, skull to shinbones.

Final score wa 4 to 3 in favour of Rach's team, or 3 to 4 in favour of Kel and Shaz's, depending on who you asked. They wa still bickering ont either side ut net when Miss finally noticed and shouted, "Go and get changed, please, ladies." They surged intut changing rooms hot, sweaty, enraged. Clustered between benches and coat racks, they shouted in twos and threes, fingers pointing in faces.

Amidst all t'furious back and forths, Rach marched up to Shaz. "You wa *cheating*," she said, as if there wa no worse sin, jabbing a finger into Shaz's chest.

"Dunt fuckin poke me, love," said Shaz, and pushed Rach's shoulders. Rach pushed back. Shaz wa half a foot shorter than Rach and three stone lighter. She lost her balance, fell backwards, head banging intut coat pegs behind her. Searing bash bash int back of her skull, two metal pegs digging in. Shock of it radiating through her: dull, ringing ache down her neck, through her temples. Felt like two fangs had punctured her scalp, sting of their bite pulling water into her eyes that there wa no way in hell she wa gunna let fall.

"She pushed me!" Shaz appealed tut whole room, looked round at all t'lasses in there. She wa panting like she'd been forra run.

"She pushed me first!"

"You all saw that, dint ya? That fuckin yeti pushed me."

Everyone, even t'boffins, responded int traditional way, since even boffins wa Donny lasses. They formed a circle round Shaz and Rach, chanted Fight! Fight! Fight! Fight! Fight!

"Come on then, ya pussy," said Shaz. "Fuckin *hit* me if you're gunna hit me."

Rach could feel crowd's appetite forra show—Fight! Fight! Fight!—feel Shaz's challenge goading her. "I'm not smacking a cheater," she said. "Wunt wanna sully mi knuckles."

"*You're* one who tells lies, love, not me."

"Oh aye, when have I ever lied to you?"

Kel, who'd been pushing her way through crowd, emerged at Shaz's elbow. "We know you don't really need to go FP, Rach," she said.

"You don't know owt! I ant had a period in three months! I'm gerrin morning sickness! Just because I don't slag it about like *she* does—"

Shaz's hand pulled itsen into a fist, two knuckles raised like her brother had taught her, and whapped Rach ont nose.

Impact seemed to Rach at first like more sound than feeling, crack like someone slamming a loo seat. Silver spots burst across her sight. She teetered sideways, hand flying out to catch hersen against coat rack. Then pain came like scald, like wetness. It spread ovver her face, sent her body into shivers.

Kel grabbed Shaz's arms, pinned them behind her back. But Shaz dint need restraining. She'd already sin crimson flooding Rach's top lip, plop-plopping onto Rach's white T-shirt. She'd already sin tears streak Rach's cheeks. She wa already sorry for everything she couldn't undo.

After—after bell'd gone, after goths and boffins had left, after school had emptied around them—Kel, Rach, and Shaz sat ont

264

benches, not looking at each other. Rach's nose dripped red like it wa counting seconds.

"Well, *I'm* not gunna be t'first to talk," said Kel.

Rach and Shaz caught each other's eye. Their mouths flexed into smiles.

"What?" said Kel. "I'm not."

Rach and Shaz laughed.

"It wont a joke!" said Kel. Then she gave in and laughed wi em, even though she couldn't see what wa funny.

Rach and Kel sat together again ont bus home. They hadn't gone back to normal—there dint seem to be a normal to go back to—but fight had shook them all into an uneasy truce. Rach's nose hadn't broken. Bleeding had stopped after a few minutes of her pinching bridge, blotting red on a fistful of bog roll. She wa mad at hersen for crying in front of Shaz, but that wut only mad she had left in her.

"Riiight," Rach said to Kel, drawing vowel out and up to indicate she warrabout to ask a hypothetical. "Let's say, right—let's say two lasses go down on each other, yeah?"

"Yeeeah?"

"Is it classed as sex?"

"Why do you ask?"

Rach shrugged and looked out window. "Just weird, innit. Like, if a lass guz down on you, and you've never had sex wi a lad, would that class as you losing your virginity?"

Kel shrugged, *No idea.* She warra bit embarrassed, not because they wa talking about sex, but because she dint know answer. Kel had worked hard all her life to seem like she always knew everything she wa meant to know—song lyrics, soap opera plotlines, names of sexual acts.

"I think it only counts as your virginity if you bleed," said Kel. She believed this even though she dint bleed on her first time. She'd been disappointed, after, when she'd not found one drop, not one trace of red anywhere. She reckoned she must be defective, made wrong.

"Have you slept wi a lass, like?" Kel asked wi a grin. She couldn't imagine owt more unlikely than Rach gerrin it on wi a lass, let alone cheating on her boyfriend wi a lass. Rach always looked uncomfortable whenever Shaz and Kel gorra bit thespian.

Rach laid her forehead ont window, vibrations ut bus engine shaking her brain. "I don't know," she said, in a voice tiny enough to go unheard.

They went back to not gi'in a shit about volleyball. Like they'd emerged from a drug binge, dint recognise selves they'd left behind. Who *wa* those lasses, trying so hard to win. Since when did owt matter that much.

Few weeks later, year elevens went on study leave. Shaz barely saw Kel and Rach, who wa either revising or hanging out wi their boyfriends and their boyfriends' mates. Mid-June, they wa deep intut exam period, stuck inside trying to get their heads round French verbs and fractional distillation and whatever riddles they wa meant to be solving in maths. Shaz felt impossibly lost, sure she'd never mek up fut three months of school she missed while she warrint clinic, not if she tried all her life.

Weather warmed and lightened, mekkin them all eager fut summer to come, and sad fut summers they'd already had. When Shaz couldn't look at another isosceles triangle wi'out wanting to screw practice paper into a ball and stuff it in her gob, chew it to pulp, she texted other two: hay bales warrint farmers' fields again—did they wanna go in on some voddy and some tinnies, get smashed ont bales like old times? Other two texted back instantly: they did. They really fucking did.

They unearthed their bikes from their sheds and garages, rattled down tut fields that evening, backpack straps straining, heavy wi their stash. They relished sense of naughtiness, of being out when they wa meant to be revising. It wa that point int year when evening swept bright blue around them, as if it had no intention of turning into night. Blush-pink clouds threaded weightless through sky, mekkin them all feel suspended, like time had stopped. Sweet smell ut hay and prospect of drunkenness med giddiness fizz inside them as they approached bale stack, standing alone int centre of a shorn field like it wa waiting for them. They ditched their bikes int dirt, climbed ontut bottom row ut stack, and sat in a circle cross-legged, stalks pricking their thighs through their jeans. They clinked cans and cheersed to "girlies." They glugged, reminisced. Every summer, they'd come down here. When they wa little, to gossip and mek up dance routines; then, since they turned fourteen, to get drunk and stare at stars, to feel world recede like a falling tide.

Shaz watched flush of Rach's cheeks deepen, wondered if she should try and talk to her again about night they lost themsens wi each other. Shaz wanted to know if Rach liked it as much as she had, if Rach mebs even wanted to do it again. But Rach wa brimming wi an energy, an excitement, new swank in her shoulders, and once she'd had enough to drink, she shared some juicy goss: her and her fella had finally done it. She cloaked it in bluff, obvs, maintaining fiction that they'd been doing it all along, but Kel and Shaz could see change in her, knew this time it wa real.

"Bloody *recks* an' all, though, dunnit?" she said. "Nobody tells you how much it hurts." She seemed ecstatic about this pain. She seemed more sure of hersen, like her feet had found firm, even path of certainty. Dentist had capped her tooth, so she could talk and smile naturally. Cap wa such a close colour match you could scarcely see t'join. "He wanted to go again," she said, "but I wa like, *hang* on a minute, love, I'm red raw, here." She laughed, big and open, and Shaz and Kel laughed along wi her.

Watching Rach luxuriate int telling, how pleased she wa to be regaling them wi tales of this sex, Shaz felt like she'd been erased from t'record, scribbled ovver, replaced wi someone more worthy. She wa just a horrible, regrettable blip.

She realised, then, that all through study leave, any time she'd thought of Rach, she'd thought of him—hoping Rach'd dumped him, hoping she'd fallen out of love. Hoping Rach would never sleep wi him, never mek him person who'd always be remembered as her first.

Rach broke off to swig her lager. Kel took advantage ut pause to tell Shaz about what'd gone on when she went round neighbour's house to clean Lambrini out ut rug. She'd not had chance to talk about it at time: they'd all morphed into volleyball monsters.

While Kel'd been on her knees, raking a soapy pan scrub across patch ut rug they'd soiled wi their boozy games, she'd remembered Shaz's dare, gorrup courage to ask neighbour if she knew where her dad wa now. "She reckons that after t'miners got laid off, he might've moved to America." Kel said "America" like its syllables contained magic.

"A*merica?*" said Shaz.

"Yeah, so I think I might go there misen."

"What, to find him?" Shaz laughed. "You do know how big that country is?"

"Not to *find him*, bellend, just—" Kel shrugged. Not to *find him*, obvs. She wont thick. She knew she wunt find him. Dint mean she dint wanna follow him.

"How you gunna get there, like?" said Shaz.

Kel shrugged again, like she hadn't gi'en it any thought, when she'd actually gi'en it loads. "If you go uni, they have study-abroad programs, don't they?"

Kel'd never mentioned uni before. None of them had. Even though they'd never spoke word aloud, they'd all three had sense forra while now that it wa summat Rach and Kel would probs do but not Shaz. Rach and Kel's mams thought they ought to go. Shaz dint think her mam expected her to do owt in particular.

"What you talking about uni for, you boff," said Rach. "We ant even finished us GCSEs."

She sent Shaz a supportive smile, but summat about knowing it warra supportive smile—knowing Rach wa trying to be kind— med Shaz want to vanish intut growing dark and never return.

When Kel hopped down off bale and headed fut tree line in search of a place to slash, Shaz tried to smile at Rach and found hersen blushing. Found hersen shy. They swivelled round, propped their backs against next tier of hay bales, feet lolling in front of them. They wa nearly a body's width apart. They stared out. Edge ut field wa dissolving intut twilight.

Shaz sparked a fag, passed it to Rach, sparked another for hersen. "Ah'm glad fo' ya," she said. "Glad it's going well between you and your lad."

"Honestly, Shaz, I'm happiest I've ever been."

Shaz wondered if Rach knew she still sounded like she wa quoting a rom-com. She shuffled closer to Rach, till their knees touched. She pulled Rach into a side hug. Rach dint lean or turn intut hug; she stayed upright, stiff. Shaz laid her head on Rach's shoulder at an odd angle, till her neck ached, till it wa obvious that Rach would let Shaz hug her, but she wont gunna hug back. Shaz pulled away, retreated to her end ut bale, downed voddy straight from t'bottle, trying to banish little cry that wa welling in her chest. Fighting breathless sucked-out feeling like she'd been socked ont spine and winded. She med a promise to hersen that she'd never gi Rach power like that ovver her again. She'd never gi anycunt power like that.

She watched Rach fiddle wi a strand of hay, watched her tek shallow, cautious puffs of her cig, tried to imagine what Rach would be like when she wa older. Bossy, funny, always right. She'd mek a good secondary school teacher, a good mam. Shaz tried to imagine her little Kel braving big bad States all by hersen, thousands of miles and several planets away. She couldn't imagine warrit wa like to dream up ideas as big as America, to believe you could just pick up and drop yoursen into a new life.

"What are you thinking about?" Rach asked.

Shaz took a long drag of her ciggie, blew out a whip of smoke. "Nowt, just how weird it is that we've actually left school." How weird it wa that after t'summer Rach and Kel would be going sixth form wi'out her. That they had one summer together left before Rach and Kel's lives would become mostly sixth form and their sixth form mates and their bezzy-bitch boyfriends. How weird it wa that they'd already stopped meaning to each other what they used to mean.

Kel heaved hersen back ontut bale, a broad-petalled purple flower perched behind her ear. She had another two stashed in her pocket that she held out to Shaz and Rach.

She said, "Let's climb tut top."

Rach protested ont grounds that she wa too drunk and bale stack wa too high, too rickety, too death-trap-esque.

"Fuck it." Shaz took another swig of voddy. "Come on, Rach, dunt be a fanny *all* your life."

"Yeah, come on, Fanny Features," said Kel, giggling drunkenly.

Rach rolled her eyes in pretend annoyance, clambered to her feet. She and Shaz tucked their flowers behind their ears, flicked their fag ends off intut dark. They all stuffed their jeans into their socks, stared at bales towering ovver them. They anchored their hands ont tier above and hoisted themsens up.

Reckoning

If you knew that one of your oldest mates wa married to a rapist, would you tell her?

What if you'd kept it from her for fifteen years?

What if you dint tell her when she wa fifteen, just started seeing him. You dint tell her before she moved in wi him intut two-room flat above chippy that smelled of frying oil and malt vinegar, or before amethyst engagement ring shaped like Princess Di's, or before hen do weekend in Blackpool—before tiaras, Jägerbombs, willy-shaped sports whistles—before wedding, before she bought her three-bed semi wi him. Before she set her heart on a life wi him.

You'd never said word "rape" out loud. You'd only just started lerrin yoursen think it. Your lass, only person you'd ever told, had been coaching you to use proper term, to call it warrit wa, to stop trying to believe it wa summat else, summat smaller, summat wi a different name. You couldn't mek word cross your lips—and you couldn't imagine ever saying it to Rach. She wunt thank you, would she. She wunt wanna know, and wunt it be cruel to tell her now.

For years, you'd hardly had to ask yoursen these questions, since you and Rach barely spoke. But when Kel cem home, back from America

271

for good, Rach wa dead set on a reunion. Organising reunion took a fortnight, a group chat, a dozen Google searches, and at least one private message thread, which wa tekkin piss considering you wa only off Donny forra drink. When organising began, you wa laid ont settee, phone two inches from your nose, telly on to drown out neighbour's telly coming through wall on one side—he wa eighty-five and deaf and watched *Countryfile* at a hundred decibels—and young family's screaming row coming through wall ont other. You preferred it when young family wanted each other dead, like; that wa better than when you could hear them plotting against you and your lass, cooking up ways to mek "fuckin dykes" move out. You tried to block it all, focus ont convo going on int group chat, which years ago yous'd named FEMINEM, after all-girl rap group yous formed int dinner queue one day in year nine.

FEMINEM

RACH

Alright girlies really looking forward to celebrating KELS RETURN!

Haha we stole her back from Yankeeland woohoo!

I recks we do a pub crawl of every place we used to drink in back int day.

Will be a proper laugh what do you reckon

KEL

Back when yous went round wearing sem glittery eyeshadow that always looked perfect on Rach and Kel but gathered int creases of your hooded lids. Yous'd nip into Superdrug before hitting pubs, do your makeup wit testers, doll yoursens up for free. Feeling wild, limitless, like yous wa really *living*, like gerrin off your tits on a neet round Donny wut pinnacle of being alive. You tapped a slow reply.

FEMINEM

> Half of those pubs arent even there anymore

RACH

> Alright mardarse I'm only trying to think of summat fun for us to do 😄

> Just sayin theres a lot boarded up now

Donny's more bar than town, like, and yous used to drink in all of them. Even though loads had shut, Rach wa still proposing more pub crawl than anyone's thirty-year-old liver should be asked to handle.

You wont *not* happy Kel wa back. You'd been dezzy forr'er to come home all years she'd been gone. Kel dint update her socials like Rach did, so you couldn't picture it, Kel existing ont other side ut Atlantic. It warra blank. You never liked it, Kel knowing your world completely, cuz it wa sem as always, just a bit worse since Recession and austerity and Brexit, but you not knowing owt about hers. And you couldn't feel excitement of seeing Kel again wi'out feeling sick. What would happen tut friendship now? Could yous go back to hanging out all t'time? Easy to stay mates when you only see each other forra piss-up every few years. Now yous'd have to find out if friendship could stand everydayness. What if you ran out of chat three hours in. Fuck would you do wit rest of forever.

FEMINEM

RACH

Anyway we've got to do it right, proper night out round town

Because this is mi last night ont lash forra while . . .

She added three dots so you'd know she had summat to announce.

KEL

Oh aye how come?

RACH

We're going to start trying 🐵

KEL

No way! 🙀 🙀 🙀

RACH

Mad innit 😲 we said we'd wait till we wa settled in us jobs and saved enough forra deposit ont house and we've been in our place two year now so we've decided it's time.

KEL

Omg! That's mint Rach I'm reyt happy for ya!

🤰 🤰 🤰

Kel sent more emoji triplets, more exclamation marks, but you'd already sprung off sofa, headed fut kitchen. You slammed phone down ont work top, flicked kettle's switch, dropped a round Tetley's bag into your mug. Your millionth cuppa ut day. You used to drink tea to fill your belly up, stop it whining for bread. You loved angry bubbling ut kettle, noise filling room till you dint think it'd ever boil ovver, then—click, dead gentle, switch went down, water settled. Satisfaction. Forra second.

Your tea wa always bitter cuz you wunt let yoursen add sugar. Hadn't let yoursen since puberty, but you could still taste it missing. Too wound up to wait fut tea to cool, you sipped too early, scalded your tongue. Bumps sprouted ont spongy pink surface. You swore at empty kitchen, at your flayed tongue, at mug slopping hot tea ovver your knuckles.

You took ice cube tray out ut freezer's top shelf, which wa jammed shut wi frost, which you had to hack away at wit bread knife. That felt good. You rapped tray ont counter till a cube popped out in a shower of chipped ice. That felt good an' all. Nowt like a bit of kitchen violence to slam all your feelings out. You rolled cube ovver your tongue, trying to soothe it. Another old trick of yours, suck ice cubes all day, fool your brain into thinking it's been fed. You tried not to dwell ont past, ont little lass you used to be, fighting battles in your head no-cunt knew about. You tried not to remember everything you could never tell.

But a babby? Rach wa gunna have a *babby* wi him?

Int group chat, Rach wa listing pubs that wa still open.

FEMINEM

RACH

There's still loads to go at like Tut, Black Bull, Spoons, Leopard.

Leopard? Fucking *Leopard*? You closed chat. Ice cube melted. You bashed out another, sucked. Why would Rach try and mek you go Leopard? Surely she knew that wut pub you were working in when—ovver two years ago, now—you lost control of yoursen, threw a pint glass at Rach's husband's band. Lost your job, got barred from Leopard for life.

You'd assumed Rach's hubby had told her where, when, how—gi'en her his version, spun a story that you wa just a mad bitch, chaotic. You'd assumed that wa why she'd been funny wi ya ever since, quickening rate gap wa widening between yas, falling out of touch on purpose. You couldn't gi Rach or Kel your version, not wi'out telling them why you threw it. You had to let your best mates think you'd lost it, glassed a bloke for no goodfuckin reason.

You switched to your private message thread wi Kel.

> No way am I doing a bloody pub crawl

> 😎 Its just drinks, innit. Let her call it what she wants

> Might just not come

> Yous two just go

> Doubt she wants me there anyway

> Dont be daft you've got to come

> It wunt be us wi out you

Kel's three dots bounced for ages, as if she dint know how to arrange her next words.

> Just let her be a pain int arse, at least we don't
> have to organise owt

> She can plan all she wants, I'm having two
> drinks and gerrin last bus home

You said it to yoursen like a mantra: Two drinks and last bus home. Two drinks, last bus. You couldn't afford more than two anyway, and you couldn't afford to get drunk around Rach. Couldn't trust your tongue. Wi too many bevvies inside ya, there wa no telling what you'd say.

Int weeks leading up tut reunion, Rach filled FEMINEM wi plans, messaging whenever she remembered a specific drink yous used to order in a particular bar—*We've got to go Biscuit Billy's for vodka red bulls! We've got to go Boiler Rooms forra shot of black sambuca!*—and asking where could yous go forra decent cocktail. You wa Googling "cocktails Doncaster" before you'd even realised Rach had sucked you intut planning. You gev up scrolling results when you saw that Yelp's top hit for "Doncaster cocktail bars" warrin Sheffield, city down road that warran actual place, not a town that only existed cuz no-cunt but Kel had ever thought to leave. And Donny had still claimed Kel int end.

Kel wa sick, apparently. Forced to gi up her job in Boston, move back in wi her mam. She wouldn't say what she wa sick *wi*. You hoped she dint mean homesick. You hoped to god she dint gi up her life ovver there cuz she missed knocking about wi thee.

Night before reunion, after another day of death-by-micromanagement-by-group-chat, you wa busting to vent by time your lass gorrin from work. She warra carer at old folk's home in Thurnscoe, so she always cem back knackered. £8.50 an hour, thirteen-hour shifts, helping old ladies wash and go tut toilet. You kissed her lips, chilly and chapped wit wind, pulled her beanie off, ruffled her bleached mohawk, put your warm hands round pink tips of her ears.

"Now then, Buggalugs," she said, as she always did, summat you loved from her but would've hated from any fucker else. Your lass wut biggest part of your life now. Besides Rach and Kel, your mates'd either got babbies and evaporated, or it turned out they weren't really mates int first place, just people you worked wi who hated sem things—early shift, emergency tax, line manager—and once you dint work together nomore, there wa nowt left to say. You and your lass used to go into Donny tut gay bar once a fort-night, got matey wit bar staff and t'regulars, till it shut down. Since then, your big treat warra trip into Donny every month or so, to go tut new Taco Bell that'd just opened int Frenchgate.

While she unloaded ya teas from an ASDA bag—microwave jalfrezis, bottle of Irn-Bru—you chatted her ear off about this stupid neet out and Rach's stupid plans. You couldn't shurrup about it while she heated each curry in its black plastic tray, raising your voice ovvert microwave's whir. You wunt stop while two of yas ate, not even when you gorra slurp of curry sauce on your cheek, and your lass took a photo to show you it looked like a willy, which'd normally mek you laugh, but this time med you dead-eye her and say, Do you mind, I wa talking. You couldn't shurrup while yous watched your Skandi drama, or while you brushed your teeth together int narrow bathroom, you sat ont loo, your lass stood at sink in boxers and a sports bra, lean tricep twitching as she brushed, and you still going, Problem wi Rach is she has to be in charge of absolutely fucking everything, while your lecky toothbrush raged in ya gob, paste foam blobbing onto your bed tee.

Your lass spat intut sink and said, "Reyt, are you ready to tell me what's really upset ya?" She wa dead good, your lass, at knowing when you wa ranting about one thing but upset about summat else. You wa slowly gerrin used to her calling you out, but it still rankled. No-cunt else had ever bothered calling you on your shite. Apart from Rach. Rach had been calling you out since yous wa eleven. You switched off your toothbrush. You could hear young family's sound system belting Crazy Frog song, which they played twice an hour, one of their many genius schemes to get shut of thee.

You willed ya mind quiet. When all your spiky thoughts had settled, you told your lass about Rach's plans to start trying. "How can ah let her have a babby wi him, wi'out knowing?"

Your lass crouched down, laid her forr'ead on yours, as if your two brains could tackle problem as one. She cupped nape of your neck wi her hand. Shiver of calm down your back.

"You reckon telling her's reyt thing to do?"

You shrugged, put your hand on her nape, cool firm of her under your palm. How could you wreck Rach's life, though, reyt when she'd got everything she'd always wanted. Which wut kindness— tell now, or tell never.

"What do you reckon she'd want you to do?"

"Well, if I knew that!"

"Alreyt, then warrabout you? Do you need to tell her fo' yoursen?"

You tried to imagine it: not carrying secret, not having it wedged between you and ya mates. How light you'd feel. How free. And if Rach and Kel could stand it—if they could believe ya, still love ya after you'd told—then wunt you know friendship wa real? Wunt you know you could trust it? But Rach'd go mad. She'd call you a liar. She'd call you a spiteful bitch. She'd never so much as look at you again.

"There's always Mexborough," your lass said, straightening from her crouch.

Whenever there wa summat yous dint wanna face—past-due gas bill, your mounting payday loans, drinks wi her folks—yous'd joke about fleeing to Mexico, till that turned into joking about flee-ing to Mex*borough*, next town ovver from yours.

You whipped her ont thigh wi a flannel, mekkin her laugh and whip you back. Your way of thanking her for lerrin you bang on all neet, for never losing her temper when you talked too much for too long about wrong thing.

You kept testing her, like, waiting forr'er to crack. A habit you couldn't shed. Most of your other partners'd had a *reyt* temper on em. Or warrit summat from further back, summat you absorbed int womb. Wont every Donny cunt always half cocked forra scrap?

Reunion day, you wa waiting ont bus stop bench by quarter past five, by t'blue shutters ut China Kitchen, plyboarded window ut Sally Army. Plyboard wa smothered in a collage of flyers: glued down and wrinkly, stapled loose and flapping, faded, glossy, torn. A hot-pink piece of A4 caught your eye. It wa rain spattered and half ripped off, but you could still read black bubble letters: "Arms-Out Simon 15th Memorial Rave." It'd been there months, you realised. You'd looked at it loads of times wi'out seeing it.

You gorra weird ripple feeling, like you warrat seashore stood on a gusty cliff edge. Arms-Out fifteen years in his grave, and you feeling sorry for yoursen for carrying a secret that long. Surely you could just keep carrying it. There wa worse things. Your fingers gripped bench till t'ripply topple feeling faded.

You wa glad, anyway, that your town wut kind that remembered its dead. Glad you wont only one who couldn't let go ut past.

You gorrup off bench to let a young lass sit cuz she looked knackered pushing two babbies in a double buggy. You dead-eyed bloke int flat cap and sheepskin coat who dint even fake like he'd gi up his seat. Reminded you of sneaking intut cinema to see *Titanic* wi Kel and Rach when you wa eleven—bit where ship wa sinking, all those blokes shouting "women and children first." You feeling glad you warra lass, cuz you'd always get first dibs ont lifeboats. You thinking it wa safer to be a girl. How long you believed that. How many years it took before you stopped being thankful when men said "ladies first," simpering grins hiding their true meaning, that safety wa theirs to gi and theirs to tek away.

You watched oncoming traffic, hoping to see 219 peeping round corner, not X19 gunning stret down Barnsley Road. Usually, you hoped fut opposite: 219's route wa fifteen minutes longer, tekkin you winding through Barnburgh, Harlington, High Melton, pretty country villages wi nice pubs and tall houses, then through Rach and Kel's village, before wheezing ovvert North Bridge into town. Tonight you dint wanna be too early, just late enough that Kel would already be there, but not so late that you'd piss Rach off.

Of course X19 cem first and opened up, door clanking, engine sighing. You helped young lass lift buggy ontut bus, held her babbies' spitty cakey hands while she packed it intut luggage rack, then climbed tut top deck, sat at front where you could watch road coming at you. You tried to keep your nerves muzzled, tried not to think about moment you'd clap eyes on each other, pressure on them first seconds—pressure to well up wi joy. Your phone buzzed relentless, them two swapping updates and ETAs. You muted FEMINEM, hid your phone in your handbag.

A group of teenage lasses sprawled ovvert top deck's back benches, passing a phone between them, howling ovver whatever meme or YouTube vid wa going viral. You dint have memes int early noughties. You barely had internet. But you remembered that belly-ache. That cackle wa just the same. One lass wa informing rest about how many calories there warrin cum—There's ovver a thousand, reyt, so you'd all better spit if you wanna stick to ya thousand calories a day. You remembered gi'in Kel and Rach sem wisdom, except int noughties it warra known fact that number of calories in a blow job wa sem as a ham-and-cheese bap. Kel used to think you knew everything, used to look at you and say, *Reee*ally? wi full trust and belief, no matter what shit you spouted. You would've done owt to kidnap that look at carry it wi you. Back then you tried to eat five hundred calories a day, loathed yoursen whenever you went ovver, whenever you gev in, binged three BK Bacon Double Cheeseburgers in a row.

You wa itching to turn round, tell these young lasses not to be so hard on themsens. As if you'd stopped being hard on yoursen.

"It's low-fat," you said, ovver your shoulder.

Lasses' chatter stopped sharp, like they'd only just realised they wont alone.

"You what?"

You turned round: six of them, all eying you wi suspicion, all wearing so much makeup they'd painted on sem face—sem black Scouse brows, sem contoured cheeks, sem ovverdrawn lips. You wanted to gi em all a hug.

"Jizz is a low-fat food, innit. Only half a point at WeightWatchers."

"Oooh," one said, as if speaking to a dementia-riddled old bid. "Reyt. Ta." They gi each other eyes and shrugs that meant *Who the fuck's that?* and *No fucking clue*, and went back to teaching each other how to have sex wi'out gerrin fat.

You faced front, smiling to yoursen; you wunt have listened either. You wished they'd got your joke, though, wished they'd known you wa trying to mek em laugh. Front window wa steamy now, everything outside hazy. Grey road tunnelled at you. Street-lights blazed amber ribbons through dark. Must be coming up on York Road. Nearly there.

What if you wont enough for them anymore. What if you couldn't still mek Rach and Kel cackle. What if they fake laughed at your shit jokes. What if you all pretended to cry when you saw each other. You pictured Kel forcing tears of happiness at sight of ya. Your heart slipped your rib cage, tumbled into your boots.

Off at North Bridge—held kids' cakey hands again, helped lass wit buggy down again—wind whisking your hair, breathing on you damp and fresh. You walked down by t'Minster, which warra church, till Donny decided to put in a bid to be a city, started renaming everything. Church became "Minster," Donny College became "University Centre Doncaster," but so far Her Majesty's Crown Office had sin through t'ruse. You peered intut Minster's shadowy grounds, to see if there warra clutter of youths amongst graves gerrin rat-arsed on White Lightning. Of course there wa—a dabbing of pale faces and baseball hats strung across old wall yous used to sit on to get rat-arsed, no idea that wall wa actually sole remnant of a Roman fort, no idea it'd been sat there two thousand years. You hadn't even known Donny wa that old, never thought forra second somecunt would've bothered invading t'place. Far as little Shaz wa concerned, it warra wall, wannit. Broken off, uneven, weeds pushing between misshapen stone. You bet it wa just a wall to these kids an' all. Just somewier to sit, drink, spit, smoke. Mebs that's what Roman soldiers used it for. Mebs they wa just as bored as yous.

When you got tut Black Bull, Rach warrat bar alone. Black Bull wut dingy old-man pub Rach wa adamant about starting wi cuz it wa where yous used to start when you warrat school. It hadn't changed: sem torn mauve benches, sem brass medallions nailed to mahogany walls, sem bar stools occupied by grey, deflating, life-weathered regulars. Rach had chopped her hair chin-length, delicately streaked it wi bleach. She wore a shortish black dress, sequinned, looking like she warroff to a party. You felt scruffy in your jeans, your pilling blouse. Rach waved at you, her body twinkling.

Three shots of silver tequila waited in a line ont bar top, slice of lime balancing on each. You reminded yoursen: two drinks, last bus.

"My treat!" Rach said, startling heavily bent octogenarian sipping Guinness ont stool behind her. Still early, only six, so it wa mostly day drinkers wi their shopping bags, their dirty plates left ovver from lunch. Rach hugged you so tight her arm yanked your pony back. "Missed you so much, lovely," she said into your taut scalp. You might've said it back if your mouth wont full of her hair, if she wont pinning your handbag to your ribs. You might've meant it, if you dint suspect her hug warra touch *too* tight. You might've felt yoursen unfolding, longing fut closeness Rach wa pretending still existed between yas by holding you so fiercely.

Wi Rach's sequins scratching your throat, wi her saying summat above your head in a giddy reunion voice, wit familiar smell of her, hunger for closeness growled inside ya.

Rach let go, turned to catch barman's eye. "What you having? I'll get first round in."

Second round, she meant. Tequila shots wa still sweating ont bar top.

"Ah'm alreyt, me. Ah'm only stopping out forra couple."

"Pint of Diesel?" Rach asked, remembering what you drank when you wa sixteen, mix of cider, lager, and blackcurrant cordial, sweet and lethal enough to please a teenager's tongue. You hadn't hankered for that in years. You dint hanker now. Rach wa jittery, gaze flitting between you and barman, sending you twitchy smiles every time your eyes met. You dint know what to mek of her nerves, whether she wa just anxious fut neet to go well, or if she wa nervous round thee. Scared that any second you'd detonate. It med you even more convinced her hubby had bad-mouthed you, med up a story about wharra mad cow you wa.

Before you'd had chance to tek your coat off, Rach'd flagged barman, purra pint of Diesel in your hand. Shots wa still waiting. And you'd have to get next round, then it'd be Kel's turn, then it'd go round and round and that wa how you gorrin trouble.

"Ah can't tek a shot, it'll do me in."

"You're not driving, are you?"

Rach knew you dint have a car, never owned one in your life.

"Ah've gorrer get last bus."

"Like *fuck* you're gerrin last bus! We're gunna go Walkabout forra boogie." She swung her hips to demonstrate. You knew Walkabout warra clothes shop now, but you dint point that out. Rach would only mek a new plan to drag yas to Berlin's, or Courtyard, or—god help yas—Flares, '70s-themed bar on Hall Gate where teenage lads and retired women drank BOGOFf Tropical Reefs and gorroff wi each other to "Dancing Queen."

"We'll just get taxi home," Rach said.

"It's twenty quid back to mine."

"No worries, we'll work it out."

You knew that "we'll work it out" meant you waint decide how to split fare till it wa three a.m. and Rach wa already staggering out ut cab at her house, thrusting a sweaty palm of pound coins into your hand that barely covered her share.

"It's Kel's first night back," Rach said, as if that fact could magic more money into your wallet. She held up her pint; you clinked glasses wi her, tried to match high pitch of her "cheers," then took too many sips of your sickly purple concoction, till half ut pint wa gone and you could already feel it in your knees.

"Should've known she'd be late," you said. "What's she like."

"Oh, drives me batty." Rach did a big mock eye roll, a big mock sigh.

"Nightmare gerrin her to reply to texts these days an' all." You wa warming to your theme, now you'd hit on summat yous could bond ovver. You could put your glass down, tek your coat off, breathe. "She dunt text back for weeks, so you keep asking her if she's alreyt, and all you get is three heart emojis."

"Yeah." Rach's tone shifted, eyes swerved from yours. "She's almost as bad as you."

Fuck's that meant to mean, you wanted to know. Rach wut one who stopped responding to your texts years ago, mekkin out she wa too busy to see ya. What wa she mad at *you* for? Nope, no—you wa gunna keep it chatty and light. Two drinks, last bus.

When Kel walked in, first thing you noticed wa how tiny she wa. Must've lost stone and half since you last saw her, and she dint have a lot spare to start wi. She looked beautiful and sick. New lines swept beneath her eyes, pillowy sleep-deprived puffs of skin. You wanted to hold her face and stare at it, drink int surreal fact of her. It warras if Kel warra stranger who looked just like somebody dead. She looked all her ages at once: eleven, fourteen, eighteen, twenty-three—it warrall in there, but mixed wi summat you dint recognise. Same wi anyone you knew from school and dint see much. They popped up on Facebook after fourteen years of not existing, and they dint look like thirty-odd-year-olds; they looked like children wi wrinkles and chub added on.

Kel smiled, and there she wa, your Kel, sem round cheeks she'd had forever. She threw her arms round your neck and you hugged her back, scared of how little *her* there wa—she wa more coat than body—and then there wa tears fucking up your mascara. Kel's eyes looked watery, but nowt broke ovver onto her cheeks, and you wanted to think she wa holding back real joy, but you daren't let yoursen believe it.

Kel hugged Rach what seemed like way longer, way tighter, two of them rocking side to side, and you couldn't help feeling what you always felt when they shared summat wi'out ya—that you'd never mek up fut early years, Rach and Kel growing up ont sem street since they wa babbies, already bezzies before you met them ont first day of comp. Dint matter how much time passed, you knew you'd never match that.

Rach gestured at tequila shots wi an arcing hand as if to say, *Voilà!* Reminded you of a Yelp review you saw when you wa looking up cocktail bars, some bloke on a rant about Premier Inn claiming they wa full, till he demanded to speak tut manager. He wrote, "And viola! Suddenly there's a room free after all." It med you laugh, thinking of this bloke in a reyt rage, naming random instruments: *And trombone! Bassoon! Euphonium!* You wanted to say it now—Viola!—but you wont sure if you could mek it funny. If they dint laugh, you dint think you could bear it.

Rach purra shot glass in Kel's hand and one in yours.

"Waheeey," said Kel. She wa grinning, but it looked to thee like smile of one of them theatre masks, freakishly fixed and wide.

"Let's get wankered!" said Rach.

You couldn't tek shot. You couldn't pay Rach back, and you'd have to find your way home on your tod, and you wa old enough now to be afraid of that—to not wanna be a flailing muddle of limbs and spirit, stumbling, med of rubber, looking forra body to press against. There warra time when you'd've been one insisting on tequila, insisting on licking salt off someone else's hand—whichever lad or lass you wa flirting wi—mekkin them lick salt off yours. You used to think it wa sexy. Good job you couldn't remember most of what you gorrup to. Long as you got home wi all your fingers and toes intact, you considered it a mint fuckin neet. How you dint die, all t'shit you put yoursen through, little Shaz's mad ambition to grab oblivion wi both hands and shek it loose, leave her vulnerable body out int town centre, in dark alleys, in taxis, int middle of nowier. You dint know what she wa after—if she wanted to destroy hersen, or just pummel hersen wi as much life, as much living, as she could gerr'er mitts on.

That lass wont you nomore, but her scars still decorated your body. Broken toilet lid wa still slashed across your left palm, falling off your high heels ontut tarmac wa still trapped int dodgy ligament of your right knee. Scuff on your wrist from that neet you couldn't talk about. Slimmest white line still showed, reyt across vein, so faint only you could see.

"Right then, ladies." Rach held up her shot. "Sink these, sink those pints, then we'll do Olde Castle, Vintage Rock Bar, Tut n Shive"—she counted them off on her fingers—"Bailey's, Leopard—"

"Ah'm not going Leopard," you said.

"But we've gorrer go and drink Tropical Sourz and lemonade," said Rach.

You couldn't believe how many rituals yous used to have, or that

Rach had remembered them all. You searched her face forra motive, forra flash of pretend innocence. Did she know what she wa asking you to do? Wa she mebs even hoping bouncer would turn you away in a blaze of shame? It'd been two years; management had changed since then. But you knew you couldn't hope that none ut staff would recognise ya.

"Ah'll be off home before you head there."

"Don't be a fanny, it's my night!"

"Yeah, we've gorrer celebrate," said Kel. "At least one of us is finally gunna be a grown-up!" Kel daubed her joy on so bright, med sure her eyes wa flaming wi so much happiness, you wanted to ask how she really felt, what pain she wa covering up. You could see smugness in Rach's face. She'd done everything reyt, and now she had what she wa always meant to: house, husband, kids next.

"Ah thought tonight wa menna be about Kel. You're not even pregnant yet, are ya?"

"Tonight *is* about Kel. I just thought you'd be happy for me an' all."

"We are," Kel said. "It can be a joint celebration." She laid her index finger int crease of your elbow. "We can celebrate Rach as well, can't we?"

You put your hand ovver Kel's finger, nesting it, felt warmth of your two bodies connected and tried to tek strength from it.

You raised ya shot glass. "Tut little twat who's about to split yours." You said it deadpan—serious, not serious—hoped they took it as a joke.

They raised their tequilas: "To splitting twats!"

You clinked and licked salt and guzzled, slammed ya glass down first. You wa first wit lime slice smarting roof of your mouth.

Yous set off to tour town's scuzziest bars, starting wit places yous used to go Fridi afternoons, when you warrat college and Rach and

Kel warrin sixth form, them two in their school ties and still ger-rin served. You had a drink in each one till you wa starting to feel full. You inched round Donny's gap-toothed streets, boarded windows beside newer spots that had been done up to look like American speakeasies, but still kicked out sem nineties dance tunes yous used to jump around to at parish hall discos. There warra festival atmosphere, takeaways oozing funfair smells, deep-fried chips and chicken wings and summat battered but sweet. Bodies everywier, yous dodging round young lasses and older women wi high heels and high hair and blushered cheeks, decked out in their best little dresses. Packs of lads shouting and jeering amongst themsens, their love coming out like cruelty. One lad said to his mate, as they wa walking along eating from Styrofoam boxes, "That is a fat arse!" and pointed at it—"Fat, fat, fat, fat, *fat* fucking arse!"—then pulled him into a sweaty hug and kissed his forr'ead, dropping chips all ovvert pavement. Takeaways wa rammed wit day lot, them that'd been out since midday, sopping up booze wi stodge, prepping their bellies for round two. Streets wa rammed wit night crowd trying to catch up, racing towards shit-faced, towards higher and higher spirits. They'd keep at it till their spirits hit a rolling boil and spilled ovver, sizzled into fight. You could feel it coming, simmering int air.

Down Silver Street, yous tried Aruba but found it boarded up. You stopped in front of it, staring, Rach and Kel saying, Come on, let's try somewhere else. You worked Aruba forra while years back, till manager gorra bit gropey one neet during post-shift drinks. Hulking old converted warehouse, tall windows hidden by chipboard. Silver Street wa heaving in your day, but crowds wa thinner now that centre of Donny nightlife had drifted a few streets up. On your Fridi and Satdi neet shifts, police had already barricaded Silver Street by seven o'clock, parked riot vans either end. Set of bored-looking coppers inside, waiting fut coming carnage. Aruba's marquee had been tekken down—and now you thought about it, place had been about five different things since you worked there: Space, Che Bar, VDKA. Your lass still called it Revolution cuz that's warrit wa in her day. Above bare patch where these many names had sat, ovvert second-storey windows, "Alfred Hall Ltd" stood in red letters, as if building had only ever been a warehouse, as if all that dancing and chugging and shagging int toilet stalls and chucking up int urinals never happened. As if there never warra beer cellar beneath bar, as if your manager never cornered you in there, never pushed you up against wall.

Rach directed yas to a new bar down Priory Walk, but it'd turned into a kebab shop, so yous went next door to Spoons instead. Spoons dint play music. Quiet med you aware of how drunk you wa gerrin, how soft and slidy your vision, how lispy your tongue. Yous dint have to shout to mek yoursens heard, but lack of a soundtrack meant more pressure to mek decent conversation. Rach declared it wa her round again, but you asked her not to get you owt cuz you warroff in ten minutes anyway.

While she muscled intut three-deep crowd at bar, you and Kel bagged last free sofas, two loveseats either side of a coffee table, ends pressed against window. Other side ut window, an alley divided Spoons from kebab shop, where lads wa stuffing doner shavings into their mouths.

You wa glad to get Kel alone forra minute. You sat ont sem sofa, leaned into her arm. "You alreyt, then?" You looked into her eyes wi meaning—she'd been loud and giggly wi Rach, but you could see she wa purrin it on. Summat warrup.

"Yeah, proper mint night so far, innit?"

"Thought you wa menna be poorly." You laid your hand ovver her stubby fingers, her bitten nails. "You can be real wi me, ya know. No point stopping out if ya not up forrit."

Kel stared into you, dark eyes searching yours as if hunting for proof that you really wa gi'in her permission to *be real*, to be whatever version of hersen had emerged int years she'd been gone.

Rach lowered hersen ontut opposite couch, breaking Kel's eye contact. She wa carrying a wine bottle and three glasses. You nearly asked her why the fuck she'd brought a glass for you, but managed not to. You dint wanna sound ungrateful. You dint wanna drink that rosé, though, even if yous did *always* drink a bottle of rosé in Spoons when you wa sixteen. You already felt like you wa two sips away from too far gone.

"Amazing, innit?" Rach laid bottle and glasses ont table. "How long's it been since we warrall together and it's like no time has passed. Just like old times, innit?"

Your body felt tight, as if someone wa pumping you wi air. Now Rach had said so, it wa like yous had to act as if everything wut same, like years hadn't moulded yas into odd shapes that dint quite fit together. Rach wa asking Kel to be sem old Kel, sweet and chilled out and up for owt. She wa asking you to be sem old Shaz, Party Animal Shaz, No Prisoners Shaz, Come On Then Ya Cunts I'll Tek You All On Shaz.

Kel pulled her hand from under yours. "I'll be reyt wi a few more drinks inside me," she said in your ear. "Pay forrit tomorrow, like, but"—she shrugged—"fuck it!" She slathered Donny back into her voice thick, way your nan spread marg on white bread. She laid her *u* sounds down round and low, a sound so fat you could chew it. But you could still hear Yankification at corners of her vowels, ends of her sentences bending up.

Every time she cem back, she cem back different. A bit less like you, a bit more like them. She did her best to hide it, but it wa there, in her wonky accent, int way she sometimes said "That's so funny" instead of laughing, way she'd started asking folk what they "did for work" instead of just gerrin to know them. Comments she med about Donny as if it dint belong to her. Like a few years ago, when she wa laughing about a billboard she'd sin int train station, tiny paddling pool propping up an enormous cartoon shark. Caption read, "Doncaster College: Be a Big Fish in a Little Pond." Kel thought that wa hilarious, but you couldn't see what wa funny. Sem wit mural next tut ring road, "Love, Cope, Give, Hope." "What's that," Kel'd said, smirking, "Donny's answer to 'Live, Laugh, Love'?" Yeah, mate, you thought, we cope wi'out much living.

Rach filled everyone's glasses wi a flourish, like it wa champagne instead of Denbies sparkling rosé brut, only rosé on offer now that Spoons refused to sell owt but British booze. All those years yous drank in Spoons, no idea who you wa gi'in your money to, till t'owner cem out as a Brexit wanker. Brexit warranother thing you'd promised yoursen you wunt bring up round Rach. Easier to look her int eye while you only *suspected* she'd voted leave.

Yous clinked, cheersed, poured Blighty's finest rosé into your mouths.

You said, "Ah'm heading off after thissun."

Rach mimed checking a watch she wont wearing. "Packing in before ten o'clock? Not like you to admit defeat."

"Kel's not well, we need to gerr'er in bed."

"I'm alreyt, me! Proper up forra dance, it's been ages."

"Leopard next, then?"

"What ya wanna go there fo'?" you asked.

Rach's smile set. "For old time's!"

It wa wishful thinking, wont it, that Rach might be trying to mek you go Leopard so you *had* to talk about neet you threw t'pint glass? You wa kidding yoursen, wont ya, that a part of her knew there wa more tut story—that she might actually want you to tell her t'truth?

"Fucksake, let's do it!" said Kel. "Honestly, Shaz, if I need protecting from *fun*, I'll let you know?" There it wa—her upward curl, America turning Kel's answers into questions.

You took your wine in gulps, trying to finish quickly so you could go. Kel and Rach got bigger and gigglier, arms gesturing wider as they talked, till Kel's hand swooped into a passing bloke's crotch and she had to say, "Oop, sorry!"

Rach and Kel laughed and dove intut remember-whens: Remember when you fell into that bloke in Walkabout and he wa screaming that you'd broke his willy? Remember when that lad broke up wi you in Walkabout because you burped in his face? Remember when you fucked that lad int Walkabout toilets, cracked your head open ont cistern?

They wa snatching at any remember-when they could reach. Afraid of silence. It wa never silent when you wa kids—it warra lattice of threads you wa always weaving, cutting each other off mid-thought wi an Oh, by t'way, or a Speaking of, or an Oh, I forgot to tell ya! Then someone would slice into a By t'way wi another By t'way, till there wa six conversations going at once that yous ducked in and out of, never dropping one.

You'd already heard about Rach's kitchen renno, her "holibobs" wi her hubby ont Costa del Sol. You'd heard about lad Kel wa seeing in America after her husband left, an "ethical non-monogamist" who liked to slap her about in bed but "not in a bad way," apparently. Now they wa raking ovvert past. Sem cycle yous went through whenever Kel cem back forra visit.

How come they never asked what wa new wi thee? They dint know you wa starting a new job next week, a proper one—you wa gunna be a support worker for kids wi autism. You liked idea of it, helping kids. But you'd've never dared think you wa qualified if it wont for your lass, urging ya, believing in ya. They dint even know you had a girlfriend. Rach's face always gorra funny tic whenever you mentioned a lass you wa seeing, her nose twitching like a rabbit's till you changed subject. But she warrall gasps and enthusiasm when you wa seeing a lad. Just one more thing you felt like you couldn't tell her.

Rach divided rest ut bottle between your glasses.

You raised yours and said, "Thank fuck we took back control, eh? Ah wa sick of drinking champagne, me." You took a long swig and felt pressure give, an inch of that tight air let out.

"I'm sorry this wine doesn't meet your standards, Shaz." Rach said it wi a smile, like it wa banter.

"No, ah meant—thanks for gerrin it, like. Ah wa just joking."

"At my expense."

"Brexit's not your fault. Is it?"

Yous stared at each other across table, summat intense and complicated flaring int heat of your held gaze.

"People voted ont facts they wa given and believed to be true."

"Facts? You mean t'lies they *wanted* to believe."

"No-one knew what wa gunna happen, so there's no point being nasty to each other now."

"Oh aye, so people are going hungry, but we've still gorrer be *nice* about it?"

Stop it, Shaz. Stop it, stop it. Booze wa mekkin you snap back before you could rein yoursen in. You needed to chill, drink water. You checked your phone: quarter past ten. Still time fut last bus. You needed to gerroff home to your lass, sober up, sleep till everything you'd promised yoursen you wunt say stopped bubbling into your mouth.

"Let's move on, shall we?" said Kel, and steered you into a chat about her younger coworkers in Boston, who she called "Gen Zee-ers," rich American lasses in their early twenties who'd grown up wi new ideas about sex and gender. "They've got loads more options than we did, ant they?" Kel said, meaning anyone younger than yous. "Everyone's a feminist now."

You thought about them lasses ont bus, their painted faces and their bad sex facts, trying their hardest to grow intut only version of themsens they thought they wa allowed to be. Feminism had took one look at Donny and thought, Reckon I'll gi this a miss.

"Well, I'm not a bloody feminist," said Rach. "I just think we should all be equal, do you know wharrah mean?"

A plump, milky-fleshed arse pressed itsen against other side ut window, inches from your face. A young lass had gone down t'alley looking for somewier private to piss, dropped her kegs, and leant up against glass, thinking it warra wall.

"Oh aye!" You pointed tut bare bum that had just wandered intut middle of your feminist debate.

"Fucking hell!" said Kel.

"Should we bang ont window?" said Rach.

Half of Spoons had caught sight an' all, chuckling and pointing and saying, Oi oi!

Int kebab shop across alley, lads noticed her, gi her a round of applause. Lass looked up at them, wee steaming round her stilettos. She laughed, gi em a royal wave, finished her piss. She wiggled to shek hersen dry, pulled up her kegs, staggered back tut street to gerron wi her neet, no idea that behind her an entire pub had just gorran eyeful. No knowledge ut pair of oval prints she'd left ont glass.

Yous warrall howling together, then, all three of yas laughing hard. Rach caught her breath first, launched into a story about when she warrat uni in Leeds, lived ont route of a famous pub crawl. Her flat warrin a converted end terrace behind an eight-foot stone wall. Some lass ont crawl had gone behind wall forra slash when Rach cem home and found her, runnel of wee cutting across Rach's drive. "And I went, 'Excuse me, love, what do you think you're doing?' And she went, 'Fuck off back to London!'"

"And what did you say, again?" asked Kel.

"I sez, 'I'm from fucking *Donny*, mayte. And you can come in and use mi loo, next time, I'll put kettle on, duck!'" Rach and Kel laughed again, and you wanted to laugh wi em. You wanted to be all wrapped up in a shared laugh.

"Can't believe you've just done that," you said. "We've all just watched a lass accidentally moon an entire pub and you've managed to turn it into a story about when you warrat uuuuni"—you imitated long nasal *u* sound Rach had started saying "uni" wi after her first semester. Most of Rach's "uni mates" *wa* from London or private school or both. You went on a neet out in Leeds wi em once but couldn't stand way they talked, buttery and clogged like they'd got summat lodged up their nose. Couldn't bear way they looked at ya, like you warra scrap of gristle not worth feeding tut dogs. "Ah could go rest of mi life wi'out hearing one more fuckin story about uuuuuni."

Fucking hell, that felt good. Your mouth felt wild, unbuttoned. Your heart pumping fast.

Rach blinked, shook her head like you'd poked her int eye.

Kel stared intut middle distance as if looking fut words that'd paper ovvert moment, stop yous all stumbling into summat nasty and grim, summat too far gone to save.

You could feel it, then, your relationship sliding into a new country, feet squelching through new muck. Finally off down a snicket friendship had never took, leaving pretend behind, just truth and bare knuckles bracing int wind.

"Ooh!" Rach purr'er glass down, clasped her knees. "I forgot to tell you all t'juice I got other night!" She wa smiling big and weird like this wa some reyt gossip you warrall gunna gerra reyt laugh from. "Went out wi our Louise other week for her birthdi, right, and there's all these people from school I ant seen in ages—Simmo, and that lot—and honestly, all t'gossip they had, I dint wanna go home. I stopped out till five a.m. just to hear it all."

"Go on, then," said Kel.

"What's goss?" you said, feeling suspended ovver that cliff again. You'd expected Rach to come back at you wi summat cutting, to say it wont *her* fault you dint go uni. But here she wa, pretending you'd never said owt. You wondered if you *had* said owt.

"Get this, right, Emma Smith"—Rach paused for effect—"has been diagnosed—wi ADHD!" She danced her eyebrows up and down like this wut most salacious thing anyone had ever heard. You waited fut punch line. It dint come.

"Girls get diagnosed later than boys," said Kel. "Because their symptoms are different. I saw summat about it on Insta."

"Yeah, I know, I just thought it wa interesting—anyway, what else did they tell me? Oooh!" Rach's face lifted again into glee. "Remember Loz?"

Not really, you thought. Most of this lot wa from Rach and Kel's primary, and you'd never got to know them at comp, and you deffo ant spoke to them since you left school.

Kel said, "Oh, yeah, how's she doing?"

"*Well*, her kid—get this—nearly went *blind*." Again, Rach paused so her words could sink in. Her words hung int air around you. "But he's alright now. Anyway, how mad's that?"

You gorrit, then: Rach wa doing owt she could to keep neet going. She wanted this—mebs *needed* this. Needed yous to be close. She just dint know how to mek it happen. And she'd never know why you couldn't gi her closeness, no matter how much you wanted to.

"*And*—I can't believe I forgot this one—Sean Gardiner's dead! Overdose!"

"We already knew that," Kel said. "Simmo posted 'Goodbye, mayte, you're wit angels now,' or summat, on Facebook, wi a picture of Sean. You saw that, dint you, Shaz?"

"No."

Numb part of you opened, a hole, small pillow of sad pushing up through your booze haze. Seany Gardiner *did* go to your primary. You'd known him well before Rach and Kel.

"Could've sworn it wa you who told me," said Kel.

Rach laughed. "Mad, innit."

"He warra lovely lad," said Kel.

"And everyone fancied him," said Rach. "Everyone fancied Sean Gardiner, bless him."

"Could've sworn you told me this, Shaz." Kel touched your shoulder. "You alright, babe?"

"Why are you laughing?" you said to Rach.

"It's just mi nervous laughter. I'm just anxious." She tried to get hold of it, and couldn't, smothered giggles tormenting her mouth.

"Stop fuckin laughing." You put your wineglass ont table, slung your handbag ovver your shoulder. "Some lad dies that I actually care about and it's just gossip to thee, cheap fuckin thrill." You warrup, legs loose wi drink, winding through crowded tables, knocking chairs and knees, mekkin fut door. You pushed out ontut street, ignoring Kel's cries behind ya—Come on, don't let it ruin us night. You quick-marched down Priory Walk, past Subway, past closed and dark former Walkabout. If you hurried, you'd still mek bus. You turned onto Printing Office Street. No bars down there, no takeaways. Only eerily up-lit mannikins keeping watch from shop windows, echoes of folk shouting somewier far off, a bass line's distant pulse. Rach and Kel hurried after ya, heels clonking against flagstones. Not what you needed—you needed them to let you walk away before you said owt else. Before you proper tore everything down.

Rach got to you first, firm fingers round your wrist, yanked you to a halt.

You pulled yoursen free. "I'm obviously spoiling everyone's neet, so just let me go."

"You're not spoiling owt," said Kel. "You'll spoil it if you leave now."

"We wa having a nice night, wont we. Why've you always gorrer be t'drama queen?"

"Why are *you* tryna force me to go Leopard when you know I'm barred."

"I'm not trying to force ya."

"Then why are you obsessed wi going thier?"

"I've barely mentioned bloody Leopard."

"Ever since you got wi him, you've been different."

That wont true, you knew, once you'd said it. But it wa near a truth. It wa hiding one.

"Ever since I got wi who?"

"Your fuckin husband."

"You *are* joking?" Rach looked at Kel sideways, as if to say, *Help me out*. Kel wa doing her best to keep a neutral face.

Of course it dint mek sense to them. How could you still be mad about summat that happened so long ago.

You needed to walk. You paced street, three steps forwards, turn, three steps back, till you felt like you'd gorra hold of yoursen. You looked Rach int eyes. "Let's be real, things ant been sem between us since we left school, and you've barely even *spoke* to me in years, and ah never knew wharrah did wrong, and it fuckin hurt, to be honest." Closer. Truer.

"I dunno what you want from me, Shaz. I have tried and tried wi you, I really have."

"*How* have you?"

"Well, for one, I texted you last year after we bumped into each other in town, asked you out for drinks, and you never texted back. And *that* fucking hurt, to be *honest*."

"Yeah, but you never fuckin texted me when I actually *needed* ya."

"Oh aye, when have you ever needed me, like? When have you ever needed anyone?"

"When ah lost mi job at Leopard, forra start—when ah got arrested, when ah fuckin phoned you from police station."

"Yeah, you phoned int middle ut bloody night and I still picked up."

"And what did you *say* to me?"

Rach shook her head like she couldn't believe you wa this bitter.

"Ah bet your fella told you a *reyt* tale about what happened that neet. And ah bet you just took his fuckin word forrit."

"He's mi husband, of course I took his word."

"Wi'out bothering to ask for my side."

"What have you got to say about it, like? You assaulted mi husband's best mate. Amount of arguments we've had in our house, every time I mention you. Mi hubby feels *betrayed*, Shaz, that I dint sack you off for good. You're lucky I'm still speaking to ya."

"Oh, well, fuck me, ah dint realise ah wa menna be *grateful* that you'd stoop to fuckin talk to me." Your words wa coming out choked now. There wa spit on your chin. "Do you really wanna have this chat? Cuz I'm ready if you are, darlin."

"What you threatening me wi *now*?"

"Am ah *fuck* threatenin ya, I'm just saying, you don't wanna know what really happened."

"Right, let's have it," said a voice from below. Kel wa sat ont kerb hugging her knees, eyes closed. "Yous two are only fucking mates I've got left, so you better just gerrit all out right now." You'd never heard Kel talk like that, never known her to tek charge. "I mean it. Sit the fuck down."

You and Rach plonked your bums ont concrete either side of Kel.

"Are you gunna tell us what's up wi you, then," you asked her. "If we're all gunna be honest. Are you gunna tell us why you're back in this shithole wi us silly bastards?"

Kel kept her eyes closed, her face solemn. "I'm not tryna keep owt from you, I just—" Her nose and eyes crinkled into an almost cry. You could feel it, underground rivers of summat in Kel's core, some bottomless rage or fear or grief. She got control of it; her face de-crinked. "Look, I'll tell you what's going on wi me if yous two can sort this out. Right?"

Yous all stared intut black ut tarmac, studied petrol stains and bits of rubbish.

"Right," Kel began, wit manner of a judge. "Rach, what's your hubby been saying?"

"I'll be honest, I don't wanna talk about it, I just wanna move on."

"Don't you think, though, that it's only fair if Shaz gets to tell her side?"

"Rach dunt wanna hear my side."

"I am still here, ya know!"

"Ah know, but I'm telling ya, you don't—you'd never forgive me."

"Surely that's for me to decide."

You shook your head. Where would you even start? You thought about that dimpled pint glass, heavy in your hand, curve of its handle, ridge ut rim beneath your thumb. Glint as it left your fingers, flew ovver heads, across pub. Band's front man crumpling at knees, body hitting stage, blood weeping from his hairline. Rach's husband peering intut dark, looking for thee, his fingers fixed across fretboard of his bass. His outrage exaggerated by stage lights, his face crags of amber and shadow. And everything that cem before, all them years of holding it in, trying to reckon wi it on your tod. All them old feelings you'd tried to destroy, everything you'd tried to let go of since you'd met your lass and your little life together had med you feel like mebs one day you could be happy.

"Fuck it." If you dint tell Rach now, you'd just keep exploding, raging ovver her every mistake, punishing her as if she wut one who'd forced you silent, as if she'd held her hand ovver your mouth all these years while you gasped for breath. You left your body, watched yoursen from a distance, huddled ont kerb in a welt of lamplight, as if, now you'd started, you couldn't stop yoursen doing what you'd swore you'd never do. "Remember that day, summer of year ten, we wa tanning and gerrin drunk in mi backyard, and lads showed up?"

Other two nodded: *Yeah, probs, think so.*

Of course they couldn't remember exact day. Why would they? Yous wa fifteen; that whole summer wa gobbled up in a glory of sunshine fogged by vodka. You reminded them ut details they'd forgot, details that'd held fast to you and never let go: everyone wanted a barby, but there wont any scran, so yous three rock-paper-scissored for who had to go tut shops wit lads for baps and sausages, and you lost, playing scissors to Rach's rock. You and t'lads left Rach and Kel int yard, went off on your mish.

"We ended up down at cornfield."

"Are you gunna tell me you slept wi him?" said Rach.

"Ah'm gunna tell you he raped me. Him and his 'best mate.'"

There it wa, word you'd never said. Left your lips and entered world. You'd gi'en birth to it. You wa back in your flesh, pulse storming, brain ringing wit word, wit shock of hearing it in your own voice.

Kel stared at tarmac.

Rach kicked at an empty Quavers packet dirtying int gutter. She laughed, a single *ha*, puncturing silence like a pencil point stabbed through paper. "Can you just not stand that I'm happy? Is that warrit is?"

"Are you happy?"

"I just told you we're about to start trying forra baby." She laughed again. "I have got sick of tolerating your bullshit ovvert years, Shannon, I really fucking have. But somehow I never thought you could be *this* vindictive."

A force in you, a welling, a wall. Summat like white noise rising up.

"Well, ah've told ya now. Do what you like wi it." You stood, walked fast int direction ut bus station, steaming down Printing Office Street. Missed last bus, so you dint know where you wa going. Just not here, just away.

"We coulda been there for ya," Kel called behind you. You kept walking, tried not to listen. You couldn't let yoursen think about warrit would've been like, having Kel to talk to, how different it might've been if only she'd known.

"If it's true, why dint you tell us back then?"

You stopped. You leant your elbows on a wheelie bin that wa parked ont pavement, laced your hands around back of your neck. Did Kel just say *if* it's true?

When you *did* try to tell Kel, drunk, sneaking a ciggie behind function room at Rach's wedding, she'd just shrugged, said summat like, Shaz, I've sin you smashed, you're anyone's. Then she disappeared back to Yankeeland, leaving you wi her words spiralling through ya thoughts, gerrin twisted up like strands of hair round a bobble. You'd even tried to warn Rach off him, int early days, convince her she deserved better, that she should find a better bloke. But who could stop Rach when she'd gorra plan? Her first real boyfriend, her first love. Boy she'd selected to tek her virginity. She couldn't hear you ovvert whirring of her own happiness, her determination to mek her life run on schedule.

"She dint tell us because it dint fucking happen." Rach spoke as though Kel warr'er only audience, but raised her voice to mek sure you heard. "She's just stirring shit as fucking per."

You turned back towards them, Rach's silhouette in shadow—she'd gorrup, leant hersen against a wall—Kel still squatting ont curb int lamplight, shoulders hunched.

"If it's true why dint you tell us about them? Why did you lerrus fuck about wi em?"

If it's true. *If* it's true. Your brain replayed Kel's words like a skipping CD.

Rach said, "It's *not* fucking true, though, is it?"

Just walk away. Walk a-fuckin-way. Get home to your lass and move on.

But Kel wa looking up at you, knees pulled to her chest, looking too young, too old, too thin, too lost, too knackered. Ghost of eleven-year-old Kel, still looking up at thee forran answer.

You sunk down ontut kerb, next to Kel, let your head hang between your knees, took a breath. Then you told them everything you'd carried around wi you for years, every word you'd never said, each one boulder-heavy, weight of it lifting as it left your mouth. You told them your booze-blotched memories ut neet it happened—too drunk, you know now, to consent—and, next day, Rach's future husband and his bandmate coming round your house, mekkin promises that everyone would hate you if you ever told anyone what yous had done. Especially Rach, they'd promised. Rach would *proper* hate you. At time, and for years after, you believed t'lads wa looking out for ya, trying to save ya from losing your mates, from gerrin branded a slag.

You told them about lonely trip to family planning fut STI swab, pregnancy test, and how, years later, t'lads played a gig at Leopard. You, int dark, clearing tables. Them ont stage, lit bright, singing a funny ha-ha song about a slaggy lass they Eiffel Towered in a cornfield.

While you talked, you watched Rach, hovering at edge of your vision. She wa hardening into marble, back rigid, arms crossed, eyes glazed. When you finished, silence fell. Nobody moved, nobody rushed to fill gap. You wa weightless, levitating. You thought mebs you'd stay this light forever, this empty, this open, no matter what cem next.

Wordlessly, Rach stirred from her lean, sat down ont other side of Kel. Kel slid one arm beneath Rach's and one beneath yours, connected yas, elbow to elbow. Three of you sat there forra while, one long chain.

Eventually, Rach said, "I'm sorry I gossiped about Sean Gardiner being dead. I dint realise you knew him that well."

You waited for her to say summat else, owt that'd let you know what she wa thinking, if she believed ya, if she hated ya, if you'd ruined her life or saved it.

"S'alreyt, ah never told ya."

"What warr'e like as a little kid?"

You'd prepared yoursen forra torrent of ugly names, for her to call you a liar, for vows never to speak to you again. You hadn't prepared yoursen for her to change subject like you'd been talking about weather. What *wa* this? Wa rage still coming, still cooking inside her?

"What warr'e like?" You shook your head again, searching forra story that could sum Seany up. "Year five, reyt, disco int parish hall, this lad promised me a slow dance, then decided he dint wanna. His mates tried to mek him hold mi hand, but he warr'avvin none of it. I'm nearly crying, reyt, cuz he's acting like ah'm too minging to touch. Anyway, Seany danced wi me, din'e? So ah wunt be sad."

304

Yous danced to "Words" by Boyzone, your first slow dance wi a lad. Song's piano intro plinked into your head, then. You ant heard that track in twenty years, but you wa sure you could still sing every line. "It wut nineties, wannit, so Seany had little blonde curtains, bless him. I thought he looked like Nick Carter out ut Backstreet Boys."

Kel and Rach sang, in unison: *"Backstreet's back, alright!"*

It wont reyt funny, but yous all laughed. Your cackles echoed off former-Walkabout's windows, raced through yas like an electric charge, binding yas. Yous filled your lungs and laughed twice as much, like you could cancel out all t'bad stuff if you laughed hard enough. Yous laughed so long you forgot what wa funny, laughed just to laugh, just to mek sound, just to feel bellyache, just to run out of breath.

When yous finally stopped, breathing heavy, you picked ya story back up, determined to finish, do Seany justice. "Halfway through t'song, reyt, he tilted his head to one side, I tilted tut other, and we kissed. Not a proper snog, like—no tongue—just an open-mouth kiss. Ah think we knew what snogging looked like from t'outside, but not what wa menna be happening inside." After that, yous wa "boyfriend and girlfriend" forra while. You went line dancing at parish hall on Tuesdi afternoons, and Seany would hang round outside, wait till you warron brek. You'd sneak out, do open-mouth kissing wi him, coming at each other in slow motion, heads cocked. Practicing, trying to get moves down. He always brought his pen-knife. You liked thrusting it int air, pretending to threaten your enemies. You had to stop going to them dance classes when another lass cem out, caught you wi a boy and a knife and said she'd tell dance teacher, so you thrust knife at her. You dint mean to threaten her wi death; you just got carried away wit power ut knife, and wi Seany, how special he med you feel.

Trying to bring his face into focus—his shy grin, his freckles— filled you up wi music, wi that slow-dance song that felt grand now, noble, med ya memories grand and noble an' all: that hall, them disco lights, that trestle table holding bowls of Cheesy Wotsits, acid-red bottles of fizzy pop. Your arms round Seany's neck, sweat greasing places your skin touched, doing that side-to-side rocking kids do, like they're trying dead gently to throw each other overboard.

Wi all this swelling inside ya, it dint feel reyt that you and Kel and Rach wa just sat there ont kerb down a dark street. You said, "Where's still doing karaoke in town?"

Of course Rach knew. She'd med fifteen backup plans in case conversation flagged and yous needed a distraction, or in case mood swept yas into furious celebration.

Yous med your way back through crowds—rowdier, denser, tripping and sloshing between bars—down through clamour of Bradford Row, Donny nightlife's new beating heart, a once deserted pedestrian walk-through that had become throng, become lung-shuddering sound systems competing, become a many-bodied writhing creature. You picked your way through tut Social, new bar that you could tell wa fut alternative crowd by t'flooded loos and sticky beer-slopped floor. DJ booth int corner, lyrics ont projector screen ovvert stage, middle-aged woman int spotlight belting out "Total Eclipse of the Heart." Other punters squeezed into booths, spilling ontut dance floor, what Rach kept referring to as a "proper weird mix of people," dead girly lasses wi their spray tans and lash extensions, next generation of indie boys wi fluffy hair and rock star pouts, androgynous people in mullets and piercings and loud-print shirts, middle-aged mams, middle-aged dads, a grandma in winged eyeliner, a drag queen wi a towering turquoise wig. All swaying tut music, singing along, grabbing dramatic fistfuls of air.

While feeling wa still inside ya, while you still dared, you went stret up tut booth and put your song in, then took Jägerbomb Rach handed you, downed cough syrup sugary nonsense, slammed your glass ontut bar. DJ called your name. You took mic, then you warrup ont stage, and piano intro that'd been swinging through ya head wa filling whole pub. Some ut crowd waved lighters. You could hear Rach and Kel cheering for ya—Go on, lass!—so you followed words ont screen as they switched from white to yellow, and you wa right, you did remember every line, lyrics packed away inside ya, somewier dark and dusty you'd forgot existed, sat patient, waiting for you to need them. Your voice wa coming out ut speakers instead of ya body—you couldn't believe it wa coming out of you; *you* wa mekkin that sound; you wa mekkin those folk listen. You wa only sure that alien voice wa yours cuz you could feel low notes vibrating your throat.

And you wa living—*you wa really* living, *Shaz*—Seany meant summat, you meant summat, and you hit chorus wi everything you'd got. "*This world has lost its glory*," you belted, and they wa right, weren't they, Boyzone? There warra bare truth to that. When *did* glory ut world get lost? You'd found it again; you'd found glory there, in that moment, int middle of Donny town centre on a Satdi neet, int streets screaming wi bloody aggression and drunken delight, int reek, int beer and kebab stink, int piss and vomit and spit.

That warra lot to get from a nineties boy band ballad that dint even have a key change, but that's what you wa gerrin. Music ended, dropped you back into yoursen. You smiled sheepish at crowd's whooping, scurried tut bar, Rach and Kel cheering for ya: Nice one, mate! Rach bought another round of shots—No, honestly, my treat.

You searched her eyes fut anger you wa sure wa coming, but Rach looked exactly like a woman having a reyt neet out wit girls. No worries, no fears fut future, no fury, no grief.

DJ transitioned from karaoke to a set of pop rock classics. Dance floor filled, everyone bopping to Bowie's "Let's Dance," Prince's "Kiss." Everyone happy, open, two-stepping in their circle of mates at first, then turning to dance wi a stranger forra chorus, looking for eye contact, smiling, singing at each other. Rach wanted to dance, but Kel wa leaning all her weight against bar, her smile so forced it wa more of a wince, exhaustion slowly sealing her eyes.

"Do you wanna go home?" Rach asked Kel.

"No fucking way! I wanna dance! I just—" She med out like

she'd be fine at bar by hersen, that you and Rach should go dance wi'out her.

"As if we're leaving ya," Rach said. "Hang on." Then she war-roff, cruising dance floor's perimeter, on a quest, ever a lass wi a plan.

You put an arm round Kel's shoulders, your mouth to her ear. "I ant forgot, you know. If you don't tell us what's up, how can we help ya?"

"I know, I know. Please just dance first? For Rach?"

Rach returned carrying a bar stool. She led Kel tut dance floor, sat her down ont stool at dance floor's edge. You and Rach shimmied next to her, Kel trying to join in. At first, she stopped every time she thought you and Rach wont looking, let her arms slack, slumped against stool's backrest, till Queen's "Don't Stop Me Now" cem on and music got inside her. Then she wa chair dancing like no bugger has ever chair danced, waving her arms tut beat. You expected her to catch a load of funny looks, but the smilers smiled at her, danced wi her like there wa nowt odd about her.

Opening notes of "Common People" sent a current of energy through crowd. If any song wa South Yorkshire's national anthem, it wa thissun. Whole pub flooded dance floor, arms round necks and waists, elbows poking faces and lower backs, everyone's breath yeasty, everyone singing every word. A euphoria took you all ovver, you and Kel and Rach and all these drunk sweaty strangers who wa hugging each other like family. One bloke pulled Kel's chair, wi her still on it, intut dance floor's centre, got down on one knee, ser-enaded her. She smiled, a proper grin, closed her eyes, whirled her arms above her head, looking fut first time all neet like she felt alive. Third verse's climax hit, and everyone jumped up and down, yelling words: *How it feels to live your life* . . . Rach pulled you in, arm round your shoulders . . . *With no meaning or control* . . . you held her hips wi one hand, pumped your other fist int air . . . *And with nowhere left to go* . . . no boundaries now, no borders between yas . . . *You are amazed that they exist* . . . just rush, just surge, just cling, just hold, just breathe, just shout, just jump.

Gone three a.m., you and Kel let Rach steer yas tut kebab shop, then you all let your arses get cold ont kerb again, bum cheeks numbing till it felt like your coccyx wa bare pressed against concrete. Scoffing your burgers and cheesy chips, attacking Styrofoam boxes in your laps, mekkin squelchy chewing sounds. Your body hungry fut stodge's oily weight. You let yoursen eat, eat fast, eat messy, let burger juice drip pinkish down your fingers.

You wa craving t'crooks of you lass's body now, bend of her knees tucked behind yours, just wanted to be home curled up wi her. You wanted to wake up early enough to mek her beans on toast before she went on shift.

"Shall we go Taco Bell one day next week?" you said. "One's just opened int Frenchgate." You thought Kel might like summat from t'States, might be impressed that Donny's gorra Taco Bell now an' all.

"Oh god, it ant, has it?" said Kel. "Every time I come back England's got more American. Taco Bell's proper dirty, man. In America, right, it wa 89 cents forra cheesy double beef burrito." She took another bite of her burger. "Nowt should be that cheap," she said, wi a full mouth of meat and bread.

"Oh, shurrup about bloody America, you," said Rach, even though Kel'd hardly mentioned America all neet. "Let people enjoy their Taco Bell. I love a cheeky Taco Bell, me." Rach caught your eye, like she wa lerrin you know that yous warront sem team.

You felt silly, then, for mekkin such a fuss about Seany, lerrin yoursen get carried away wit Boyzone song, wit singing in public, for fucksake. You ant sin t'bloke in ovver a decade. He'd been dead six months and you dint even know. You dint even have him on Facebook.

It wont Seany you wa upset about losing, warrit. It wut little lass who swayed wi him int disco. Little Shaz, whose dad wont dead, who hadn't starved hersen half dead, who'd never passed out int corner of a club or woken up wi sick on her sheets or had a fella who liked to smack her about. Whose kegs had never been pulled down in public, whose boss had never felt her up, who'd never worked an endless river of wank jobs for wank pay, who'd never been raped in a cornfield.

Kel licked her greasy fingers, laid her head on your shoulder.

"Honestly," you said, "has tonight battered you out? Has it med you more poorly?"

"I'm alright for now. Alcohol numbs it, gives me energy." Her skull dug into your collarbone. She shifted, leant more of her weight on you. "I dint wanna tell ya because I just wanted us all to have a nice night. But I probs won't be able to gerrout of bed fut rest ut week. Could be a fortnight. When it's really bad, I ant even got strength to gerrup and go tut loo. It's like someone's holding me down, pinning me tut bed. I just have to lie there int dark, wait forrit to be over."

"Fucking hell, Kel," said Rach. "Come here." She wiped her hands down her tights, pulled Kel's feet onto her lap, so Kel wa curled across you both. Rach stroked Kel's leg. You stroked her hair.

A fight broke out across street, int taxi queue, scuffle between two old bald blokes in tracksuits. One bloke brought a beer bottle shattering down ont other un's head. Whole queue erupted: group of lasses squatted down in heels and bodycon dresses to check ont injured bloke, who wa slumped against wall bleeding from his scalp; some ut younger lads started ont old bloke who'd done t'glassing, burying him in a circle of swinging fists. Other lads tried to stop younger lads pummelling shit out ut old bloke, till they warrall trying to dodge and land punches, shoves, headbutts, kicks. Any lass not tending tut bleeding man stood at edge ut battleground shouting, Gi oo'er, this is gerrin silly now, this is gerrin beyond a joke.

Yous watched till you heard ambulance siren, knew bleeding man would be alreyt.

"How long have you been feeling this poorly?" you asked.

Kel closed her eyes. "Months. It's been really hard over there by misen. I dint wanna tell you I wont doing well because I know you dint want me to go int first place."

Rach looked at you ovver Kel's head. "Woman," she said, "as if we'd ever stop you doing summat you wanted to do."

"We wa glad to be shut of ya," you said.

Kel giggled, though she wa crying now, mascara-laced tears down her cheeks. "I dunno what happened. I wa fine after t'divorce—I wa relieved to be out of it. Then I cem down wi flu or summat, in bed forra few weeks wi a bug, and since then I just haven't felt back to normal. It's like there's a tap in me that's been left running and all mi energy keeps leaking out."

"Have you been tut docs?" you asked.

"Doctor sez I'm not ill. He sez I just need to fall in love again. But he's not inside me, is he? *I'm* inside me, and I feel like I'm losing misen, like I ant got control of mi own body. I feel like I'm disappearing in front of everyone, and no-one can see what's happening. No-one gets it. No-one believes me."

She wa right, you dint gerrit. You'd never heard of anyone coming down wi a bug and never gerrin better. But you *did* know invisible. You did know drowning on dry land while everyone else got on wi breathing.

"We believe ya," you said.

"Course we fucking believe you." Rach said it wi so much warmth, so much love, that you looked across at her, let yoursen hope that you'd find her looking across at you, hope that she might've half meant it for thee.

Rach wa looking down into her lap, watching her own hands stroke Kel's legs, wit care and focus of a mother. She kept her gaze fixed there, as if determined not to look up, determined not to feel your eyes waiting for hers.

At first, you thought next-door's telly woke you, fucking *Countryfile* already, which meant you'd missed your lass's alarm going off— missed chance to mek her breakfast and kiss her bye. But beneath intense, doom-strumming cellos of *Countryfile*'s theme music, beneath posh yah-yah-yahs of its presenters, another noise wa pushing through. A knocking. A bloke delivering a parcel, mebs. Or young family trying a new tactic to drive you barmy. You rolled ovver onto your lass's side ut bed, which wa cool but still smelled of her, pulled her pillow ovver your head, waited fut knocker to gi oo'er and go. You ant had a hang-over this bad in years. Last neet's food and drink wa swishing and slith-ering inside ya. If you gorrup now, you'd immediately have to vom.

Knocker kept on knocking.

"Fucksake, fuck *off*," you shouted intut mattress. It did nowt to dissuade whoever wa stood on your front step. Mebs your lass had forgot her key again. You crawled slowly backwards, down t'length ut bed, and off t'end, dragging duvet wi ya, swinging it round your shoulders like a cape, wrapping yoursen in your lass's smell. Int bathroom, you chucked up, flushed, then plodded down t'stairs tut door at stairwell's bottom.

You opened door ontut usual view: dog-walkers strolling, road droning wi traffic, terrace row across way, snicket leading tut terrace row behind, sun actually mekkin a half-decent attempt at poking through misty clouds—you had to squint and shield your eyes wi your hand—and Rach. Rach in last neet's sparkly sequin dress. Her slinky bob wa frazzled now, tormented, her mascara smudged into greyish smears beneath her eyes. Her heels wa muddy, her tights torn. She smelled of old booze and smoke and manure.

"Sleep under a bush, like?"

"Are you gunna let me in?"

You hesitated, thought about slugs int kitchen, black mould invading front room wall, your cracked concrete yard, windows that still dint have blinds, your thirdhand furniture, fact that house wut exact size and shape ut council house you grew up in. Not that it *warra* council house nomore. Now it had a landlord whose favourite hobby wa upping your rent.

You stepped back, held door open. You sat Rach down ont settee int front room, went to throw up again, then med two cups of tea and carried them through, still wearing your duvet cape.

"We ant gorrany biscuits."

"S'alright, I can't eat."

You set teas ont coffee table, sat down next to Rach. She wa staring at her cuppa like it might leap up, toss hot tea in her face.

"How come you know where ah live?"

"Heard you gi'in cabby your address."

Cabby had dropped Rach off outside her house before tekkin you t'seven miles back to yours, Rach's sweaty palm of pound coins in your hand.

She told you that after t'cab left, she stood looking at her front door for ages, like she wa frozen, like there warra force field around house she couldn't penetrate. She set off walking, int black ut neet, then grey-blue ut dawn. "Tried to tek a shortcut through farmers' fields and got lost about five times, then I stared at your bloody front door for ages, crouched down in that snicket like a weirdo."

"You went through farmers' fields in your high heels?"

"No-one's saying it wa mi best idea." Rach flopped against settee back, as if spent, as if every yard of them seven miles had caught up to her at once. "What am I meant to do? How am I meant to go home and be normal?"

You kept your eyes ont chimney breast, which had long since had its fireplace plastered ovver. It hadn't occurred to you that if you shattered Rach's idea of what her life wa, you'd have to help her mek sense ut pieces. Why wa this your job? Why not go to Kel? But Kel would be in bed, locked inside for days, weeks. Dint mean it had to be you, though. You wa allowed to tell her she wa asking too much.

Crazy Frog song cem blasting through t'other wall, drowning out poshos on *Countryfile*.

"Soz," you said, raising your voice ovvert noise. "Neighbours are tryna annoy us into moving out. They think lesbians are allergic to cartoon amphibians wi floppy willies."

Rach flinched at word "lesbians" like it warra slur. You'd never called yoursen one in her presence. You'd barely called yoursen one in your head.

"Fancy a smoke?" asked Rach.

You nodded, even though you knew it'd mek your hangover better for five seconds, then mek it loads worse. Owt to gerrout front room, away from head-mashing sounds. You led her through kitchen, out ontut bare yard, both carrying your untouched teas. You dusted off two plaggy garden chairs. Fence wa high enough that you couldn't see young family's kids trying to kill each other int next yard, but you could hear their squeals and grunts and gi oo'ers.

Rach handed you a fag and a lighter, and you both sparked up. You savoured nicco rush, till smoke teased your belly into sending acidy nausea up your throat. You ant sin Rach smoke since she wa sixteen, but she drew hard on hers three times before she blew out.

"I remember that song."

"We're all still tryna forget," you said, thinking she meant Crazy Frog, which had looped through everyone's minds nonstop during summer of 2003. Summer, you realised now, yous all left school, started drifting in your different directions.

"Not that song, you daft apeth. The one they wrote about you." She took another drag, tapped ash ontut concrete. "I watched them play that bloody song in every grotty pub in South Yorkshire. I asked him once who lyrics warrabout. He laughed at me and said, 'No-one,

314

don't be daft, it's just a song.' And I knew he wa lying then. I fucking *knew*. I could see it in his face. But I didn't wanna know, did I. Didn't wanna press."

She smoked in silence. A little bird flirted wit fence post, fluttering on and off, its pouchy yellow breast a bright splodge against concrete's grey.

"I wa so sure I'd never get divorced, me. I thought all you had to do wa choose right first time. I thought people just weren't trying hard enough." Rach leaned forwards, pushed her fingers into her forr'ead. Sun disappeared behind cloud, mekkin yard chilly and dark. "I med plan so long ago, didn't I—mortgage, kids, an' lot. Spent all these years determined to make it happen. Never once stopped to ask misen if it's what I want. Like, do I even *want* kids?"

"Well"—you nodded at neighbours' yard—"that lot's enough to put anyone off."

Rach stayed hunched ovver, staring at her stockinged feet.

"Do you wish I hadn't told ya?"

She wa so quiet and so still for so long, looking like she wa praying wi her neck bowed, head balanced on her fingers, you thought she might stay like that, a praying statue int yard forever. Mebs you shouldn't've asked. Warrit too much to ask.

Rach stubbed her cig ont ground, straightened, sparked another cig. "So that lass I saw leaving your house earlier, that's your girlfriend, is it?"

"She'd've been off to work, yeah."

"I never thought you'd end up wi a lass." Rach smiled, but it warra broken smile. It tremored. "I just thought—" She trailed off.

"—ah liked slagging it about wi anyone who cem along?"

"No, you dick." She smiled properly. "I just—I don't know what I thought." She hadn't looked at you in ages, but it felt like a different kind of not looking to last neet's, like instead of shutting you out, she wa trying to hold hersen in.

"What do you mek of Kel's thing?" you asked.

"No clue. Seems like she needs supporting, though, dunnit. Like, whatever happens wi us."

You nodded. "We've gorrer be there forr'er."

You wondered if Kel'd think it wa worth it, int days to come, when she wa trapped inside her body, in bed, int dark, listening to her pulse jackhammering in her ears. If she'd regret dragging hersen round Donny wi you cunts fut millionth time.

"Do you want me to leave him?"

You thought forra minute, trying to work out what she wa really asking: would you feel better if, would it set things right if, could we be mates again if, or some other if, some past she wa hoping yous could find your way back to, some future she wa already trying to gerra glimpse of.

"I don't need you to do owt. If you wanna stay wi him, stay wi him."

Between your fingers, a column of ash balanced on top ut cigarette's filter. You let butt drop tut ground, then felt bad about leaving a mess for your lass to find, nipped back inside, grabbed dustpan and brush.

While you wa down on your knees, sweeping ash and fag ends, gerrin your duvet dirty, Rach said, "You're happy wi your girlfriend, then?"

You rocked back on your haunches, laid dustpan down.

Your lass wa more safety than you'd ever known, and still sometimes your life together felt too rickety to trust. If you fell out, broke up, it'd all vanish. You'd be back sleeping on your sister's settee, further than ever from only thing you'd ever wanted. A door that wa just yours, that you could lock behind you, a room no-cunt could enter unless you let them.

"Reckon I am, to be fair."

Or you warrat least ready to let yoursen try.

"I'm happy for ya." You could tell Rach meant it, but she couldn't keep sad note out her voice. "Why wa I in such a rush to be normal? To have everything I wa supposed to have?"

"You reckon you're normal?"

"Shurrup, you." Rach laughed, helped you up, took dustpan from you, knocked it out int wheelie bin. Yous went back inside, dumped your undrunk teas int kitchen sink.

"Seriously, though," you said, "that's wharrah liked about you int first place. You dint gi two shits what anyone thought about ya when we wa eleven, you just did your own thing."

"You could've bloody told me that. I spent most of mi time tryna be more like you."

"Fuck would you wanna do that fo'?"

Int stairwell, Rach pulled on her mud-battered shoes. "I thought you knew what you wa doing." She looked up at you wi a cheeky grin that sent one spreading ovver yours.

You held door open. She stepped out intut day, then turned back to thee.

"I don't, by t'way. I don't wish you hadn't told me."

It dint feel good like you'd thought it would. Dint feel like light or air or sugar rush or weight off or free.

"Do you remember what you said to me? When I called you from police station?"

You'd never forget. Shaz, she'd said, you deserve everything you get. She'd meant legally, like, but at time you heard other meanings, heard her laying blame for every shit thing that'd happened to you at your own feet. How many times you'd imagined confronting her wi these words, spitting them back at her, mekkin her feel as small as she'd med you.

You could see in Rach's face that she dint remember, that her words hadn't tattooed themsens onto her memory like they had yours. There wa no spark of guilt or regret in her; she wa just looking at you anxiously, her nose doing its rabbity twitch, like she wa pleading wi you not to tell her more than she could cope wi.

She took a step or two backwards, towards road. "I'll text you later, alright, lovely?" she said, cocking her head to one side, eyes hopeful, waiting.

You pulled duvet back round your shoulders, held Rach's gaze.

You *wa* happy wi your lass, yeah. But you couldn't survive off your lass alone. You needed mates round you who knew you little, knew you unbruised. Who could retell your stories, your mad times, your glorious fuckups. You needed to hug, laugh, gossip, dance. Say, Remember when, and That wont what happened! Reyt, warrit wa wa, and fall out about minor details, memory slips, all your who-where-whats. You needed to feel full, like you've gorra whole history, a whole life.

You nodded: yeah, she could text ya.

Rach's arms wa round your neck, then, knocking your duvet cape tut floor. Cold rushed round your legs. She clung, squeezed, clung, squeezed again. You wondered what she wa trying to say, what words she wa squeezing into your body. You squeezed her back, held her hard as you could. Felt yoursen unfolding. Longing.

Don't, Shaz, you told yoursen, staring ovver her shoulder intut road. Don't ask her, or yoursen, or anyone what might've happened if you'd been able to tell sooner—that year, that summer, that neet. How your lives might've been different. Don't ask who Rach could've become if she'd let hersen, who you all might've become if you'd been allowed to grow into whoever you wa gunna grow into. Don't. You can't drive yoursen mad wi that kind of what-if.

While Rach hobbled off across road, down snicket, you leant against door frame, breeze stroking your hands, nose, ankles. Sun spilled ovvert cloud again, ray cutting reyt across your face, mekkin you wince, mekkin you feel poached, alone in a shaft of hot yellow. Your belly nagged, growling for stodge, salt, fat. But you wont ready to go in and put brekkie on. You watched folk pass—biddy in a plaggy rain bonnet, dinky lass sucking an ice pop—and cars zip by, windows glinting like memories, like good ideas, like sensations firing electric through your brain.

Acknowledgments

The description of Gatecrasher One as "Gehry-esque" comes from *Sheffield* by Ruth Harman and John Minnis. Stacey Sampson reported in *Vice* that after Gatecrasher's fire, locals could taste smoke in every postcode. I came across the maxim "you cannot thread a moving needle" in Elinor Cleghorn's powerful, illuminating, and horrifying book *Unwell Women: Misdiagnosis and Myth in a Man-Made World*. The full statement is attributed to the nineteenth-century British gynecologist Robert Lawson-Tait: "no man can affect a felonious purpose on a woman in possession of her sense without her consent [because] you cannot thread a moving needle." "Shake a bridle over a Yorkshireman's grave and he will rise and steal a horse" is one of the many charming adages about Yorkshire folk recorded in *The Great North Road: The Old Mail Road to Scotland* by Charles G. Harper. *Savage Courtship* is a novel by Susan Napier. Kel remembers a line from "Beasley Street" by John Cooper Clarke. Songs referenced include "Children of the Night" by Nakatomi, "Are You Ready to Fly" by Dune, "Cheeky Song (Touch My Bum)" by the Cheeky Girls, "Words" by Boyzone, and "Common People" by Pulp.

Acknowledgments

I owe endless thanks to my agent Henry Dunow for taking a chance on me when this book was only part formed and for seeing value in tales of the escapades of teenage girls from a deeply unfamous former mining town. Thank you for your unparalleled enthusiasm, insight, kindness, and expertise, and for being with me every step of the way. I owe the same to Elizabeth McCracken, for your extraordinary wisdom, guidance, and generosity. I don't know where this book—or I—would be without your mentorship.

Thank you to Veronique Baxter for championing the book in the UK and ensuring it found the right home and to Emily Hayward-Whitlock for handling screen rights so brilliantly. My US and UK editors, Caroline Zancan at Holt and Rose Tomaszewska at Chatto, and the teams at both houses, for embracing my Donny lasses and for expertly ushering the book towards its best self.

To the publications that gave first homes to some of these stories: *Granta*, *Solstice Literary Magazine*, and *Everywhere Stories: Short Fiction from a Small Planet, Volume III*.

The institutions whose gifts of time, space, education, and money made writing this book possible: GrubStreet Center for Creative Writing, Wellspring House, Bread Loaf Writers' Conference, the Anderson Center, Tin House Summer Workshop, Hedgebrook, the Ragdale Foundation, *Prairie Schooner*. At the University of Texas at Austin: the New Writers Project; the English department; the British, Irish, and Empire Studies department; the Michener Center for Writers.

To my creative writing students at GrubStreet and UT Austin; Mary Cotton and the winter 2014-15 team at Newtonville Books; my 2017 Bread Loaf waiter cohort; my Anderson Center roomies; my Hedgebrook and Ragdale cohorts; and Team Nana, my 2022 Tin House workshop buds.

The teachers and mentors whose influence lives in everything I write: Daniel A. Hoyt and Dr. Katherine Karlin at Kansas State University, Michelle Hoover at GrubStreet's Novel Incubator Program, Dr. James Smith at Boston College, Stacey D'Erasmo at

Acknowledgments

Bread Loaf, Nana Kwame Adjei-Brenyah at Tin House, and the brilliant faculty I learned from at UT Austin and the Michener Center, including Lisa Olstein, Chad Bennett, Laura van den Berg, Paul Yoon, Mitchell S. Jackson, Molly Antopol, Deb Olen Unferth, and Bret Anthony Johnston. Edward Carey, thank you for your support and enthusiasm; your belief in this book helped me believe.

My NWP/Michener MFA sibs: Rob Macaisa Colgate, Gabrielle Grace Hogan, Annie Robertson, Molly Williams, Zack Schlosberg, Emeline Atwood, Rickey Fayne, Alejandro Puyana and Brittani Sonnenberg, Shaina Frazier, Maryan Nagy Captan, Willie Fitzgerald, Laurel O. Faye, Bismarck Martinez, David Grivette, Brynne Jones, Stephanie Macias Gibson, Carrie Wilson, Justin Bui, Felipe Bomeny, Megan Kamalei Kakimoto, Jackson Holbert, Hedjie Choi, Beverly Chigozie Chukwu, Lauren Aliza Green, and the whole gang. Thanks for post-workshop drinks at Crown & Anchor and Posse East, writing nights at Epoch and Cherrywood, the check-in texts, the Parlor sessions, the backyard parties. Thanks to Avigayl Sharp for giving me safe harbour in the middle of a pandemic. To Amanda Bestor-Siegal and my Coven, Ellaree Yeagley and Juan Fernando Villagómez: there's no Texas without you.

My Boston fam, especially my BC cohort Lauren Bell, Nikki Siclare, Hannah Taylor, Sara and Kelly Danver, Brooke Nusbaum, Steph Haines, Matt Messer; Chris Boucher and *Post Road* magazine for my introduction to the publishing world; and the GrubStreet community, including Shilpi Suneja, Cara Wood, Deborah Good, Bonnie Walch, Kathleen Gibson, Kim Libby, Shuchi Saraswat, Dariel Suarez, Sean Van Deuren, Shubha Sunder, Jenny Xu, Desmond Hall, Rachel Barenbaum, Bob Fernandes, Louise Berliner, Andrea Meyer, Kelly Ford, Alex Marzano-Lesnevich, Lisa Borders, Steve Almond, Chip Cheek, Christopher Castellani, Sonya Larson, Lauren Smith, Lauren Rheaume, Hanna Katz, Eve Bridburg, among many others. To Stacy Mattingly; Eson Kim and Damon Avent; Sharissa Jones, Daniel Medwed, Mili and Clem: for all the joy of our conversations, for always putting me up and putting up with me, for holding me together in rough times. To Alison Murphy, for everything, but not least those Monday night ciggies on Boylston.

No thank you to the Epstein-Barr virus. You can get t'fuck.

To my music teachers Mr. and Mrs. Moore, John Ellis MBE, Kate Ashwood, and Kristina James, and the many musicians and orchestra leaders I played alongside at Ridgewood School, the William Appleby Music Centre, and the Doncaster Youth Jazz Association: thank you for growing and sustaining the institutions that make music accessible to Donny kids.

Thanks, always, to the Donny lads and lasses who created childhood and blundered into adulthood with me, including Lucy (& the Rounds!), Helen, Tilley, Dav, Mel, Tom K, Welsh, Squiff, Afro, and many others; and bandmates Leigh, Peo, Luke, Danny, Mathew, Jussey, Bri, and Gooey. To my HERCKS crew Harri (and Dave!), Em, Rachi, Charles, and Mo: just while I'm sober, I wanna say I love you, and I'm grateful that we stuck together all this time. Many thanks to my platonic husband Thirsty Hirsty for taking me on my first night round town and for joining me on many a boozy "research trip" since. Your sacrifices are not forgotten.

In memory of Sean Towers, Neil Gardiner, and Peter Butler.

To my grandparents: Betty, for your wisdom; John, for your eccentricity, your storytelling, and the gift of my first dictionary; Marj, for your affection; and Ben, for your interest in local history, which taught me the value of the people and places around me.

To my family, for giving me the freedom to pick my own path. Special thanks to Ed for naming Arms-Out Simon and for being the funniest person I know.

About the Author

Colwill Brown was born and raised in Doncaster, South Yorkshire, and is now based in the United States. She holds an MFA from the University of Texas at Austin, where she was a recipient of a James A. Michener Fellowship, and an MA in English literature from Boston College. Her work has appeared in *Granta*, *Prairie Schooner*, and other publications and has received scholarships, awards, and support from the Tin House Summer Workshop, the Bread Loaf Writers' Conference, Hedgebrook, the Ragdale Foundation, the Anderson Center, GrubStreet Center for Creative Writing, and elsewhere. For over a decade she's lived with ME/CFS, a debilitating neurological disease triggered by a virus that, due to systemic medical neglect, currently has no treatment. A proud Donny lass, she claims to have played bass guitar in (nearly) every rock venue on South Yorkshire's toilet circuit.